## PENGUIN BOOKS
## SULTRY DAYS

Shobhaa Dé describes herself as an 'obsessive-compulsive writer.'
Columnist, commentator, and author of fourteen books, she
lives with her family in Mumbai, a city that she considers a
'character', not just a locale, in her work.

She is currently planning her next book, a novel.

# Sultry Days

### SHOBHAA DÉ

**PENGUIN BOOKS**

PENGUIN BOOKS

Published by the Penguin Group

Penguin Books India Pvt. Ltd, 11 Community Centre, Panchsheel Park, New Delhi 110 017, India

Penguin Group (USA) Inc., 375 Hudson Street, New York, New York 10014, USA

Penguin Group (Canada), 90 Eglinton Avenue East, Suite 700, Toronto, Ontario, M4P 2Y3, Canada (a division of Pearson Penguin Canada Inc.)

Penguin Books Ltd, 80 Strand, London WC2R 0RL, England

Penguin Ireland, 25 St Stephen's Green, Dublin 2, Ireland (a division of Penguin Books Ltd)

Penguin Group (Australia), 250 Camberwell Road, Camberwell, Victoria 3124, Australia (a division of Pearson Australia Group Pty Ltd)

Penguin Group (NZ), cnr Airborne and Rosedale Roads, Albany, Auckland 1310, New Zealand (a division of Pearson New Zealand Ltd)

Penguin Group (South Africa) (Pty) Ltd, 24 Sturdee Avenue, Rosebank, Johannesburg 2196, South Africa

Penguin Books Ltd, Registered Offices: 80 Strand, London WC2R 0RL, England

First published by Penguin Books India 1994

Copyright © Shobhaa Dé 1994

15  14

Typeset by Vans Information Limited, Mumbai
Printed at Baba Barkhanath Printers, New Delhi

For my children—
Ranadip, Radhika, Aditya,
Avantika, Arundhati
and Anandita—
finally, a book by me that they can read.

# One

God wasn't at all what I'd expected him to be. He spoke with a vernac accent and smoked smelly beedies. He also changed my name the moment we were introduced.

'Forget it, *yaar*,' he said, chucking his beedi into a half-drunk cup of tea. 'I'm not going to call you Nisha. It's a ridiculous name. From now on, you'll be my intoxicant, my *nasha*.'

I wasn't impressed. Not initially, at least. But I didn't dare say anything by way of protest. One didn't do that with God.

The college canteen was dark and stank. It was pouring outside and most of the professors had stayed away from classes. There was nothing to do. The only option was to have a plate of greasy, frilly cutlets with a messy dollop of carrot ketchup all over them. The place was crumbling, with bats flying in and out of the high, Gothic windows.

God was holding court in his favourite corner. I'd never really liked him but I must admit to a deep fascination. A sort of infatuation towards him that simultaneously attracted and repelled. It wasn't just his nine-day stubble that put me off. It was his entire manner. I used to wonder whether he ever attended lectures. He was always in the canteen. Always, always. And smoking those God-awful beedies. His friends varied. Especially the girls who hung around his table. I couldn't imagine what attracted them to him. Most of the time they were the ones who paid for his special chai, bought him his beedies and even offered to subsidize haircuts. Oh yes—his hair. I hated that too. Matted locks—which I was sure were full of lice-nests and other creepy crawlies. One hand of his was invariably engaged in scratching. The hand didn't stop at the head. I'd never seen a man who itched so much. Scratch, scratch, scratch… his hand tore inside his filthy shirt and scratched up a bloody pool. It travelled down to his groin, up to his armpits, right round to his back. Sometimes he'd pause mid-scratch to make some point and then start all over again. He really was most revolting.

And I? How must I have appeared to this animal? A prissy little good girl who carried far too many books around. Pretty enough, I suppose. But not special.

'You look so frigid, *yaar*,' he told me within three minutes of our being introduced. 'Why don't you carry a hot water bottle around?'

2

Everybody laughed, especially the girls. I was dumbstruck. Too taken aback to retaliate. Not that I could think up something smart enough. The chai-boy came around just then.

'Mushtaq, get the poor girl something hot to drink before she freezes,' someone shouted.

I picked up my stuff and walked stiffly out of the canteen.

Once I'd ducked into the library, I felt safe. I could dive into my books and pretend to read. I could strike my favourite pose and not be found out. The librarian knew me by name. I fitted in here, just like the other introverts and wallflowers around me. I didn't know why I felt awkward in company. There wasn't anything particularly wrong with me, though you wouldn't know it by the question that was most often asked of me.

It used to start first thing in the morning. The moment I walked into the dining-room for a cup of tea, my mother would look at my face anxiously and ask, 'What's wrong?'

I'd want to yell, 'NOTHING,' but that wasn't done around our house. Father would follow shortly. I'd hear him enquiring en route to the kitchen, 'Is Baby up yet?' And then, on seeing me, that irritating question, 'What's wrong?'

Was it my expression? Did I look troubled? In pain? Depressed? Maybe it was that birthmark of mine. It had to be that. I was born with worry lines between

3

my brows. The doctors had assured my parents that they'd get fainter with the years and eventually disappear. But they didn't. They grew darker and gave the impression that I was constantly frowning or scowling. No wonder the teachers at school ended up writing the same remark in the report book, year after year! 'She needs to cheer up and take more interest in extra-curricular activities.'

My best friend (the only friend I had, actually, and I lost her as soon as I began to hang around God) tried to tell the others that I wasn't in a bad mood, it was just a birthmark. Nobody was convinced. 'What sort of a birthmark is that? We've never heard of anyone born with a frown.'

I still haven't learnt to live with it—the frown. And often when I catch sight of myself in a mirror I'm startled. I nearly ask myself, 'What's wrong?'

God was the only one who thought my frown was 'cute'. 'I like it, *yaar,*' he told me, and for that moment, at least, I'm sure it disappeared. 'Hey! Where did it go?' he asked in mock alarm touching my forehead.

That was the first time he had touched me and I jumped.

'Don't electrocute her, *yaar,*' his ugly friend with the horribly stained teeth laughed.

'Leave the kid alone,' declared God before picking up his beedi packet and sauntering out. Someone settled his bill.

'Why is he called "God"?' I asked a boy in my class.

'That's his name,' he answered.

'Don't be ridiculous,' I said. 'How can anyone be named "God"?'

'Not God-God. His name is Deb. Deb means God, or so he tells anybody who dares to ask.'

That made sense, though he was the first Deb or Dev I knew who had decided to be so literal about it. I liked the name God. Deb. Or Dev. I only wished God wasn't so dirty. What Deb needed desperately was a bath.

My mother, being the eternal romantic she was, had named me Nisha or 'night' since that's when I was born. My father, my sweet, doting father, insisted there was a full moon out when I arrived. Thank God both of them were considerate enough not to have called me Poornima. I've always hated that name. Nisha had a pleasant ring to it. I liked the way it sounded. It made me feel very sensual and sultry... but only in my fantasies. I thought of the other girls in my class who had awful names like Mona or Prema. What would God have changed those to, I wondered.

He had had (yes HAD) several girls by the time he got to the second year at college. 'I started early, *yaar*,' he told me. 'I was a randy little bugger at five.' His early explorations apparently began with a neighbour's servant girl. 'She smelt so much... oof... but so did I.

5

It was quite a feat trying to do anything with both of us holding our noses. It used to irritate me that *she* also held hers. I'd pull her filthy hand away from her nose and shout, "Why are you holding your nose, you dirty thing? You are only a servant." She, being three years older, would pinch me hard on my bottom and threaten, "If you say that again, I'll go and tell my memsaab what you were doing to me!"'

God's stories used to fascinate me, I could listen for hours while he boasted about his exploits. In between stories, he'd lift up his thigh and let go, without any embarrassment whatsoever. The first few times I was too polite and formal to react even though I felt I was being gassed to death. I'd just sit there unable to move or, like the servant girl, to block my nose. I learnt to open my mouth and breathe in through it the moment God's leg went up. I must've looked pretty stupid with my jaw hanging open.

'You know, you resemble an imbecile sometimes,' God commented once. 'Why don't you shut your mouth? It makes you look kind of stupid.'

It was years before he found out. By then I had learnt to anticipate the blast. I could see it coming even before he lifted his leg. After a point, we stopped laughing over it. I began to show my irritation.

'You are being *bhari* inconsiderate, you know,' I said to him on one occasion. 'How would you like it if I did it back to you?'

6

God didn't feel insulted. He scratched himself thoughtfully and said, 'Try it... I'd probably not even notice. Why do you make such a fuss over a fart, *yaar*? You've too many hang-ups. Must consult a shrink—why don't you?' I knew it was no use explaining to him that a shrink had nothing to do with malodorous fumes choking me—so it was best to forget the whole business, as it was with almost everything else. God had made that clear from the start.

'Look, I don't want any of your fancy stuff. It does not impress me. If you want to hang around, it's OK. But don't expect me to change-wange for you. I am what I am—take it or leave it.'

This was before I'd even thought about 'hanging around'. It was his presumption that I would fall in line just like all the others. But as usual God was right, of course, for that was precisely what I did—in time.

In the beginning, I was nothing more than a devotee. He treated me like one. I hated the patronizing tone, the kindness and condescension. It irritated me no end when his friends would snigger as I approached their table. 'Where are the offerings? What? No offerings today? How can you come empty-handed to a temple? Go back and bring something. Even a packet of beedies will do.'

God would grin maliciously and wave me off. '*Jao, Jao... kuch ley ke ao* (Go on... get something).'

It was humiliating and awful. But I took it. And I learned to like God, though I was probably more fascinated by him than anything else—initially. And I think he liked me.

There were things about God which appalled me. Like the first time, looking at a girl in class, he had said, 'She needs a carrot.' I hadn't known what he was talking about.

Foolishly, I asked him.

'Forget it, *yaar*. You are such a tell-tale that if I tell you, you'll go and tell her. Not that I care. But she'll probably think I'm interested in offering her mine.'

I still didn't catch on. I turned to one of his buddies, an obnoxious person with gingivitis and asked him what God was talking about. With a leer, he demonstrated it using his fingers and forearm. I was too shocked to react.

God turned to me and said, 'Next time don't ask silly questions, OK?'

I learnt very quickly that I had to bury whatever little ego and pride I had if I wished to hang around God. His attitude towards girls was simple—use them and leave them. There were enough takers around—bold girls whose jaws never stopped working on the thick wads of gum in their mouths. For them God represented some sort of an anti-hero and they probably fancied themselves as sexy molls. As for me, I was plain moons-truck. And for once in my life I wasn't going to lose out by default.

I still don't know and cannot explain where I got the courage to go for God in such an obvious way. I had had crushes before—silent, brooding ones where the chap never ever got to know. But with God, my entire behaviour altered. He had that effect on me—and on several others. I fancied I could see beyond the put-on menacing facade, the strutting around, the fake bravado. And I fancied that God fancied me—in his own clumsy way, of course. All I needed was a sign—even a small one.

'Opposites attract, Nasha,' he tossed at me airily about a month after our first encounter. And then, embarrassed by the confession, he chased me away saying, 'Samosas—get four. The big ones, OK? And don't forget the chutney.'

I'd been accepted. And I felt deeply honoured.


God's father was called Comrade. At first, I thought it was some sort of a joke. But no, God Sr. was a card-holding commie. Being very committed, he didn't want his son to be a fellow-comrade. Neither did God's mother. They wanted him to 'make' something of his life. What precisely that could be was unclear to all of them.

When God was sixteen he decided to be cheeky and find out. 'Does that mean you've made nothing of your own life... Comrade?' he asked his father.

His brother, Toro, nearly gagged over his chai-biscuit. But God's father was unshaken.

'Ideals, my boy, ideals. I had them... still do. I believed... still do. You don't. I don't know what you value. It is up to you to find out. But the Party doesn't need people like you. Even if you want to join it you won't be accepted because you are a taker. The Party wants givers.'

'So where has "giving" got you?' asked God. 'A rat-infested hole we have to call a home? If you chose ideals, why did you have a family? Ma and you could have suffered in bliss by yourselves. How do you think Toro and I feel about not having good clothes? No pocket-money? No place where our friends can come? I'll tell you how we feel—angry.'

'That's enough. Now go and help your mother with the buckets.'

God said to me that he didn't feel bitter any longer. Only cynical. 'Comrades!' he'd snort while passing a morcha. '*Lal nishan, zindabad,*' he'd shout mockingly at the protestors.

'Who pays your fees?' I'd asked him once, rather indelicately.

'I do,' he said without any self-consciousness.

'Meaning?'

'Meaning, I work as a freelance reporter... and do other stuff... correcting proofs, galleys... that kind of thing.'

'But your English... I mean, you went to a vernac school.'

'That has nothing to do with it. I was reading Chaucer and Karl Marx at ten. Don't ask me whether I understood any of it, but those were the only books around the place. Besides, how about *your* English, my dear Miss Snooty? How well do you conjugate? Forget it, *yaar*, all your convent crowd is full of crap, you people put on a *maha* accent to cover up for your poor language. I bet I can write better than all the guys in your class. Or mine. I'd got a scholarship—to Columbia. Have you heard of that university? 1 couldn't go because Comrade didn't have the money to pay the air-fare. And he didn't want to borrow. I tried telling him that had either Toro or I been a daughter he would've had to pay a dowry to marry us off. Where would he have got the money from then? But he ignored me and said, "First graduate in India. And then show off abroad." After that, I lost all interest in studies, *yaar*. But not in languages—I'm fluent in German, can understand French and read Spanish. But what's the point? I'll stagnate here like everybody else. So... now you know where my fees comes from. Any other questions?'

'Yes—from where did you get those fancy jeans?'

'Oh these? I bought them off a junkie at Colaba. You know Dipti—the fruit juice place? We used to go

11

there for a lassi after doing *bakwas* in the night. Grass dries up your throat. I met this guy—he was from Heidelberg. He couldn't speak English and a pusher was trying to con him. He kept muttering in German. I felt sorry for the guy and I spoke to him in German. His face lit up. I told him the pusher was trying to sell him junk. I guess he felt grateful. We started chatting. Dipti shut shop and we strolled off towards the Gateway.

'It was a beautiful night. We sat on the parapet watching the lights of the ships in the harbour. He talked of his family, his university, his dreams. It was too much, *yaar*. I bought him some chai. He must have been touched— because he asked me whether he could give me something in return. Poor fellow, he had hardly anything left. Everything had been stolen—his camera, bags—everything. I felt bad, *yaar*, but I couldn't help it. I said, "I want your jeans."

'He looked so happy as he stood there in his chaddis. "Here—take them," he said. I took off my pants and tried them on. They weren't a great fit… but I'd always wanted imported jeans. I knew this was the chance. If I hadn't taken it, I would've had to wait for ten more years. I didn't feel as if I was taking advantage of him or anything. Damn it, I'd given him my pants in return.'

I don't remember the precise day that God decided we were 'going together'. I think it was during a coffee morning at a college haunt, the Bistro. The jazz group was playing "Take the A Train," and God was drumming on the table with a lighter. 'You are OK, *yaar,*' he said to me, without breaking his rhythm, 'I mean, I don't mind you hanging around. I can't stand frustrated females generally. But you... you're all right. Stick around, baby.'

His awful friend, Guru, winked and made the victory sign. I sort of guessed God's little speech had made the whole thing official. I looked around the restaurant to see whether anybody there had noticed—it must have been so obvious that we were 'going steady' now. But nobody looked back at me.

Being God's girl was challenging. It was also pretty lonely. Most of the time God wasn't there and I had to sit around with Guru waiting for him to show up. All the others dropped me the moment they knew we were on. The few friends I'd made melted away as soon as they got the message that God came first. Or worse, that God would probably join us. The girls would move away hastily at the sight of him strolling up the courtyard. I couldn't understand this. It seemed so mean. God was good. And at least he wasn't boring like the other boys who wore Wrangler jeans and chewed gum. God must've sensed my unease.

One day, while walking back after classes he said, 'Look, *yaar,* it's OK if you want to split. The scene's getting heavy. I'm not used to having a female hanging around. Guru also feels funny when you are there. You're a sweet kid and all that. But all this steady-weddy business is too much. Why don't you see other guys... you know... that guy with specs, what's-his-name? Krishna—or someone else? You'll get a guy, I'm telling you. You haven't tried, that's all.'

I didn't want to go for other guys, damn it. God was all I wanted—had ever wanted in a boyfriend. He wasn't like the other boys. He had character—you know? It came out at different moments. Like the time he stood up to Rakesh whose sole claim to fame was being the only son of a sugar baron.

Rakesh had been indulging in a few sneaky tricks with the girls—the old kiss-and-tell routine. One of his victims complained to God. The confrontation between the two took place in the college canteen. Rakesh called God a 'commie beggar'. God retaliated by dubbing him a 'ball-less eunuch'. A few punches later, Rakesh, looking like a bloodied rat, begged for mercy. God dragged him across the basketball court and flung him at the insulted girl's feet.

'Say sorry to her, you dog,' he snarled.

I thought the whole thing heroic and old-fashioned. Rakesh was bigger and richer. But it was God who had scored.

His general attitude towards me was one of calculated indifference. But on days when I skipped college or bunked lectures, my absence registered with God. At our next meeting he'd narrow his eyes and look at me.

'Where were you yesterday, Nasha?' he'd demand. I'd suppress my secret thrill (he'd noticed!) and give him some vague answer. This would get his goat further. And I would get the reassurance I was looking for. Though, I must say that with God, it was I who wore my heart on my sleeve. It was I who made my feelings clear and took the initiative. No games. Not even an attempt to play hard to get. God had only to say the word, and I would be his. His what? Slave, sidekick, girl. It hardly mattered.

On the day he spoke to me about finding someone else my heart sank by the second listening to him. What was he saying? I would die without him. I'd go mad with grief. How could he feel that way when I was so happy? 'I'm not looking for a carrot,' I finally heard myself say.

God laughed. He actually laughed a happy laugh! 'OK,' was all he said. 'OK.' The sweetest words I'd ever heard. And that was it. It was settled. I was God's girl.

# Two

I took up a job with a mediocre ad agency straight after college. Just because I'd graduated with English honours and didn't really want to study any further, I had decided to go out and get myself a job, any job. And as everybody knows, when there's nothing better going, join advertising. If your bullshit sells—nothing like it. If not, you can still get by. Not shine as a supernova, but crawl along, jumping from one agency to the next, till you join the huge firmament of senior mediocrities like yourself. By then, you at least have the ad jargon mastered and several cute tricks under your belt. Unfortunately, these little numbers didn't excite me. There were other trainees in the same batch who had orgasms during the so-called creative brain-storming sessions. I just couldn't feel all a-flutter over a new brand of sanitary napkins that the agency was out to promote. Whether the protective shield was blue or pink—what the hell did it matter?

'Oh, but it does. It makes all the difference. Blue is the colour associated with safety,' the creative director would say, hands flapping. 'Pink? No, dearest ones, it cannot, but cannot, be pink. That's too close to blood.'

So, we'd all rush off to the studio and stop the final artworks which had the pink shield.

The art director resembled a crow and was called that, but in Marathi. In the Bombay agencies, most of the paste-up boys and lay-out girls are Maharashtrians. No sin. But most inconvenient, unless you spoke Marathi, since they didn't speak any English.

Kawla (Crow, the art director) was detested by everybody. But everyone agreed that he was talented. He came up with visuals that were knock-offs but which didn't look like copies. That qualified him as being an 'original ideas man'. It was invariably left to me to explain a client's brief to him since I was the only Marathi-speaking person on the 'other' side. I dreaded these encounters since Kawla insisted on carrying on a conversation in his version of English. This would lead to suppressed titters as the slaves in his galley pretended to align copy while listening to us. My Marathi was pretty shaky, but it was still better than his English. Kawla would resent my speaking to him in his native tongue since it implied that he couldn't express himself in 'Ingreji'. So, we'd struggle on—me in broken Marathi and Kawla in fractured English. It wasn't easy discussing sanitary napkins (with or without loops) or cold wax hair remover under the circumstances.

Kawla disapproved of God, who often burst in on us and laughed openly at our exchanges. He'd pointedly pull out a huge handkerchief and hold it to his nose while God puffed at his beedi. Most of the others in the studio would stop whatever they were doing to watch while God asked me to 'lend' him a tenner. Since I always left my handbag in the cabin I shared with the trainees, the entire exercise would become very obvious. Even the peons knew. After a few months, when we'd all got used to each other, the smarter of the two peons, Dhondu, would rush to my table to pick up my bag the moment he saw God coming. Nobody liked Deb, not even Anu, the telephone-operator-cum-receptionist. But then, I suppose, Anu didn't like anybody. And she listened in on all calls. She was also caught intercepting mail on several occasions. Any reprimand only added to her surly behaviour. She behaved like it was outrageous for anyone to expect privacy. I'd often walk into the office to find her reading my letters or even just holding them up to the light (what she hoped to see that way, I'll never know).

'What rubbish!' she exploded when I dared to protest. 'Who's interested in you and your letters?'

'What about phone-calls? I know you listen whenever Deb calls.'

'As if anybody would want to hear your stupid conversations. In any case, all he ever calls for is money.'

'There! I caught you. How did you know that if you hadn't heard us?'

'Everybody in the office knows it—why pick on me?' She sulked and stopped talking to me after that.

God wasn't at all bashful. '*Theek hai* (OK), *yaar*,' he said to me when I told him. 'That female has problems. She looks frustrated. She needs a good screw.'

I hated God when he said stuff like that. It was his explanation for everything. Any woman who didn't instantly fall into one of his slots was 'frustrated' and 'in need of a screw'.

Comrade often courted arrest at Flora Fountain or Kala Ghoda, where all processionists were halted by baton-wielding pandu-havaldars. Sometimes he was accompanied by Toro. Years after I discovered who he was, I saw him being dragged off into a waiting police van, kicking and protesting all the way. The agency overlooked the busy square and I had a bird's-eye view of the whole thing. Seeing God's father yelling *'inquilab zindabad'* so lustily impressed me a great deal. It also made me feel very tender towards God.

In fact, by now almost everything made me feel that way towards him. I'd be doodling on a scratch pad waiting for orders— 'Give me a paragraph on plastic mouldings… I need some body copy'—and suddenly, I'd spot a hairy beast at the beedi shop at the corner. 'God!' I'd exclaim to myself, feeling thrilled. The thought of writing rubbish about plastic mouldings after that wouldn't be as awful. Sometimes, God would rush up the stairs panting: 'I need some beedi-money, *yaar.*' There was nothing apologetic about the demand but curiously it would actually make me feel grateful. And each time he touched me for money, I'd feel a stirring of enthusiasm for my lousy job. At least it gave me a salary which I could use for him.

Occasionally, very occasionally, God's selfishness would bother me. Once, walking back from the office, I stopped at a sandal store (like Imelda Marcos, I had a shoe fetish—and still do) to gaze with longing at all the gorgeous new styles. He impatiently prodded me to move on, 'Forget it, *yaar.* You don't need any chappal-wappal. Come on, let's go get me an umbrella. I get drenched waiting for you to show up.'

I didn't dare tell him that one of my secret childhood longings was to own a cupboard full of shoes in every conceivable colour. Particularly red.

On my fifth birthday, I'd wanted a pair of bright red point-toed shoes. The kind that those pretty, goldilocked English girls wore in *Women and Home.* I'd plucked up the courage to ask my mother for them. But Mother being Mother thought in terms of 'wasteful expenditure'. She insisted I should buy black or white ones so that they'd double as school shoes.

'But I don't want school shoes,' I'd wailed, 'I want *party* shoes.'

'We don't have parties in this house on birthdays—you know that—it is unlucky. Do you want something to happen to you just because of your obstinacy? Supposing I got you red shoes and you had a party... supposing a horrible thing happened... an accident or something. If your dress caught fire on the cake candles... won't you feel bad? All because of your red shoes. So... no red shoes—you understand?'

No, I hadn't understood one little bit. I was crushed and disappointed. I didn't mind sacrificing my life for the shoes. The candles, the cake, me aflame... I didn't care. I wanted the shoes.

I had tried appealing to my father. It didn't work. He was a mama's man. I had to settle for black shoes... but my father had tried to arrange a compromise. 'Let's buy red socks,' he had suggested brightly.

I had been crying too hard to reply. In any case, I didn't want red socks. Only red shoes. The shopkeeper, obviously moved by the sight, had run out of the shop and brought back a red lollipop. I had flung it on the floor and continued to sob. Ever since that episode, I have had a mental block... red shoes are associated with trauma. Somehow, I secretly believed my mother's prediction. I was convinced I would die a horrible death the moment I stepped into a pair of the forbidden shoes. Yet, I couldn't stop coveting them.

I tried to share all this with God. But he wasn't at all interested in my childhood. 'It sounds so corny, *yaar*,' he snorted. 'You must have been a crazy kid.'

And so, we walked past the shoe shop and headed for the umbrella counter in the huge department store. 'Let's pick up one of those automatic Japanese jobs, *yaar*,' God said. 'The *desi* ones are useless.'

God had expensive tastes in most things. He'd spend hours looking for a perfect pair of loafers. 'If they aren't hand-stitched, they aren't worth wearing, *yaar*,' he'd comment, while I haggled with the impassive Chinese shopkeeper over the exorbitant price. I loved buying things for God. It gave me a sense of belonging. Gifts were a bond—perhaps the only one. Gifts—which he took entirely for granted.

And although he poured scorn on the Commies, he did believe in the philosophy which was understandable given his background. I didn't mind being called a capitalist pig, but I didn't like his calling my father that. For his part, my father couldn't stand the sight of God or the sound of his voice on the phone.

'What do you see in that worthless fellow?' he'd ask. 'He has no future. He has nothing. No looks. No money. Nothing.'

But that was precisely why I liked him. And, unlike other boys, he didn't *want* to work. I thought that was terrific. He actually rejected work. He had contempt for it. I told my father that with a lot of pride, during an argument. He nearly fell off his easy chair in anger.

'You fool! How can you say something so absurd? What will that man do in life? Beg? Become a pariah? Has he no self-respect?'

Undeterred by his reaction, I mumbled, 'You don't understand, Papa, he is a genius.'

'Genius at what? Living off other people? When will you see sense? You know how your mother and I feel about him. He'll ruin your life... just wait and see.'

How come both of them didn't realize how strangely those words worked? All you have to tell a young girl is that some boy is going to ruin her life—and presto! the chap becomes irresistible! I wanted to say, 'I'd *like* Deb to ruin my life. I *want* him to ruin it. I don't care if he wrecks it. I love him.'

But my father's white knuckles clutching the chair stopped me. 'Idiot!' he said, reading my thoughts. 'Heaven knows what you see in such a fellow? We will have to show your horoscope to Shankerao. There must be a *mangal* in the marriage house. You were born under a bad star. This man has some power over you. He must be a hypnotist. Filthy fellow. He stinks. He looks dirty. And he wants to be a beggar. Yet, my daughter, my foolish daughter, calls him a genius.'

Most people felt that way about God. And I thought that there was something the matter with them. How

23

come they couldn't recognize his qualities? His talent? God could quote from the Upanishads. He had read *Don Quixote* in the original Spanish. He knew how to pronounce and eat escargots. He could tell you all sorts of interesting things about insects. Or rain forests. He knew all the Beatles songs by heart. And was on first name terms with several painters and poets. He could cook and sew. And he knew how to fix the world's best fluffy omelettes. Dogs, cats and other animals were instinctively drawn to him. He could tie a tiny bandage around a house sparrow's injured leg. Or repair a torn wing with cellotape. I'd watched him bottle-feed nine hungry boxer puppies when their mother had died delivering them. He was fantastic with electronic gadgets. He enjoyed the opera as much as Bade Ghulam Ali. And he had seen *Citizen Kane* fourteen times. He'd read Ayn Rand when he was twelve years old and could quote extensively from Allen Ginsberg. He had a scrapbook full of Mcluhan's verses which he had illustrated himself using psychedelic ink. He'd stitched me a blouse once, using bandhni scarves and mirror-work pieces. While walking down a dirty road, he'd spot a gulmohur tree in the distance and stop to admire it. He created hair-ornaments for me using fresh green leaves, marigolds and twigs. He'd point out the patina on an old brass pot lying under a thick layer of grime. Or improvise on a vanilla ice-cream cone by sprinkling Bournvita over it.

How could I describe all this to my father or my mother? To them he was just a bum. A stranger who'd squeeze me dry of all that I owned. Mother would warn me, 'You may be the only child, but if you ever marry that man we'll cut you off completely. You won't get a paisa. We'll give the flat away to my brother's daughter. I won't let you have even my old saris or the steel almirah. Go, live with that scoundrel and suffer; if that's in your horoscope, what are we to do?'

God said he wasn't interested in wealth. He insisted that money was only a means to an end. He couldn't help it if he had very refined tastes in all things. He liked beauty and as he put it, 'Beauty comes with a price tag. Quality costs.'

While the others in his group carried khadi jholas full of radical literature, pamphlets and magazines, God preferred a saddle-stitched, all-leather satchel. 'It's more practical, *yaar*. Holds more things. Lasts longer,' he explained.

He was right. His friends had to replace their jholas every three months. The satchel saw him through three years. It was the same with pens and scratch pads. 'The writing process becomes easier if you have the right implements,' he'd say, taking out his silver Cross pencil.

And there were other unexpected things as well. God's hands and fingernails were surprisingly clean and neat. Once, I caught him filing his nails. He was embarrassed

25

at first, but recovered quickly enough. 'Nails are a big bore, *yaar*. They get in the way.'

I didn't say a thing.

He dipped into his satchel and pulled out a beautiful manicure set which he tossed at me carelessly. 'Here... use it. Your nails could do with some buffing.'

Often I'd catch him munching something absently. 'What are you eating?' I asked him the first time I heard his jaws moving noisily in a theatre. We were watching *Sundance Kid* and I was trying hard to pretend that Robert Redford didn't affect me since God had dismissed him as a 'blond pansy with a wart'.

'Calcium,' said God shortly.

'What do you mean "Calcium"?' I asked.

'Haven't you heard of it? It comes in various forms... chalk, lime and so on.'

'You mean you are eating chalk?'

'No... I'm eating something more refined—tablets.'

'Why?'

It's good for the nails,' he said and passed me a handful. After that, we'd munch calcium tablets companionably through a movie while the others ate popcorn. It was things like this that made God, God. Only, nobody really understood or cared.

In addition to his nails, God was particular about his lips. Whatever be the season, God carried a chapstick

around in his filthy pockets. This he would whip out at
the unlikeliest moment and apply evenly on his dried
lips. The first time he did it in my presence I looked
away in embarrassment. God looked extraordinarily
silly rubbing a chapstick on his lips. But he wasn't at
all embarrassed.

'It's OK, *yaar*. You'd better get used to it. My lips
start cracking if I don't use this bloody thing.'

'Why don't you try giving up grass?' I asked him.
'Maybe those ciggies don't suit you.'

'Give up grass? You must be *pagal, yaar,* completely
mad. It's like asking me to give up … urinating.'

'Must you be so crude?'

'What's wrong with pissing? It's natural, *yaar*.
Everybody does it. Don't you?'

'But you make the most natural function sound
obscene.'

'It's all in the mind, *yaar… chalo chhodo…* forget it.'


God was contemptuous about almost everything. But
my parents, particularly my father, came in for special
treatment. 'What is he, *yaar*? Just a stooge of his white
masters. What has he done for himself, *yaar*? Fuck all.
Screwed the country, that's all. Selling substandard rubbish.
Things are going to change, baby, just watch out. Tell
your old man, they're coming for him. I'd like to see
him then. What will you do when that happens, Nasha?

When the party's over, *sub kuch khatam, yaar.* You'll have to travel in buses and trains like the rest of us.'

God just hated the sight of my father's car. It was a smart, grey Ambassador with white towelling on the seats. Our driver wore the company uniform with the logo emblazoned on the epaulettes. 'Is he a slave, that *chootiya* driver of yours? Has he no shame? No self-respect? Looks like a bloody *bandar* (monkey) in that uniform.'

I used to ignore these taunts and digs as much as I could. But sometimes God could get terribly vicious and cross all limits.

Once, he spotted my mother in the car. She was dressed for her twice-a-week bridge session at the club. He looked at her long and hard and finally announced. 'Your mother, *yaar*—what she really needs is a good screw.'

'Oh, shut up! How dare you?' I screamed. 'You and your filthy mind. What would you know about the needs of ladies—you who have no background, no class, you filthy bastard,' I spluttered.

It didn't faze God at all. 'Getting all uppity with me, are you? Cool it, *yaar*. No need to get so angry. I didn't really mean it. All I'm saying is, poor woman seems a lonely lady. Cold. *Thanda.* Get the picture? Now I know what makes you an ice-cube. *Theek hai, yaar.* Even ice-cubes melt at the right temperature. Relax. Have a fag.'

I was violently angry. I thought my mother was looking especially pretty that day. She was wearing a fetching pink sari which suited her complexion. Her nails looked like dainty shells and her hair had been freshly set by Lizzie.

'Is she wearing a helmet on her head or what?' God asked nastily.

'It's called a bouffant, and it suits her beautifully,' said coldly. 'But how would you know about such things?'

That was supposed to be a cutting remark directed at his own mother, who he'd told me resembled a washerwoman or a brothel-keeper, depending on her mood—'When she feels all fancy, she puts huge flowers in her hair and kaajal in her eyes. Her tits hang out of her choli and the paan in the mouth makes her look like a whore. At other times, with her sari carelessly tied, she looks like a maidservant. But it's OK, *yaar*, my father looks like a handcart puller from Lohar Chawl.'

I couldn't get over how candid, even ruthless, God was in his descriptions of his parents and their lives. 'I don't believe in all that reverence-sheverence shit, *yaar*,' he'd explained. 'After all, parents are people too. What's so special about them? They screwed and made you by accident. Does that mean you should be grateful to them forever? *Chhodo, yaar*, forget it—I only hope they were having fun while making me. Otherwise, what's the point? Hey... have you ever seen your folks fucking?'

29

'How can you talk like that, Deb. It's disgusting.'

'Which means you have—haven't you? C'mon... confess, *yaar*. I won't tell anybody. Promise.'

'No, I haven't. And even if I had, I wouldn't tell you.'

'I've seen mine. Want to hear about it? It was when all of us used to live in a small kholi. You know, the type of chawls your driver probably stays in. There was no privacy, *yaar,* no space. What could the poor things do? They'd put me and my brother on the charpoy and lie down on the floor. When they thought we were asleep, they'd get on with it, as quietly as possible. But the old guy's grunts always woke us up. I'd nudge Toro or he'd nudge me. Then it would be a free show.'

'How shameless of you! Don't you feel bad now?'

'No chance, *yaar.* Everybody does it. Even animals. After some time, we stopped watching. There was nothing new. Same old stuff. It became so boring that we'd close our ears to stop the grunts from disturbing us. But one sight has stuck. Often, we'd find our mother on top, and that used to look quite funny.'

'I don't want to hear anything more. Stop it. Just stop it. You have no respect for anyone or anything. I really don't know why I tolerate you.'

'That's simple, *yaar*—you love me.'

✳

Till I met God, my father had been the most important man in my life. He worked for a multinational which sold a range of useless products. I loved watching him preening in front of the mirror before leaving for the office. It was a routine that rarely varied. The part that I liked best was when he carefully selected his aftershave. My father was fixated on smell. One could gauge his mood from the after-shave he picked. At least, my mother could. When I was a kid, the choice of men's fragrances was limited to just two or three popular brands like Old Spice. To those, my father had added English Lavender and 4711. He mixed and matched perfumes skilfully so that, depending on the combination and the ratio, each day produced a fresh fragrance. He hoarded his colognes and after-shaves, not even allowing my mother to splash on a few drops. 'You have your own. Leave mine alone,' he would say.

The house used to smell heavenly in the mornings, especially my parents' bedroom. Mummy's sandalwood soap-smell with just a hint of Miss Dior—her favourite perfume. Unlike my father, who really indulged himself in this department, my mother was miserly. She was very stingy with her bottles, dabbing on a drop here and a drop there. The heavy, expensive stuff she'd reserve for the nights when they went out to company dinners. These were obviously very important occasions for my father, who'd be very tense while applying the cologne-of-the-evening on the neat folds of his Swiss handkerchief. He'd also get impatient with my mother while she adjusted the soft folds of her chiffon sari (French for the really big events, Indian for those in the minor league).

My father's ideas of a well-dressed wife were pretty fixed—she had to be draped in pastel-coloured chiffons worn with a sleeveless blouse. Jewellery to be restricted to a discreet row of pearls, a diamond ring, bracelet watch and small ear tops. Matching shoes and handbag were an absolute must. Also, manicured nails (fingers and toes), and lacquered hair. Make-up, especially lipstick, was of vital importance since he firmly believed it was a sign of sophistication and no stylish woman should ever be seen without it. He also had another hang-up—but here, my mother drew the line.

'Elegant women always wear stockings,' he'd tell her.

'Under saris?' she'd ask.

'Why not? I've seen many Parsee ladies wearing them,' he'd say uncertainly.

'Well... I'm not a Parsee.'

And that would end that particular round. I'm not sure my mother's ideas about well-dressed women coincided with my father's. They came from entirely different backgrounds, for one. My mother was from Gujarat. My father had been born and brought up in Bombay. My mother, in Ahmedabad.

I would've loved to know the story of how they met and married. But my mother had never encouraged intimacy though we got along quite well most of the time—and sometimes she could even be fun. She was a different person in my father's presence—far more subdued and silent. Not that he was an overbearing man or anything. But he had his own ways of shutting her up. Not rudely. Just firmly. I suppose they loved each other. Sort of. I'm sure my father loved my mother, at least, in those days. About her, I can't say. That was one taboo area. In any case, my mother wasn't particularly demonstrative. Neither was my father, but he didn't actually shrink from physical contact the way my mother did. She stopped holding me when I was five years old.

'You are a big girl now,' she'd said, 'stop behaving like a baby.'

Papa continued to plant a vague kiss or muss up my hair absently till I was much older. I missed companionship. I missed having brothers and sisters. I asked my mother once why she'd stopped with me. The question had made her most uncomfortable.

'You ask such silly questions. Well-behaved girls don't talk like this,' she'd said and walked out of the room.

I'd found her reaction most strange. In my mind, I'd asked a perfectly legitimate question which deserved a straight answer. I tried again with my father.

'Well… did you ask your mother?' was his immediate response.

'I did, and she refused to tell me.' Maybe I shouldn't have said that. He clammed up too.

'Have I asked something silly?' I carried on. 'Why are both of you not telling me?'

'It's like this, Nisha... your mother and I were very young when we married. Your mother was little older than a child herself when you were born. She found it difficult to handle a baby. Your mother is not a very strong woman... you know... physically. The strain was too much. You took a long time to arrive. She was in bed for three months before and two months after your birth. When you were an infant, you used to cry a lot and keep Mummy awake all night. She had a difficult time, even though we had Didi who had just arrived from Nepal. So, we kept postponing having another baby—till it became too late.'

I didn't like this version at all. I wished he'd told me something else. Even a lie. I wished he'd said something like, 'We loved you so much, we didn't want to share that love with any other child.' Parents in books and movies always said that. By being truthful (if he was being truthful, that is) he'd made me feel guilty and awful. As though I was to blame for my mother's health. And that it was all my fault she fell sick so often.

❋

When God and I started seeing each other regularly, I told him about my father's explanation.

34

'He's lying,' he said flatly. 'Take it from me, there was some other reason, *yaar*. He must have been too busy scrambling up the corporate ladder to screw your mother.'

'Don't talk like that about my parents,' I shouted.

'Why? Are their names inscribed in the scriptures? Stop being absurd, baby. Grow up. Reality, *yaar,* it's a very ugly thing.'

God was right about reality, of course. He was right about nearly everything. When we weren't together, I would try and see him as he appeared to others. To my parents, for instance, he was thoroughly detestable. Coarse, unkempt, ill-mannered. He knew it and even revelled in it.

'So, what did Mr Multinational say about me to his beloved daughter, his *ladli beti*.... Hey—that's a nice little pet name for you—I'll call you L.B. short for Ladli Beti—how about that? Does Daddy like his darling's bum of a boyfriend, huh? Poor Daddy, wouldn't he have loved to see you married off to some marketing manager—a man with a future and no past. An MBA from Harvard. Or at least Ahmedabad. The sort of creep who hands out visiting cards with his degrees embossed in bold type. Ha-ha. I've ruined his neat little plans for you, haven't I, baby? I love it.'

My parents soon began to pretend they didn't know of God's existence. He was never referred to by name and his calls were rarely taken. The question of giving me his messages, therefore, didn't arise. The servants caught on quickly enough. Only Didi was sympathetic. If she ever picked up the phone, she'd promptly hand it to me silently. Not the others.

'Sack those bloody *chamchas* (sycophants) before I send my goon-squad over to murder them,' God yelled one afternoon. He'd called to inform me that our date stood cancelled as he had to rush to the Esplanade Court to fish out his father from the clink. 'The jailbird is at it again,' he said. 'I had to borrow dough to bail him out. Such a pain, *yaar*. Think of all the beedies I could have bought with the money.'

This used to occur regularly and was thought of more as an inconvenience than a disgrace. God had a rich uncle. Rich by his standards that is. Each time his father got hauled in, God had to go and touch the uncle for bail money. This was one thing that depressed him, but there was no alternative. 'We always pay the swine back,' he said, 'I'm sure he swindles us. I have a feeling he charges interest.' God's mother took all the shenanigans in her stride and carried on like a jailed husband was no big deal. There were other aspects to her life that she also bore stoically. Often, she had to sleep in the common balcony of the chawl when their room was taken over by union workers. Toro, God's brother, was responsible for supplying tea. Over a kerosene stove, a huge kettle full of water would be kept on the boil, while the men argued and debated late into the night.

'Such shit, *yaar*. All *faltugiri*, all nonsense. When will my father learn that they can never lick the system? Total waste of time. Your old man is a *chaalu* chap. He knows the rules of the game all right. But tell him to watch out. One day he might find himself gheraoed. I've been hearing things. Do you know how they run that company? Have you seen their balance sheets? No? Then go home and take a look. *Saalas* think they're fooling everyone. Selling adulterated stuff at fancy prices. We will take care of him—warn that tight-ass father of yours.'

That tight-ass father of mine was far too busy with the launch of a new detergent to pay the slightest attention to union noises. He was travelling constantly, which used to bother my mother.

'Baby, talk to Papa. Tell him about all the plane crashes in the papers. Why is he killing himself for the company? What has it given us—or him—besides a roof over our heads and a car with a driver? Papa will get ulcers—I read in the *Reader's Digest* that stress leads to intestinal ulcers. Have you noticed how often he belches these days?'

'Maybe Papa enjoys his work,' I suggested brightly.

'How can anyone enjoy selling soap powder?' she asked.

I didn't know what to say. Her remark made me wonder about their relationship. My mother didn't respect my father. She didn't make it obvious, but she gave herself away with comments like this.

She was a finicky housewife. Almost obsessive in her attention to detail. When she wasn't ordering the servants to dust away an imaginary speck from somewhere, she was nagging Didi to clean out all the cupboards. *Jhadoo-pochcha*, sweeping and swabbing—she woke up each morning with that as a mantra. She thought she was doing her duty as a housewife. A thrifty one. She may have imagined that Papa approved of her 'involvement' in the running of the house and compared her attitude to that of the other 'company' wives who left it all to servants. Like one of them used to remind her, 'Why not, darling? Since the bloody company pays for the servants, let them slog. You work too hard. You are the only senior executive wife who does not join our kitty club. OK, *baba*, if you don't like rummy, play bridge with us. We are willing to learn. But it's important to mix. The M.D.'s wife was saying the other day—Mrs Verma doesn't mix around. Think of your husband's career… take it seriously, *yaar*. People in Personnel are always watching.'

My mother would try to defend herself by saying that she didn't have too much spare time.

'Why? You don't work or anything. It's different if you were like Mrs Mehta. She has a good job. I would say, even a better job than her husband—poor fellow, he's still stuck in the audit department. That too, without a promotion in three years. In her case, it's different. She has to travel also—then who'll stay with the children? Like that, Mr Mehta is very co-operative. My husband would never allow me to attend office, and travel—no chance. You have only one child—that too, a daughter. So, what's the problem? Soon, she'll also be married off. Then you won't have to bother about her.'

Once again my mother would start explaining the servant problem in our area.

'Forget it, darling. Servant problems are everywhere. But I don't bother. My kitty comes first. We are not only housekeepers, after all. If there is no servant, then forget work, *yaar*. You can order food from the club—nobody will notice.'

'My husband will,' my mother would say.

'That is your problem. But if I were in your place, I would just tell him that if he'd wanted to marry an ayah, he shouldn't have married you. We bring a lot of status to our husbands and they should realize it. We also have a role to play in their careers. See the M.D.'s wife—how active she is. Office sports, social welfare club, officer's mess, rural development programmes, creches and *balwadis*, also flower arrangement classes and cake baking… she does so many things. It was because of her that he became the M.D.'

On one occasion when the Managing Director's wife was once again being held up as a shining example of a corporate spouse, because of the number of so-called relevant activities she engaged in, my mother forgot her customary discretion as a 'company wife' and blurted out, 'Is that the reason? And I'd always thought it was because of the ex-chairman. Wasn't she his mistress for years?'

'I don't know, *baba*. Don't involve me in office gossip.'

# Three

God's entry into the 'literary' circuit was through proof-checking. Apparently he was very good at it. 'The best, *yaar*,' he used to boast.

Proof-checkers were a fast-disappearing breed. It was simpler to get a writer than a proof-checker. God was surprisingly responsible too. He took his proof-checking very seriously. It didn't take long for his reputation to spread. Reams and reams of galleys began to arrive at his doorstep. God decided to hire an assistant to help him. A bright schoolboy from the chawl.

'Any fool can proof-check,' he said. 'I'll teach him the basics in a week and go over his stuff once before submitting it.'

Pappu, the underage proof-checker, turned out to be an eager learner with an eagle eye. Between the two of them they'd clear anything between a thousand to two thousand rupees a month. God was quite fair with Pappu and paid him per galley.

It was around this time that God discovered that he could do more than read other people's proofs. He had a natural gift for writing. It started with poems. I didn't understand poetry and had always thought that for anything to fall into this literary category, it had to rhyme. God guffawed when I told him.

'*Chhodo, yaar.* This stuff is not your scene. You'd better stick to reading Mills and Boon.'

I hotly denied reading Mills and Boon (though I couldn't resist them).

'Cool it, baby. Read whatever you want to, but leave my poems alone. They'll be too heavy for you.'

'Stop being so condescending. As if I can't understand what you write. What is so great about it, anyway? Any fool could write something meaningless, which doesn't even rhyme, and call it poetry.'

'*Achcha?* Then you'd better come with me to the next poetry-reading session.'

And that's how I got to meet the grand Dirty Old Man of the arty-farty literary circuit.

The sessions were conducted in dingy halls where the organizers didn't have to pay any rent. Everybody sat around on uncomfortable folding chairs or on the floor. The Dirty Old Man would preside over the evenings with his cutesie-of-the-moment at his side. He liked them young and dumb. Others who were present regularly were a fairly motley lot of struggling writers, a Grande Dame of Verse, frustrated copy-writers and self-styled critics. Each session was broken up into various stages, including one reserved for visiting intellectuals and another for first timers. Sometimes, a flute or a guitar would also feature. It was at my third session that I discovered that God was musically inclined. He could play both the flute and the tabla exceedingly well.

'Why didn't you ever tell me about it?' I asked, when he suddenly pulled out a bansuri from his satchel and started playing it softly... beautifully.

'No big deal, baby,' he interrupted his playing to say, 'sometimes I feel I am Krishna reborn.'

A pretty scruffy Krishna. But that hardly mattered when his lips were on the flute or his fingers on the tabla. It was easy to forget his ruffian-like appearance, his unrefined ways, his crude jokes as the melodious notes from the simple reed held with such delicacy in those manicured hands wafted over our small group and cast a spell on those listening. God was a naturally gifted musician but a surprisingly shy one.

'It's nothing, *yaar*. Just some too-too-poo-poo I picked up from the old woman,' he'd say.

It was much more than that but God was uncharacteristically modest about it. Maybe he didn't want to put himself on the line and find out just how talented. I could understand that. And like he put it, 'I play for myself, *yaar*, not to impress the fucking world.'

✳

God had been longing to acquire a motorbike for years. It would enter our lives later. Along with the flute and chapstick, this new monster was to become a permanent feature of God's existence. But right then— 'No dough, baby. I'm not a rich man's son. My old guy has always used public transport—generally without buying a ticket. I've done the same. But a motorbike would change my life. I'd be able to save so much time.'

'And do what with it?'

'Who knows? Goof off... listen to Bade Ghulam Ali. Go whoring.'

'Do you really?'

'Do I really—what?'

'Go... you know... go to those sorts of places?'

'What sort?'

'You know what I mean. Why do you want me to utter bad words?'

'Look, *yaar,* don't give me all this bullshit. Why don't you say it—brothel. It's a simple word—try... bro—thel... see? Easy!'

'OK, do you visit brothels?'

'Every night, *yaar*... I hope to meet your father there. Ha! Ha! It's a joke, OK? Relax.'

'No... but seriously... have you ever been?'

'OK, seriously... I have—once or twice.'

'Where?'

'You know, you ask too many stupid questions. Where? What diff, *yaar?'*

'I'd like to know. What was it like.'

'Honest answer?'

I nodded.

'Horrible, *yaar*. Couldn't do a thing. Those bloody *randis* are such cold-blooded professionals. All they want is to finish it off and get you out of their filthy beds.'

'Then why did you go?'

'Don't be mad, *yaar*. Everybody goes.'

'You mean all the chaps in office… ?'

'Not the stupid types. But the real guys… naturally.'

'What for?'

'*Aré…* it's obvious, *yaar*. That is the first lesson in life to be learnt… there's no such thing as a free fuck. Everything costs. Understand?'

'Couldn't you wait till you got married?'

'Wait? For eternity? Who knows about marriage-sharriage, *yaar*. I'm happy as I am.'

'But you'd expect your wife to be… you know… untouched. No?'

'No. Makes no diff, *yaar*. Let her also enjoy herself. Why make such a fuss over one square centimetre?'

'What does that mean?'

'Leave it. Some other time. I don't want your Multinational to accuse me of corrupting you.'

'Tell me just one more thing. Do you still go?'

'Oh God! Even my mother doesn't ask me so many questions!'

'Do you? Just say "yes" or "no".'

'No.'

'Thank God!'

'Anything else?'

'Yes—do you see other girls behind my back?'

'Definitely—thousands of them.'

'Liar.'

When God got his bike, (with money borrowed, scrounged or stolen, I never found out) our lives changed. It made him feel powerful. And confident.

'Her name is Bijli,' he told me.

At first, I thought he was only joking. But no. Bijli was a person to God. She had feelings. She was the one 'woman' who understood him. Years later, he explained Bijli's role in his life to me.

'She was everything, *yaar*. Mother, sister, lover, daughter. I could count on her. I knew that if I looked after her, she'd look after me. And she was faithful. No other man ever rode my Bijli while she was mine.'

I found the whole thing pretty crazy. Especially his talking to her, I mean, *it*.

'I get lonely on the road, *yaar*. I enjoy speaking to her.'

'But isn't it unnatural?'

'What's so unnatural about it? Bijli is lonely too. I can sense it when she's feeling neglected. Or blue. She purrs differently. She responds differently.'

'Like how?'

'You wouldn't understand.'

'Try me....'

'Did you ever have dolls as a child.'

'Of course I did. I still have my favourite ones.'

'Did you talk to them?'

'Yes, of course I did.'

'Didn't you feel close to them? Weren't they real to you?'

'But I was a child then. It was a childish reaction. A universal one. But that stopped. When I was... let's see... about seven or eight years old.'

'What about dogs? Cats? Don't you find people talking to their pets? And do their pets "talk" back?'

'How can you compare Bijli—a motorbike—with a pet? Pets are alive.'

'Don't you see—Bijli is alive too? She is not just a motorbike. She is not just a machine. Why can't you understand that?'

'People will think you're mad. Can you imagine what the others on the road must be thinking?'

'Who cares, *yaar?* Do you? I love Bijli and she loves me... *bas,* matter ends. Why should I bother about what all these *chamchas* on the road must be

thinking? Anyway… how does it affect their lives? Or
yours? Do you feel jealous?'

'It's not a question of jealousy. I just think it's
not normal.'

'What is "normal"? Who decides that? You? Society?
Mr Multinational? Comradesaab? Let's drop the topic,
yaar. I don't want to discuss her. Come on, I'll take
you home.'

Maybe I was going crazy too. I thought I caught
Bijli giving me a dirty look!

✴

The poetry-reading sessions were getting on my nerves.
The D.O.M. (Dirty Old Man) was such an obvious
phoney, I was surprised God couldn't see through
him. His cronies and he called themselves the
Anglo-Indian Poets Association. Each time God dragged
me to these affairs, I'd sit around feeling hostile and
helpless. I thought the poetry was putrid. Often, a
blousy woman in her mid-forties would preside over
the evening. I used to find her gross and repulsive.
She had beautiful eyes but with a touch of madness
lurking in them. The rest of her was bulky and awkward.
She preferred to wear coarse cotton saris with
bush-shirt like blouses. Her hair was matted and wild.
God found her divinely sexy. So did most of the others.
And so did she herself. Her poems were pornographic.

48

Or that's how they sounded to me. I couldn't understand how anyone could rhyme 'orifice' with 'Gin-Fizz'. She would sail into the hall, supremely confident of her sexuality. Men of all ages would be drawn to her... to her what... smell?

God said, 'Just go close to her and breathe in. Instant orgasm, *yaar*.'

'What rubbish!'

'Sorry—you aren't a man. I forget that sometimes. But try it, anyway. Sandalwood, coconut oil, musk, perspiration, sambhar— it's all that and something else... maybe stale sex... she's some thing, *yaar*.'

'You fellows behave like dogs in heat. It's disgusting! Why have me around? You can spend the evening going sniff, sniff, sniff. And if that bores you after a while, you can zip out and chat with Bijli. I really don't know why I hang around.'

'She's old enough to be your grandma, *yaar*. Cool it.'

'That's why I find the whole thing so disgusting.'

'Mother-complex. Heard of it? According to Freud, every son wants to screw his mother.'

'Shut up! You talk like a pervert.'

'Beware, I might be one.'

There was another, younger woman around as well. She was batty too, but in a different way. Strong white teeth in an ordinary face. Bad skin. Straw-like hair. And dark wide eyes that weren't still for a moment.

She was said to be the D.O.M.'s current passion. She behaved more like his servant. The D.O.M. and God had beedies as a bond. The slave-girl carried the D.O.M.'s in her embroidered silk bag.

'I am a poet,' she'd announce dramatically to a person she'd just been introduced to. 'I'm working on my first major collection.'

The D.O.M. would take a minute off from looking important, to tweak her cheek indulgently. 'Talent. My girl has talent.'

Chandni (that was her name, I'm not sure whether her parents had given it to her or the D.O.M.) was the chai-girl at these sessions. About thrice during the course of the evening, all the thirsty poets would reach into their pockets for small change and hand it to her. Chandni would rush out and come back a little later with small glasses full of over-brewed, over-sweetened tea.

On a special occasion, like someone's birthday, crisp dosas from the Udipi restaurant across the street would be ordered strictly by contribution. At other times, the sex queen, Sujata, would get 'tiffin' from her house. Once or twice a year she'd invite everyone to her spacious flat to listen to visiting poets from far-flung places, who'd read their stuff in their native tongue. These were considered the high points of the Association's existence. Sujata would play Mother Hen and gather all her chicks to her bosom—literally. I was surprised to discover that Sujata had a family.

A very conventional one at that. All of them——her timid husband and four daughters, doted on her. However, she had made it plain that she had gone beyond them and that she'd stopped playing wife and mother long ago.

'My duties are over. They are on their own now,' she would explain. 'I have played the roles I was expected to at the appropriate times. Now... I'm on my own. And they are on their own. This is my life. I want to live it my way.'

Her way included a succession of lovers, both male and female, who were paraded under the noses of her family.

'Yes... they accept,' she would say, calmly. 'Why shouldn't they? I've been a good wife and mother. I'm still here, living in the same house. They are grateful. I could easily have left and gone away. So many men have longed to make me theirs. I receive marriage proposals all the time... even now. But no. My place is in my own home.'

Her home was comfortable in a bourgeois way. If her daughters found her conduct embarrassing, they certainly hid it well. She filled the room with her presence and they followed her every move, their eyes shining with adoration.

'What a fortunate woman,' I said to God. 'How lucky she is. Any other husband would have thrown such a wife out of the house.'

'She's not just any ordinary wife... she's Sujata. She's like an empress or a goddess. Don't equate her with any *altu-faltu,* commonplace female.'

'I wasn't talking about her. I was wondering about them—her family. How come they accept her behaviour?'

'What's wrong with her behaviour? She is beautiful, man, just beautiful. She follows her instincts. She makes her own rules. She's not a coward. She cares two hoots for so-called "society". I admire her guts, *yaar.*'

'But didn't her husband have a nervous breakdown or a heart attack or something some time ago? And didn't he nearly lose his job when she published her first book of vulgar poems?'

'Vulgar poems! Really, *yaar.* You'll never appreciate art. Those poems were not vulgar. They were truthful. She performed a striptease of her soul. She bared everything. She stood naked in front of the world. And you are calling that vulgar?'

'My mother was so shocked. I remember her telling my father, "That woman must be a nympho." I remember this very clearly because that was the first time I'd heard that word. So, I asked my parents, "What does 'nympho' mean?" And they'd looked at each other and said, "It means... it means... a woman who is suffering from breathing trouble." So I said, "You mean, like asthma?" And my father replied, "Exactly. Now finish your pudding." Ever since then I've always felt sorry for her—thinking the poor woman can't breathe properly. Imagine! Even after I found out the meaning of the word "nympho"!'

'You are absolutely right, *yaar*. Sujata can't breathe... she is suffocating. But not physically.'

I was a total misfit in God's arty circle. Most times I'd try and be as unobtrusive as possible. Sujata noticed me after nearly ten sessions. Suddenly, her eyes strayed towards where I was sitting, fiddling with my dupatta.

'And who is that sugar mouse in the corner?' she asked imperiously.

The group was experimenting with play-reading that evening and God had been given some dramatic lines. He looked up from his book and assured Sujata, 'Oh... she's nobody. I mean... she's just a friend.'

'Well, dear friend of Debu's, stand up and be identified,' she commanded.

'You heard her, *yaar*,' God yelled out. 'Get up... she won't gobble you up.'

I detested him at that moment. And all the rest of the unwashed bodies.

Chandni giggled and said, 'My, my... she's so shy. Hey! That rhymes.'

I didn't know what to do. The rehearsal had come to a standstill. Everybody was waiting for me to do something. I laughed nervously.

'Don't giggle stupidly, *yaar*. Join the crowd,' God ordered.

I thought I saw a collective sneer at my gaucherie. It was the D.O.M. who finally rescued me. He broke the tension by reciting a poem—an appropriate one. Everybody applauded as the focus shifted from me to him.

Chandni came up and sat down. 'Deb is such a talented guy. You are lucky. Nana is thinking of giving him a big break soon.'

'Nana' was what insiders called the D.O.M. I noticed tiny hairs peeping out of Chandni's permanently flared nostrils. They were unattractive.

'So, what do you do, Neeta,' she asked, feigning interest.

'Nisha,' I replied.

'What?'

'My name. It's Nisha.'

'Oh yes… I knew it began with an "N"—Neha, Neeta, Nidhi… something of that sort.'

'Nothing.'

'What?'

'I do nothing. I mean, nothing interesting.'

'You aren't into poetry, creative writing, painting… that sort of thing?'

'No. I'm working as a trainee.'

'A trainee what?'

'Oh, they are still trying to figure that out.'

'I see,' she said without the slightest interest and turned to a young man wearing granny glasses.

'I loved you as Cleopatra. That was so clever!' He got up and bowed elaborately.

'I wanted you to play Caesar, but Nana didn't approve.'

'Nana… forget him, *yaar*. He's becoming slightly senile. Imagine getting possessive in his old age. Too much trouble.'

Nana was staring at Chandni while she flirted with Granny Glasses.

'He's looking,' warned the young man.

'Let him look. What can he do? Fight a duel?'

'No, *yaar*. But who needs hassles with the old boy?'

'Tell you what? Pass me your phone number. I'll call you when Nana goes to Greece for the International Poets' Meet.'

'Aren't you going?'

'Not this time. I had enough of them last year.'

Chandni had just enough time to grab the piece of paper before the D.O.M. came across to claim her. He looked at me thoughtfully through his half-moon glasses. Wiry hair that stood on end all over his head made him resemble an ageing gollywog.

'Virgin,' he declared looking steadily at me. 'In this day and age. Obscene. Perfectly obscene.'

Chandni stared saucily at God and giggled, 'Nana—why don't you take over from Debu?'

I picked up my stuff and ran out blindly. I wanted to kill them all. And God. I heard his footsteps behind me. 'Cool it, *yaar*. Don't be so hyper. Forget Nana. He tries that line with every new bird. Ask Chandni if you don't believe me.'

'I don't care. I don't have to ask anyone anything. I'm sick of the lot of you. Pseudo bores. You should see yourselves... so serious about your pretensions. So pathetic.'

'OK, OK. Have a dosa. I'll pay for it.'

'Stuff your dosa along with your poems. I may not be a part of your pseud-crowd... but even I can tell that your poems are rubbish. They stink just as much as Nana the Banana. What's more, he has toe-jam.'

The promised break for God did materialize after all. The D.O.M. was all set to launch a literary quarterly. He needed two things desperately—a sponsor and an assistant editor. God felt honoured when he was roped in for the second slot.

'Imagine!' he gloated. 'Me! An assistant editor to Nana! Let that bitch Chandni stew. She thought he was going to hand the whole thing over to her. But Nana knows she's good for just one thing—if that. Nana can smell out real talent.'

I didn't join in in his enthusiasm.

'Jealous, baby?' he asked.

'You must be joking. I'm worried about you.'

'Worried? What for, *yaar*? You worry about stupid things. What's wrong with *Plume*? Oh yes—I forgot to tell you—that's the name Nana came up with. Sujata loved it. One of her daughters has designed the masthead and logo. We've even found someone who may be ready to back it.'

'Really? Who?'

'That blue-haired old bag—Lady Kiss-My-Ass Shirinbai. Remember, we had met her at an organ recital once? Parsee loony. Dowager Dingbat. Loaded. Doesn't know what to do with the stuff. Her late husband—God bless him—had literary aspirations. So did their son, Freddie, the one who died a couple of years ago in that ghastly road accident near Panvel. Both the father and son had done the Oxbridge *chakkar* and used to contribute boring articles to those rags. The old girl is keen on setting up something to perpetuate their memory. She is sitting on a pile, as I told you—the Dadabhoy Trust runs into crores. This will be a piddly amount for her. I bet she spends more on her annual doggie parties where assorted pooches are served sirloin steak and caviare out of silver dog-dishes. Anyway... Nana plans to take the proposal to her.... Freddie used to be quite active when he was at Xavier's. He edited the college mag, headed the literary circle and all that. He was also madly in love with his Jesuit professor—but that's another story.'

Poor Lady Dingbat. She was quite a character around town, dressed in nineteenth century finery, her tiny feet shod in delicate lace shoes. She couldn't get around as much as she would have liked to ever since her stroke, but when she was wheeled in anywhere, it was a grand entry all right. Her heavily rouged face with the hooded eyes painted turquoise over the lids, the lips covered with scarlet lipstick, the hair coiffed and lacquered into place like a blue helmet and the gnarled hands with fastidiously manicured nails, all contributed to the image. She wore stockings through every season and nobody had seen her toes in years.

'It's terribly low class to display bare feet,' she'd once declared at a garden party startling the guests.

Her collection of magnificent *garas* (Chinese silk embroidered saris) was the envy of the Parsee community. And her jewellery was really impressive. It was rumoured that she dripped emeralds even when she was 'receiving' just her solicitor. And each Wednesday when she rode regally in her blue-to-match-her-hair Daimler to the Willingdon Club for her weekly bridge session, all the 'boys' and bearers would line up in the porch like a guard of honour. She was gracious and kind. And an easy touch. Her generosity had been well exploited by all those around her and it was believed that her personal maid had amassed a small fortune milking her employer over the years.

She bathed in a large, sunken marble tub filled with warm water at a precise temperature and perfumed with half-a-gallon of her favourite cologne from the House of Grès. In her time, all her underthings were custom-made in Paris out of the finest silk. It was said that a famous couture house had once considered creating a fragrance named after her. Yet, Lady Dingbat was a fierce nationalist as her late husband, Sir Hormusjee, had been. They lived like European aristocrats and behaved like royalty. But both of them had actively participated in the freedom struggle, giving generously to the fledgling Congress Party.

'We stopped short of courting arrest, my dear,' she was fond of saying, 'since I reminded Homi that the jails here did not have thunderboxes.'

There was a time when they had installed a French chef in their kitchen and milady's personal maid was an impoverished Austrian princess. Their parties, held on the family estate atop Napean Hill, were attended by maharajas and barons, dukes and duchesses, along with the crème de la crème of Bombay society. An English orchestra played waltzes on the lawns while millions of fairy lights twinkled on the trees. At these banquets Lady Shirinbai invariably served native food.

'Let them sample our splendid cuisine and go back and tell the people that we Indians dine better than they do. Savages—what would they know about the fine art of making a perfect biryani?'

But now the old girl had become a bit of a joke even within her own community. She was exploited and ridiculed by the very people who lived off her. The grand old home was almost totally in ruins except for the wing in which she lived with her dogs and servants. Apart from a faithful retainer, Gómes, from the old days, who padded around softly in a frayed uniform, all the others were recruits from the current brash breed. Their uncouth ways regularly shattered the old girl's sensibilities, but, as Gomes would remind her gently, 'Things are not the same anymore, madam.' Things certainly weren't, and Lady Shirinbai spent her days stroking her favourite dachshund and remembering earlier times when servants were faithful, discreet and invisible.

Her weekend salon was the one social grace she hung on to, though even here the kind of people who now called on her had undergone such a change… and with them, so had the conversation—good conversation. Lady S could still remember some precious *bon mots* dropped with genteel refinement decades ago. But she was training herself to be more philosophical about the changing scenario. She accepted people in her home these days, who would have earlier been dismissed by her butlers in the anteroom.

'Riff-raff,' she'd sniff privately to Fifi, her darling dachshund. Anyway, she needed company—not just any company, mind you—and how choosy could she really afford to be now? So, they'd troop in to drink her sherry, eat croquettes and canapes, gossip a little and depart, taking a whiff of Shirinbai's lavender home with them.

Lady S and her ways—these were subjects of heightened interest as soon as the D.O.M. and his circle had targeted her as their golden goose. As God told it, it had all begun at one of Shirinbai's salons—to which the D.O.M. had been invited as a guest.

# Four

It was to be an evening with a little light music played on Shirinbai's grand piano by an effete young man recently back from Juillard. Bomsi was a gifted pianist and his parents had great plans for him. They were sure that with a little encouragement from Lady S, Bomsi would be launched in his chosen career as a concert pianist. Shirinbai was, after all, a trustee of the only decent auditorium in the city. What better debut could Bomsi have hoped for?

The D.O.M. arrived at 'Windermere', Lady Shirinbai's home, for the elegant affair looking far from elegant himself. Not that it mattered. Nobody expected him to look anything but scruffy and abstracted. He had cultivated a vagueness of expression that was meant to convey a deep preoccupation with matters other than the ones immediately on hand. Except that his shrewd, beady eyes behind the thick lenses observed everyone and everything. He had decided to leave Chandni behind, afraid that her crudeness would pollute the refined atmosphere. It was a wise decision, for as soon as he entered Shirinbai's magnificent drawing-room, he spotted someone. He could tell that she was feeling lost and self-conscious. He decided to use his infallible ploy—the one that always worked with nervous young girls. The D.O.M. invariably scored a direct hit when he played Grandpa.

'Trust me,' he'd say after a few minutes of conversation. 'I was in college with your dear grandfather.'

Occasionally, someone would look startled and exclaim, 'My grandfather never went to college,' to which the unflappable D.O.M. would mime the doffing of an imaginary hat, bow low and purr:

'Pardon me, mademoiselle, I must've mistaken you for another lovely young lady I once dandled on my knee.'

By then he'd have this one giggling and eating out of his grimy hands.

Sure enough, Ava wasn't any different. Within minutes he had appropriated her from right under the noses of half-a-dozen young hopefuls who'd wasted time sniffing around her instead of zeroing in. Ava turned out to be Lady S's long-lost grand-niece from England.

The D.O.M. grilled her discreetly till he got her story out of her. She was an heiress and recently orphaned ('Perfect,' thought he). Lady S had offered to put her up during her stay in India, which was of an uncertain duration.

Ava was in search of her roots after the death of her parents in an aircrash. She had been born and brought up in London and looked and behaved like a proper English girl. The D.O.M. noticed her faint moustache and began to salivate. He had a thing about women with soft down on their upper lips. The one Chandni sported almost bristled. He sat through Bomsi's recital occasionally patting Ava's soft hands in an avuncular way. She didn't recoil. Nor did she seem to mind the dampness of his palms. When it was time to 'mingle' as Lady S put it ever so sweetly, the D.O.M. approached her with his arm linked through Ava's.

'Charming! Charming! What a beautiful young lady we have here,' he announced.

Lady S's left eyebrow went up by half-a-centimetre as her fan stopped in mid-air.

'And who do we have the pleasure of having with us tonight?' she asked.

The D.O.M. introduced himself using elaborate phrases and exaggerated gestures. He ended up by quoting Keats, 'Your favourite poet, I understand.'

Lady S didn't give a thing away. She turned to the bearer and asked, 'Croquette?'

Unfazed, the D.O.M. persisted in his efforts to impress her. Time was rapidly running out and Ava was beginning to look around.

'May I beg five minutes of your precious time, Ladyship?' he asked, bending from the waist.

'You may indeed,' she sniffed and indicated the adjoining study. The D.O.M. stood aside and bowed her in.

Once seated at her husband's magnificent mahogany table, Shirinbai faced the D.O.M. and raised both her eyebrows. He pretended to be transfixed by the enormous portrait of Sir Hormusjee behind Lady D.

'Wonderful. Just wonderful. The eyes. The bearing... quite, quite remarkable.'

'You wish to state something?' Shirinbai enquired.

'Ah... yes... but I forgot momentarily... so mesmerized was I by your late husband's expression. I had had the great pleasure of meeting him just before he so tragically passed away. God bless him. A great man. A great city father. I propose to start a campaign to name this road after him. Perhaps we could also erect an appropriate monument.'

'You are a poet,' said Shirinbai, ignoring his speech.

'Well... yes... that is... I write verse.'

'In English, I believe.'

'Why... yes indeed... in English.'

'How does it compare with Keats?'

'Well... Ladyship... I am embarrassed, abashed... I don't quite know how to respond. It would be far too immodest for....' he left the sentence dangling.

'Favourably then?'

'It is for you to decide, Ladyship,' he said with a semblance of a blush.

'Recite.'

'I beg your pardon, Ladyship?'

'Recite what you consider your favourite poem. You do have one, do you not?'

'This is a rare privilege indeed, Your Ladyship. Alas! I am far too taken aback to recall even a line.'

'Try,' she urged almost sadistically.

'Ahem... that is... I haven't brought my book with me. With your gracious permission, perhaps I could impose on your time and hospitality another day and read out some of my earlier poems to you?'

'Perhaps,' she said airily. 'Cognac? Port?'

'No no, thank you, you are too kind, Ladyship. What I wanted to see you about was this....'

And without further ado he thrust a dummy issue of *Plume* at her. She recoiled like he'd thrown a snake at her.

'What on earth is this rag?'

'It's a literary quarterly, Your Ladyship. Your late son—may his soul rest in peace—had been deeply interested in supporting this project. I have taken the liberty of setting down the outline for the proposed publication of *Plume* for your kind perusal. We will consider it an honour if you would be good enough to read the contents and agree to be the founding publisher and chief patron. It is primarily to encourage young poets. There are no outlets for them in this country, you see. Most of them give up out of frustration. It is in the hands of kind people like yourself to do what must be done to keep English poetry alive in India.'

Lady S took her time to glance through the dummy issue before reaching across the desk and picking up a cigar. 'Indulge me, won't you? A terrible habit.... My doctors have warned me. But I'd rather go down puffing when the time comes.' With that she puckered up her mauve mouth and stuck a Havana in it.

❋

The first issue of *Plume* was scheduled for a December release when the weather would be just right to hold the function under the branches of an enormous banyan tree in Lady S's vast compound. God had taken the whole thing very seriously and was working furiously on the layouts. Drawn by Lady S's patronage, many aspiring poets had crawled out of the woodwork and presented themselves to the D.O.M. who in turn directed them to God. And for the first time since I'd met God, he actually immersed himself completely in productive activity. The D.O.M. had briefed the team.

'We don't want a tacky publication printed on toilet paper. Poetry is prayer. Treat verse with the reverence it deserves. Don't spare effort... or cost... get the best. Concentrate on layouts. Get someone prominent and controversial to design the cover. We'll try and persuade Peter Cockburn to come for the release of the first

issue. That will please Lady Dingbat too. She was s
aying they'd met the bard when her dear husband was
stationed in London during the war years. It will provide
the right touch. An ageing poet laureate on his last
legs... his links with India... after all, he has been a
sort of patron saint to us.'

God asked me whether Kawla would be interested in
moonlighting.

'I can ask... but he's such a pain in the ass.'

'He's good and he'll be cheap. Cheaper than the
greedy Goans in the business. Two accepted campaigns
and they all think they're ready to bag the CAG awards.
Lazy buggers. Kawla is diligent and unsophisticated.
We'll be able to brief him without feeling funny about
it. I hate to deal with egotistical bastards.'

'What about the cover?'

'Let's ask Iqbal—nothing like it, *yaar*. If he
agrees—we are made. Lady S will pay any price provided
we can convince her—and if we get Iqbal, that won't
be a problem, though she'll probably want Belu for
the job. You know, Bawaji-Bawaji and all that.'

'Belu is pretty good too.'

'OK, but not in the same league. Besides, Belu is
much too straightforward. No *tamashagiri* with him.
With Iqbal one can be certain there will be a lot of
*stuntbaazi*. That's half the fun, *yaar*.'

Kawla agreed… but reluctantly. He put down just one condition. He would deal with me and not God.

'That phellow… sorry, madam, but that phellow is useless.'

I worked out a fair deal for Kawla. I didn't see why he should be short-changed just because he, like most Maharashtrians, was too inhibited to discuss money and suffered from low self-worth. Iqbal was a much harder nut to crack. I was nervous about meeting him since he had such an awesome reputation. He was known to be arrogant, temperamental, unpredictable and disgustingly attractive.

God and I used to spot Iqbal at his favourite restaurant, the Surai, which was just across the street from Bombay's one and only art gallery. When he wasn't travelling abroad, Iqbal was a permanent fixture at the Surai where he had his table and his cronies, fellow painters, always waiting. Iqbal was a tea addict and consumed up to twenty cups in one session. Behind the casual front was a shrewd man who had watched world trends in contemporary art and picked up several clues.

He knew how to market himself. He had mastered the art of being a hot commodity. Critics panned his work… but not strongly enough to stop the stampedes at his openings, which were invariably sensational and spectacular. He was also exceedingly handsome (at thirty-something) and knew it. The Surai's regulars would narrate the most incredible stories about Iqbal's exploits. The man's hunger for beautiful girls matched his thirst for tea. He loved both equally, though often the tea scored. He'd be sitting over his fourteenth cup chatting with his friends when his wandering eyes would suddenly settle on a fresh-faced college girl digging into a paratha. He'd quickly weigh the options—another cup of tea or a quick seduction first. Nobody knew what he said to his women and he never revealed it. An ex-girlfriend had tried to demolish the legend by 'revealing all' in a city glossy created precisely for such reading. But her attempt at blowing his reputation had only added to his appeal. His line, according to her, was so commonplace, it was really quite funny.

'Iqbal thinks he can win any woman over by saying, "You are so beautiful. I'd like to paint you." Pause. "Naked."' If that was indeed his line as claimed by the thwarted girl, it worked fantastically. He hardly ever came back to his table alone. And when he did bring the girl with him, they stayed around just long enough for him to finish his tea. Rumour had it that he didn't take his conquests anywhere close to his studio. 'That's a shrine. I'd be committing sacrilege. Studios are for serious painting. When all you want to do is bed the woman—you take her somewhere else,' he had once said. The 'somewhere else' would often be the storage room of the art gallery across the road from the Surai. The owners were not just his agents but close friends too. Chitra Gallery was run by a homosexual couple, though that was supposed to be a secret. Both the men were such macho studs to look at, it was hard to believe that they didn't like girls. Especially since girls liked them. Iqbal would often joke that he was going to 'convert' both one day by offering them the best of his women. But it never happened. Billoo and 'Boxer' (actually Bhasker) were utterly devoted to each other and had been together since school. There was simply no question of either of them looking at a woman. Not even at another man, for that matter.

Iqbal was very close to B and B and insiders of the art world often talked about the surrealistic canvases Iqbal had painted of both of them in very intimate postures. Some found these paintings unbelievably erotic ('What's wrong with celebrating the male body? What's wrong with immortalizing man-man love?') Others were shocked and repulsed by the explicit pictures. Billoo and Boxer guarded them with their lives and only the privileged few had ever set eyes on them. Iqbal invariably referred to the duo affectionately as 'B & B', 'Billoo & Biwi' or 'Those homos'.

B & B adored Iqbal and promoted him aggressively. It was said that they were the real brains behind the astronomical prices of Iqbal's works. 'Even his bloody doodles cost a lakh these days,' cribbed collectors while B & B laughed all the way to the bank. They were also the ones with a canny eye for gimmicks. Encouraged by them, Iqbal cultivated an image for himself that was hollow and phoney but one that worked beautifully—and profitably—for all three of them.

'He is the only painter in India who can get away with murder,' B & B would giggle. 'He is wild and outrageous. The sky is the limit for him.'

Iqbal generally played along with all their mad suggestions. Each time his show opened, he'd hog the headlines for a week. B & B would make sure of that. Each show worked around a theme which B & B dreamt up. They'd control everything down to Iqbal's 'costume' for the occasion. In between his major exhibits, they'd get him to do 'statement' shows that were supposed to be artistic comments on events in India and the rest of the world. Every show of his was a sell-out, despite the crazy prices and the patchy quality of his work.

B & B were also shrewd enough to keep Iqbal, monumental ego and all, in his place. They had a second-line painter in the wings whose main job was to act as a foil to Iqbal. Basu was a resettled Bengali who lacked both Iqbal's lupine looks and his ferocious appetite for publicity. Connoisseurs insisted that Basu was a better painter... and that was precisely the sort of debate that B & B loved and encouraged. It meant additional sales and the maintaining of the right balance.

'It's nothing but a strategy to keep Iqbal in his place,' critics would declare. But that was just what the gallery owners were after.

Iqbal ignored Basu and pretended he didn't know of his existence. But Basu was obsessed with Iqbal. B & B cashed in on this weakness and used it to exercise absolute control over Basu. They knew that if they wanted to get a rise out of the Bong all they had to do was to goad him on about Iqbal's success, his next show, his latest conquest. Basu, driven to inarticulate fury, would vent his violence on canvas... painting fast and furiously. Out of this seething rage emerged his best work, which B & B flogged immediately, making sure to keep Basu's prices at least thirty per cent lower than Iqbal's. Sadistically and only in the presence of a few trusted art-lovers, B &B would chortle, 'Checks and counter-checks. Squeeze one fellow's balls, the other fellow's ego—and what do you get? MONEY!'

Basu led an isolated existence in his modest two-room flat in Dadar. He stayed away from the press and rarely granted interviews. He was a solitary brooder without much of a personality. His other problem was that he didn't speak English too fluently. And when he did, it was with a heavy Bengali accent. This made Basu very self-conscious and reticent. His approach to art was radically different from Iqbal's. He viewed it as something much beyond a calling or a vocation. Art was religion and he revered it.

What Basu was best at was portraits. 'He paints a person's soul,' his admirers would rave. Yet, for all his reverence towards his calling, Basu was driven by his hunger to catch up with and go beyond Iqbal. In terms of fame and success. About the quality of his work, Basu was never in doubt. It was there that his absolute confidence came to the fore. 'I paint with integrity. Not to create a sensation,' he'd reply when asked to explain his work. What Basu really needed was a woman.

And for a few mad months, Basu decided that woman was me. God feigned indifference.

'OK, *yaar*,' he said to me, chewing on an unlit beedi. 'I don't own you or anything. It's OK if you want to look around, experiment, find out your market value. But if you ask me, that bloody Bengali fucker looks a no-can-do.'

God had the males of the world neatly divided: the can-dos and the no-can-dos. To that he'd added a third category: 'the *gandus*' (homosexuals). Very few men made it to the can-do category.

His assessment of Basu turned out to be totally off-the-mark as I discovered late one afternoon at the Surai. Basu, after weeping copious tears into his tea, told me dejectedly that his 'laab' for me was driving him crazy. Between sobs, he recited poetry, sketched on a paper napkin, and kissed the palm of my hand noisily. Perhaps encouraged by my tolerance, he finally reached for my other hand under the small table and placed it squarely on his erect penis saying, 'Feel my member, it is thaarsting for you.'

I hastily withdrew my hand and looked up to see whether any of the waiters had seen anything. I thought I detected a definite gleam in that bastard Badshah's eyes. I shot to my feet and mumbled something stupid to Basu before fleeing. Feel my member, indeed!

I never told God about this. Besides, Basu had obviously got the message. He stopped talking to me.

❁

'He's such a weirdo, *yaar*,' God said about Iqbal after the first meeting. 'He was excited by the idea of doing our first cover. But he has some completely mad ideas. He wants us to find him a model who will be willing to act as his canvas.'

'What do you mean?'

'He wants to paint all over her... calligraphy done with a plume.'

'Body language?'

'Something like that.'

'Is it going to be hard finding someone?'

'Are you crazy? Who'll do it, besides some impoverished whore from Kamathipura... ?'

'That's an idea. Why don't we find one then? I've always wanted to go there again.'

'Again? I'm surprised you even know about the area.'

'My school was nearby... just a couple of kilometres away. We used to have a daredevil of a girl in my class who took us there. God! How I admired her guts! Just imagine—she got thrown out in the final year because she had an abortion.'

'Now you're telling me... just what sort of a school did you go to anyway?'

'I hated it with all my heart. But it was the sort of school favoured by multinational executives. My parents killed themselves to get me in. No, not because I was retarded or anything but we came here on some sort of a transfer in the middle of the term, after my father's short posting in Calcutta. All the children from Marks and Schmidt were in this awful school—a Protestant mission run by frustrated spinsters.'

'No wonder you are so wonky.'

'What's so wonky about me?'

'I don't know, *yaar*—don't ask me heavy questions.'

'No. Tell me, please. It's important.'

'You're so repressed, *yaar*. All screwed-up.'

'Thanks a lot, friend.'

'Anytime, *yaar.*'

'So, are we going or not?'

'Where?'

'To look for a whore.'

'Oh, that. I'd almost forgotten. *Chalo,* let's go.'

# Five

The first thing that came back to me as we approached Kamathipura was the smell. A peculiar, icky smell which I, as a schoolgirl, associated with rotting vegetables in an uncleared garbage dump. It wasn't that, of course. Bombay's red-light area smells of dirty sex. Putrefying, coagulating semen on filthy sheets. This is the stench that hangs over this narrow stretch of road in the heart of the city.

When Babli had suggested a conducted tour of the place in our tenth standard, her idea had been received with shock, horror, fascination and instant acceptance. There were six or seven of us in a vague kind of gang. Babli had always drifted around in search of a friend but had never found one she could hold on to. At the time of which I speak, she had decided to try me out. I was thrilled, in a way. Thrilled that someone like her found it worth her while to cultivate me. She was so bold, free and mature. She wore kaajal to school and

77

defied the lizard-white missionaries. She slung her sash low over her hips and sashayed around the basketball court like a stripper in a nightclub.

Babli seemed to have so much fun, really. At the time I got to know her, she had a motor mechanic boyfriend who'd come to the school driving a different fancy car each day. We didn't know that he was only 'borrowing' from the garage. Or that he'd spent most of the day on his back under one of them, oiling various parts and replacing spark plugs. We would die in awe as Babli scaled the wall in one graceful leap and jumped into the waiting car. She liked rogues.

When Peter changed gears and left the nearby garage, Babli replaced him with a Punjabi caterer—a married man, nearly twenty years older. He was the one who knocked her up after performing an improvised marriage with her at the Mahalaxmi temple.

That afternoon, she arrived after the lunch break with a garland of flowers around her neck and a red bindi on her forehead. I let her in through the tiny backdoor which was meant for servants bringing tiffin for their *babylog*.

'What have you done? Where were you?'

'Please call me Mrs Gupta, I'm married,' she said solemnly.

I pulled out a hanky from my pocket and handed it to her. 'Rub that bindi off—someone might see you.'

'Let the world see me,' she said dramatically. 'I have nothing to hide. I'm not ashamed.'

'Don't be silly. Miss Fielden will be coming on her rounds any minute… she'll kill you. And me. Let's go to the loo.'

'You go if you are so scared. I will tell Miss Fielden the truth.'

'Nobody will believe you. She'll send you home. You'll get a pink card. Your parents will be called. Forget it… let's go and take all this off.' Reluctantly, she agreed and by the time we got back to the classroom there were only traces of sindoor in the parting of her hair.

It was three or four months after this that she began to haemorrhage during the Geography class. At first, all of us thought she was having a particularly heavy period. The teacher asked me to go with her to the small room adjoining the principal's office where there was a bed and first-aid kit. The nurse on duty took one look at her and rushed to summon an ambulance.

Babli's face was fast losing colour. Our class teacher came running and rushed to the school office to phone Babli's parents. Minutes later an ambulance rolled up. Almost the entire school rushed into the courtyard to see what was going on. Babli was placed on a stretcher and taken away. Some of the smaller children chanted, 'Dead! Dead! Dead! She's dead! dead! dead!'

They were nearly right. Babli had lost so much blood by the time they got her to the hospital that the doctors gave her only a slim chance of pulling through. But pull through she did. It is a sight I'll never forget... Babli lying on the stretcher with thick, blackish blood like a muddy, running stream, leaving a trail down the main stairs. She didn't come back to school and that day was never discussed even between friends.

But had it not been for Babli, none of us would have known that an area like Kamathipura even existed. She was the one who gave expert instructions to Minal's driver and told him where to go. On the way, we had picked up ice-cream cones. When we got to the street with the cages, we forgot all about the ice cream as we hung out of the car windows and gawked at the prostitutes.

In our excitement, we forgot about the driver, a doddering old man who'd been with Minal's family for thirty years. Impassively, Laxman drove the car through the overcrowded lane while pimps and idlers jumped out at us and beckoned lewdly.

'Let's stop the car and walk around,' Babli suggested.

At this point, Laxman spoke up (he understood English but pretended that he couldn't). He told his 'baby', that he would certainly not stop his car in this *randi gali,* the street of whores (I hadn't heard the term till then) and that if she insisted, he'd tell her mother. So, we had to satisfy ourselves by driving through.

With a great deal of persuasion, we coaxed Laxman into turning the car around and driving back. 'Promise, we won't ask again,' Minal beseeched after a lot of prodding from the rest of us.

Laxman growled, 'If anything happens to the car or to any of the *babylog,* I'm not responsible. Remember that. I'll tell the *seth* that baby forced me.'

We absolved him of all responsibility in the matter and continued to gaze with unblinking fascination at the half-clad women hanging out of the unbelievably small cages which were their workplaces. They wore such strange costumes—thigh-length skirts with sari cholis or just brassières on top.

'They stuff their bras,' Babli told us knowledgeably. 'Most of them don't have any boobs.'

Some of the girls couldn't have been much older than us. They were tiny, fragile and fair with lustrous, long hair. 'Nepali prostitutes,' said Babli, 'they cost more because they are fair.'

'How do you know?' someone asked her.

'Peter comes here regularly. He only goes to the Nepali girls—they are clean and hairless. Not like those ugly ones from Bihar. Those are half-price.'

'Peter told you?'

'Of course. He tells me everything. He says the Nepali girls are the best.'

'Best at what?'

'Don't ask such questions,' Laxman interrupted again, speaking sharply to Minal. 'I will tell the *sethani*. Such dirty talk! *Babylog* from good families don't say such things. *Baap ré*! I will tell your father also. I will refuse to take such girls in my car—it doesn't matter if the *seth* asks me to go. In thirty years I have never driven through this place. What will your mother and father think? I'll be held responsible.'

Babli told Minal, 'Tell him to cool it. OK, OK. Enough of his *lecturebaazi*.'

Laxman was livid. He pulled up along the sidewalk and told Minal. 'I will not drive if that baby doesn't keep quiet. I've had enough.'

We told Babli to shut up. She hissed. 'Babies! All of you are such babies,' making it sound like the worst imaginable insult. 'I was going to take you to a restaurant here which sells the best baida-roti in town. Only five bucks. Now forget it. Let's all go home and have a bath.'

'I don't mind coming with you,' I heard myself saying. 'Let's get off.'

'Are you mad? You are wearing school uniforms. Someone might see you and report you. What will happen then? We'll all get into trouble.'

Babli suggested a way out. 'Look, why don't we remove our sashes and badges? That way, nobody will be able to tell which school we're from.'

I was game, but Minal put her foot down.

'OK, girls,' Babli brightened up once again, 'if you don't want a baida-roti, let's at least have a fag.'

❋

Going back to Kamathipura after so many years and with God was an entirely different experience. He seemed so much at home, so familiar with the area. He even exchanged greetings with the paan-beediwallah at the corner and sauntered casually into a cold drinks stall and ordered a soda.

'Relax, *yaar*, nobody is going to devour you. Besides, you don't look like a potential *randi* even though I look like a professional pimp. I doubt I'd be able to get a good price for you in any case, you ice-cube. The Neps have cornered the market. Fair skin, no hair, no boobs—like I told you—one Nep in the brothel and all the other whores might as well quit.'

We walked down slowly 'surveying the merchandise', as God put it.

'Why don't we go to your usual place?' I asked brightly.

'Oh shut up! Take you there and ruin the fun forever?'

'*Ladka chahiye ya lakdki* (Do you want a boy or a girl)?' a dwarf with a red scarf around his thick neck called out from a dark stairway. '*Sab maal milega* (You can get anything you want),' he beckoned.

83

'Why not?' said God, and started singing, 'I want to be in Kamathipura... everything free in Kamathipura... OK by me in Kamathipura...' to the tune of "I want to be in America".

The dwarf toddled up and took God's hand. *'Chal hatt, bhadwa* (Get lost, pimp),' God snarled and shook him off. Undeterred, the dwarf continued to trail us, keeping up his little chant—virgins, Nepalese, little boys, little girls, homos, hijdas, blacks, even blondes.

'Let's ask him for a blonde,' I begged of God. 'Are you mad? He'll take us for such a ride, we'll be reeling. It's all cash down in Foras Road—so, just keep your mouth shut and follow me.'

Since it was off-duty hours, the prostitutes were lounging around on rickety charpoys parked in the middle of the busy road. Handcart pullers, bullock-carts, cabs and cyclists, negotiated their way carefully past their prone figures. Some of them called out to us in a friendly way and offered boiled eggs and tea. 'Why do all of them eat boiled eggs?' I asked God.

'Because they are cheap, nutritious and convenient,' he answered shortly.

In a while, he spotted a familiar looking madam. 'Hey, Rukhmanibai... namaskar,' he greeted her.

She stopped her paan-making activity long enough to look up at him. *'Aré,* Comrade *ka bachcha... kaisa hai tu, saala* (how are you)?'

'*Sab theek* (OK),' he answered and went up to offer her a beedi. '*Phoren* cigarette *pila* (Give me a foreign cigarette),' she taunted.

He sat down next to her and asked, '*Kuch naya maal hai* (Have you any new recruits)?'

For some reason she thought he was offering her a new recruit and that it was me. She gave me a quick once-over and shook her head firmly. '*Nahi chalegi* (Won't do).'

I hadn't made the grade. I'd flunked! I felt most insulted and humiliated. Not good enough for this gargoyle with blood-red teeth and thick furry tongue! Indeed! God patted my head affectionately and said, '*Bachchi hai*—*chhod do uski baat* (She's just a kid—forget about her).' Then he got down to business.

She was suspicious. Of course she had the right girl, but the whole thing sounded very fishy. Some man wanted to paint her naked body—all right, but what about screwing her? No? Then how could they settle a rate? There was no separate tariff for just painting one of her girls.

'Half-day, half-night or whole night?' she asked.

'That depends.'

'No, no, no. That depends on *me*—not on you. She's *my* girl.'

'Let us see her first, then we'll fix up the price and time.'

'She's resting just now. Had a busy night. French ship in town. Chameli is very popular with the *gora log*. Dark, thick hair everywhere, that's why.'

'So when can we see her?'

'Come back tonight. Try tomorrow. Up to you.'

Just then a young girl clad in a gaudy lungi peeped out from behind a curtain. She was wearing a bright pink bra, five sizes too small for her. 'Chai?' she asked flashing a set of fine white teeth.

God jumped up. 'I want her—that's her. That's the one I want.'

The madam restrained him with one hand and shooed the girl off with the other. *'Jao! Jao!'*

Someone from inside the dimly-lit house called out, 'Chameli—*kidhar hai tu? Tera bachcha ro raha hai* (Where are you? Your child is crying).'

The same girl emerged again with an infant on her hip. She was smoking a Gitane.

'That's her, isn't it?' God said. 'Let me talk to her.'

The madam signalled wildly to her to go back into the room, but the girl stood around smoking, swaying her hips gently to keep the baby quiet. She was staring at God thoughtfully. He looked like he was in a trance. The madam spoke to her rapidly in Tulu and turned to us. 'She isn't interested, I asked her.'

God turned to the girl. She winked at him and put out her tongue—just the tip. It was as pink as her bra. 'You're lying,' he said to the madam. 'She wants to do it.'

'I just told you she doesn't. And if you don't move along now, I'll call Bahadur.' She wouldn't have had to shout. The bouncer was squatting nearby smoking a hookah and having his ears cleaned by a man who specialized in doing just that. The girl intervened at this point and said something rapidly to the madam. God hadn't been able to take his eyes off her.

The madam asked him, 'Are you going to introduce her to some filmwallah?'

'Yes, sure. I know lots of them,' he lied glibly.

'Look… if she joins films, I will get a cut. She and I have this understanding from the beginning. No nonsense. No cheating. If you try and hoodwink me, I'll break every bone in your body—understand?'

God was ready to wipe the madam's filthy feet with a scented towel by then. He would have agreed to anything. The girl flicked her cigarette away and stuck her forefinger into the infant's mouth. It began to suck at it noisily. 'Hungry,' she announced and walked into the room. Thick, dark hair covered her back like a satin curtain. God was on the verge of collapsing.

'Shit! She is so bloody beautiful,' he said hitting his palm with a lighter.

'Yes, she is,' I agreed. Amazing. I wasn't jealous at all.

❈

My parents were having their annual party. They always celebrated their wedding anniversary with an elaborate dinner. It was one occasion my mother dreaded and abhorred. But it had to be gone through. Weeks of careful planning went into it since my father used to invite what he called the 'big shots'. Senior executives, important clients, advertising agency people who handled the company's account, bank people, and a few of his juniors, who were expected to help with the drinks and snacks.

When I got home from Foras Road, my mother was in the bedroom, weeping.

'What's the matter?' I asked her. I was quite alarmed seeing her like that. She rarely cried. Or laughed, for that matter.

'Oh, it's nothing. Really. Why don't you go and wash up?' she said in an embarrassed voice.

'Has the soufflé collapsed?' I asked, imagining that there couldn't be a worse disaster.

'No... not the soufflé. But my marriage.' And she burst into loud sobs that seemed to emerge from the pit of her stomach.

'What?' I screamed and started to shake her. 'What are you saying?'

'Your father doesn't love me anymore. He told me so this morning.'

'Don't be ridiculous,' I said. 'Papa told you that? He must have been tired or tense or something.'

'No, Baby, he was very calm. But I don't want to discuss it right now. I must first calm myself… and then there's the party tonight. Papa will get most upset if the party flops. You know how important it is to him.'

'Don't be ridiculous, Mummy. How can you go through a party in this condition?'

Mummy rushed to examine her face in the mirror, 'Oh my God—is my face OK? Look at my hair… Papa is going to kill me.'

'Forget your face and hair, Mummy… just tell me it's not true. Tell me it was only a silly fight.'

'I wish I could say that—God! I wish that it was true. But a Sindhi woman! Can you imagine? A Sindhi! Someone from his office—a divorcee. Those are the worst types. Ruin their own marriage first and then ruin someone else's. But what I can't get over is, how could he fall for a Sindhi? You know how he feels about them? He always used to say Sindhis have no class. That they are crude and lacking in taste. You remember the holiday in Goa two years ago? Remember those people in the next villa at the village? Sindhis? Remember what the women were wearing—shiny clothes with broad plastic belts. And high heels in the sand! Remember, how we laughed? Especially Papa. He even commented on their bleached moustaches. And now….'

'It's not possible, Mummy. He must have been angry with you or something. He loves you. He loves me. He wouldn't do this.'

'I thought he loved us too, but obviously I was wrong. Anyway, let's not talk about it now. Go and get dressed. Please wear a nice salwar-kameez. And don't let Papa know that you know.'

I went back to my room in a state of shock. I wanted to phone God immediately. The whole day had been too much. And now this! I knew that God wouldn't be very sympathetic. Or even interested. But I had to tell someone. I felt dizzy and sick and lay down on my bed.

Didi, our old maid, came into the room and asked whether I was unwell.

'Limbupani, Baby?' she enquired with concern.

I waved her away but she wouldn't budge. She urged me to dress quickly before Papa got home. Obviously she didn't know anything. Or maybe she did. She belonged to the old school of servants, trained never to show their reactions no matter what the provocation. I remembered now how, years ago, I'd wanted desperately to know why my mother was crying constantly and what the doctors and nurses were doing in our home for nearly a month. I was certain Didi knew but she wouldn't tell even after my pestering her to. Instead, she'd just make me sit in her lap and rock me gently, singing ancient Nepali lullabies. This time too, I knew her lips were irritatingly sealed. Only; this time I probably knew more than she did. I felt strangely triumphant. I finally managed to get rid of her and went to my parents' room.

I knocked on Mummy's door before entering and found her sitting listlessly in front of the dressing-table. She resembled a faded rose and even smelled like one. 'It was nice living at Mount Pleasant Road,' she said in an absent sort of way. 'Ahmedabad will be hot now... very hot. Ba will be surprised to see me.'

'What are you talking about?' I asked.

'It's all right, Baby, you won't have to come. You can stay on at Nilgiri Apartments. Remember when we used to stay in Vile Parle? No, of course you can't, you were too small. We didn't have a car in those days. I used to travel by BEST buses. Your Papa also. Our sofa was made of blue Rexine and we didn't have a bathtub in the bathroom. No fridge, no gas, no washing-machine, no air-conditioner... imagine. That was before Papa joined Marks and Schmidt as marketing manager. Then we moved to Malabar Hill... and everybody felt so jealous. Do you know I didn't possess a chiffon at that time? Only mill saris—Khatau, Bombay Dyeing—the type that Didi wears these days. Ba was so proud. She'd tell our relatives in Ahmedabad, "Veenaben has done so well for herself... she lives at Malabar Hill in Bombay. Big building with automatic lift. Servants, car, driver, everything!" And now it's all finished. Finished because of some Sindhi woman. That is the worst part. Had she been Punjabi, I would have understood. Maybe your father missed his language, his food. Maybe I

91

should have made his type of khana more often. But you know how strict they are at Ba's home—no onions, no garlic. At least I'd started eating those... but how could I possibly eat mutton and chicken? I'd tried fish once—the smell was so horrible. I thought I'd throw up—right there—in front of the bosses. Your father had looked at me and smiled understandingly. He was a nice man actually, he didn't make me feel small in front of important people.'

'Don't talk like this, Mummy... all in the past tense. Papa isn't dead or something.'

'Isn't he?' she asked vaguely. Her expression scared me. She wasn't really there at all.

The party went off as all the other parties had in previous years. Everybody brought ugly baskets full of unnatural-looking flowers, or presents wrapped in handmade paper. My mother went through the evening gracefully, and I felt very proud of her. She wasn't looking her best, and her make-up hadn't come out right, but that was understandable. My father was far too animated and jolly. I thought he must have looked artificial and a little ridiculous to the others. But nobody seemed to notice. Or so I thought. My father suggested a 'spot of dancing' and called the servants to move the furniture. Someone started singing, "For he's a jolly good fellow", and soon everybody joined in.

I looked at Mummy anxiously. She looked like she was about to faint. I went and stood by her. She clutched my hand tightly and whispered, 'They all know.' And I asked her how she knew.

'I can tell. Besides, Mrs Bawa came up to me and said, "How nice that you decided to have the party this year too, we weren't sure you would."'

'That doesn't mean a thing.'

'Of course it does. I've always hated that woman... lipstick all over her teeth, sweat under her armpits and a bra two sizes too big for her. She had the guts to say that to me!'

'Papa doesn't look upset.'

'Why should he look upset? He's getting what he wants.'

And I thought to myself sadly that perhaps, in a way, she was getting what she wanted as well... only she didn't know it. Not just then.

I was troubled about this depressed state and spoke to God the same night. (Yes, despite his appearance and the dump he lived in, he did possess a phone!) There were times when he was thankfully receptive to such conversations. He told me not to worry too much about Mummy.

'Women go through these things, *yaar*,' he said, 'even the old woman at home behaves funnily sometimes. But she settles down soon enough. Leave her alone. It's just a damn phase. Women get into these *chakkars*. Nothing serious. She must be menstruating. Ask her.'

I did. And Mummy denied it hotly. I think she was outraged by the suggestion that her low mood had anything to do with her periods. But she didn't want to discuss it further with me.

'It will pass,' she said coldly. And I left it at that. I got the feeling that Mummy was in the throes of re-examining her life, her marriage, her priorities. And like God had suggested—'Give the broad some space, *yaar.*' Which is exactly what I did.

# Six

Disappointingly for God and the rest of the Poets Association, the encounter between Iqbal and the whore didn't materialize. Eventually, they had to settle for a naughty doodle. They thought Iqbal had done it for free till he phoned the D.O.M. and asked to be paid for it. 'Don't you know—just my signature sells these days.' The D.O.M. was too stunned to respond and decided to take it up with the rest.

'Serves us right,' giggled Chandni.

'The filthy bastard,' said Sujata. And everybody agreed it was the most mercenary act possible.

Meanwhile, Iqbal had agreed to give an interview to God. I wanted to go along, since Iqbal fascinated me (as he did nearly every woman who knew of his existence). God had been commissioned by the editor of a leading fortnightly. The editor, Nandan Kapoor, was a failed poet but an immensely successful journalist. He was half-jealous of God and half-patronizing. 'Do me a great cover story and I'll make you in one stroke,' he'd told him at his studiedly arty office.

God had come back from the meeting entirely unimpressed. 'He's a fart, *yaar*,' he said decisively.

'Then how come he's considered such a hot-shot in his field?' I asked.

'Don't be naïve, stupid. It's because he's such an asshole. Nobody takes him seriously. He gets by... you know... buttering up the right people—staying on the right side of his maliks.'

'It can't be that simple. A lot of readers find him very talented. He has quite a fan-following. He's always called to address the Rotary Club—my father was telling me....'

'Fuck what your father was telling you, baby. He's another asshole himself. What does he read besides balance sheets, huh? And the stocks and shares news? Tell me, has that man ever read a book? Or listened to music? Rotary Club! Who belongs to it? Social-climbing businessmen who want to get their mugs into the evening papers. What do they do there? Eat five star khana, gas around, gossip and pretend they're listening to whichever sacrificial goat they've managed to rope in as a speaker. Nobody can hear what the fellow is saying since all the Rotarians are busy belching and farting after the heavy food. One day I'm going to rip them apart in print.'

'Are you sure your new friend—the great Nandan Kapoor— isn't using you? Why can't he interview Iqbal himself?'

'Oh, he thinks Iqbal will clam up with him. Nandan has that effect on people. He overpowers them. He thinks I'll be able to disarm Iqbal and get some good quotes.'

'What are you planning to ask him?'

'I haven't worked it out yet... but nobody is interested in reading his views on art. I'll get him to bitch about other artists and discuss his sex-life. Maybe pose nude with his mistress. He has one—not that he's faithful to her. But he likes his women old and fat except his one-night stands who have to be virginal college kids. He says he's a classicist who appreciates Rubenesque beauty. Pendulous breasts, a big arse—that sort of thing. He's game for stunts, so I'm sure he'll agree. We can shoot them in some mad setting... maybe a bathtub. Or maybe in Borivili Park with lions and tigers.'

Eventually, God had to settle for a more mundane picture. Iqbal was all set to strip since he loved his own body. But the demure lady shied off. What God finally got was a wedding portrait type of photograph, but at least the world got to see what this mysterious woman looked like. Iqbal spoke about her candidly and with rare, uncharacteristic tenderness. He reserved his venom for the other painters.

'A monkey's shit is more artistic,' he declared when asked to comment on Basu. 'Let him paint ghosts. His portraits give everybody nightmares anyway.'

God asked him to pick out his favourites and Iqbal laughed, 'It's like asking me to sift through a pool of gurgling crap... forget it.'

I sat through the interview in a daze, taking it all in... drinking in every word... hanging on to Iqbal's pronouncements in a semi-trance. I jumped out of my skin when he suddenly turned to me and asked God, 'Is this the little whore whose backside you wanted me to paint?'

God was as startled as I was and for a minute both of us were speechless. 'No, no... this is my friend—Nasha... I mean, Nisha... she's just a friend. She helps me with the tape-recorder, lights, reflector... that sort of thing.'

'Body *achchi hai, yaar,* pretty good. *Kapde utaar do...* go on, take your clothes off.'

God turned to me and asked in an offhand way, 'How about it?'

And I heard myself saying, 'Sure. Why not?'

Nothing happened. God was stumped and Iqbal just stared. Then God arranged his expression carefully and asked Iqbal to excuse us. He took my arm roughly and pushed me into Iqbal's kitchen. I noticed that the sink was like a gutter. Full of unwashed pots and paint brushes.

The garbage pail was flowing with rotting papayas and the fridge door was open. Somebody had scribbled 'Fuck you!' on the wall behind the gas range, in orange fluorescent paint. God pushed me against a shelf and hissed, 'Are you mad? You want to strip in front of this maniac and have yourself photographed?'

'Why... I thought you'd approve,' I said deliberately and insincerely.

'I just said that in front of him because I knew you'd refuse.'

'Or did you say it only to humiliate me?'

'Look, there's no time to stand here arguing. Let's go out and tell him it's not possible because you have your period.'

'But I don't.'

'I know you don't—but let's tell him that and finish off the interview.'

'Coward.'

'What did you say?'

'I said "Coward".'

God raised his hand. I saw his broad, flat palm coming towards my face. And ducked. His hand hit the sharp spout of a battered aluminium kettle and cursed. I ran out and smiled brightly at Iqbal who had started painting a canvas conveniently mounted on an easel by the window. *Kya hua?* Chickened out? Tell your boyfriend not to worry... I like mine old and huge. You are cancelled on both counts. Now run along, the two of you... I have work to do.'

❄

Iqbal's interview created the necessary sensation and Nandan Kapoor was gloating over it for weeks. The art world was up in arms and God became a byline to reckon with.

As for me, I was drawn into my mother's sad world, full of self-pity and doubt. I didn't know what to make of the bomb she had dropped. My father continued to be 'normal' and pretended nothing had happened. After a point, I began to wonder whether my mother had imagined it all.

'Don't be ridiculous, Baby—of course it's true.'

'But has Papa brought it up again?'

'No, why should he? He's waiting for me to make the first move.'

'Have you spoken to Ba?'

'Yes. She told me to come to Ahmedabad immediately. But it will be so hot there.'

I couldn't believe this. My mother was postponing the decision to leave my father because the weather wasn't to her liking! I was getting worried about her. Sometimes I'd go into their bedroom and find her talking to herself and folding her saris over and over again. The saris she'd once told me she couldn't stand.

'I hate chiffons. Nobody in Ahmedabad wears chiffons. They are such Punjabi status symbols. I've always worn cotton saris. Handblock printed, bandhni, leheriya—prints of that sort. Your father doesn't approve of them. He says they are meant for sweeper women—he thinks cottons don't go with his new status. He always points to the other company wives and says, "Look at how Rina dresses—so immaculately. Soft colours. Always in silks." It's no use telling him that silks make you sweat. Nobody wears silks in Bombay except during December. But he feels silks look "expensive". He doesn't know that these days good cotton saris are equally costly.'

Beneath Papa's surface normalcy, I began to detect some changes. And even if I hadn't, Mummy would have pointed them out. For instance, he now came home much later and worked over weekends more often.

'It's her. That Sindhi woman. They all know black magic. She has cast a spell on your father… *jadu-mantra*… I'm sure of it. He is completely under her control. But it can't last for long. Sooner or later he will come out of the trance and realize his mistake.'

I'd listen to her rantings as sympathetically as possible. And even when these took place in front of Papa, it was obvious from his vacant eyes and empty smiles that he wasn't with us at all. Sometimes he'd rush to pick up the phone during dinner or on a Sunday afternoon, and my mother would look at me significantly. 'It's her!' she'd mouth silently and stiffen. Father would speak with his mouth buried in the receiver and return looking distracted.

I was curious about this woman who had captivated him. And told God that I wanted to see her. 'Whatever for? Waste of time. If you really want to break it up, think of a strategy. I'll check with Comradesaab. He usually manages to come up with something or the other. My mother too. I suppose they have plenty of experience....'

Comradesaab came up with two suggestions. I found one brilliant and the other scary. Blackmail. And roughing up. The first one seemed easy. God could write a couple of dirty letters threatening to expose her. If these didn't work, he'd warn her that he'd send them to the bosses. If even that ploy failed, Comradesaab would send his fellows to gherao her somewhere and frighten her. God told me, 'Just leave it to the experts, yaar. Sit back and watch the fun. She'll get cold in no time and that tight-ass father of yours will come running home. In any case, I can't see what any woman could find in an idiot like him. Such an ordinary bugger. Have you seen him naked recently? Does he still have his equipment?'

'Don't be disgusting. Just do what you have to. I hope it works. At least for my mother's sake.'

'I'll outdo myself... don't worry. If words fail me, I'll seek Sujata's help. By the way, have you seen the way she has been eyeing my crotch lately? I think the lioness is hungry....'

As a matter of fact, I *had* noticed Sujata's new-found interest in God. She'd taken to being very coquettish and physical. Her hands were invariably on his thigh when she plonked herself next to him. Once I'd even seen him removing her sweaty palm very deliberately from his lap and she'd dug her elbow into his ribs and giggled. Shameless woman. And depressing too. For I suspected her interest in God had to do with his elevation to associate editor of *Plume*. His articles and interviews had also begun to appear here and there since his interview with Iqbal for Nandan Kapoor. He had also been offered a regular column in a Sunday paper, to cover the arts. Sujata wanted desperately to be written up since she'd been largely out of the news for nearly five years. She was one of those who believed in direct action. Soon enough she came to the point.

'When can you interview me?'

God hadn't been prepared for the question and was stumped for a moment. 'I'll have to check with the editor.'

'What for? I thought the arts page was yours.'

'It is. Even so. Besides, we have worked out a schedule for the next six months.'

'Rubbish. No paper works so much in advance. Or are you playing hard to get? Is there something I can do for you in return?' And with that she did the obvious—let her Venkatgiri sari-pallu drop from the shoulder. Her eyes took on the practised look of seduction. She let one crinkly lock of hair fall over one eyebrow. She looked pretty bizarre and far from the femme fatale she was playing. 'I knew your editor pretty well,' she added. 'In fact he and I were lovers ten years ago. He worshipped me,' and she giggled. 'Champak blossoms. He always brought them for me. Wrapped in green leaves and tied with a string. I could speak to him directly... but that wouldn't be nice. Why don't you be a good boy and do this for me? I'll give you sensational quotes.'

God didn't dare tell her—not right away—that her quotes, sensational or otherwise were of no interest to anybody any longer. That all her candid revelations about her conquests, real or imagined, shocked nobody in these changed times. And that, in any case, it was unlikely looking at her—bloated, ageing—that there would be any takers either for her poems or her body. A cruel but accurate assessment of Sujata's drawing power, in and out of the boudoir. Maybe she knew, but pretended not to. Sujata needed her delusions, or else she might have gone mad.

God played it gently, cautiously. While he was detached enough to see Sujata through the eyes of the rest of the world, he continued to lust for her explaining, 'Must

104

be some sort of a mother complex, *yaar*. Besides, she is still very fuckable... and her smell... *wah*... it's the same fucking smell, *yaar*. Can't resist it.'

He told her he'd work on the editor and get back to her. She added with a final sidelong glance, 'Remember... it will be an exclusive—and in colour. I have a photographer in mind—he's young, talented and totally in love with me. I don't want to be clicked by just anybody. They make me look... different. They can't capture my soul. Not that I want to look a glamour puss. But why end up looking a hag? Some photographs can be so sadistic. It's jealousy, of course. Wrong angles. Bad lighting. The last time I allowed some unknown to click me—I ended up looking like Medusa. So... it's done then. I'll write a couple of new poems specially for you... naughty ones... OK?'

❀

As *Plume* got noticed, God attracted many ambitious, good and bad poets. There was one acid-dropping brooder, Lucio, who used to waylay us no matter where we went.

'Such a fucking bore, that mutt, *yaar*. Why doesn't he get lost? I think he's got a crush on you.'

Poor fellow. I used to feel very sorry each time I saw his emaciated figure lurching towards us. He was also an aspiring musician, being a Goan. Everybody from Goa strums a guitar whether or not he or she can sing, but Lucio was different. He actually did sing rather well despite having an unnaturally high-pitched voice. He also wrote his own songs. But God didn't have the time or the interest.

'Don't encourage him, *yaar*.'

'Why not? I thought the purpose of this project was to encourage budding poets and writers.'

'That's absolutely right. But this rascal is neither a poet nor a writer—he is a junkie and free-loader—in that order. Get it? If you want to "encourage" him, take him home to Pearly Shells.' Pearly Shells was God's name for my mother. 'Only, you can bet your ass Pearly Shells won't throw him even a bone.'

God was right. The first time I took Lucio home, Mummy took one look at Lucio's glazed eyes and suppressed a scream. She asked me in Gujarati who he was. She thought he was a pickpocket I'd rescued from the street. I tried to tell her that he was a poet and singer. She refused to let me go on. 'Just throw him out before your father gets home.'

At this point, Lucio surprised both of us by saying in fluent Gujarati, 'But before I go, may I have a glass of water?'


I liked Lucio. He reminded me of a stray kitten. I felt protective and loving towards him. I wanted to feed him porridge, clothe him in soft linen and shield him from the world. Underneath the layers of grime, he had a sensitive, fine-boned face with a full, sensuous mouth. It was difficult to say how old he was. I guessed he was twentyish. His slight frame was attractive too, particularly his slim, hairless torso with a silver crucifix dangling between nutmeg-coloured nipples. God was suspicious of Lucio, though he didn't come right out and say he couldn't stand him. Lucio seemed to like God but he very obviously preferred me. I'd listen to his almost girlish voice as he sang sad Goan love songs.

'Bloody pansy,' Guru would snort while God sneered.

Soon Lucio started leaving little notes for me at the agency. My reputation for attracting weirdos was fast gaining ground and Kawla's scowls of disapproval were getting fiercer. For some strange reason, I was referred to as Bai by the art department. What did that make the other women? I guess it had to do with the Marathi connection. Once, I heard Kawla telling one of his boys, 'Naik, that Bai is really weird.' Naik stopped pasting a bromide of a water pump on the artwork he was handling to look up and mutter in agreement.

All the artists had one or two fingernails that were at least an inch long. Generally, it was the nail of the little finger, and often it was painted red. I used to wonder how their girlfriends or wives felt about this funny nail. I asked one of them, who replied with disarming candour, 'They don't notice it.' I wanted to pursue the thought further but felt embarrassed. How could they not notice a mini weapon on their man's hands? Didn't it come in the way? Why did they grow it? What precise purpose did it serve? 'We need it for paste-ups, Bai, you won't understand... rubber solution, small types that fall off, this nail is very useful.' I'd go into the studio and watch them deftly slipping the lethal nail under a bromide no bigger than half a centimetre—yes, I had to agree the nail served a purpose—but oh! how ugly it looked.

God wasn't interested in discussing nails—other people's that is. Lucio was. Lucio was interested in everything. He would listen with his head cocked to one side, fingers fiddling with the crucifix. He wanted to know everything. Little things, and soon I started treating him like the best friend I wished I'd had at school but never did. Lucio was involved and attentive. He noticed when my hair was shampooed or if, occasionally, lipstick strayed to my teeth. He wasn't a physical person—not with me. And if he had to point out a pen mark on my cheek, he'd indicate it by making sure his fingers remained a micro millimetre from my face. Lucio noticed my clothes, my make-up, even my pre-menstrual pimples. I'd mention this to God and say, 'Isn't Lucio sensitive?' and God would laugh derisively, 'Sensitive, my ass. Moony—that's what, stupid bugger. Must be a queer—lipstick, pimples, saris... ha!'

God found fault with Lucio's singing voice too. 'He sounds like Barbara Streisand,' he commented. 'Bloody fairy—no man sings like that.'

And then I found a way of putting Lucio's musicality to some use when I asked him to come for a recording. The agency was in search of new voices for jingles. A new cola was about to be launched. The client was a fastidious old sod who'd gone through stock tapes of voices in our stable and rejected the lot. 'Too high. Too low. Too thick. Too deep.' The campaign was built around a fantasy. It involved a princess held captive in a castle. The jingle was supposed to be her song about freedom. There was a prince involved (naturally), who hears her beautiful voice floating past his ears as he rides through the woods. Drawn by its dulcet sweetness, he goes in search of her blah... blah... blah. We did a track with Lucio singing in his charming falsetto and it clicked.

Soon Lucio was in great demand to do female voices. This upset the two jingle-queens in the business. Lucio's response to the war raging within the jingle-makers was uncomplicated and open. 'Hey man! What's the hassle about. Let them do the men's voices.'

The girls weren't amused. Especially the one with the right connections. She'd married into the business and it upset her no end when her composer-husband opted for Lucio. 'He sounds like Joan Baez, man,' he told his stunned wife. 'His voice is romantic... soft... he is a natural. One rehearsal and we are ready to record.

No fuss! No tantrums. He hits the right note without missing a beat. Come on, baby, can you match that?'

The miffed singer was in no mood to hear her husband singing Lucio's praises. She considered switching to the rival camp. It would have meant the end of her marriage, but the other man had promised to stage an extravagant musical just for her. Lucio stayed out of the wars and continued writing me lovelorn notes.

❋

My mother was cracking up. The signs were all there. It was the uncertainty that was killing her. Was it on or was it off? Had she really heard my father telling her the marriage was over? Had he meant it? And, according to her, he refused even to discuss the whole business. She'd stopped wearing chiffons and I suppose that was her way of protesting. She'd also stopped going to the hair-dresser for her weekly facial and hair-set. I asked her why.

'What is the use? In any case, you know how gossip travels, particularly in that salon. Everybody goes there. Most of the Company wives. I'm sure all the girls know. I can't face Lizzie and the rest. What will they think?'

'Why don't you find a new salon?'

She seemed horrified at the idea. 'Don't be ridiculous! I've been going to Fleurs de Paris for more than fifteen years. I can't start looking for a new place. I'd be so embarrassed! Imagine getting your armpits waxed by some strange female. This place is clean. It smells of antiseptic and eau de cologne. They use fresh strips of cloth for each client. Have you seen how filthy the other places are? Eeks! Someone else's hair on solidified wax. Enough to make you throw up. My friend got such a terrible rash. You know how delicate my skin is. I get an allergy just thinking about dirt. No soothing lotion. No talcum powder. Not even a fresh towel to wipe oneself. And have you seen those women who come for pedicures just to have their calves caressed by hefty fellows sitting at their feet? So vulgar! No, no—I'd rather stay this way.'

I hadn't realized till then just how vehemently my mother felt about the issue. 'But what about Papa?'

'Papa can go to hell....' The remark escaped before she knew what she was saying. It was too late to retrieve it. She looked at me shamefacedly and said, 'I'm sorry, Baby. I shouldn't have said that.' The phone rang just then. There was an agency party on Saturday to woo a potential client. Steal him from another agency as a matter of fact. On the spur of the moment, I asked my mother if she'd like to come with me. And she astonished me by saying 'yes'.

❋

The party was to be at the agency head's home. Roy D'Lima was a strange man with an even stranger wife.

He held the advertising business in such open contempt that one often wondered what he was doing in a business he so obviously loathed. He loved giving interviews about his hatred for his profession; and whenever he was asked why he didn't quit and do something else he had a stock answer. At that precise point in the interview he would remove his antique, tortoise-shell spectacles ('My grandfather's... hand-crafted') and heave a mighty sigh. The woes of the universe, the sigh conveyed, rested on his well-exercised shoulders. 'Bread and butter. That's it. I need the money to fund my other interests.' That was a cue for the next question—an obvious one: 'What other interests?' 'Oh—let's just say, one prefers to be discreet and modest.' If the interviewer was fool enough to let it go at that, the poor man would feel vanquished. He'd bring up the topic tangentially in some other context. 'There's this book I've been working on....'

The book had become a joke in the agency. He'd been working on it for a decade and a half. Most people knew that the best way to reach Roy was to ask, 'So, how's the book coming along?' He'd go through his specs-removing-and-sighing routine before replying. 'Oh—it's getting on. I manage around five hundred words a day. Naipaul does four.' The topic was shrouded in mystery. Was it an autobiography ('How boring,' was the standard reaction, 'who's interested in his life besides himself?'), was it an exposé on the business he hated? Was it a novel? What kind of a tome would take this long?

Like all the other hot-shot ad guys in Bombay, Roy did theatre. And he took it very seriously indeed. While others may have dabbled in acting for the love of histrionics, Roy insisted he was in it out of a deep sense of commitment. "Theatre as an instrument of social change," was a pet subject that he had laboured hard to batter into a feature-length article that he got his agency boys to peddle to various publications. He liked to think he was making 'statements' through the plays he chose to sponsor, direct and act in. His articles managed to see the light of day since most papers and magazines regarded them as fillers with a P. R. angle. 'We carry his shit and we get three colour double-spreads. It's a terrific trade-off.' He didn't care if it worked that way, so long as his name (and photograph—the same one he dished out everywhere) appeared from time to time. He was very particular about his media image. Nobody was allowed to click candid shots while an interview was being conducted. 'You tape on your recorder. I'll tape on mine,' he would state.

He had his agency photographer do his yearly photo-session. It was a tense day in the office when the boss' shot was being set up. No interruptions, no calls, no disturbances. A peon was posted outside the studio while Roy changed in and out of outfits. Kurtas for casual features, pin-stripes for press conference handouts, open-collars for semi-formal interviews and track suits for fitness articles. The photographer did nothing beyond physically pressing the shutter-button. Roy handled everything down to the props. He preferred a Pashmina shawl over one shoulder with a potted plant out-of-focus for the kurta picture; a bookcase with leather-bound volumes for the pin-stripes; a bay window for the open collars; and a handsome Doberman for the track suit. Any suggestion that a few could be shot outdoors would immediately be shot down. 'You can't control the lighting outdoors. Besides, I'd feel ridiculous.'

His wife, Karen, assumed the role of art director and supervised the photo-sessions. When she arrived, the office froze. She was an overbearing, imperious bitch who had once been the office telephone operator. A few employees from those days had dared to call her by her first name soon after her marriage to Roy. Karen had exploded! 'I am Mrs D'Lima now,' and that's how everyone addressed her (even though her husband was known by his first name). Roy fancied himself as a brooding intellectual. His theatricality was so much a part of his personality that it was difficult to know when he wasn't rehearsing for a role. His wife was equally self-absorbed but in a different way, since her preoccupations weren't the same. She was a political junkie. Power turned her on. It didn't matter whose. She fancied herself as a closet revolutionary and loved making wild statements about the state of the body politic that nobody understood. 'I am for the underdog,' she'd declare, sipping her whisky-water thoughtfully. The two of them led separate lives, putting in joint appearances only on the opening nights of his plays or at 'important' social events in the city. She was quite a woman in her own right with exotic good looks that couldn't be traced to any ethnic group. 'I'm one-eighth Turkish—my great-grandmother was a naughty girl—one-fourth Khasi, one-sixth Goan and one-third Himachali,' she'd explain, getting her arithmetic all wrong. 'She's nothing more than a scrambled egg,' Roy would articulate (he never just spoke, he always articulated) while she crinkled up her chinky eyes—'the Khasi part of me...'—and reached for a Marlboro Lite.

Their house was done up in what she liked to call an eclectic style. She'd brag modestly that the duplex didn't require the services of a decorator, as she was a pretty talented one herself. Roy would swing away on an enormous Rajasthani jhoola in the bonsai-filled terrace and stare moodily at the sea in the distance. Their parties were of two kinds—ad-and-arty or media-and-politics. The latter were always more fun since Karen attracted and invited crazy bods on the fringes of some anarchic party or the other. 'As intelligent people and opinion-makers,' she'd say, 'it is our duty to support the Opposition.' Roy didn't think it a wise stand from a business point of view, but enjoyed the uproar and controversies these parties created. His parties were as phoney as the profession he was in and were used to sound out potential clients or flatter the old ones. For entertainment he'd have an audio-visual going in the 'den' (all admen have dens in their homes). Reluctant guests would be firmly propelled into the stuffy room and told to observe how the hottest agency in town functioned. 'Don't you dare get bored,' Roy would whisper. 'Pay attention. I'll ask questions later. You flunk one and I minus a drink.' People weren't always sure whether Roy was trying to be funny or not. In any case, his parties were like his campaigns—stolen and stale.

❉

God and I discovered Roy's real passion at his party. She came in rather late dressed in very little. Roy jumped up from his jhoola and went to greet her with the mandatory two kisses at the door. Karen stopped her conversation, but only for a second, before going up smoothly and saying, 'Hello, gorgeous! Just look at you!' There was a cutting edge to the last remark that escaped no one. Maitreyee flashed her narrow green eyes and blew the room a kiss. Her hair was streaked gold and purple, and she wore a swirling ghagra with a backless choli. 'My *metrani* (sweeper-woman) wouldn't be caught dead in it,' hissed a guest.

We'd heard about 'M', the great love of Roy's life, and I'd been dying to see her. Apart from the eyes, she wasn't really special, except for her enormous vitality combined with that irresistible quality very few men are immune to—flirtatiousness. She fanned and flattered male egos shamelessly and without much pride. Her track-record, known to all, included a crazy maharaja who'd given her a monstrously big American car that guzzled more gas than she could afford, and a Parsee millionaire who had shocked everybody by presenting her with a litter of poodles when she'd been expecting something slightly more substantial—like an apartment. There she was then, with a car she couldn't pay the petrol bills for and hungry puppies she had nowhere to keep. 'The story of my life,' she'd laugh brazenly. From Roy she expected nothing beyond the occasional campaign or fashion show and genuinely seemed to like him for himself. As she put it, 'He's the only man I know who reads the *Financial Times* and can quote Balzac. I feel so intelligent in his presence. Tell me, folks—is intelligence infectious?'

Karen had no choice but to tolerate her. Roy had made that very clear. Besides, M had her uses. Outstation politicians salivated at the sight of her. She represented the 'available Bombay woman'—brazen, bold, brassy. And she helped out whenever Karen needed something special—a painting, a thumri singer, an Odissi dancer. M knew everybody and she got around. Delhi for a ghazal evening, Ahmedabad for an all-night sammelan, Lucknow to take in a Kathak performance, Madras to check out the Cholamandalam scene, Bangalore for a fashion show, Calcutta for a festival of Ghatak films, Cuttack for Chhau in the open air and back to Bombay, where she was into everything. Her energy-levels were astonishing. 'Uppers,' insisted the women who felt exhausted just watching her.

M's interests varied with the season. She was fickle but frankly so. 'Is there some special virtue in consistency?' she asked a visiting executive from New York who had dared to question her. Roy loved M in the only way he could. He was far too self-centred to invest more than just a portion of himself. But if she was sick or in need of air-fare, he'd send her chicken broth and money—the exact amount with a request to send him the stubs. But M also knew she could count on him in an emergency. Like the time she went hurtling through the windscreen of a friend's car while driving back from a party. Nobody came up with either the money or the blood she required for transfusions. Nobody except Roy, who gave her both. But Roy being Roy, had drawn the line at paying for a nose-job after she had recovered.

'So long as you can breathe through the damn thing, I see no reason to fix it.'

'But, Roy darling... can't you see what's happened to it? It looks like a squashed pakora,' she'd wailed.

'Then dip it in ketchup and serve it to your guests,' he'd snapped before leaving a tearful M in the hospital room. It didn't take her long to find someone willing to not just finance a new nose but perform the surgery himself. Dr Bharucha was the best-known plastic surgeon in Bombay. M soon had him running circles around her. 'He's willing to give me new tits, a new bum, a flat tum-tum... anything... all on the house. Such a sweetie, my Fali,' she'd giggle, but stopped with the nose. 'I look just like Cher in *Moonstruck*,' she had announced at her nose-job party.

After the party, I asked my mother what she'd made of the evening. I had expected her to turn up her nose, sniff and say something like: 'Your father would never approve of these people... they are so... so obvious and loud... you know?' Instead she nodded her head vigorously and beamed, 'My God! That was great fun, I must say... you do work with some interesting people, don't you? Roy? Is that his name? Of course it is. Charming. Very charming. And that other young person whose operations he finances. Simply amusing. So lively—yes, so lively.'

I was frankly astonished and rather pleased by her reaction. I decided there and then to take her along with me to the next mad party. Mummy needed diversion. And you could always count on ad types to provide it. Dammit, that's what they got their fifteen per cent for—diversions.

# Seven

God's idea of a great time was to go to Manori beach and shack up in one of the villas. It wasn't an inexpensive way to relax and I certainly couldn't afford to finance it. Not twice a month.

Besides, my bi-monthly disappearances were causing major problems at home. I'm sure my mother knew what I was up to. She'd register a mild protest and unconvincingly threaten to involve Papa in 'disciplining' me even though she knew he was far too busy scrambling up and further up in the organization to get overly-involved with my escapades. Besides, I could always trot out an ad-shoot (caught in monsoon floods, car breakdowns, no access to telephones, minor accidents) excuse. Of course, I wasn't fooling either of them, but we all needed these little games to maintain the facade of a tuned-in family.

I still felt passionately about God. We'd crossed the crucial one-year mark of being together, which surprised all the people who knew us—separately and as a couple. He continued to drive me up a wall with his demands and erratic conduct—but I hadn't met anybody else who interested me even half as much. God knew it. And used the information to manipulate me. If he had any genuine feelings for me, he didn't articulate them ever. But in his own rough fashion he conveyed that he cared—as much as he was capable of caring for anyone. His insensitive remarks about his parents and brother used to bother me—especially when he referred to his mother as 'that old hag. And it wasn't as if he disliked her or anything. Toro was always *'saala chootiya*, while his father came in for heavy sarcasm— 'Leader' sometimes, 'Unionwallah' at other times.

I often wondered why God went out of his way to project himself so negatively. He wasn't such a terrible person. I'd seen him perform various acts of kindness at the most unexpected moments. Somehow, he didn't like me to see this side to him—he obviously felt embarrassed and would immediately turn offensive. I was used to it—his on-now-off-now moods.

Though we were spending a great deal of time together, I was getting more involved in my career than I'd bargained for when I took the job. Our 'dirty weekends' provided a safety-valve. It was also the only time I got to be with God without hangers-on milling around. This was important for me, especially our intimacies—physical ones I mean. He was the first man

I'd *known,* had carnal knowledge of, as they say. And God, for all his crude public conduct, was a tender lover who took care not to hurt me.

It wasn't as if we spent all our time in bed. I could listen to him talk for hours. He must have enjoyed having such an entranced audience, even though he feigned boredom and contempt for my company.

'What *yaar,* Nasha. You are such a stupid female. I don't get a kick talking to you,' he'd announce, yawning deliberately.

'Look for someone else then,' I'd reply with a smug smile.

'Fuck it... too much effort. One stupid female is as good as another. Besides, your body and mine are fit-fit.'

Whether or not he meant it as one, I took that as a supreme compliment. I guess our bodies were kind of 'fit-fit'. I rather enjoyed our couplings in impersonal hired rooms. But, even on my newly bloated salary, I couldn't afford to give God a great weekend four times a month. His beer bill alone came to three hundred bucks. I hated paying for those awful belches later.

In any case, I wasn't a particularly physical person. Surprisingly, neither was God. He talked about sex a lot—particularly in the presence of his cronies. But when it came down to it, he was willing to give it the pass. Was it out of laziness, or was he as under-sexed as I was? Who knows. His lack of passion suited me fine for I had never ever really come to terms with pre-marital sex. It wasn't something I could swap stories about with other girls either. Talking to Mummy was out of the question too. It was left to me to work out this troublesome problem—to go all the way with God or stop at 'fooling around'. Our first few times were awkward and deeply embarrassing. Eager to please God and yet terrified beyond words at actually doing it, I was withdrawn and stiff. God sensed my unease and backed off. Fortunately, he spared me the wisecracks.

Dealing with the guilt was difficult. I'd started feeling like one of those 'bad' girls. I was sure everybody 'knew'—especially people at office. It was only after 'it' actually happened (not at Manori but in an empty office Comradesaab had dispatched God to on a minor errand) that I found out just how overrated 'it' was and how exaggerated my fears. Whether it was God's ineptitude or just my guilt, but I never did learn to enjoy 'it'.

'I'll have to find a richer broad,' he said to me, when I told him I was strapped for cash one month.

'If she'll have you,' I said half under my breath.

'Getting nasty, are we?' he asked and jerked my arm so roughly that I thought it had come out of its socket.

'Stop it,' I said, a sharp pain travelling down to my fingertips. 'It's your wretched background. How can you be anything but low?'

'Listen, woman, don't give me any of your upper-class, multinational shit. If this deal doesn't work for you—scram.'

Which is what I did. My resistance lasted for two weeks. A well-timed two weeks as it turned out, for I met someone I really liked at a presentation.

Anil Bhandari was a marketing guy who'd just set up a hot-shop of his own. I had reached his office earlier than the others and we got talking. He'd just returned after a long stint in one of the best marketing agencies in America and was keen to put his expertise to work back home. He spoke with a faint accent and wore sexy spectacles. The sort Warren Beatty started to sport in public after he crossed forty. Anil was in his early thirties and mockingly referred to himself as a 'first generation yuppie'. He was on the fast track and had his priorities all worked out. Priority number one was Success. He never said 'money' since that sounded 'vile' according to him.

He started his day, yuppie-style, with an energetic work-out at the Oberoi Health Club followed by a jog down Marine Drive. I asked him why he didn't drive his air-conditioned Maruti to the Mahalaxmi Race Course and jog there instead.

'I am a serious jogger,' he answered solemnly. 'I care about my waist-line as much as my bottom-line. I don't want to blow kisses as I work my way round the course. I need to conserve my energy for better things.'

Anil provided such a contrast to God—he was clean, for one; and so motivated. 'Life is a turn-on,' Anil said soon after we met at the presentation. 'I want to make the most of it—don't you?'

Till then, I hadn't really thought about what it was that I really wanted to do, besides drift in a lazy kind of way. Anil wore pin-striped, button-down collar shirts with large arm holes. And reverse-pleated trousers with turn-ups. I thought he looked very smart and chic. 'The big look—it's very in right now,' he said to a woman I loathed—an account executive called Aarti, who wore cut-away sleeved choli blouses without shaving her armpits. She smoked Charms holding the cigarette awkwardly between her fingers and blowing smoke out of her nostrils. Her kaajal was invariably smudged and she always wore thick handloom saris which created puddles around her feet during the monsoons. I'm not sure why I disliked Aarti but I suppose it was one of those instinctive things. I'd stare at her thick neck as she slopped around during brain-storming sessions and wonder whether she was suffering from goitre. I'd told God once that she looked like she had thyroid trouble.

'She must be on the pill,' he'd said dismissively. 'Fat cow—what she needs....'

'No, don't say it—a carrot?' I had prompted.

'I was going to say—a razor.'

Aarti had a thing about Anil and made it very obvious. His market research agency had a loose arrangement with our agency. He was at the office at least three times a week, all slick and sexy in his Italian fit shirts and baggy trousers. He smelt of Aramis or Drakkar and used Studio Line gel in his hair. Behind the Warren Beatty glasses were eyes the colour of melting chocolate. The one thing I didn't like about Anil were his white, cotton socks.

'But they go perfectly with tan top-siders,' he said when I mentioned them. And then added, 'Back where I come from, white socks were almost compulsory. Only hicks wore colours.'

Anil's office was neat, modern and well-organized. He preferred the American open system to cabins and cubicles. His office could be rearranged in minutes with a flick of a screen or two. The furniture was modular, with swivel chairs and efficient filing systems. The walls were in primary colours. 'Brights... they cheer one up,' said Anil. 'Psychology of colours—all designed to lower stress and encourage concentration.' And there were potted plants all over which looked plastic. 'Nonsense. They are living things—touch them and see. Plastic is a real no-no, don't you know?' His attitude towards his colleagues was informal and relaxed, but I suspected the whole thing was a pose. 'I'm easy about some things,' he said, 'but I expect people to deliver. If they don't... they can cheese out. I pay my guys more than they'd get in any other comparable set-up. And I want my returns.' I admired straight talk like that.

Aarti was coming on strong at the presentation. Her sleeves this time were more deep-cut than usual, and she kept raising her arms constantly. ('It's the animal in her,' God had once observed. 'Hair can be quite a turn-on if it sprouts on the right person.')

Anil was conducting the show in a laid-back, in-control manner. His Punjabi accent slipped through occasionally, but his slight drawl managed to overpower it. It was good to hear someone speaking fluently, easily. I'd got quite used to God's thick accent and the frequent mispronunciation of the commonest words but it had taken a long time.

Aarti giggled and giggled through the presentation, jangling the two hundred silver bangles she wore on both arms from wrist to elbow.

'Anil—you're so cool, *yaar*. You never get het up.' He looked at her with a flattered gleam in his brown eyes. 'You should model, *yaar*. You look sexy. One of our clients has been asking for a new face. Think about it, *yaar*. It's a range of men's toiletries. Very up-market. Suits your image. It's called Manhattan Men's Cosmetics, with an after-shave called Fifth Avenue. What do you think, *yaar*? Solid idea, no?'

I wanted to kill her for looking at him like she was going to lick his earlobes that minute.

Anil turned to me and said, 'What do you think?'

It was so unexpected and my concentration was so much on his earlobes, I didn't know what to say. So I said, 'Great. I'll be your agent.'

'*Aré, chhodo,* Nisha? You, an agent? Leave it to me. I'm the pushy one.'

Anil shrugged and smiled indulgently at both of us. He had a smart pen in his pocket and I liked the files in his hands. But one detail was slightly askew. He was wearing an ugly coral ring on the forefinger of his right hand. And another one with a yellow stone on the second finger of his left hand. A superstitious yuppie? The two didn't blend.

❋

'What's wrong with yuppiedom?' Anil asked.

'Nothing. It's just… what's the word… so derivative… you know… so borrowed,' I answered.

'Isn't that true about so many things in your life too? The music you listen to. The books you read. Some of the clothes you wear. Don't kid yourself. We are all after the same thing.'

'Not if the "same thing" includes clichés like compulsory CD's and PC's and membership at the right clubs. Not if you feel you are devastated unless you have the right label on your T-shirt and your running shoes cost more than my salary.'

'It's all relative. Why attach a moral to everything? It's a running shoes hang-up for me and maybe it's a fancy silk sari hang-up for you. Don't tell me you don't feel snobbish about certain things? I've seen it so often. Why do you criticize people who put plastic covers on their car seats and have a showcase full of imported souvenirs in their houses? Why do you look down on Vimal saris and fake silver jewellery made to look antique?'

'That's different.'

'Oh yeah? Why? Just because *you* say so. Well, come and check out my pad. It isn't fancy. It isn't big. But I'm not going to be there next year. See how I have used the space. Come and look at my doo-dahs. Even if I say so myself, I think I have a pretty neat set-up. OK, so I can't afford Iqbal's canvases on my walls or Chor Bazaar lamps on my ceiling. But, baby… you watch me… I'll get them soon. Big time—that's where I'm headed. Meanwhile, it's the real thing or nothing. I don't have cheap knock-offs to impress or fool people. I don't have melamine tables or plastic cups and plates. I don't give my guests paper napkins at parties. And I don't keep cloth flowers in Taiwan porcelain all over the place. Oh yes… no synthetic lace curtains, no fake fur rugs… and definitely no silly stickers on my car that read "I am a recycled Porsche".'

No. Maybe not. But how was a stuffed Garfield on the rear windshield any better?

Anil asked me home on a Saturday night—spelt nite?—when serious yuppies take time off to unwind, relax and have a spot of sex. Good for the system. The yuppie handbook said so. But it would be a change from eating at some crummy Irani joint at Colaba with God and paying for it. Besides, I'd never been to a bachelor's home before. Anil had boasted that he didn't employ any full-time servants since his place was full of convenient gadgets he worked himself. 'You will see—it's easy. I have a super food-processor, a microwave oven, dishwasher and washing machine. I vacuum the place once a week… no hassles.'

Was this a date? A real one—yuppie-style? What was one supposed to wear? I didn't have the right clothes. I didn't wear designer jeans or Reebok shoes. I didn't go to aerobics classes. I wasn't getting ahead professionally and didn't care much whether I did or didn't. I used public transport and jostled my way through sweaty crowds. I wasn't living on my own and had no plans to. I hadn't been to a wine and cheese party in my life and couldn't tell a Camembert from a Brie. I didn't own very much, not even an exercycle. And I continued to prefer home-cooked, calorie-laden food to salads and fruit juices. OK, I was sufficiently 'into nature' in that I enjoyed picnics to the lakes around Bombay, but I didn't have a pet cause to call my own. I didn't care sufficiently for Bombay's street-children or slum-dwellers. I wasn't paying towards the upkeep of a panda or a

Puerto Rican orphan. My face was clean-scrubbed and make-up free only because I was far too clumsy to apply eyeliner or lipstick. The watch on my wrist was an HMT, not a Swatch, and my underwear was Indian.

It turned out to be educative. Anil impressed me with his efficiency and hospitality. Everything was just right in his Studio as he called the one bedroom-kitchenette apartment in an ugly high-rise. It was one of those buildings that had an idiotic name, Pantheon, which made me giggle at the irony of it all. It was built on a plot acquired from a Bohra family gone to ruin. Where once there had been a grand mansion with an enormous portico now stood this eyesore with a silly name. The view was pleasant enough. If one got up on a chair in Anil's tiny kitchen, one could see the harbour. One could also see the immense sprawl of slums with Dalit Panther slogans and flags all over. The stench of rotting fish, from Sassoon Docks, increased and decreased with the tide—but it was all-pervasive and constantly present. Despite this, Anil had used a great deal of imagination and talent to put his little home together.

The decor was 'ethnic' in that he had raw silk on his settees and Shyam Ahuja throw cushions. He'd splurged on a Ravissant silk quilt which was on one wall. There were fresh rajnigandha flowers in ceramic vases and Lalit Kala Akademi prints everywhere— 'Till I can afford the originals,' he remarked confidently. A large Dhokra lamp at the entrance complemented the simple chatai on the floor. 'But we do produce such exquisite things. One has to restrain oneself from buying like a maniac. I've stopped going to the state emporiums in Delhi for this reason. I always come back loaded with stuff I don't need and have no place for. In fact, I have some beautiful Orissa appliques stored in the loft. And those palm leaf fans from Bengal. Other things too.... What I'd love to have one day is a Gurjari jhoola. But in this pokey little flat I'd end up fracturing my knee just moving from one end of the room to the other.'

The place was uncluttered and functional, making the handkerchief-sized living-room appear larger than it was. The dining-table was fitted into the wall and could be pulled down when required. One corner was his 'work station' which was like his office—modular.

I was curious about his bathroom, because bathrooms reveal so much about their users. Anil's was spotlessly clean with a cheerful shower curtain that had a rainbow on it. 'Got it at Macy's—that and the shower head with speed controls. A waste here, since the water pressure isn't sufficient,' he laughed. His shampoo was imported—'Neutrogena, it suits my hair type'—as was the gel squeeze-tube on the small shelf under the mirror. I wanted to tell him to discontinue gel since it led to scalp infections and hair loss. But I felt too shy. (I did tell him that, when I got to know him better: 'Try a combination of water and Brilliantine—much safer.')

His after-shaves stood in a neat row with Dior's L'Homme occupying pride of place. 'I'm dying to try Fahrenheit but it's too bloody expensive. So is Kouros,' he said. There was no hair in the basin or in his brushes and combs. The toothbrush was French. 'Funny that the French who never brush their teeth should make the best toothbrushes,' he quipped. His towels were Turkish and there were no dirty underpants lying around. The soap dish was dry with a Pear's cake in it—'It's the mildest. My skin breaks out into a rash with other brands.' And his shaving stuff was in a leather case. 'No electric shavers for me—I told you—my skin is like a baby's,' he confessed. There were other cosmetics like cleansing creams, face scrubs and Clinique's skin freshening lotion. He spoke unselfconsciously about his fortnightly facials and the face packs he preferred. 'No chemicals. Cucumber or yoghurt works well for me. I occasionally do a papaya pack myself when I'm having it for breakfast. Or I pulp a peach and slap it on,' he told me. I liked his being so open about his beauty routine, when women were so secretive and coy about theirs.

He was equally candid about his passion for cooking. 'I love trying out new dishes. I'm an experimental cook. Gourmet stuff... you name it... I've tried it. My speciality is omelettes, I can make over twenty kinds with different fillings—fluffy ones, flat ones, rolled up ones... you must come and have breakfast one Sunday. I'll give you the works—fresh orange juice

with champagne—how do you like that? Mushrooms
sautéed in butter. Eggs any which way you like them.
Stewed prunes... creamy porridge with hot or cold
milk, fresh fruit, sausages, even steak if you have the
appetite for it. Then we can laze around and listen to
jazz or opera, I love both, or Indian classical—Kishori
Amonkar, Jasraj—do you like them? I smoke a joint... but
only rarely. On special occasions. No hard liquor for
me. I put on an inch round the middle immediately.
Far too much effort to work off two whiskies... not
worth it—I love good wine—I've chilled some for
tonight. A good, not great, Chablis. I've planned the
music—Jean-Michel Jarre—futuristic and wild. Why
don't you relax and tell me more about yourself while
I toss a salad and get the shrimps going?'

I realized that I would have to be a non-vegetarian
for the night but that was the least of it. I was transfixed.
He seemed to love what he was doing in such an innocent
way. He took so much pleasure in wiping his precious
long-stemmed wine glasses and setting the table. The
napkins and place mats were again from Shyam Ahuja
in beige and pink shades. He had pink carnations in a
terracotta bowl to match. The plates were American
China—'Can't afford Limoges—but will someday.' The
cutlery was Scandinavian stainless steel.

The conversation was so Wall Street it wasn't funny.
Anil talked about 'inter-facing' and 'doing lunch'. He
'met with' clients and friends and conjugated words

normal people generally considered nouns. But he was sweet in his earnestness and deft with his fingers. I enjoyed the meal, but I'd enjoyed watching him cook it even more. He talked about his American experience with something bordering on awe. It had obviously affected him deeply and in the most positive of ways.

'I dig India,' he said, 'make no mistake about it... but, man, America! That's another, way-out experience... something else.'

God seemed an alien at that moment. A creature from another galaxy. I imagined him as one of the *Star Trek* crew or a monster from one of the sci-fi quickies. God had given up cooking and sewing long ago—it didn't go with his image of a macho journalist. I couldn't wait to tell him about Anil's expertise in the kitchen. It was easy to predict God's reaction. He'd say, 'That bloody fairy... I'm not surprised, *yaar*. The guy looks like a bawarchi. He can't talk... have you heard his voice? Pansy! Sissy *hai saala*. Hijda! He probably embroiders in his spare time... ask him.' I personally didn't think there was anything non-macho about cooking or sewing for that matter. In fact, I found the idea rather sexy.

Anil wore an apron which said 'World's Best Cook'. He kept all his pots and pans within easy reach, hanging from hooks over the range. 'Heavy copper bottoms... they distribute the heat evenly.' He used wooden spoons for stirring and a fork to beat the eggs.

'Salad dressings are my speciality... and I make super strawberry margaritas,' he said, as the CD played Puccini.

We talked about our families and he mentioned his without any self-consciousness. 'My dad was an accountant in some crummy firm. I was a pretty good student. Straight A's in the US. It was great out there I tell you... what a life!'

'Why did you come back then?' I asked.

I'm realistic. And I'm ambitious. Sure, I would have done well enough for a few years and then what? I wanted to come back home and set up my own shop. Hell, I decided, if I was going to bust my ass, I might as well do it for myself... but let's not talk about me. What about you? What's a nice girl like you doing in a sloppy ad agency?'

'Frankly, I don't know. I kind of enjoy it. It's not too demanding. The pay's OK. The people are fine. I have enough time to do other things... you know, see plays and stuff.'

'And stuff? Does that include someone called Deb? Don't get mad... I think I should know. This isn't the sort of evening I spend with just any girl, you know. I've been thinking. It's time to settle down. My folks have been at me. They've even tried to fix me up with some highly eligible girls from our community. Educated ones. Dowry thrown in. Can you believe it—I'm worth thirty lakhs in the marriage market, only because of my foreign degrees.'

'With that kind of money, you could go places. Move into a bigger apartment. Expand your business. How come you are passing it all up?' I ventured.

'I've asked myself all these questions. There's just one answer—I can't do it. I will not be able to spend my life with a stranger. Though I'm terribly old-fashioned about a few things—like I don't expect you to go to bed with me tonight—but an arranged marriage is completely out for me. Are you surprised to hear that?'

'No. Not really. I didn't think you were a raging sex maniac or anything.'

'No. But most Indian girls have even stranger notions about a foreign-returned fellow. They think they are very fast and on the make.'

'Well... you're the first specimen I've come across. So I really have no idea.'

'But Deb. The guy you hang out with. Don't ask me how I know. Agency grapevine. Everybody knows. You two seem an unlikely combination. I don't mean to be rude, but he isn't your type. You don't belong to the same class.'

'It's difficult for me to discuss Deb. We have nothing in common. And yet....'

'It's all right. You don't have to explain. Have another glass of wine. I'll change the music. How about the Beatles? I love them.'

And to the familiar beat of "It's been a hard day's night", Anil and I finished the bottle, shook hands, said good-night, and parted.

I saw Anil twice more during my two-week estrangement from God, but after that I couldn't say no to him. He was too much a part of me and I agreed to see him again. The next morning Bijli and he came to collect me. Papa had already left for work. There was trouble brewing in one of the company's toilet soap units. Mummy was talking to herself and rearranging the contents of her dressing-table for the five-hundredth time. I didn't pay attention any longer. A couple of times I'd noticed weird sadhus sitting in a trance outside her bedroom. Mummy had flipped so completely that there was no point in even asking her what was going on. Any more mother-daughter combination at firm parties was obviously out of the question. Didi had also taken to muttering to herself. It was a loony-bin. Papa stayed away for longer and longer hours. Even the sparrows that used to come in through the window each morning seemed to mope and not chirp as they used to. Like my father, I hardly hung around at home. I couldn't bear the atmosphere. Mummy would swoop down on me the moment I entered. Her conversation was so incoherent, I couldn't unravel her remarks. I didn't think they were worth the effort in the first place.

As I climbed onto Bijli, God said, without turning around, 'How would you like to become a goddess?' and revved the engine. Before the question could register, we had zoomed off down the stretch in front of my home and straight into the chaotic traffic at a roundabout without signals. The wind was strong, God had his helmet on, and I was still trying to make sense of that toss-away remark. Did it mean what I thought it did? Was it a proposal? Was God feeling ill? Was he stoned? He leaned over and started his standard conversation with Bijli, while the motorbike purred away contentedly. He always spoke in whispers to her and it was the only time his expression softened.

I yelled over the sound of BEST buses scraping past our ears and pedestrians darting daringly in front of us, 'Are you asking me to marry you?' I must have really been hollering since a couple in the Maruti next to us stopped looking bored for a second and actually allowed themselves to smile a little. God was being impossible. He pretended he hadn't heard. I tapped on the fibreglass dome covering his head. And asked again, but a little more softly this time. He'd heard me. I know he had.

He waved his hand and shouted, 'Shut up, woman. I can't hear you. Want to create a *hungama* on the street? Let me concentrate on getting out of this shit-hole.'

How typical of God. I couldn't resist a tummy squeeze. I would have bitten his ear if it hadn't been covered.

I hopped off at the agency and saw Roy driving up in his Volkswagen. He looked harassed and barely nodded at us before going off to park.

I waited a moment, then asked, 'What did you say near my house?'

'Nothing.'

'Of course you did. Liar. Say it again.'

'Get off my back. You must be growing cuckoo like your *pagli* mother. Hearing things.'

'God, please. P-L-E-A-S-E. I know you asked me to marry you. Why do you feel so ashamed now? Everybody gets married. Even communists and poets.'

'Shut up, you silly woman. Who said anything about marriage? I was *lagaoing* line, that's all, don't take it seriously.'

'Isn't it a bit late in the day for that?'

'Marriage! Huh! You should marry that pansy with the fairy hair. He's more your type. You can discuss advertising and marketing in bed and get your orgasms reading feasibility reports. I doubt that you'll get them any other way.'

'So you did get jealous.'

'Jealous of that half-cock? Don't be ridiculous. Tell me—how did you spend your evening at his place? Not that I'm interested. No... let me tell you. He talked about America and you drooled over his pizzas.'

'He didn't give me pizzas.'

'No? Then what? Hot dogs? Hamburgers?'

'No. He made divine pasta with shrimps and a superb salad.'

'Go diddle yourself... eat pasta and salad for the rest of your life. You don't deserve real food.'

'But it *is* real food!'

'Yeah? Maybe for pansy buggers like him. I don't have the time to waste discussing this *behenchod's* cooking. I can't keep Sujata waiting.' And with that he roared off with Bijli leaving a trail of exhaust for me to choke on.

Lucio was sitting in the foyer upstairs. He glanced up at me and shook his head. 'Hey... what's the matter? Old man getting tough?'

'Nothing. What's up with you?'

'Oh... nothing really. I was free and Nitin had mentioned some new jingles you guys were planning, so I thought I'd pop by and check the scene.'

Suddenly something snapped inside my head and I heard myself screaming, 'Why don't you leave me alone? I need time for myself. Why do you keep barging into my office like this? You know jolly well there aren't any jingles. Why can't you find some other diversion?'

The telephone operator stopped listening in to whichever call she was snooping on and sat up to watch. I was beyond caring. I didn't even know what I screamed, except that it was horribly cruel and shrill. Lucio stood there with this delicate fingers on the crucifix. He waited for me to stop.

'Hey... take it easy. Cool it. Why don't we go somewhere? Let's go to Rhythm House and listen to the Rolling Stones. Come on... you need a break.'

I suddenly felt ashamed of my outburst and agreed meekly to the suggestion. Besides, it was the best idea he'd had in a long time. Rhythm House was just round the corner from the office. I ran into the studio and told Kawla I'd be back in a while. He glared at me. 'But who will check these artworks? Urgent, madam. Client meeting at 12.30.'

'I'll be back,' I said. 'Promise.'

'*Kamaal hai*... one minute that other phellow comes here on a motorcycle. Now this phellow also comes. And you go... is this office or a maidan?'

The other artists had stopped slouching over their drawing boards. I noticed that Naik's long nail had broken.

'What's happened to your nail?' I asked him.

Kawla interrupted: 'Why phor you want to know? You do your work phirst, we will do ours. That D'Lima will be coming to check just now. I will report the matter to him. Why I should take responsibility? If the artworks don't go, I will say phrankly that madam came here and bunked off. If you get a phiring don't ask me. We don't want any hassles here. I will talk at weekly meeting. Too much nonsense goes on and the art department gets the blame. Come on, boys, what you're staring at simply? Do your work... do your work. Let madam and that loafer go and drink coffee in a hotel, how does it affect us?'

Without waiting to hear any more, I picked up my bag and ran out.

'If that other phellow comes back asking for money, what I will tell him?' Kawla mocked.

'Tell him I have gone out with some other phellow and he can look for money somewhere else,' I replied.

'*Besharam... besharam* (shameless),' I could hear Kawla saying. My little scene had provided the art department their cheap thrill for the day. And as for the telephone operator, she didn't need to listen in on any more calls that morning. She was far too busy making them.

After I returned from my little outing with Lucio, I discovered the real reason why everyone in the office was in such a flap. Apparently, Roy's daughter, Janine, had run off with a sacked driver and shacked up with him at Bombay's notorious Antop Hill. Roy couldn't make up his mind about what had upset him more—her elopement with a menial or that she wasn't located at the 'right' address. Antop Hill—I mean, you couldn't think of a worse area. It was where all the hoods and dons of Bombay's burgeoning underworld hung out. It was a locality so notorious that even cops and crime reporters gave it the pass. And there was young Janine, his pampered, pussycat of a daughter, brought up on soft-centre Godiva chocolates and imported toilet paper, living in a ratty jhopdi with a rakish driver.

Roy was so completely devastated by the news that he didn't give any interviews for a week. Karen gave up gold and bought just one great outfit for herself from Ritu's Boutique. Everybody at the office realized that this was major.

'We won't pick up any new accounts at this rate,' moaned the senior accounts supervisor.

'Forget new accounts, yaar... we might lose the old ones.'

Aarti giggled and giggled fingering her underarm hair disgustingly. 'It's nothing more than a class war, yaar,' she drawled. 'Terrible nexus between the haves and have-nots. So what if he's a driver? He's also a human being.'

'So, go live with a bhangi if you want to, yaar. Prove your point and save us your lectures,' said Ronnie, the 'hot' precocious copy-writer who, I was certain, couldn't have been older than fourteen. The top talents in the business were getting younger and younger—like starlets in Hindi films. It was very 'in' to hire acne-marked teenagers who specialized in writing hip copy, 'for the growing youth market'. Ronnie's lines didn't go beyond 'cool it, babe', and his ideas for visuals were straight lifts from American magazines like *Taxi*. But Ronnie earned more in a month than an accountant in a bank drew annually. 'The Brat', as he was affectionately known, was Roy's pet-of-the-moment and could do no wrong.

Soon after the elopement (which made it to an eveninger) Roy sent for me in his 'Creative Cabin'—so described because it was designed to distract. Roy sat casually behind an enormous teak desk from Chor Bazaar, which he said had belonged to his great-grandfather (a lie!) and was originally housed in their huge family home in a small village of Goa. His chair was a gigantic affair—weathered leather in tan tones. A collection of pipes was stacked on one side of the table, with antique silver nut-crackers on the other. His Buddha collection in all materials (ivory, agate, onyx, enamel, ebony, lapis, even gold) were displayed in a high-security cabinet at one end of the room. Roy liked to disarm visitors to his cabin by its impressive decor. 'It has been accessorized by my wife,' he'd say easily as people gawked in admiration. There was nothing in the room to suggest that it was either an office or an adagency's work station. How could anybody discuss business with a magnificent pool table occupying most of the space anyway? Roy would encourage juniors to 'toss out a few ideas' while fooling around with the cues. I'd been told that if I wished to clamber up the ladder of success in this agency, I'd have to play snooker. I'd tried... but clumsily.

'Aah—Nisha,' he'd greet me, 'come on in... how's the game progressing.' I'd look stupid, shuffle my feet and confess that it wasn't. 'No sweat,' Roy would assure me generously and pick up a cue himself.

But this time it was different. He looked sombre and defeated as he sat slouched in his chair chewing on a pipe. He had taken off his Gucci loafers and was wiggling his toes in purple socks. 'Your friend... the young man who keeps touching you for money,' he began, without attempting to conceal the crudeness of the remark. 'I hear he has a lot of influence... or his old man does. He's some sort of a *neta* or something—isn't he? A leader... trade unionist... local dada... whatever.'

I didn't say a thing and continued to stare fixedly at a bronze dog on his table.

'Well, as you know... Janine... that is... oh hell... I'm sure everybody knows. I need your boyfriend's help to get my darling back. My wife is completely wrecked by this horrible affair. We trusted the rascal... and this is what he did to us... to our honour and prestige. A driver! It's disgraceful. I hope our clients don't get affected by the news... it is being circulated, isn't it?' I still didn't say anything. 'So, my dear? Why don't you ask that fellow to see me, we can take care of him if you know what I mean... there's money to be made here. I'm willing to pay... anything... within reasonable limits, of course, to get my daughter back.'

'I'll speak to Deb—that's his name.'

'Yes... Deb... when can you arrange a meeting?'

'When he's free.'

'Good. But what do you mean by "when he's free"? I was told he was a bum. That he did nothing besides sponging on you. Pardon me for being so blunt. But that's the office gossip.... I do get to hear things, you know.'

'Yes. I suppose you do. It's quite all right. I don't really care what everybody thinks of him. But Deb happens to be a very talented writer... he's not a bum.'

Perhaps it was the sharpness of my tone, for Roy apologized immediately. 'I didn't mean to offend you. But you know how it is... office grapevine... that sort of thing. An image tends to stick... particularly if you are an adman. But I *do* apologize.'


'What does that bastard expect me to do? I don't care if his precious daughter fucks herself to death with an escaped convict, frankly. So beat it. I'm not interested in phoney sob stories.'

I pleaded with God to meet Roy, just once. 'It's my job, Deb. I don't want to get the sack. What will we do if I'm jobless?'

That made sense. Even though God was earning enough he still thought it his birthright to touch me. 'What do you do with your own money?' I'd asked him, summoning up enough courage to do so from time to time.

'Oh, I keep that for important stuff.'

'Like what?'

'Projects,' he'd replied vaguely, but with an important, mysterious air. 'You know... Narmada Valley... Bhopal... Chipko.'

God strutted into the office the next morning looking officious. He asked the bitch at the board if he could see Roy and she all but laughed out loud. 'See Mr D'Lima?' she mocked. 'Do you have an appointment?'

'Screw appointment-shappointment. The problem is his—do you get me... *he* needs *me*. Just do your job and tell him I'm here.' It must have been his menacing tone that did it.

She buzzed Roy and told him in terrified tones, 'Sir... it's that man. Miss Verma's... that is, Nisha's... er... boyfriend. He is saying he wants to see you.' A moment later, she waved God in wordlessly, astonishment all over her mean face. A minute later she summoned the peons and told them the day's news. They immediately rushed into the art department and yelled it out in Marathi. Kawla dropped his brushes and exchanged a significant look with Naik, who was busy chipping the ice-cream pink nail polish (his wife's) from the long nail (which had grown back) of his little finger. During God's brief chat with Roy, no work got done at the agency. Even I couldn't concentrate on the latest designer tiles in the market, which perfectly matched the designer potties and basins (coffee-coloured) that we'd launched six months earlier.

'What did he say?' I asked God the minute he emerged.

'Shit-head. Scum. Skunk. Worm.'

'Did he call you all those names?'

'Don't be mad, *yaar*. How could he? He needs me. I had to stop him from licking my chappals. He was grovelling at my feet like the bloody dog that he is.'

'What does he want?'

'Oh—nothing very much. Simple stuff, *yaar*—he wants the driver's head on a platter... like the Roman emperors or Shahjehan or someone.'

You mean, he actually wants it? I mean, literally?'

'Murder. That's what he has on his mind, baby. Blood.'

Does he think you are a murderer?'

'Maybe. He asked....'

'Asked *what?* "Look, can you murder someone?" WHAT did he ask? Tell me!'

'More or less.'

'And what did you reply?'

' "Sure. I do it all the time," I said, "but what's in it for me, pal?" "A lot," the shit-head replied. So I continued, "How much is a lot?" He went on, "How much do you... well, charge?" So, I tried Hindi film *stuntbaazi* and asked again, "How much is your daughter worth to

you?" "Plenty," said the dog. "Can you put a price to it?"
I said. "You do that," he replied. Can you imagine, *yaar?*
Finally I told him he'd got the wrong man. And he looked
as if he was going to die there and then. "Do you know
someone? I hear your father has connections…." I said,
"Well, pal, you heard, wrong." He was ready to beg.
"I need a *supari*-killer, a contract chap—know what
I mean? I thought you might be able to help me. I'm
willing to pay a great deal of money. But I want that
bastard dead. I don't care how much it costs to hire
someone. Get me a contract killer, and I'll look after
you… and Nisha." I would have spit on his face. But I
thought of you… of us. We need the bread, *yaar.* So I
just said, "I'll see what can be done," and left it at that.'

'You mean you can organize it? You'll get someone
to bump the fellow off? DON'T. Please don't. It's a
crime. Don't get involved.'

'Baby—don't tell me what to do. I know this business.
You want to get rid of someone—come to me. But
bring the lolly with you. Nothing for free, remember.
Not even love.'

# Eight

The weather got all of us down but God had been unusually moody and listless ever since Roy tried to hire him to organize a hit-man for the driver.

If God was behaving like a swine, I wasn't faring much better. It had to be the bloody weather. October, the worst month of the year in Bombay, was on us. Even air-conditioning didn't help. The sweat never stopped—it just evaporated faster in an icy room giving everybody the chills. Humidity levels were so high, I felt dehydrated and drained most of the time. The heat was getting to everybody and affecting each person in strange ways. I found myself snapping at Didi—something I had never done before. And God was beginning to get on my nerves. Maybe his new association with Sujata had something to do with it.

He wouldn't talk to me, and this was frustrating for I was dying to know how his extended interview with Sujata (yes, he had finally agreed to do it) had gone. However, if God was uncommunicative, Sujata was not. At the next 'rap session' for *Plume,* she pounced on me, 'Oh you sweet little thing... so virginal and pure. How does darling Debu survive?'

I wanted to say, 'With women like you around, it must be easy.' But I kept quiet and started a conversation with Chandni, who startled me by saying, 'I was just like you when I met Mr Mascarenhas.' I always found it funny when she referred to the D.O.M. in such a formal way. What happened when they were in bed? Did she squeal, 'Oh, Mr Mascarenhas, that felt so-o-o good?'

Chandni nudged me. 'You know, I didn't know what semen was... I mean... what it looked like, when I met him. I'd only read about it in books. So, one day I asked him. He was so touched by my trust that he said, "Here... let me show you... get me some soap." And just imagine what he did? He masturbated... right there in front of me. It was the most beautiful thing. That is called love. Now do you understand how it is between us?'

I nodded and tried to change the topic but Sujata waded in again, 'Men are such adorable beasts, aren't they, girls?'

Chandni smiled and said, 'Grrrrr!'

'Take Debu, the tiger. That's what he is... a real tiger. Nisha, I'm surprised he doesn't cover you with clawmarks and love-bites.' With that she stretched her thick neck which was covered with small black warts, and put up her unruly hair. Purplish bruises below her ear matched the sari she was wearing that evening.

Two weeks later, her exhaustive interview appeared. She was at her shocking best, talking blithely about her lovers and how they inspired her verse. It was so pedestrian and fake that even God felt ashamed. She'd given him a photograph of herself that was twenty years old. Plus a poem—a highly erotic one—titled simply "For Debu, my tiger".

'She'll drop you now,' I told God when I saw the piece. You aren't of further use to her.' He pretended he didn't know who or what I was talking about. But Sujata didn't drop him. If anything she became possessive and demanding, hunting him down and practically tearing his clothes off. She pressed poems and lovelorn notes on him daily and kept arranging trysts that he didn't keep. Surprisingly, I felt detached and distant. Unbelievably cold, in fact. It didn't affect me, or I didn't allow it to.

It was then that I wished my job had been more enjoyable, more fulfilling. The ad scene was full of creepy characters who spoke in a language I couldn't always understand. I was working on a campaign I detested wholeheartedly. It was for a fruit drink that hardly qualified as one. And the client had pre-determined ideas about the launch.

'Let's recreate California—lots of sun, surf and sex,' he kept repeating in what he thought was a West Coast drawl. He wanted the best photographer, the best models, the best locales, the best copy... but at a cut-throat price. 'Spare no expense, gang,' he repeated, with a pocket calculator in his hand. 'Keep it straight and keep it oomphy.'

I was roped in to find the right props and people. 'Why me,' I moaned.

'Because you don't threaten the female models. Some of them have egos thinner than their skins—you have to handle them carefully, especially when you go on an outdoor shoot.'

That was the big incentive—Maldives. Nitin, a squeaky-voiced executive, had come up with the idea of shooting there—'The closest thing to California,' he squeaked to the client. There was much excitement at the agency. Who would finally make it for the junket besides Roy and Karen, of course? Kawla was ecstatic, 'Phree trip. Art director must go. How those phellows will be able to visualize otherwise? *Aré, majaa aayega* (we'll have fun).' It was understood I'd go... and that was about the only attraction that stopped me from chucking in my resignation.

I set up an appointment to meet Pebbles Prabhu reputed to be the world's biggest swine and the most irresistible photographer in the business. Pebbles had a wild reputation. It was said that he chewed up half-a-dozen models a day and still had the energy to sample some more. He was a rough-talking hunk with wolf-like eyes with absolute mastery over his medium. He was brilliant. And impossible. The story of his colourful life read like one of the storyboards we often worked on at the agency. A rags-to-riches type, he had arrived in Bombay from Singapore without a penny to his name. An orphan who had been brought up by a benevolent uncle, Pebbles exuded a raw, rough-edged sexuality that most models in the city found impossible to resist. He was linked with the best of the lot and in ad circles it was rumoured that he changed girlfriends as often as he changed bedsheets. Pebbles wasn't a conventionally good-looking fellow—thickset and bull-like. Neither did he speak particularly well. If anything, his low, crudely-worded mumble was practically incoherent. But he had the girls flocking. 'He's mean and treats them bad,' said our model co-ordinator, an Anglo-Indian lad whose voice had never cracked. (Poor William, he'd spent his young life dreaming of Australia and trying his best to pass off as an Irishwoman who'd been accidentally born in the wrong country with the wrong sex. Lucio got along famously with Willie and they often got stoned together.)

Pebbles roughed up his models all right and they begged for more. His photo-sessions were so notorious that most first-timers took mommies and boyfriends along for protection. They lost their careers at that very moment. Pebbles would take one look at the escorts and growl, 'If you need bodyguards with me, you can go fuck yourself. I don't have the time to waste on you.' The more brazen ones who survived the initiation went on to grab the best deals in town. Pebbles was a monster in arenas other than the sexual. He got the bread he asked for, and so did his girls.

His 'woman' at the time was the top model in Bombay, a reserved, bespectacled, scholarly sort when she wasn't in front of the cameras. Nobody could figure out this particular hook-up Malini was an out-of-towner, a Bangalore girl who had come to Bombay to become a lawyer. It required Pebbles to see beyond her mousy facade and discover the face of the decade. Malini had the right bone structure to make fantastic pictures. 'Her calcium deposits would give a chalk factory a complex,' Willie used to giggle. Once the glasses came off (along with most of her clothes) and she had her face painted by talented make-up wizards, Malini looked sensational. The transformation was so startling that most times she went unrecognized on the street. Pebbles adored her and pushed her for every campaign that came his way. The other girls didn't feel too threatened since Malini was obviously in it only for a short-term stint. She was a bit too bright and far too indifferent to the glamour of their world to last the course. Yet, she was all over the place, including TV commercials, and within her first year, had made enough money to buy herself a second-hand Maruti Gypsy.

I decided to take Lucio with me for the meeting with Pebbles.

'Are you sure?' he asked softly. 'The guy may not like it.'

'Look, Lucio, I'm only going there to fix up the Maldives shoot... not to bed him.'

'Who knows....' Lucio said vaguely and picked up his satchel.

We ran into Anil at the door, 'Hey, howya doin'?' he said, and I thought he was being funny.

Lucio groaned and muttered, 'Man... what a creep.'

'Say... I've been meaning to touch base with you. New Year's Eve will soon be here. I thought we could bring in the whole show together. Make a night of it.'

I was thrown for a bit. New Year's Eve seemed so far away, with over a month to go. 'Gosh, Anil, I can't think that far ahead. Check with me later.'

'Reservations. We've got to make reservations.'

'Where? What for?'

'Oh! I thought we'd do it in style. Maybe have a drink somewhere special, dinner at the Club or the Rooftop Place. And then party the rest of the night away.... I have quite a few cards stacked up... clients, friends... combine a bit of P.R. with all the fun. How does it sound?'

'Dismal,' said Lucio close to my ear. And before I could reply, he piped up, 'Actually, she's spending it with me at the Byculla Mechanics' Ball.'

Anil nearly dropped his tan leather portfolio. 'No, she's not. Nisha… give me a break. Are you really going to hang out with greasy mechanics that night?'

'Sure,' I heard myself saying. 'I do it every year.' I linked my arm through Lucio's and tripped out.

Pebbles wasn't formidable at all. I rather liked him. It must have been such a strain to play Tarzan all the time when he was really Winnie the Pooh. I found him open, accessible and surprisingly ill-at-ease. Malini was hanging around in black leotards, her hair oiled and tied into a tight bun. She was reading an Asterix and eating a green apple.

'Why don't we discuss the assignment with her,' Pebbles suggested. 'She fixes up everything.' Malini looked up from her comic book and raised her eyebrows. 'Come on over,' Pebbles urged, 'we have a big shoot ahead of us, Maldives.'

She reached for a scratch pad, picked up a Bic and walked over to where we were. Within minutes, she'd figured out the logistics of the exercise and done some rough costings. She told Pebbles who she thought would fit into the 'look' of the campaign (besides herself) and he went along with all her suggestions docilely. I thought it very sweet that he never called her by her name but always 'she' or 'her'. Malini rushed around the studio running through their impressive filing cabinet and showing us the portfolios of potential candidates— 'we need someone with fizz'. 'Nice teeth—she has the best teeth in the business. We'll need them. Lots of laughter…. This one isn't great looking—but she has super legs. We can use her body and cover her face. This chap… let me see… dandruff… we can take care of that. Wrong jaw. That can be fixed too. Oh—here's Aarti—she's cute—looks great in a bikini. No bikinis? Oh, of course, the new government cover-up policy. OK. How about this one… yeah… good tits, nice eyes. She looks like a younger version of Dimple… same sort expression. Too much gum, we can't have her. That one has chopped off her hair, she looks like a shorn puppy—forget her. OK, let's go with this bunch. They look good together. Muscles, boobs, biceps—everything fits. A couple of them are enthusiastic modern dancers. Maybe we could work in a small sequence at a disco or the beach.'

Terrific, Maldives was on. Maldives was happening.


God was even more sarcastic than usual about the Maldives trip. 'What are *you* going there for? If you think you'll make it with Pebbles or whoever that sham is, forget it. You aren't a model or a starlet.'

'Why don't we change the subject and talk about you? How's the next issue of *Plume* coming along? What's happening on the arts page? Have you met Iqbal?'

'The very fact that you have to ask me all these questions shows how indifferent you are to my life. It is all you, you, you. You and your fairy boyfriends, you and those foolish models, you and that bastard boss of yours.'

'Don't be unpleasant, Deb. What's the matter? Broke?'

'*Chhodo, yaar*—I make more than you do these days.'

'Then why are we fighting?'

'Fighting? Who's fighting?'

'Deb… you haven't played your flute for such a long time. Why don't we spend a quiet evening catching up and listening to your melody?'

'I don't know, *yaar*. I'm not free in any case. Have to go to the Lala's house to see his cars and paintings. You can tag along if you want to. But don't bring Lucio.'

'Which Lala? You mean the guy who lives in that absurd-looking bungalow and behaves like an eighteenth-century feudal lord? What's a good commie like you doing with him?'

'I've been asked to work on a profile. He's quite a character. Just like a Hindi *phillum, yaar. Aa jao,* you'll enjoy yourself. I'll tell him you are my *chamchi.*'

'I'm surprised at you, Deb. These were the people you used to detest at one time. Didn't your father organize a lock-out at the Lala's factories three years ago? And now you are accepting all sorts of invitations… I don't know. You have changed. You are becoming like everybody else. No wonder you don't have the time to play the flute. I wouldn't be surprised if you've even stopped talking to Bijli.'

It was true that God had changed more than he cared to admit. He was out at some five star clip joint or the other night after night. Often, he'd begin his day with a breakfast-meeting at the Shamiana, with a quick lunch at China Garden, a cocktail party in an opulent setting and, if he had room for dinner after stuffing himself with chicken tikkas and shami kababs, then a bite at an all-night coffee shop (with beer), before going home to his shabby chawl. I found all this very disturbing and difficult to understand. God was selling out.

'I have always been a sponger, *yaar,*' he admitted.

'But that's different, Deb,' I said.

'In what way? I consider these outings as perks... fringe benefits of my job. Frills, Nasha, frills. Why make such a *tamasha* out of it? These people need me—do you think I don't know that? They want to use me. They get what they want—and I get to have a good time. It's OK, *yaar.* No *lecturebaazi,* understand?'

I wasn't convinced. Only, I didn't want to get into an argument. God was behaving like a mortal, like all the other journalists in town, a bum who shamelessly sold his pieces for a few pegs of Scotch and a five-star evening. He'd started dressing differently—flashy horrible clothes that looked absurd on him. He carried Dunhill packs around which I knew he hadn't paid for. He dropped names constantly, particularly one name—and that scared me.

Yashwantbhai Dawani was a powerful political broker, known for his ruthless wheeling and dealing. In the right circles, he was referred to simply as the Collector. He controlled the purse-strings of his party and arm-twisted huge 'donations' out of industrialists and businessmen. Everybody knew about his modus operandi, yet nobody dared take him on. Yashwantbhai courted and pampered the press since he was aware that the right mentions in the right papers would consolidate his image within the party.

God had come into contact with him at one of Iqbal's art openings. 'Come and see my collection, *yaar,*' Yashwantbhai had said to God, throwing his arm over God's shoulder. 'I think you are the best reviewer in town.'

I was sure he hadn't even heard God's name till then but God had been immensely flattered.

'Did you hear what he said?' he asked me later that evening.

'Don't fall for it, Deb. I'm sure he says that to everybody.'

'Rubbish! You are such a wet blanket, *yaar.* Always pouring cold water on everything.'

I reminded God that Comradesaab and Yashwantbhai had been locked on a collision course for over a decade and that God's father would be horrified to learn that his son was hobnobbing with this hateful man.

'The times are changing, *yaar*. Comradesaab is against the whole world. What's wrong with Yashwantbhai? He was so charming.'

'Wait till he finds out whose son you are—he'll be even more charming.'

No, I didn't like what was happening to God at all. We were beginning to see less and less of each other now that he didn't need to touch me for cash that often. He was getting ahead professionally, meeting all the VIPs in town, interviewing culture-vultures and generally being wooed by 'all those who mattered' in the high-life of the city.

The Lala was a harmless man. An eccentric and self-styled connoisseur for whom time had stopped a century and a half ago. He lived so completely in the past that he seemed far removed from today's realities. Except when it came to money. Nobody knew where and how he had made it and he certainly wasn't very forthcoming about its origins. He rarely granted interviews and even the business press hadn't managed to ferret out any telling details about his vast wealth. He surrounded himself with his fine art pieces, jewels, paintings and antiques, rarely venturing beyond the portals of his palace-like residence. A lonely, unusual man, his only 'friends' were faithful family retainers and the pedigreed dogs that roamed his estate. There were stories galore about his single status, since it seemed such a waste that someone like him should die without an heir. People wondered who he was going to leave his fortune to—the servants, the dogs or charity. The Lala could be wildly generous with total strangers and miserably stingy with those around him, especially his office staff. Most days, he directed his world-wide operations from the privacy of his enormous bedroom. On the rare occasions that he did deign to step out, he carefully selected a car that matched his cufflinks. He struck terror in the hearts of his executives but was kindness itself to his countless drivers and their children. What was the point in amassing so much when there was no one to either share it with or pass it on to, people wondered, when they caught a glimpse of him cruising down the Bombay roads in a stately fashion. The avaricious women of Bombay had not given up on him even though he had made it perfectly clear he wasn't interested. The matchmakers from his community tried to find him a suitable partner month after month, but the Lala wouldn't budge. 'I will enjoy my wealth myself—here and now. After I die… who knows what will become of it? And who cares? I don't, so why should anybody else?'

It was whispered that he had once been in love with a close cousin back in their village in Rajasthan. The two of them had made a pact as children to get married when they were older. But it wasn't to be. As was common in their part of the world, Padminidevi had been married off at the age of fifteen to a man from the neighbouring village. It was a romantic tale, and the few who had actually visited his home, swore that he had her name engraved on every marble slab and brick of the house. And that all the fabulous jewellery he kept buying from the vaults of now impoverished maharajas, was meant for her—for the day that she would come back into his life and become his. It wasn't confirmed but people also claimed that he had the weavers of Benaras spin gossamer-fine saris of the sheerest kind every year during Diwali. These too would be lovingly stored in gigantic Chinese camphor chests, never to be worn or seen again.

God was very intrigued by him. 'He's like a character out of a movie, *yaar*, or a cheap novel. I'm glad I've got the opportunity to interview him. *Saala dekh lega kya baat hai.*'

I was fascinated too. He reminded me of Jay Gatsby.

'Forget it, *yaar*. He's only a nut. A rich nut. If I can get him to adopt me—just think how much money there would be!'

'I thought you weren't interested in it.'

165

'In what?'

'Money.'

'It's OK, *yaar*. It has its uses. I'd buy myself a luxury yacht like that Khashoggi fellow and sail around the world. All the chicks would flock to me.'

'Then what would you do with Sujata?'

'What's the matter with you, *yaar?* Why bring that old hag into this? Anyway, these days she's seeing some poet-shoet from Botswana. Could be Zaire. Don't know. He looks like a gorilla.'

'So does she.'

'He wears huge robes.'

'So does she.'

'He writes horrible poetry.'

'So does she.'

'Stop saying that all the time, *yaar*, you really piss me off.'

❂

Lucio was having problems at home. He didn't want to discuss them, but I could tell he was troubled. 'The usual Goan story,' he smiled, 'drunk father, oppressed mother, too little money and too many children.'

'What are you planning to do?'

'Nothing. Any ideas?'

'Why don't you sing professionally—I mean, not just jingles, but you know—songs and things.'

'Yeah! Who'll give me a break?'

'You have to make a start somewhere. Let me talk to a couple of jingles types—the ones who sing at the Taj and Oberoi in the night. Good money there.'

'Sure but such long hours. I'll collapse.'

'No, you won't. Not if you eat well and stop hashing.'

'I wouldn't be able to face life without hash. You know that.'

'Try it. It might surprise you.'

It was that very night that Lucio was told by his father, 'There is a huge sea around Bombay. Why don't you go and jump in it?'

He did just that. Only, poor Lucio didn't succeed even in this. When he was fished out of the sea at Nariman Point, he had a lot of water in his lungs, but he wasn't dead.

God and I went to see him at the municipal hospital. He looked like a ten-year-old urchin, his tiny frame curled up on an ugly aluminium cot, his small wrists dangling over the edge lifelessly. 'Hey, man,' he said, 'I blew it again. Didn't I?'

My heart went out to him, lying there so pathetic and helpless. I wanted to help him, I really did. But what could I have done—I had none of the contacts that I built up later, nothing to call my own. And I had enough problems to deal with. I couldn't take on the role of friend, philosopher and guide. I couldn't even play mommy temporarily to the sickly waif.

A couple of days later I went to see him again, this time to tell him about the Maldives. He looked so weak and depressed that I was strongly tempted to cancel the whole trip.

'Lucio, please, for my sake, hang in there till I get back. It'll just be for two weeks,' I pleaded.

He just looked at me with those sad eyes, and said nothing.

When I got back from the Maldives, all tanned and looking healthy, Lucio had left. He had left the city, carrying his guitar and his torn clothes, and no one knew where. And I never heard from him again.

'You know, if you weren't so stuck up and snooty, we could make a damn good pair, *yaar*,' God said thoughtfully, as we sat at 'our' table in the Surai drinking pudina chai.

'What do you mean?'

'You could come to all the parties-sharties, *yaar*. Have a ball.'

'Deb, I'm not interested. I would feel out of place. It's not my scene. Don't you feel awful? Like a Cheap Charlie, eating and drinking at other people's expense, all the time?'

'I've explained that to you, *yaar*. These people will lick my chappals for publicity. You don't know how they beg me for just a line, a paragraph, a mention.'

'These very people will readily spit on you if you ever lose your arts page or the other stuff you do.'

'Forget it, Nasha. You don't understand power. Today that's all that counts. Power. And we who wield the pen, have it.'

'Fine. But be careful. That same pen can become a jack-knife. That man—Yashwantbhai—he gives me bad vibes. He is dangerous. Watch out for him. Ask your father.'

'Father, huh! What does that toothless tiger know of the Politics of today. He only does *bak-bak* and organizes gate-meetings. Nobody takes him seriously any more. He is finished.'

'Wasn't it Yashwantbhai who broke all his strikes last year?'

'So what? That feud is between them. It doesn't concern me at all.'

'How can you trust a man like that?'

'It's not a question of trust. Haven't you heard of a lovely phrase that goes you-scratch-my-back-I-scratch-yours? Two-way traffic, baby. I believe in that. He needs me, the *chaalu* fucker. And I need him. Not now. But I will some day. I want to build up a bank of favours... and then ask him to pay up when the time comes.'

'What makes you think he isn't thinking along the same lines himself?'

'He probably is.'

'Then?'

'Then what? One of us will have to call the bluff. Right now we are playing blind and the stakes are high… next year, when the election fever is at its height, Yashwantbhai's ass will be twitching. That's when he'll come crawling. I have a lot of dope on him and he knows it. With Comradesaab's contacts and my own in the underworld, there is enough to nail the fellow. The land-scam scandal is just beginning to hot up. He thinks nobody knows about his involvement in it. Crores, baby, crores. I have the details. Dossier upon dossier. Taped conversations, notes, everything. His biggest ally is that smuggler in the Gulf—Isamia. That's where the money comes from and goes to. Yashwantbhai has jacked up the percentage of his pay-off. Isamia isn't happy. There is sure to be a showdown soon. That's when Yashwantbhai will need my services. And my father's. You'll see. He'll come to us. Meanwhile, he has asked me to send him a couple of new chicks. "Send me good stuff, *yaar*," he told me. I said I wasn't a pimp. He laughed, "Communists, pimps… same thing, bhai. In one way, or the other, you are a *bhadwa*." I will show him what a smart *bhadwa* can do. I'll get the bastard.'

'Or he'll get you.'

'Not a chance,' said God and lit a Benson and Hedges.

# Nine

My yuppie friend, Anil, was still around looking like a Benetton ad. His dressing was getting sharper and sharper and he had knocked off his sideburns altogether. He looked a little like Charlie Sheen in a baseball movie I had just seen or maybe like Sheen in *Wall Street*, I'm not sure. We'd exchange a self-conscious 'Howyadoin?' and carry on. I still liked him, but I also knew I wasn't ever going to fit into his scheme of things. I was surprised he had thought I might in the first place. I often saw him rushing off to 'take in a spot of tennis', with all the right gear.

One day, I saw him with a girl dressed like Steffi Graf in a tennis skirt that barely covered her shapely bottom. He waved his graphite racket at me jauntily before climbing into a smart jeep. I could see Kawla and his boys crowing from upstairs. I could read their thoughts. 'There goes a *bakra* and here comes a fool. She will learn the hard way when the broke bums in her life ruin her completely.' I didn't feel any regret at all.

I plodded up the agency stairs (we were in a dilapidated building that threatened to collapse each monsoon). The bitch at the board signalled something with her eyebrows. I followed her glance and found one of the most beautiful girls I'd ever seen sitting in the tiny lobby; her long legs stretched out languorously in front of her, she was smoking in a lazy sort of way.

'Hi-yee,' she said. Her voice was high and childlike.

I thought she was joking, so just to be friendly I said, 'Hi-yee,' back to her.

'I'm Shona. I was asked to see you.'

'Oh yes—the model from London.'

She continued her baby-speak. 'Yeth,' she lisped, 'I only got here a couple of weeks ago.'

It was becoming a strain for me to carry on baby-speaking back to her. It was only a few sentences later that I discovered she wasn't fooling—that it was actually the way she spoke! Amazing. Here was this statuesque wonderwoman wearing an enormous buckled belt that would do a buggy horse proud and she was stuck with a lisp plus an irritating, infantile, sing-song accent that shattered the image of a cold, aloof, alabaster goddess.

Shona was one of the girls we were considering for a new campaign as yet quite hush-hush. But I realized immediately that she looked far too sophisticated and soignée for it. Willie took one look at her and squealed, 'Divinity!' He had to stand up on the settee to kiss her. Shona was nearly six feet tall in her stockinged feet. They loved each other on sight (Shona was an Anglo as well, though she insisted she was the product of a Bengali mother and a 'proper' British father). They made a comic couple—Willie with his squeak and ear-stud, Shona with her lisp and sexy mole. Willie wanted Shona for every ad the agency was handling. At their first meeting itself, he quickly recognized that Shona was wearing a skilfully cut wig. Shona's major beauty flaw was a forehead that was as large as a *papad*. She always wore wigs. Willie thought of it as a plus rather than a minus. 'She can look so different—from Cleopatra to Sridevi. The most versatile face in the business.' And with a great body too.

Shona shot to the top of the heap in no time at all. Her face was everywhere. About her body, she was very coy. I thought that was strange, considering she claimed she'd been modelling in London before coming here.

'I'm an old-fashioned girl,' she simpered when Willie asked her. 'My mother's family is very traditional. You know she's distantly related to the Tagores.'

I sniggered at that one since every pretentious Bengali claimed a kinship with Bengal's first family. Willie reasoned with me. 'You people think all Anglos are *chaalu*. As if our girls have no morality or something.

If Shona doesn't want to show, let's not force her. She's a well-brought-up, modest girl. So many of the other females are far more cheap—what about that Sindhi chick? And that Gujju *maniben*—the one who has joined the movies? And that one—the Punjaban who posed under a waterfall? Forgotten? You people feel so superior. You really believe all Catholics are fast. That their girls can only make good typists, air-hostesses, shop-girls, crooners and models. We have our own rules. Nobody sleeps around like you think....'

He would have gone on but I put a restraining hand over his mouth and said, 'Ssshh! Someone will hear you—and then what will happen to the model market?'

He was still livid, 'Model market! See how you talk. As if our girls are cattle... sheep. You don't respect us. Anytime you want a girl for some shitty nude ad, you ask me to round up my friends. Well, at least Shona has shown you that we also have our dignity. Don't think I haven't noticed how Nitin and you discuss models. "Oh that one, Lorraine—she'll do anything. Susannah—she'll drop her knickers for anyone. Jessie? Did you see the shots she has done for the new soap? The pictures stopped at the pubic line."'

Just to make him feel better I said, 'Well, Willie, it's true we badmouth some of the dare-bare girls, but it doesn't have a communal bias to it. What can we do if girls from your community have the best figures?'

174

Willie snorted and stormed off to the peon's room to smoke a joint. I went back to doodling meaningless headlines for a television company.

Anil met Shona quite by accident. It was at a major presentation.

The agency was all keyed up with the Ad Club Awards right round the corner. It was the time of the year when competition was at its keenest. Everybody wanted to slit everybody else's throat. It was believed that every big agency had a mole in it, that is, a sneaky someone who leaked campaign strategies to rivals and orchestrated hostile takeovers of prized accounts. We were being paranoid at ours since we had lost two major clients in the past six months. Five of our best speculative campaigns had also found their way into the creative departments of other agencies. This was to be a do-or-die presentation with all stops pulled out. The Brat Pack in the copy department was jittery and chewing more gum than usual. Roy had temporarily forgotten about Janine and the driver. I still had God on my mind, but he was on hold.

Anil had handled the in-depth countrywide survey. The product? A new newspaper which had the backing of one of the largest industrial houses in India.

There had been internal debates galore about the *need* for another daily. Hours spent on arguments about its format and target audience. According to Anil, there was a definite readership for a Paper of this kind—up-market, monied, educated and yuppie: like him. He had recommended a campaign that appealed to this segment. The copy had to be sleek and false—like Madison Avenue in its heyday. One creative chap had come up with something snappy but couldn't decide on whether or not to use a model. 'Graphics don't work in India,' the account exec had declared, his voice sounding like Moses' must have while bringing the Commandments down from the mountain.

A compromise was finally reached. We'd do two approaches, one using a model (Shona), the other, an illustration. Roy wanted Shona to sit in on our run-through, since he claimed we'd need her for the whole package (TV spots, etc.) if the deal went through. I thought otherwise. Roy wanted to ogle her and to impress the client who was known to have a glad eye.

Anyway, there she was, all demure and elegant in a tailored pant-suit with enormous shoulder-pads that made her look like a Martian. Or a vintage Joan Collins. Anil was in yuppie formals, unstructured khaki jacket with the sleeves rolled up and baggies held up by polka-dotted suspenders. He looked rather dishy.

Aarti nudged me in an obvious way and said, 'Look at that! You lucky thing!'

'Don't "lucky thing" me, he isn't mine.'

'No?' she asked looking delighted and relieved. 'Then it's open season.'

'Good luck,' I said sincerely.

Shona didn't say a word to anyone. She continued to smoke and look dreamy. Anil was at his American-marketing-whiz best as he pulled out charts and graphs and finally zapped us all with a sleek audio-visual, computer graphics, rock music and all. A big round of applause greeted him when he finished with a flourish and stood there basking in all the attention, his thumbs stuck into the cute suspenders. Shona was busy adjusting her shoulder pads. It must have been her complete lack of interest (apart from those looks, of course) that got Anil.

He walked up to her and bowed: 'We couldn't have done this without you.' She smiled and blew some smoke in his face.

Well… to each his own way of falling in love.

Anil and Shona became the big 'item' in glam circles. He was there at all her shows and she flitted in and out of his office if only to borrow the car and make endless phone-calls. A few months into the affair Anil sheepishly stopped by my table for a cup of coffee. Unusual for him since coffee was a no-no in the yuppie handbook. He fiddled with the lucky bunny on my desk and generally looked moony. 'We are thinking of getting married in May… I wanted you to hear it from me.'

'Congratulations!' I said. 'Shona will get to eat the best omelettes in town.'

'Oh that… you remember, huh?'

'Of course I do. I'm glad for you, Anil. You two look great together. Like an ad for velvety enamel paint.'

'That sounds snide.'

'Sorry. Couldn't resist it. But seriously… you ought to consider a side career in modelling—you fit today's role model completely. In a year from now, you can produce a cute kid and then we can have the whole family on our files. Between the lot of you, you'd capture the entire market.'

'It wouldn't go with my clients at all. In fact, I'm going to ask Shona to give up modelling once we're married. She won't need the money anyway.'

'Maybe there's more than money in it for her. Maybe she loves her career. She is right at the top now. Have you discussed it with her?'

'Not yet. I'm sure she'll agree. She's such an innocent, docile girl. And what better time to give it all up than when you are at the top?'

'What will she do with her time?'

'What does any housewife do? There's so much to do around the house.'

'Not yours. You do everything yourself anyway. At least, all the tasks your machines don't do. She can't spend all day watering your house plants or making conversation with your PC no matter how intelligent it is.'

'This is a minor matter. She can take classes… learn something new. I'd like her to do that. She could even open a grooming school—with her image and all that, she could do it successfully… and from the house itself.'

Perhaps I looked sceptical. Anil hastily added, 'It's not that I don't trust her or anything. She's a wonderful girl.'

'Do you love her?'

'Yes… she's… she's a nice person,' he ended weakly.

'What about your parents?'

'Well, I haven't broken the news to them, yet. But I'm sure there won't be any problems. She's beautiful, smart… so what if she isn't from our community? They didn't expect me to marry one of the *behenjis* with oily hair, I'm sure. They must have been prepared for this. They should thank their good fortune that I didn't come back with some flakey blonde. There were enough of them ready to jump, I can tell you.'

'I believe that… the Indian Prince, with his dark, good looks.'

'You've got the picture.'


Unfortunately, it didn't quite work out that way. Something yucky happened which involved us all.

Something messy which nobody could have seen coming. Least of all Shona herself. The week before they were to get officially engaged (with the blessings of Anil's parents, clients and friends), a leading, mass-circulation weekly published nude photographs of Shona culled from a foreign photography magazine. It was her all right. There was no mistaking that. It was Shona minus her cropped wig, posing like Venus, with a few locks of her original, long hair flowing across her perfect bosom, her long, tapering fingers placed coyly over the pubis. She looked like a Madonna—chaste, pure and virginal. It was a feature on international beauties, some in the buff and some semi-clad. The magazine itself didn't fall into the nudie category but was a prestigious journal that acted as a showcase for leading photographers. Shona's pictures had been done a couple of years ago when she was struggling to find a foothold in the cat-eat-cat world of modelling in London. The magazine itself was nearly a year old. But obviously someone spiteful had ferreted it out and sat on the photograph, waiting for the right moment to embarrass her.

Anil was at our office when one of the executives flipped the complimentary copy of the weekly open and gasped. Everybody in the room crowded around, including Anil. 'Bastards!' he said. 'The bloody bastards! It's not her picture at all. Can't you people see that? It's a doctored photograph. Someone jealous wants to ruin her—someone wants to finish our happiness. Poor Shona. What will she do when she sees this? And my parents—Oh God!—my parents!'

'Think coolly,' I said to him. 'Don't fly off the handle. Let's get in Kawla, Willie and the studio boys. Let's check this out. If it is a doctored picture, you can send the weekly a legal notice and have them apologize to Shona plus pay her damages. Besides, Deb has excellent contacts there. Let me reach him and we'll take it from there.'

Anil had slumped into a chair. He was ashen-faced and motionless. 'Just what I needed! What will my clients think? I'm going to be a laughing-stock. Every time we go out now, I'll imagine that people are mentally undressing my wife-to-be.'

'Come on, man,' Willie offered, 'it's not the end of the world. Shona is a gorgeous chick. She has a great body. Let the world admire it, man! Be proud of your woman. How many Indian girls would have made it to such a feature? Look at it that way.'

'Don't talk shit, man. It doesn't work like that. Not in my world. It's OK for you Anglos. Our women don't show even their toes to strangers.'

'Then, man, you picked the wrong chick. You should've stuck to one of your *behenjis* with a ghungat down to her navel.'

'Does Shona know about this?' I asked Anil.

181

'Who knows?' he said and walked out, leaving a trail of Aramis behind.

Shona messed it up for herself still further by going to town with the doctored photograph story. 'That isn't me!' she pip-squeaked. 'It's my face but some other woman's body.'

Her statement appeared in the eveningers, which added to her troubles by publishing the offensive picture on the front page, along with her hysterical statements.

'She's mad,' God declared. 'If only she had kept her trap shut the controversy would have died down in a month or so. Now let that pansy stew. The asshole deserves it.'

'Don't be mean. Please help them. At least go and see the editor and ask him to show you the original. Find out if there is some truth in this doctored business.'

'Listen, muttonhead, I don't mind going there. I'm scheduled to drop off a piece anyway. But I don't want to make a champion ass of myself by asking for some foolish "proof". Forget it. Besides did you ask those fools who they think has done a cut-and-paste job on Shona? The *phirangs* or the local lech who edits the rag?'

'That's a good question. Let me call her up.'

Shona was asleep and it was close to noon. 'Tell her it's urgent,' I told her landlady. She came on the line sounding groggy and even more kiddish than usual. She lapsed into tearful mumbo-jumbo when I asked her to clarify and kept repeating, 'It's not me. It's not me. Help me, Nisha. Anil's so angry. What shall I do?'

'Hang in there,' I advised. 'Let Deb check this out.'

He did. The editor showed him not just the original picture published in the foreign magazine but also a set of reject prints from the same shoot. They were all of Shona all right. 'What's more,' the editor said, 'I have actually done her a favour. Here... take a look at this.' And he threw a video cassette at God. It was one of those triple X-rated pornographic films shot in a hotel room in Hamburg. 'Quite a girl, that Shona,' the editor added with a wicked laugh. 'Talented too. Very talented. You should see her in the "lollipop" sequence... if you get what I mean.'

'What are you planning to do with this?' asked God.

'Well...' the editor said deliberately, 'there's always a price for everything... master print—yours. Copies—mine. *Ho jaye*? We'll both make a buck out of it.'

'Stuff it, you old sod,' said God before walking out. He didn't leave his article behind. I liked him for that.


Shona called me up after a few days. There was nothing I could do except advise her to lie low and wait for the whole thing to blow over.

'But, Nisha, what do I do about Anil? He's too decent to break off the engagement because of this. And at the same time he can't marry me and leave his family forever,' Shona lisped.

'Then what do you think you should do?' I asked her.

'Maybe I should break it off. Maybe I should go back to England. I don't know, Nisha, I'm so confused and lost.'

I didn't feel like uttering inanities like 'It'll be OK' and I finally told her that if she needed any help she could turn to me, and rang off. In the end she did do what was best for her. She broke off the engagement, packed her bags, and caught the first flight to London. God and I found ourselves being drawn into the lives of the unlikeliest people. God, because he was now considered influential—'Such good contacts (pronounced cunt-acts) and all, *yaar*,' people would whisper to each other before clearing their throats and coming right out with the favour they were after. And me? Well, initially I was approached only because I hung around with God—'Let's first try the girl friend… and then….' Later, these same people assumed I had great 'cunt-acts' of my own. Like M. She actually worked on me—ME—for weeks trying to wangle an appointment with a fat-cat client whose account I serviced. Later she told me to put in a word for her with Roy—'Since he really values your opinion.'

M wasn't sure what she wanted to do with herself. 'Try p.r., *yaar*,' God suggested carelessly, adding, 'but don't add an "o" and an "s" after that.' If M got the joke she didn't let on. Instead, she tweaked God's nose playfully and rubbed her breasts on his head.

But I did speak to Roy on her behalf only to discover that I could have saved myself the effort. Roy had plans of his own for M. He got her a job as an upscale hostess for the super exclusive executive club started by the plush Apollo Hotel.

It was supposed to be so upper crust that even some of the most prominent 'captains' of industry in Bombay had failed in their endeavours to be 'invited' to join the club. An 'invitation' that cost over a lakh annually for the dubious privilege of wining and dining in surroundings that resembled an old English hunting-lodge, complete with appropriate prints on the wood-panelled walls. The menu was very 'nouvelle' (everybody starved) and the cellar boasted rare vintages (though most of the pot-bellies present preferred to stick to 'isk-otch'). The waiters, wine stewards and maître d' dressed like the staff of any deluxe European hotel and spoke with matching accents.

M's job was to make the monied clientele feel 'comfortable', that is, pat bald heads and flash a little cleavage around. She was excellent at it, and her appointment was considered a coup of sorts. Industrialists asked for her by name when they called to make reservations, and she was there waiting to receive them when the elevator glided up to the mezzanine and let its occupants out, straight into the carpeted luxury of the club. The place smelt rich and M loved the fragrance.

'I feel like a geisha,' she laughed when I ran into her at the hair-dressers. Her style had changed dramatically. No more purple and pink punk streaks in her hair. She wore it in a low chignon that accentuated her neck. The sari was sedate and draped around her shapely figure in a way that was sexy (a hint of navel) but not vulgar. Quite a departure from the days she wore it at crotch level and people stared surreptitiously to see if they could spot the hairline. 'No way. Sorry guys. I wax my bikini line,' she would say. M's make-up had also altered and she looked less of a classy call-girl now with just a hint of kaajal, blush-on and lip gloss. She minded not being allowed to load herself with jewellery, since she insisted she felt naked without it—'Gold and diamonds make me feel so warm.' The hotel was very strict about conduct. She was instructed to be friendly but not familiar. She could extend her hand for a handshake with members but stop them if they tried to kiss her. Under no circumstances was she to be caught smoking or drinking on the job. 'I don't mind the drinking... but I hate rushing to the loo every half an hour for a fag,' she confessed.

Roy was very proud of her. It hadn't been easy to fix her up at the Apollo but then what are good client-relations for? He had been handling the Apollo account for years and very successfully at that. It was one account he was possessive about and which he serviced himself. He approved everything personally, from the copy to the visuals. He made the presentation and naturally, he picked the models (M earlier, Shona later). He knew everybody from the top downwards and was on first name terms with the big boss—an elusive, low-profile man who was always referred to as 'The Boss', never by name, even by his closest lieutenants. Somewhere down the line there were two dragon ladies (Vampire One and Vampire Two, as they were called) who actually managed the day-to-day running of the show. Each of them was a fearsome creature, highly motivated, alarmingly ambitious and unbelievably ruthless. Roy had managed to steer M past them without ruffling too many feathers. In the trade this was considered to be nothing short of a miracle.

Once she got in, M used her considerable charm and common sense to woo the witches over to her side. They were smart enough to recognize an asset when they saw one. It was decided that M was to be handled with velvet gloves and allowed to do her job her way.

Karen, understandably, wasn't overjoyed by this development. She felt upstaged and cheated. Over the years, Roy had managed to wangle a neat deal for Karen with Apollo. A deal that included Karen's 'talents' as a discerning buyer of doo-dahs and *objets* for the hotel.

Naturally, Karen made a fat commission on every piece she flogged, plus she managed to get quite a few exclusive *objets* for her own personal collection in the bargain. It was a great deal. Karen managed to hold her own despite the antagonistic vibes sent out by the two vampires. She went on extensive buying trips or had the local dealers crawling around her splayed feet, hoping to hawk something to the group. This was big bucks territory. Karen enjoyed the clout this provided her with and didn't let go a single occasion to show off the latest acquisition. Since she had managed to stash away so much for their personal use, Roy decided to buy her a godown to store the stuff. Karen shrewdly calculated that there was just no point in hanging on to everything. But if she had to flog her wares, she wanted to do it in style, though Karen's ideas on class and style were even tackier than the ghastly visiting card she flashed around (black with gold-embossed lettering).

Everybody knew that Karen had a side-business going from the godown. There were catty contemporaries who insisted there was nothing Karen wouldn't sell (for a price, naturally) including the kurta off her back. I'd overheard someone talking about Karen's modus operandi once.

'Really now... how crass can that woman get. She uses her home like a showroom. I'm certain all her furniture has price tags on it. And those false antiques too. A guest has merely to comment that something looks good and Karen promptly jumps on the person and offers to transport the piece home. "It's yours, darling," she says grandly, making out as if it's a gift. The next morning her tempo is at the doorstep with the desk, chair, cupboard, statue or whatever. She phones a little later and asks sweetly whether the person received the goods. "By the way, darling," she adds, "you owe me eight-and-a-half grand." Don't know why people continue to fall for her hard sell. She tried it with me once, and I said, "Thanks a lot, darling. The painting's great. But really, I'd rather have the original." You should've seen her face! She thought she could pass off a knock-off at some ridiculous price. Forget it. Not all of us are such idiots.'

Office gossip had it that Roy's new beach house at Marve was furnished entirely with stuff flicked by Karen. They'd got the most amazing bargains for a pittance. Enormous stained-glass windows from an old Parsee home, old jharokas and carved wood screens from a demolished haveli in Jaipur. Magnificent miniatures from a Rana who had run up monumental gambling debts in Monte Carlo, bronze bulls from a sculptor who had run into hard times and of course, Iqbal's best works from his 'brown period' when he only painted whores dressed in brown, with eyes that looked like they'd been gouged out by wild dogs. Karen had had a minor

Shobhaa Dé

thing with Iqbal in the days she'd worn her hair long and her boobs hadn't begun to sag.

Vampire One and Vampire Two detested Karen's constant interfering in their departments at the hotel but since the boss seemed so fond of her, and since she did manage to deliver in her own way, there wasn't much either could do about her skimming the cream off most of their deals.

Vimla or Vampire One was a woman from Madhya Pradesh who had an intimidating presence. She was physically gross and moved with all the grace of a battle-tank over rough terrain. She'd made it from bottom up, starting in the housekeeping department and moving on to banquets, public relations and finally the top of the heap, in personnel. Since she did all the hiring and firing for the group, nobody dared cross her. She moved through the premises with minions falling along the wayside, her hook-nose and beady eyes making her resemble a hungry vulture in search of prey. She wore flowing frocks to work ('nighties' as the front office girls dubbed the strange tent-like garments) and didn't have a single known friend. Her private life was a mystery. Hotel gossips said she sometimes summoned a particularly smart-looking waiter from one of the restaurants to her house, a house she shared with half-a-dozen smelly, vile-tempered stray cats and a mentally retarded brother.

Determinedly single, she referred to herself as a 'bachelor girl' and hated it when anyone tactlessly called her a widow, which she was.

Vimla was an archetypal workaholic, with the compulsory ulcer to go with the tag. She lived on milk and antacids, which she swallowed round-the-clock. Her office hours just stretched and stretched, which was hard on her staff, particularly the male, south Indian secretary, who worshipped her. She couldn't stand the sight of him and had forbidden the poor man from eating his idli-sambar at the desk. 'My office smells like a bloody Udipi restaurant,' she told him. 'Go to the loo and finish your lunch. Or eat something decent, like sandwiches.' Vasudevan didn't dare tell her that his wife didn't know how to make sandwiches. In fact, she'd never heard of them. 'She is coming straight from Madurai,' he confessed to colleagues. 'How she will know about sandwiches? In Madurai they only eat idli-dosas for tiffin. But simply Madam is getting angry with me.'

Madam got angry with everybody. She was a stickler for perfection and with all those years in housekeeping behind her, she could spot a coffee stain on a tablecloth from two miles away. She didn't actually carry a general's baton or a headmaster's cane but she managed pretty well with her sharp tongue and hard fingers.

'Come on, come on,' she'd urge her staff. 'Look at those roses in the lobby. Fading. Look at the menu-cards in the coffee-shop. Dog-eared.' Her interviewing tactics left few survivors. Those who managed to get past her grilling stayed the course and remained eternally loyal to her and the group. That was her biggest asset. That, combined with her reputation as a woman of integrity, if no charm.

Manju or Vampire Two, was scary, but in a totally different fashion. For one, she was voluptuous in a Punjabi sort of way; overweight, fair and flashy, she used her wily charms to utmost advantage. She had been married twice over. Once to the hotel which she had joined as a management trainee twenty years ago, and the second time round to an effeminate executive who had been a lobby manager at the hotel but had had to switch jobs once it became clear that the wife was the one who was slated for the big time and not he. 'No personality, *yaar*,' she'd say straight to his face. 'Vikki is a sweetie... but you know what I mean? He has the sort of looks that make people mistake him for a bartender. So often at parties, even our own, people tell him to fetch them a drink. But I'm not complaining. He's really such a doll. Looks after the kids. Takes leave when I travel to stay home. Vikki even cooks us all a great meal when the servant doesn't show up. You know how I hate entering the kitchen. I can't make a cup of tea... forget that, yaar, I don't even know how to light the bloody gas.'

Vikki was just the sort of milksop someone like Manju needed She was a driven careerist who cared for just two things in the world—her job and her bank account. 'I refuse to spend on *ghar-ka-kharcha, yaar*,' she'd say. 'That's my Vikki's responsibility. What's the point of having a husband if he can't pay all the bills. I don't mind buying an item or two sometimes. I got us a VCR and I contributed towards our holidays last year. If I don't save now, who knows what will happen later? Vikki could leave me for another woman.' At this point, she'd stop to hear the suppressed giggles and add, 'Don't laugh, *yaar*. He's a man, remember? All men are the same. Fools. Someday he might meet someone he prefers to me. But I doubt it. In any case, he'd never leave the kids. I'm candid, *yaar*. I don't do anything for them. Vikki does everything—bath-shath, breakfast, potty, dropping, fetching. He's the one who goes for Open Day, sports, dramatics, all that nonsense. Where do I have the time? The kids are fast asleep when I get home. And I wake up after they've left for school. But my mother's also at home, so Vikki doesn't have to manage all by himself. Thank God for that. It's a joke, *yaar*. The teachers in my kids' school ask them if their parents are divorced since they've never seen me. I'm thinking of putting them in that boarding—you know that one in the hills that's called "The Divorce School". But it's a bigger hassle, *yaar*. How will Vikki get leave to go there twice or thrice a year? I didn't want kids at all.

But Vikki—such a *buddhu*—he told me, "Darling, you just bear them for nine months, that's all. The rest is upto me." I had them *only* to keep him happy. Now Bittu and Mini ask me, "But Mummy, why don't you spend time at home like other mummies?" And I tell them, "Because your daddy does that."'

Manju was slightly more popular than Vimla. She handled projects and marketing, and was said to be a tough negotiator. Her money-sense was phenomenal and she could reel off statistics without the help of memos or a calculator. Businessmen doing deals with the hotel dreaded coming up against her. "That woman can chew the lot of us up,' they'd say after a harrowing meeting. Yet, Manju managed to stay ahead of the pack without sacrificing her sex-appeal. 'I don't believe in behaving or looking like a man in a man's world,' she often said. 'I think being a woman has its advantages—and I make the most of them.' That would be pretty obvious at high-power meetings or presentations when Manju pulverized people at the table as much with her tantalizing pallu-play as her manipulation of figures.

These two were a breed apart. They were corporate women all right, but they didn't fall into the 'New Woman' category. They missed that label by a generation. But they had enough representatives of the tribe working for them either directly or indirectly. Most of the new recruits fell into this slot. They carried the awesome weight of an MBA degree (IIM Ahmedabad or any of the better American business schools like Wharton or Harvard) on their padded shoulders. These were no-nonsense women who had 'take me seriously' written all over them. They even wore business suits to work and carried burgundy-coloured briefcases (Csango's in Bombay or Gucci from Hong Kong). They took their jobs with an earnestness that was almost terrifying in its intensity. Even the married ones insisted on being addressed as 'Ms' or stuck to their maiden names. Their male colleagues were not permitted to crack jokes or flirt lightly, which made several of them complain, 'What's the point of having females in the office if one can't fool around a little?' These sorts of remarks were taboo around these girls with their sensible haircuts, sensible make-up and sensible jewellery. 'All copied *maal* from old issues of *Cosmo, yaar,*' the other girls would joke in the loo, but that didn't stop the hep lot from going ahead with their 'look' and their ambitions.

Workaholism for women had become very fashionable. 'If men can pursue careers ruthlessly, so can we,' women declared at seminars and workshops for senior managers. 'No guilt-trips allowed here,' their instructors would tell them. 'Postpone babies or ask your husbands to share housework.' The poor husbands were caught entirely unprepared. There were a few token 'New Men' around the place but, by and large, the 'New Woman' was forced to make do with the same old man. The sort who expected his high-powered wife to make him his evening cup of tea and even sing an occasional ghazal in the kitchen while stirring a dekchi full of mutton-do-piazza.

'Not all of us are married to nerds like Manju's husband,' the women at the executive centre would say, contradicting themselves. 'I have to deal with a mother-in-law who expects me to sit for an hour-long morning puja with her, and all the other botherations. I'm the one who has to make the breakfast—imagine, alloo parathas first thing in the morning. No—my family refuses to switch to cornflakes and toast. Dinner is the same thing—heavy greasy food drowned in masala. My mother-in-law eats more than all of us put together. I have to hear lectures about what I should feed growing children. It's no use telling her or my husband that the last thing adolescents need is fried pakoras. No wonder my son's skin is covered with acne. I stick to my salads and dahi. Feel so dopey at work otherwise. Don't know how I'm going to attend the Hyderabad convention. Husband is already acting up. So are the children. As for the mother-in-law, she has threatened to ditch me and go off to her daughter's house just at that time. Bitch! That's her way of sabotaging my career. Jealous bitch. Who'll look after the servants and children if she goes? As it is, the ayah has been stealing my St. Michael's bras and perfumes. But I can't say anything. I'll be sunk if she leaves. My neighbour—remember the slovenly fat cow who does nothing but watch video all day? She's been trying to steal my servants for years. Every month she offers them hundred bucks more. And she tells them that she'll show them one Hindi film a day. Terrible! That's why we keep our VCR in our bedroom. So embarrassing to watch these Mithuns and Sonams prancing and dancing and raping each other, with the servants sitting in the same room.'

God and I laughed over these stories while telling ourselves they didn't really touch us. We weren't like them. We were different. We had depth. A sense of purpose. We were real people.

God actually believed this bullshit. I on the other hand was wracked by self-doubt.

'Don't be mad, *yaar*,' he'd say dismissively. 'You aren't like these other bitches. You have... what do you call it... character, you know?'

No, I didn't know. And I wasn't at all sure. It didn't need much 'character' to do what I was doing—earning a salary based on re-positioning semi-colons. God was lucky. He rarely questioned himself. To him the Maitreyees, Karens, Vimlas and Manjus were collectively seen as self-seeking whores. And I? I dared not ask.

# Ten

God was really getting around and moving up. He seemed to enjoy every moment of his newly-acquired status. *Plume* was all the rage and his arts column in the paper had expanded into a whole section (including a page on art cinema, which meant that he now got courted by all the pseud film makers in town).

I asked him, 'Does anybody see their films?'

He looked at me witheringly. 'Not the sort of people *you* know. But certainly—a film like Ghosh's latest—the one about a woman married to a holy stone— is seen by a wide audience of discerning film-goers. He's entering it for the Berlin Film Festival. If I hadn't picked him up and promoted him—forget it, *yaar*. He would have still been hanging around Mandi House trying to get some *bekaar* television work.'

'But is the film any good?' I wanted to know.

'Good? It's brilliant! What camera work. What concept. What acting. He's one of us—he hasn't sold his soul to the system.'

'You mean he's also a pseudo-leftist?' I said.

'Go to hell, *yaar*. You and your two-bit views. Do you know he made a brilliant documentary a couple of years ago about the plight of migrant labourers in Bombay? It was fantastic. Revolutionary. Sensitive. But the government refused to show it. They called it "slanted". I tell you—it is their corrupt, bourgeois mind that suppresses the real creative talents of this country. Finally Ghosh smuggled one print out. It was shown in Bucharest. The critics loved it. His next project is with that sexy chick from France. What's her name? That Muslim female who smokes ganja all the time and is hooked up with some German—he's a photo-journalist I think.'

'Are you talking about the one who made the famous film on the exploited hotel boys in Udipi restaurants?' 'Hahn! That female. Very sexy, *yaar*. What a woman! *Aré!* That film got raves internationally. When she went to Cannes, all the foreign presswallahs were sniffing around her. She's too much. She and that film festival female from Delhi. With these two around our film festivals are made. They know how to get ahead. They know what will click with the phirang media. Both of them are good at stuntbaazi. Do you know Fatima came to one of the shows wearing a sari without a blouse? She didn't show her tits or anything—but all the photographers rushed to click her and forgot all about the topless starlets in the fountain outside the Palais. That year was terrific. Our other committed actress was also there. She's also sexy, yaar. She'd come all dolled up carrying so many ethnic costumes and gajras with her. Bindi-shindi, jhumkas-wumkas, kaajal-waajal, whatever it takes, these women make an impact. Come on—why don't you come along for Ghosh's screening? Few people—just us—critics, friends, other film makers. We are planning to make a big noise over this film, yaar. Take the protest to the street. It must be seen. Ghosh used to work as Ray's third assistant. *Uska* oeuvre *pakka hai*. Come on, *yaar*. It will be a lot of fun. We'll go for coffee-shoffee later and discuss *Bhoj*. What a title! Symbolic. Simple. Straightforward.'

The film was so intensely boring that I switched off after the first twenty minutes when nothing had happened beyond the oppressed woman washing piles and piles of clothes on the banks of a river. The tiny auditorium was filled to capacity. There were people sitting cross-legged in the aisles. Ghosh himself was in the projection room, running his fingers through matted hair. His beard looked like it housed roaches that crawled out at night and wandered all over his body in search of sticky crumbs of leftover meals. His kurta from Khadi Bhandar could be smelt in the theatre. He'd left his satchel full of foreign art film magazines with God.

The woman next to me, Manorama, worked as a film critic for an eveninger. She was wearing a mix-and-match salwar-kameez in vegetable dye prints.

Her bindi started on her nose and ended at her hair line. Chunky silver jewellery was strung all over her frail body which was weighed down by a huge cloth jhola with Banni embroidery. She took her job very seriously, God told me. She went for film appreciation courses to the FTII at Pune and read books on Tarkovsky and Eisenstein. She'd once worked for some obscure magazine, a quarterly, devoted to the cause of promoting 'meaningful' cinema in India. She'd also once been married to the biggest bore in 'alternative cinema', a director who had made two or three disgusting films on chapattis, tube-wells and gobar gas. He'd left her for the actress who had played a raped Harijan belle in one of the films. This had been particularly shattering for Manorama, since the actress had been her roommate in the working women's hostel a few years ago.

At Ghosh's screening she was holding a pencil torch in her mouth to light up the pad on which she was scribbling notes furiously. Nobody understood a word of what she wrote, but it was generally considered 'serious criticism' as opposed to 'frivolous reviews' by amateurs who knew nothing about the 'other cinema'. Her only rival in the field was Rishi, a venomous viper of a critic who everybody knew was on the take. But he concentrated on reviewing commercial Hindi films, writing about them in a style that suggested he was doing the film makers and readers a great big favour by deigning to comment on such garbage in the first place. God detested

Rishi and it was mutual. Rishi felt miffed that God had never asked him to contribute and God in turn thought Rishi should have volunteered to do so in the first place.

'*Saala*—what does he think? That I'll go and beg for his shit? He should pay me to publish him. In any case, he makes enough money out of his reviews. Just the other day that fellow, producer-director—what's his name—Gulab—was telling me how Rishi came and asked him for a packet to write a favourable review for *Disco Lover*.'

'But why do these people pay him? Are Rishi's reviews that important? Who reads them?'

'Don't know. He writes such crap anyway. All his silly jokes and play on words. That isn't what's called a review. But his paper is powerful. It reaches more than five lakh people daily, *yaar*. That's why he can blackmail the industry. But one actor refuses to play ball with the bastard. And I tell you—he'll be the one who'll fix him. *Woh to kya superstar-ka-baap hai.*'

'You mean—Ardhendu?'

'Who else? Rishi's tricks don't work with him. In any case, nothing Rishi writes can affect A.D.'s market. He's in a class of his own. He rang up that day. I recognized his voice immediately. But I didn't want to give him much importance, *yaar*. So I played it cool.'

'What did he want?'

'His new release is coming up. This is going to be a crucial film for him. If it flops, his price will plummet. He's been through a rough patch last year. Bad health. Three flops in a row. Income tax problems. But *Ram, Rahim aur Robert,* will really decide his fate. If it's a hit, he's made. Otherwise, distributors will think again before shelling out one crore per territory for his next film.'

'What did he say to you?'

'He was very charming and warm. Called me home to his bungalow. Said, "Meet my wife and family, no party-sharty, *yaar.* Just an informal evening."'

'Are you going?'

'Why not? Definitely. You come along too.'


In time people got used to seeing me with God. I suppose we must have made a reasonably 'cute' couple and therefore party-worthy. Bombay society was perpetually starved for new faces. Anybody with novelty value was welcome. Gatecrashing was so common-place that at most big parties, twenty or more unknowns drifting in and sometimes taking the scene over, was not considered odd or even undesirable. Hostesses would boast about the number of 'crashers' after a party. It was an indication of their social popularity.

Another unusual aspect of these flashy affairs, we discovered, was the soliciting for invitations to parties that were considered THE events of the season. Weeks before such evenings, the host and hostess would be deluged with calls from long-lost 'friends' asking blatantly to be invited. 'You haven't forgotten us by any chance, have you?' they'd ask, reducing the recipient to laughing nervously and hastily extending an invitation. Others adopted more aggressive tactics. 'We were there for your anniversary last year. Why haven't you got us on your list this year?' And then there were regulars like God who were on everybody's lists.

God came under the critics / presswallahs category. Journalists had acquired a glamour of their own. No 'do' was complete without a sprinkling from the fourth estate. Not just the editors of city glossies and other glam publications, but the big boys from the big league. Those who wrote thundering first edits about the state of the nation, the need to review our foreign policy and our antiquated taxation laws. These were the chaps who mattered and around whom little clusters of glittering people formed to hear firsthand at night what the nation would wake up to the next morning. God, on the other hand, represented the élite coterie of 'opinion makers'. The scruffier this lot looked, the more seriously it was taken. God's special talent lay in dropping the right names at the right time. He knew when to bring up the topic of his cosy lunch at the Windsor (the ritziest hang-out in town) with Yashwantbhai, or lightly mention the Lala's phone call and joke about Iqbal's invitation to a biryani party at which only his favourite whores were present. This way, God managed to keep his stock up. His conversation with the pseud-crowd had a certain pattern to it. Here he talked of rare books, first editions, Godard's imagery, Kinski's kinks, Ghatak's follies, Ray's genius, Mrinalini's footwork and Bhimsen's *bhairavis*.

'Where do you find the time to mug up all these names?' I asked him, half-nastily.

'I don't *mug* them up, *yaar*. They happen to be a vital part of my liberal education,' he answered, shutting me up effectively.

At one of these interminably boring (for me) evenings at a loud-mouthed industrialist's home, I ran into a liberated Marwari lady. I'd first met Bindiya five years ago, when she'd arrived in Bombay from Calcutta, with an oaf-like, paan-chewing husband in tow. They'd stayed with rich cousins at Worli sea face for months while their own penthouse was being done up by Bombay's most high-profile socialite designer. It was during this time that Bindiya had had a quiet affair with the cousin's husband. An affair that hadn't created any ripples even within their close-knit, conservative community. How come, I'd wondered. The explanation was that such little indulgences were fine so long as they were all kept in the family.

Shobhaa Dé

'Anything goes nowadays,' another Marwari lady had told me 'Poor Bindiya. She must be so bored. Look at her husband... such a stupid fellow. She's so clever. Educated also. That's why there's a problem. He joined the family business without even finishing school. Now he's good at only one thing—making money. But Bindiya is fond of travelling, reading, music. Naturally, once she came to Bombay, she lost her senses. In Calcutta, the mother-in-law could keep her in check. There she couldn't try any of her tricks, though we'd heard she used to flirt with her youngest brother-in-law—the one who went to college. But the *saas* kept an eye on her. She wasn't allowed to go anywhere without someone from the family. It was a known fact that the driver was a spy. He reported all her movements to the mother-in-law. In Bombay, Bindiya found freedom. She should never have been allowed to come here. And no children! That's another problem. A woman with children has a sense of responsibility. At least they tie her down to the house. But Bindiya was free, and she took full advantage of it. Shopping trips, hair-dressers, jewellers, friends—in Bombay you can find any number of excuses and alibis. She became... what is that you people say... foot-free and fancy loose... something like that. Her husband didn't suspect anything. He was so busy setting up his factory. He used to be away from morning till late at night. But that other chap had all the time since his business had collapsed. His wife? What could she do? Complain and create a scandal? *Na baba,* our community wives don't behave like that. Anyway, she knew her husband was never going to leave her for Bindiya. Whether he went to bed with her or some prostitute in London—what difference does it make?'

The affair had certainly made one hell of a difference to Bindiya though. Gone were the starched organdy saris and ugly jewellery. Gone, the low nape bun with several bob-pins to hold stray hair in place. Gone were the low-heeled chappals (she was taller than her stubby hubby) and the dusky face devoid of any make-up. The new Bindiya was quite a woman—bursting with confidence and looking smashing. She always did have a great smile, but in the past she'd flash it once a fortnight. Now, she walked into the room beaming. She was wearing a very well-cut trouser suit with a Chanel (Pamella Bordes) bag slung over a shoulder carelessly. Tapered heels made her legs look like Raquel Welch's and her hair was cut in a flattering feathery style that highlighted her shapely jaw line. It was difficult to believe this was the same woman. Her husband hadn't changed at all. He still wore garish 'party shirts' from Charagh Din with a Dunhill belt holding his belly in. The trousers hung limply over his Gucci shoes and he had on a flashy diamond-studded watch on his thick wrist. The other hand was hanging on to a tin of paan masala. He had also retained his hangdog expression.

I watched them as they circulated around the room. Someone mentioned that Bindiya was now the chairperson of some prestigious charity organization that organized auctions, art shows and classical music concerts to raise funds for starving children in Bihar, flood victims in Orissa, the drought-affected in Uttar Pradesh and so on. She had organized a music recital by a new, up-and-coming sitarist from Calcutta for this evening.

Someone sniggered, 'Why is she dressed like she's going to a disco? Nobody dresses like this for a serious *baithak*. What will the artiste feel?'

Someone else replied, 'Don't be a bore. What a cliché. You mean she should have worn a temple sari with half-a-dozen gajras in her hair and kilos of jewellery all over? That's so predictable. She looks stunning in that creation.'

Another voice chipped in, 'She looks like a bandmaster. Stupid, *yaar*. What are these *medho* chicks coming to? I hear she has a computer in her bedroom and is planning to write a book about her community. Can you imagine? Her dolt of a husband won't even be able to read it. I doubt that he can go beyond signing cheques and reading balance sheets.'

Bindiya must have been perfectly aware that she was the cynosure of all eyes. But that didn't inhibit her at all. She looked supremely confident as she busied herself with the arrangements for the concert.

'She has even started smoking,' I heard a woman comment.

'Forget smoking and drinking. She eats meat. Really. I saw it with my own eyes last week. She had come for the buffet at the Oberoi, and I saw her heaping her plate with all that horrible stuff—I don't know what it was—chicken or something. Someone said she also eats cow-meat. She has gone crazy over steaks.'

There was a stunned silence at this point. Just then Bindiya came over to say 'hello' and the group of women who had been at my elbow moments ago just melted away.

'You really scare them, don't you?' I teased her. 'Do you enjoy it?'

She laughed. 'In the beginning I did. Now, I just ignore them.'

'What about their husbands?'

'Oh… those lechy creeps… they all want to go to bed with me. Real crude fellows. No finesse. They come and ask directly. Some of them say, "Oh but we thought it's OK, now that you smoke, drink and all that…."' I don't even bother to reply or explain that smoking has nothing to do with screwing. By the way, I don't drink, except for wine occasionally. But all these chaps keep plying me with liquor saying, "Come on. We know you drink. Don't feel shy. *Chalo*, have a peg. Your husband isn't looking. What would you like—rum, Scotch, vodka?" It's disgusting, but I don't blame them. I suppose they find the change in me so shocking. Sometimes I feel shocked by it myself.'

While Bindiya had successfully 'found herself', everybody wrongly assumed that her dumb husband (who was known around town either by his initials, M.B., or as Mr Bindiya) had lost himself for good. But the sly fellow had plans of his own which did not include Bindiya at all. The fool had gone and fallen in love with an actress. Not just any actress, but the reigning sex symbol—Kiki-baby—as the film press had dubbed her after a particularly sexy cabaret in a film called *Love Ke Baad Pyar*. M.B. had seen her at the première, which had been staged Hollywood-style at the Metro—complete with a police band, arc lights, red carpet and gatecrashers by the hundred.

It was a charity show for one of Bindiya's pet causes—Save the Slums. Being the moving spirit behind the glittering affair, there she was at the entrance, instructing the awestruck havaldars not to lathi-charge fans who were pressing ahead, beyond police barriers and into the foyer, to try and get as close to the favourite film stars as possible. As each limousine rolled up, a collective shriek would go up with catcalls, claps and a few lines from the film's hit song, "*Toba, toba*" (the same one that had catapulted Kiki to the top of the popularity charts). 'There's Jackie!' 'There's Anil!' 'Hey hero, come here!' 'Oh my, Sridevi!' cried enthusiastic voyeurs as they crammed the tiny lobby waiting for the big moment when the two stars of the film would show up (fashionably late by at least two hours). It was well-known that they were not on talking terms since Kiki had caught her co-star and lover, the droopy-eyed Avinash Goel, with her hair-dresser. But for this evening they'd arrive together and smile for the cameras. Bindiya was getting frantic. The time on the invitation was 8 p.m. It was now coming up ten and there was no trace of the two. She sent a lackey to call their homes to check whether they'd left. She received the standard reply.

'Saab bathroom *mein hain*. Memsaab *so rahi hai.*'

She cursed under her breath. Did these bloody film people spend all their time in the loo or in bed? The invitees were getting restless inside. A clandestine bar had been organized in the men's room, while the regular counter had run out of soft drinks and samosas. Everybody was hanging around in the lobby or falling over the balcony upstairs to spot the stars as they arrived. An out-of-work comedian had been lined up as an emcee. He tried to keep spirits up by cracking stupid jokes and mimicking the big stars. He'd stopped trying to do on-the-spot interviews with those present since the only words he could extract were 'no comment'. Bindiya's husband took a swig from his silver hip-flask and opened the top button of his stiff-fronted shirt. Bindiya had insisted on a tux, even though it was a muggy, hot evening. She herself was in an extravagant costume from the newest boutique in town, Couture, which specialized in crazy clothes at crazier prices. She'd knocked off the gold tissue turban at the last minute when M.B. had looked at her and said, 'You look like the durwan outside Khyber.' Her outfit was a big hit even without the turban and the silver-gold streaks in her hair went down as the ultimate strokes of a fashion genius.

Just as M.B.'s eyes were beginning to glaze over with boredom, he spotted her. It was Kiki-baby all a-dazzle in leopard skin and gold lamé. She was looking gorgeous and wanted the world to acknowledge it. Under a diaphanous blouson top, she was wearing a quarter cup gold bra which displayed her magnificent breasts to advantage.

Bindiya went up to greet her and gestured to M.B. to stay by her side. He hastily redid his top button, straightened his shoulders and waited to be introduced.

'Meet my husband,' Bindiya said with a hint of condescension in her voice. Kiki looked deep into his eyes, held out her soft hand, dimpled and unexpectedly leaned across and kissed him on the cheek. Or so it appeared to onlookers and so it was immortalized in photographs. But actually, she'd leaned forward and bitten him under the ear.

'Hi sexy!' she'd whispered while scratching the palm of his and with the long painted nail of her forefinger.

Why she did what she did was never clear. Perhaps Kiki did that with every man. But it was a moment that transformed M.B. It changed the course of his life. And he began, foolishly, to believe in destiny.

M.B. was reborn. Nothing was the same again. He became a man obsessed. A man possessed. A maniac and a demon. He was convinced Kiki had seriously made that remark, and he wasn't going to let it go at that. He was determined to see this through to the end.

'I must have her,' he confessed to his golf partner, Lucky, who was alarmed by the intensity of his declaration.

'Don't be absurd, old man. She's an actress... not your type,' Lucky said, trying to discourage him.

'You don't understand—I love that woman. I will not rest till she's mine.'

Lucky was an urbane, experienced playboy who had had enough liaisons to know that this one was not going to work. He told M.B. so. But M.B. would have none of it. He pleaded with Lucky to help him chart out a strategy to woo the lady.

'Find out all you can about her first,' Lucky suggested. 'Who she sees. Who she sleeps with. How often. Where and when. Get to know her weaknesses. Jewellery? Cash? Holidays abroad? Pent-houses? Cars? And then work on those. But before you do any of this, get yourself a target and a budget. How much are you willing to invest in her? You don't want to be taken to the cleaners, rendered bankrupt. So lay it on the line—the money. Tell yourself, "I will spend X-amount on her. If it works, fine. If not, I won't have ventured more than I can afford to lose."'

M.B. mulled over the suggestions and thought them extremely astute and wise. He immediately employed a detective agency to keep tabs on her and give him weekly reports.

The first one revealed that at the moment, Kiki was freelancing. She'd recently broken up with the great love of her life—Avinash Goel, the star of her recent hit film. He had moved on to another nymphet and Kiki had sought solace in the arms of a down-and-out actor, Sunju, who liked the perks of their relationship. Sunju was never going to make it as a star and the knew it. So he'd sensibly opted to concentrate on playing the available stud to any actress in need of his services. In return, he lived well, drove their cars, escorted them to parties and often accompanied them on location shootings to lush hill-stations, managing to squeeze himself into the film in a side-role. Producers looking for co-operation from the heroine didn't mind accommodating him if it meant that the women would appear for shooting on time and not bunk extended schedules. It was cheaper to find a role for the lover instead.

Apart from this pest, Kiki didn't seem to have any other hangers-on. She lived in a well-guarded bungalow at Juhu with her ambitious mother and a half-brother. They handled her finances, appointments, contracts, publicity, and often, sleeping companions. The brother also doubled as a bodyguard when she ran out of suitable escorts. It was rumoured that Kiki often felt stifled by these two over-protective and dominating people, and longed to break away.

M.B. consulted his 'guru'. What was the first move to be? Lucky considered the matter carefully while strolling along the lush green fairway of the Willingdon Club. 'Well, old chap... the thing to do is to make a classy move. Nothing obvious. Nothing crass. Remember, she is used to trash... you know what film people are like. So... I suggest you surprise her with something unusual and expensive. Not jewellery—she must be getting that from producers... but say... a Lalique vase.'

M.B.'s eyes lit up at the idea. 'That's it. A Lalique vase on a silver tray. Wonderful. I'll organize it immediately. But... how will she know it's from me? And what if she hasn't heard of Lalique? Then the whole thing goes phut.'

Lucky assured him that in all likelihood he was right. Kiki wouldn't know a Lalique from a Lohar Chawl crystal. But she was smart enough to find out... have it priced. That would impress her. M.B. agreed with the argument.

A fortnight later, the driver was dispatched after a great deal of stealth and surreptitious planning. Bindiya wasn't to know, naturally. M.B. had left his gold-embossed card discreetly on the salver, with a small handwritten note on the reverse. 'In appreciation of your great beauty and talent,' he'd stated carefully after cross-checking all the spellings. He'd toyed with the idea of underlining his phone-numbers at the office, but decided against it. The driver was instructed to wait outside her bungalow till he saw her car coming in. And only then was he to make the presentation. The driver waited. The car came. He went to the massive gates... and there the story ended. The bouncer-watchman wouldn't allow him in.

'I have brought a very valuable gift for Madam from my saab,' the driver announced.

The watchman looked unimpressed. 'Many saabs send valuable gifts to Madam. We don't let any *altu-faltus* in.'

The driver looked stricken. 'My saab is a big industrialist... *crorepati,* not one of your film heroes.'

'Get lost, messenger boy,' the watchman jeered, 'show off your saab's wealth somewhere else.'

'I will not leave till I have given this to Madam... those are my instructions.'

The watchman did a quick calculation and said generously, '*Theek hai, theek hai...* give it to me. I'll give it to Madam.'

The driver handed the Lalique vase to him gratefully. 'Please tell Madam to phone my saab. He is a very important man.'

The watchman leered, 'Of course, of course,' and shut the gate on his face.

That was the last anyone saw of the vase. In all probability, Ramu, the watchman, hawked both the Lalique and the salver to some sleazy dealer in Chor Bazaar—hawked them for a song. Enough to get him a month's supply of country liquor, some imported fags and a couple of Taiwanese jeans. Poor M.B. He waited for the call that never came. And he sacked the driver.

I enjoyed these interludes. They perked up my rather uneventful life. God said I was living 'vicariously' (a new term he'd picked up on the art circuit). 'Bullshit,' was what I had to say to that. Maybe I was—living vicariously, I mean. Things on the home-front were dull. Mummy was practically incommunicado while Papa stayed out as much as he could. I'd walk in and walk out at will—something I didn't enjoy doing. I missed the old cross-examination, I longed for suspicion; I even craved punishment—at least I would then be sure that someone still cared. It was a lot like living in an impersonal hostel. But even hostels had wardens. At my house there was no one.

God's set-up wasn't much better. The old woman still cooked meals regularly even if God, Toro and Comradesaab weren't always around to eat them. The few times God took me there left me feeling depressed

217

and ill. The small room was crammed with badly printed posters. *Zindabad* was often misspelled. The rolls of mattresses reached the ceiling ('You never know how many people will want to spend the night here—it all depends on when they secure bail,' Comradesaab had explained once). God was obviously uncomfortable there these days—and showing it.

'Don't tell me you're ashamed of your home,' I once prodded.

He looked at me witheringly. 'What a cheap remark—and so typically bourgeois,' he said. But the old defensive rage was missing.

'I have no place to keep my shirt-pants, *yaar*,' he let drop one day. Seeing my amused expression, he swiftly turned that around and snapped, 'The rain-water leaks through the roof, *yaar*. Who likes wearing wet clothes? Must tell that *saala* Toro to fix it.'

I said nothing. But I knew that he knew that I knew. God was going capitalist. But he didn't want anybody to find out. Not even me.


God was also busy wheeling and dealing for his own little acre in the Artists' Colony that the Chief Minister had grandly announced on Maharashtra Day—the first of May. It was also the busiest day for Comradesaab, since there were at least five important morchas and as many gate-meetings from dawn onwards.

It was at one of these that a stone hurled from nowhere got him on the temple. Comradesaab fell down near the factory wall, his head bleeding profusely. Nobody could say, or was willing to say, where the stone had come from. A bystander insisted he'd spotted one of Yashwantbhai's goons running away from the scene soon after Comradesaab keeled over and collapsed. Someone summoned an ambulance and tried frantically to trace God. It was doubly ironic that he was eventually traced to Yashwantbhai's office, getting his recommendation letter for the land allotment. However, there was no proof to be had of Yashwantbhai's involvement and life went on as usual.

❄

Tanya, a talented but unknown singer, had really been Lucio's discovery. He'd heard her gig at one of Bombay's newly-opened pubs which featured live bands. I remember him describing her to me and recommending we use her for a jingle. But Lucio had done his recommending subtly and it was really God who introduced her to me (and through me to the agency) after he heard her at one of Yashwantbhai's private parties.

'She can't sing, *yaar*,' God said cynically, 'but she has nice tits.' I took both statements with a pinch of salt.

I mentioned Lucio and his comments on Tanya's abilities.

'If he could spot talent... rather, if that asshole had any himself... he wouldn't have copped it,' God said cruelly.

'That's a harsh thing to say,' I scolded. 'And besides, we don't really know... he could be alive and well. Anyway, I don't know why you pick on him like this.'

'Look, Nasha, I'm not the sort of person who picks up stray kittens and feeds street puppies. Whether Tanya can really sing or not doesn't matter. The men jack-off the moment she opens her mouth. Use her....' We did.

Tanya was so fashionable, so rich and so thin that she was known as 'The Duchess' by the 'in' crowd—those of them who had heard of the Duchess of Windsor and the famous saying attributed to her ('You can't be too rich or too thin') that is. Tanya had been born Lalita, but had decided to change her name when she turned eighteen. She'd debated between Lara (from *Dr Zhivago*) and Natasha (from *War and Peace*) and finally settled for Tanya since she said it sounded 'so ancient and yet so modern'. It was a time when every little kid born around town was given a Russian name, especially kids from Sindhi and Parsee families. This had led to a great deal of confusion in local schools since at any given point there were at least three Natashas, two Tanyas and as many Laras in one class. Tanya had joined the

Russian brigade slightly late in the day, but she had no regrets. Along with her new name she'd set about acquiring a new identity. One that suited the name Tanya. A friend suggested an alternative career to the one she was training for—law.

'Tanya the Lawyer doesn't sound half as exciting as Tanya the Temptress,' advised this well-wisher. Tanya replied sensibly that as a lawyer she could easily be a temptress too. 'No, no,' said her friend, 'I can see "Tanya the Temptress" up in lights. You should be a star. A rock star.'

'But I can't sing a note,' poor Tanya protested.

'Don't be silly—since when did that stop anybody,' her friend argued. 'You can always learn. Besides, rock stars don't need to be great singers. You've got what it takes... you look like you are on drugs, you have bedroom eyes, you won't mind singing dirty songs and besides, why waste a name that means so much to you?'

She was instantly convinced and converted.

So, 'Project Tanya' was launched by the slimo who had suggested it, and what's more, it worked. She started off by cutting a demo tape of Hindi rock songs which were straight lifts from successful hits abroad. Slimo, who called himself 'India's first impresario', fixed the whole thing up himself. It cost, but like he told her—'So would your law degree, baby.' The next step was to get her publicity campaign on the road. And that's how Tanya met Pebbles and Malini.

Their first meeting was almost a disaster. Pebbles took one look at her, shook his head and turned her over to his make-up guy and told him to work her over. Present in their studio that afternoon was a snazzy Indian hair-dresser from London ('Call me Czar... I do Imran's hair. And Pamella's and Farah's... and oh... just about everybody else's'). He studied Tanya's face carefully before pronouncing the verdict: 'Far out.' This was Czar's ultimate compliment. He confessed it was he who had persuaded Madonna to go ash-blonde and for Whitney to fuzz it all up. Tanya purred, 'It's all in your hands,' as it quite literally was. Bunches of it. He took a pair of garden shears and went snip-snip-snip. Within seconds Tanya's crowning glory lay in snake-like strips all around her.

Czar ordered the make-up man to hand him a squeeze tube of gel. 'And the spray cans of frosting.' Four or five deft strokes later, Tanya was a new woman wearing her hair close to her scalp like a sleek cap with touches of gold highlighting her bird-like features. Czar stepped back and said with a flourish, 'There, she's all yours now.'

The make-up man pounced on her and got busy with the paint. It was like witnessing a miracle as Tanya's cheekbones jumped out of her face with clever contouring and her eyes looked like luminous dishes the size of a full moon. She looked beautiful. 'Clothes,' boomed Pebbles, 'what about her clothes?'

'Take them off,' said Czar, 'and we'll do her in drapes.' Within minutes Tanya had been stripped of everything except her bikini panties—'Naughty girl—you need to wax.' Czar took two lengths of studio satin and wrapped it around her small frame like a duo-toned bandage. 'How does she look?' he asked all those present. 'Like a rock-star,' they chorused. Pebbles grunted approvingly. And with that completed, 'Tanya the Temptress' was born.

Her success story was quite astonishing. With Pebbles photographing her and Malini planning each detail of the publicity campaign, Tanya was all but made. But she had to do a spot of work too. She started taking singing lessons from an Indian classical vocalist, as well as jazz classes with a Goan musician who played with a local band. Both of them discovered that Tanya had a natural musicality that only needed harnessing. And to Tanya's credit, she kept at it relentlessly, doing her *riyaaz* for five long hours a day. Slimo didn't give up either. He became her diet-consultant, physical instructor, manager, p.r.o., hairdresser and dress designer. He did just about everything short of cleaning her bony bottom.

Tanya started off with a small stint in a rooftop restaurant where she was billed as the 'New Year's Eve Sensation'. Slimo was at the lights when he wasn't transporting her costumes from the loo to the improvised dressing-room near the service entrance. Her repertoire for the evening had been carefully planned by him to include husky, throaty, undemanding numbers that required Tanya to do little more than breathe suggestively into the mike with an echo chamber attached to it. Slimo kept her lyrics very basic as well, rarely going beyond, 'Kiss me. Love me. Let's do it all night through.' These may have been standard words for English pop songs, but when translated into Hindi and combined with suggestive panting, the effect was sheer dynamite.

Slimo crowed later, 'Did you see all those pot-bellies in the front row jerking off? Tanya really socked it to them. Particularly when she started wandering all over the place with her Flo-Jo nails straying here and there. Collective orgasm *ho gaya.*'

It was a smashing debut all right. And Tanya was promptly offered a generous deal with the entire chain. Restaurant managers marvelled, 'This is the first time that a local female with no boobs has got the crowds collapsing in the aisles. Usually, we've always had to go in for foreign broads from cheap clubs. And they used to behave like such pricey bitches. Good, now we have Tanya.'

But Tanya had other plans for herself. At least Slimo did for her. 'Forget it, baby. This is small-time. We must go for bigger things. You are a star. You mustn't ever forget that.'

Tanya actually didn't need to be reminded. She was already displaying most of the symptoms—including a vicious temper. After they ran through her hotel contract, Slimo began to groom her for the stage. 'You need your own show. But for that we need a sponsor. I'll find him.' Within months, Slimo had bagged the biggest producer of musical hits in the business. Tanya was to be sold to Bombay, packaged as Barbara Streisand in *Funny Girl*. It was an ambitious, expensive gamble, but one that paid off for everybody. *Funny Girl* turned out to be a hit and that's when Tanya got her first recording offer. Slimo told her to stick to Hindi rock since that was the hot new sound with thousands of fans all over India. But Tanya decided to go it her way with a track that included chart-busters recorded by superstars abroad. It was a total flop. Tanya had learnt her first lesson the hard way. And that's when she realized she needed Slimo in her life after all.

She made her second mistake when she married him. 'Nobody wants to fantasize about a married rock star,' publicists told her.

'I'll prove them all wrong. Who says you can't be sexy and married?' she challenged. Slimo wasn't too convinced, but anyway, it was too late to retract now.

'How about a divorce, darling?' he asked her on their first anniversary. 'Not that it will change anything between us... but it will create fresh interest in you. It's you, I'm thinking of, baby.'

Tanya thought about it and said solemnly, 'But divorce is against my religion. I'm sorry, but we are stuck for life. So you might as well get off your fat bum and get me a new contract.'

To which Slimo replied, 'Talking of fat bums, baby—have you seen yours lately?'

Tanya often came to me with her sob stories. I half-listened since most of her tales sounded so crazy. She was in and out of the agency—and not always in search of work. Tanya was doing well enough without recording for us. Maybe she liked talking to me. As she put it, 'I don't trust chicks generally—insecure bitches. But you're OK.'

Each time she floated in wearing one of her 'special' outfits (fluorescent tights, cropped-off tops with gold tassles dangling from her nipples) she would create a sensation. I don't know how, but Roy invariably got to know about her presence. He'd stroll in casually to ask stupid questions— 'I'd like an update on the scooter campaign... have we wrapped it up yet?' Tanya would roll her eyes at me and mouth, 'Help!' But help was really what she needed at that point. Professional help.

Tanya tired of Slimo the Husband soon enough, but shrewdly decided to hang on to Slimo the Manager. From cutting flop tapes he guided her career to a point where she was recording a song a day for Hindi films and charging by the metre. Hindi film music has undergone a total change with pop driving everything else away. Hers was the voice that best suited the nymphets prancing around on the screen. India's 'youth' could identify with her warbling and hum along with her songs. The lyrics were simple and easy to remember. Any child could memorize stanzas that rarely went beyond, 'Yoo-hoo-yoo-hoo—I love you, I l-o-v-e you.' Slimo kept dinning it into her that she was a star now and had to behave like one. His instructions were basic—'In public, keep your distance and hire a bodyguard. In private, make sure you never remove your own shoes or fetch yourself a glass of water. Real stars have servants to do that for them.'

Her publicity was controlled by him as well and all pictures had to be approved by Slimo before they were released to the press. He was equally strict about her waistline and wardrobe. Three hundred push-ups daily with two twenty-minute work-outs. No chocolates and no rice (the two things she adored). All this, combined with her new play-back career, kept her busy. And she stopped visiting me with sob stories.


Roy never did manage to get close enough to Tanya even when he had the opportunity. Karen made sure of that. Things had improved between them ever since Janine and the driver had walked back into the fold and humbly asked for money. That was the kind of talk both Roy and Karen understood. Money, or 'financial assistance' as Roy preferred to call it. He pitched in bravely and bailed out his daughter who, predictably, was expecting by then. 'Can't let the side down—know what I mean?' he'd say to nobody in particular. Karen had discovered a brand new incarnation—the sexiest grandma-to-be in town.

Business, though not exactly booming, was stable enough at the agency. And for once Roy wasn't cribbing—or hustling for new accounts. He was far too busy reconciling himself to the fact that he was soon to become the grandfather of a sacked chauffeur's offspring.

# Eleven

We were used to handling weird clients, models and photographers at the agency, but sometimes even we were stumped. Mrs Sippy was the sort of slave-driver who expected the world to jump each time she snapped her soft, white fingers. The trouble was she happened to be a woman with all the right ideas. Her husband owned a textile mill that had started off as a one-shed operation in his father's time and was now poised to become the number one textile empire in the country. 'My one moves with the times,' she told us at our first briefing. We exchanged glances wondering who she was talking about, but soon caught on that, like an old-fashioned Punjabi housewife, she never referred to her husband by his name. But neither did she call him *'Soonte ho jee'* as some of her contemporaries called theirs. She had arrived at a happy compromise. He was either Mr Sippy or simply 'My one'.

'My one' rarely appeared on the scene. Presentations were made at his hide-out in the hills, where he spent all his weekends. Mrs Sippy had recently taken charge of the mill's publicity since she felt she knew best how to interpret 'My one's' vision. This was fine by us, since we weren't required to do very much more than execute her crazy ideas. Well, not that crazy actually. Her logic was simple. Their mill catered to the vast middle class. The vast middle class loved Hindi movies. It followed that they should have Hindi movie stars promoting their range of fabrics in situations the audience could identify with. She explained, 'I don't want anything sophisticated, understand? No gimmicks. No fancy headlines. Give me straightforward masala. If necessary, hire a Hindi film script writer and forget about your copy department. Get me the best. All I expect from you is service. Instant service. I want the top heroines and the top heroes. I want situations that duplicate our films. Give me action, plenty of action... and sex, of course. Let us have horses, dacoits, kidnappings, twins, fights and disco sequences in our ads. Make the whole thing like a dream.'

We groaned at that one. Mrs Sippy was turning into a nightmare already. Roy was aghast but impressed—by the hefty size of the account if nothing else. 'Give her what she wants. The broad wants kitsch—let her have it.'

As always, it was left to me to find the stars. The top ones at that. And then to sign them on. I didn't know how to get anywhere close to them. Phone numbers? Addresses? What was I supposed to do?

'Call one of the film magazines, *yaar*,' Nitin suggested.

Aarti chipped in, 'If you ever go to see that Pathan hunk—take me along.'

Willie pretended the whole thing was beneath him. 'Come on, *yaar*. How on earth will we communicate with those animals? Do they speak English?'

Finally, I got the numbers I was looking for and called them up. After a week of trying at least a hundred times a day at all hours, I gave up. It would have been easier to get Gorbachev. In absolute frustration and rage, I checked with a film journalist I knew vaguely who laughed at my clumsy attempts.

'Are you crazy? You actually expect Sonia to come to the line and speak to you—you, a complete stranger and non-entity? Forget it. You need someone like me. Tag along when I go for my studio round-ups. I'll introduce you.'

Roy was horrified at the thought. 'Rubbish, dear girl. That's not the way to do it. We must be absolutely professional about this. And quick. I don't want that woman breathing fire at me.' Another journalist suggested I get through to the secretaries through their *chamchas*.

'But how do I know who these *chamchas* are?' I groaned.

'Go to a film party and you'll spot them immediately.'

'Nobody has invited me,' I answered.

'Nobody will. You just gatecrash. Generally. They don't throw females out... particularly single ones.' That was said with a leer that wasn't hard to interpret. 'There's one on this weekend—that monkey's birthday—Bobo—the one who starred in *Love Ke Baad Pyar* Let's go together... don't look so nervous. Nobody will rape you. There are far too many other willing victims around at these *tamashas*.'

So there were. Dozens of them dressed in the most outlandish creations. The party was at the poolside of a five-star suburban hotel. 'Everybody will be here tonight,' my friend told me.

'Why?'

'Oh, because the producer, Mr Suresh Gupta, is the most sought-after man in filmdom. His films never flop. Super-hits, *aré*—super-super-hits. All the stars want to work with him. He's a real bastard. Filthy, illiterate, uncouth fellow—but just see how everybody will come and lick his dirty feet.'

And so it was. Well, not literally, of course, but every major star and each minor, up-and-coming starlet lined up to pay their respects to this whiz producer when he finally arrived. He looked like he had already downed a couple of double whiskies, and he proceeded to tank-up immediately. After a couple of drinks, he became quite obnoxious and started singing boozy songs. He also started pawing indiscriminately while he tottered around the poolside and I had to repress the urge to hide behind a deck-chair as he approached me. But thankfully, he didn't cast more than an inebriated look in my direction, and moved towards a tall, slim woman in a black, low-cut dress.

Suddenly, I spotted Pebbles and realized that the woman Mr Suresh Gupta was moving towards was none other than Malini. I hadn't met the two since our Maldives trip, and Malini had given up modelling to start studying for her law degree. She still seemed to be handling Pebbles' engagements, and I felt pleased to see them together.

Mr Suresh Gupta went up to Malini and said something softly. Malini glared at him through her specs and politely said, 'Fuck off.' All those close enough to hear her words, were stunned into silence. Mr Gupta's face changed rapidly from a leer to a grimace and he lurched away from her, colliding with a minor starlet and upsetting her drink.

But no apologies were forthcoming from the great film producer. Instead, he started abusing everybody present—even the stars of his films. Nobody dared object. They laughed when he started cracking coarse jokes and encouraged him to drink some more. Soon, he plopped down on a deck-chair and yelled for Sonia, the beautiful young actress he was promoting. It was a foregone conclusion that he would get all the fringe benefits of such an alliance.

Sonia was nothing more than his slave. She rushed to his side and waited for instructions. Soon she was feeding him seekh kababs dipped in tomato sauce. After a while she fetched him another drink, and sat at his feet massaging his thighs.

I looked across the pool and spotted Pebbles and Malini again. He saw me and waved, beckoning me to go over to them. I skirted the pool, dodging elbows and legs, and finally reached the two of them. Both of them seemed genuinely pleased to see me—we had struck up quite a good friendship in the Maldives—and were perhaps relieved to find someone they could talk to.

'Hi! What are you doing here? I didn't think this was your kind of a do....' said Pebbles.

'I was quite surprised to see you both here too,' I replied.

'Oh, we're here to look for new faces. Getting bored of the old ones!' laughed Malini. 'But seriously, this is quite a surprise... you're the last person I expected to see here.'

'Maybe you both can help me,' I said, struck by a brainwave. 'I'm working on a complicated ad campaign. The client wants film stars to strut about in garments made from their mill's cloth. And it is so tough to get anywhere near these bloody stars... can you guys help?'

Pebbles and Malini looked at each other. 'Tanya....'

'I know Tanya, she used to sing jingles for the agency. But will she model for us?' I interrupted.

'Yes, she's been looking for something like this. She's sick of only doing playbacks.... And once we have her, I think a couple of biggies can be roped in too,' replied Malini.

'So, is it a deal? There'll be lots in it for you too. This client is willing to pay....'

'It's a deal,' said Pebbles, and Malini nodded.

That was a load off my mind. I felt glad that I had come to the party. A minute later, however, I wasn't too sure. Across the pool a drama was unfolding. Even as I watched, I saw Suresh Gupta throw up all over Sonia—yes, that's right—all over her sari. But she just smiled and said, 'It's all right, darling. It's nothing at all.'

And he barked, 'Take it off immediately. I hate dirty clothes.'

At first we all thought he was joking. But soon it became clear that he was absolutely serious. He stood there yelling, 'Take your sari off... what are you hiding? What are you ashamed of? Haven't I seen your naked body? And hasn't the public? Come on, we all know what you look like without your clothes.'

Sonia tried to laugh it off and divert his attention. But he just stood there screaming. Suddenly, without a warning, he pulled out a small pistol from his jacket and said in a carrying voice, 'I don't like my orders to be disobeyed. If you don't remove your sari at once, I will shoot you....' He meant it. Without a minute's hesitation, Sonia undraped herself right there in front of hundreds of guests. She didn't even look scared. Her eyes were cold and expressionless. She just stood there, shivering a little, staring straight at Gupta. Nobody dared move or say anything. Finally, he laughed and put the gun away.

'Get her something to wear. She looks better with her clothes on,' he said.

Mrs Pratimaben Shah was someone who fancied herself as a saviour of lost souls—preferably from her own community. She was eagerly sought out by neglected Gujarati ladies who courted her with pomegranates and gold sovereigns. She had a soothing sort of presence, I must admit. And she was doing good things for my mother who had met her at the home of another corporate wife like herself.

Pratimaben had taken my dear mother under her wing. Perhaps she saved Mummy from going bonkers altogether. The divorce was a forgotten matter. A topic that was never to be discussed. It had something to do with my father's boss man ticking him off and telling him that ambitious corporate men did not divorce their wives. It was bad for the company's image. And if they did indulge in a little funny business, it had to be strictly out of the office and outside office hours. 'Business and pleasure (pronounced 'play-ure' in the typically Punjabi fashion by Mr Mehra) don't mix, old chap,' he had tut-tutted, pulling on his pipe, while my father stood around like a chastised schoolboy looking sheepish.

God didn't have to resort to blackmail with the Sindhi harlot—someone else had beaten him to it. 'The department is so jealous. Everybody is so jealous,' she kept whining. 'After all, I didn't go after anybody's husband. What can I do if these fellows fall for me? Why blame me? Why not blame the wives who can't keep their husbands happy?' At any rate, she soon lost interest in the affair and latched on to a widower with whom she thought she had a better future.

But the break-up didn't change anything between my parents. It was as if it had signalled the end of whatever relationship they had once shared. They were civil enough in private and definitely in public, but beyond, 'Pass the toast. What's for dinner? Don't forget we have a cocktails programme with the Purandares on Friday night,' they rarely spoke. Mother seemed less fraught. At least she'd stopped talking to herself and she had resumed getting her weekly hair-set. This pleased Didi no end, and she fluttered around her whenever my mother was going out, adjusting the pleats of her sari, patting an imaginary crease, handing her perfume.

Pratimaben had all but moved into our house. Her husband was an affluent Ahmedabad-based businessman who shuttled between the two cities ceaselessly. 'My weekend husband,' she called him. The children were both married off ('What a *lagan* we had for them. Crystal Room, eighteen courses and the decoration... too much. We hired Smitaben to do it. She arranged matkas and chatais with mirrors everywhere. Just like a Kutch village'). Now Pratimaben (who was still in her forties) was free to explore the world on her own terms and without anything or anyone to bind her down. She went abroad—'Only with Cosmos Tours. They give good Gujju food everywhere. I tell you, fun to eat khaman-dhokla in Milan. And papdi in Madrid'—during summer, and to Srinathji in winter—'Religion is so important, no? I have to go on my pilgrimage otherwise I feel guilty.' She was keen to go to Badri-Kedar and wanted to drag my mother along. But her frail health came in the way and Pratimaben shook her head, 'Poor *ben*, she doesn't eat enough. You people don't use asli ghee for your cooking that's why you lack strength. Look at me—all my food is cooked in ghee. I haven't fallen ill for a day. Now, we must instruct your cook to give your mother hot milk and ghee everyday.' Maybe she felt protective and sorry, but she was there every morning trying to involve my mother in something or the other. 'Join our Mahila Mandal. *Aré*, we do so much social work. We also have fun. We organize melas in schools with food stalls and games. You can take charge of one stall. During Navratri, we have dandiya garba-raas every night. Last day, it goes on all night. All of us dress up in ghagras and dance. We invite film stars, then we have a beauty contest, nice prizes also. Try it.' My mother recoiled at the prospect of wearing a ghagra but went along in a chiffon sari anyway.

There was nothing Pratimaben hadn't tried, including est. *'Kya* fun, *ben.* You should have seen our group. They didn't allow us to do *soo-soo,* so one fat fellow pissed in his pants.'

What did Pratimaben herself do? 'I went just… simply. To try. What's wrong? Three days of something new. I got up and shared my experiences. I told them how I didn't like my husband and I thought everybody would be surprised. But all the women there said that they also didn't like their husbands. Funny, no?' Pratimaben took all sorts of classes including public speaking. 'Who knows? One day I might become the president of my Lioness Club, or the ladies' wing of the Indian Merchants Chamber. Then I will have to speak, no? Speeches and all that. Better to have training.' She was a keen Bonsai enthusiast and had surrounded herself with stunted trees. 'See my mandarin oranges. I got a medal for this one. And my peepul tree. Good, no?' Her latest kick was to start either a boutique ('Bo-tic' as she pronounced it) or an art gallery. She wanted to rope in my mother for these projects.

'But what does she know of fashion or art?' I asked my mother, who replied vaguely, 'That doesn't matter, dear. She has enthusiasm.'

I asked Pratimaben myself. Not rudely, but with more than just casual curiosity.

'See—everybody has boutiques these days. I can get cloth cheaply from Ahmedabad, employ a darzi who can sit in the guest room, and copy other people's designs. I have no problem. Everybody copies everybody else. I can also copy from film stars—you know, what Madhuri or Juhi wears. That way I can sell to the building people and then expand. Art gallery is only in name. It is not for paintings or anything. We will hold sari and salwar-kameez exhibitions. If someone wants to show some art-wart—OK, we will allow. But not often. This gallery will make money—we will hire it out for two thousand rupees a day. Not much—I will air-condition it: Give water-cooler. Bathroom also. Nice bathroom with expensive tiles and all that. So what? People in Bombay have lots of money. They won't mind paying.'

I still couldn't figure out where my mother would come in. I asked Pratimaben. 'She is a good lady. Nice personality. She can be manager, no? I will give her good salary. She can answer phone, she is speaking English so nicely. Plus, she is also knowing Gujarati. I can trust her, no? Other women are cunning. They will cheat me. But not your mother. Poor thing—what she is doing at home? Wasting time. This way she will meet people… it is good. Your father won't get angry, no?'

My father didn't get angry. He was livid. 'In our Company wives do not work—at least not in such cheap jobs. They stay at home and organize dinner parties. What will the bosses say if their wives tell them that they saw you selling saris in some shop?' It was no use trying to explain to him that she wasn't going to be selling saris on the street. As usual, my mother gave up without putting up a fight.

But Pratimaben was made of sterner stuff. 'What is there? I will talk to him. No problem,' She didn't know what she was letting herself in for. She turned up one evening, her mouth stuffed with paan-masala wearing a thin, organdy sari with huge peacocks appliqued all over it. She had tucked in her bunch of house keys on an enormous chaabi-jhumka on her waist. It made an irritating tinkling sound each time she moved. While talking, she pulled out a gent's handkerchief from her bra which in any case was five sizes too small for her. Father could barely conceal his disgust. He stopped her mid-sentence and said, 'There is nothing to discuss. My wife is different. She cannot be seen sitting in a shop—and don't tell me it's anything else. You need a salesgirl and receptionist. My wife is not meant for such jobs. She comes from a very good family. I have my reputation to think of. Please do not try and influence her in this manner. If she needs more money for her needs, I am there to provide it. That's all.'

My mother was trembling in the other room, listening to the conversation. Suddenly, she flew in like a pretty pink parakeet. Her eyes were blazing and her voice was close to a shriek. 'I have had enough of your bullying and hypocrisy. I have kept quiet for far too long. Go to hell with your corporate nonsense. Who cares what your boss thinks? Or those bloody women think? Where were they when my world was collapsing and you were with that Sindhi whore? I know where they were—at the Club and the Gym, laughing at me. Telling each other what a fool I was. And what an ass I was married to. And you want me to bother about them? Why should I? Why should I bother about you either? You can also go to hell with your pompous talk and empty boasts. I am sick, do you hear, sick of living this false life. Varnishing my nails, setting my hair, wearing these silly saris and smiling through your office parties pretending nothing is wrong with my life. Well—it's my turn now. And you can listen to me for a change. I will go along with Pratimaben with anything I choose to do. She is my friend. She encourages me. She appreciates me. She makes me feel like someone. So you can go to hell with your lectures and your Sindhi girlfriends—you don't deserve me. And God knows what sins I committed in my last birth to be stuck with you. Whether you like it or not, henceforth I will make the decisions about my life. And the first one is that I'm taking a job.'

There was nothing left for Papa to say. He looked suddenly shrunken and small and scared. He fiddled with the telephone for a minute and then barked for some tea.

God was certainly meeting strange types these days through his film-world contacts. Yashwantbhai's men were rapidly moving into the studios and mobilizing support from disgruntled workers—the stuntmen and women, the lighting boys, the sets people. God was in and out of meetings at various locations often coming back with an obviously impressed expression after interacting with a bigwig. Of course he tried to play it down and sound blasé but, to my surprise, God was getting glamour-struck. It was on one such studio round that he ran into Feroze.

Feroze was a film-star groupie. She lived breathed and dreamed movies. Which was quite odd considering she was a Parsee. Well, a half-Parsee. Her mother was Muslim and her father described himself as 'Persian'. Why they had named their only child 'Feroze' was anybody's guess. Perhaps they'd hoped she'd be a boy. While the rest of the family (an untidily-knit joint one that occupied a sprawling bungalow in one of the few secluded, tree-lined areas left on Malabar Hill) stuck to reading Shelley and Keats, Feroze lived on a diet of film magazines.

The family was aghast. Hindi movies were for the servants. Only menials watched rubbish like that. Not refined folk. Most of the Mehtas pretended they'd never heard of an actor called Amitabh Bachchan. This used to enrage Feroze, who'd snap, 'Are you people blind? Don't you look at posters as you drive along? Don't you see newspapers? Or hoardings? Stop pretending.' To which an uncle would reply, 'We know about film stars, *dikri*, but not this riff-raff. Ask us about Deborah Kerr and Gregory Peck. Lawrence Olivier and Elizabeth Taylor. Yes... such great actors and actresses we have watched. Aah—what a scene there was in *King and I* and what acting in *To Catch a Thief*. That is what we call true histrionics.'

Hindi films were entirely out of Feroze's orbit. And yet, she was hopelessly hooked. At the age of fourteen she dropped out of school and joined up with a film unit. The family was aghast. 'Have you ever heard of a girl from a Parsee family mixing with such trash?' a hip cousin asked the family when they gathered around the table to eat dinner, which consisted of watery soup and lacey cutlets.

A grand-uncle shook his head and mumbled, 'That's what happens when our boys marry outside their community. I had warned Naval—marry a Zoroastrian girl and everything will be all right. But did he listen?'

At this point Feroze's mother, the fiery Raisa, banged her soup spoon down and left the table.

'Spoilt. That child was spoilt from the start. No discipline. Naval used to try—but what to do? Her mother didn't stop her. Do you remember when Feroze tried to cut off the cat's tail? Her mother didn't say a word. Just shielded the girl when she had deserved to be whipped. Now this is the result. Hindi *fillums*. Khodai—what will all the relatives think?'

Feroze was certain she had found her vocation. 'I want to be a director. But before I get that chance, I have to learn everything from the bottom up. You people wait and see, some day I will be great. The first woman Parsee director of Hindi films.'

A cousin sniggered, 'As if it is something to be proud of.'

Feroze's mother rushed to her daughter's defence. 'Better than you, dear. Where has your degree taken you? To the cash deposit counter of the Central Bank. And your sister. What has she done? Failed three times in Davar's College. Can't even pass a secretarial course. So much money wasted on typing and shorthand. At least my Feroze is on her own.'

Feroze was on her own in more ways than one. Enterprising, manipulative and full of a strange kind of charm, she got around to places most people only dreamt of. Nobody was sure how she did it. Did she con people into sponsoring her? Did she cheat and lie her way into film festivals? Did her gift of the gab do the trick? What was it? Feroze became a familiar and popular figure in filmdom in an incredibly short period. The filmwallahs just didn't know what to make of this mad *bawi* in her trademark jungle safari suit. She seemed smart and rich. She drove her own car—she smoked foreign cigarettes. She travelled by planes. Yet, she didn't ever have a dime in her pocket—permanently broke. 'How does she do it?' they asked themselves, baffled by a phenomenon that defied explanation.

Feroze was everywhere—at film parties, mahurats, premières, shooting, story sessions, publicity bashes and outdoor stints. It was at one of those—a location shoot in Ooty—that Feroze met Kiki. It was an encounter that changed her life. It was at the same location that God was covering for a 'serious' film monthly, that he also got to know Kiki. To everybody's amazement, Feroze and God both fell instantly in love—not with each other—but with Kiki.

'What happened?' I asked God when he came back after four love-struck days.

'Don't ask me, *yaar*. That female is like *bijli*. I was struck. Before I knew it—*khatam. Main mar gaya*. You are looking at a dead man.'

'Did she say something? Do something?'

'She didn't have to, *yaar*. One look and I became her slave.'

Help! God was even beginning to sound like a C-grade jilted lover. I debated upon whether to talk to him sensibly or just to let him wallow in his moonstruck madness. It was so out of character. So irrational. And frankly, so sweet.

'Did you get to touch her?' I asked trying to keep my voice serious.

'Hell, no, *yaar*. She has all her goons around her. Bodyguards. Karate types. In any case, she was having it off with that hairy fellow, the hero, Balwant. I had no chance, *yaar*.'

'Then why are you wasting your time?'

'I can't control myself. That woman has something. I don't know what it is....'

Helpfully, I provided some hints, 'Sexuality? Animal appeal? Availability?'

'No, *yaar*. It is something primal. I don't know. Basic attraction. Very basic.'

'And Feroze?'

'That's a weird one. Bloody lesbian. Or I don't know what she is a sex-maniac or something. She was in bed with the first cameraman—I saw them. Didn't feel embarrassed or anything. They carried on as if I wasn't there.'

'But what were you doing in their bedroom?'

'It wasn't their room, damn it—it was mine. I mean, he and I were sharing a double room.'

'Why didn't you throw them out?'

'Couldn't, *yaar*. In these filmi affairs, anything goes.'

'If she was bedding your roommate, when did she find the time to flip for Kiki.'

'Don't ask me, *yaar*. All I know is that the whole unit was talking about this mad woman.'

'Was Kiki embarrassed?'

'I don't know. Flattered, maybe. This was her first experience with a female devotee.'

'But what exactly did Feroze do?'

'What didn't she do? She was like Kiki's slave. Following her like a puppy. Sending her flowers and poems. Fetching her food. Carrying her clothes. Generally behaving like a love-lorn maiden.'

'How funny. If she was doing all that—what did it leave you to do?'

'Shut up, *yaar*. I'm not a bloody coolie. I am fascinated by Kiki. I've never met someone like her. She's instinctive and phenomenal. Such talent! Her potential hasn't been exploited. Such intelligence! Switch on the cameras and she's dynamite.'

'Are you telling me you have gone for the actress and not the woman?'

'Both, *yaar*. As a woman—what can I say that won't sound obscene? She makes me wet my pants just looking in my direction.'

'Well, you sure have a lot of competition... starting with Feroze.'

'Forget Feroze,' God said meaningfully, 'she doesn't have what it takes—she doesn't have a prick.'

That was his inelegant way of letting me know that he was sleeping with Kiki.

Eventually, it was Feroze who won out. It was a bizarre story, a fight that was fought on various sets, locations and finally, in the press. But when the time came for Kiki to choose, she opted for Feroze. 'I like women,' she explained simply. 'I like men too... but women more.'

It was a quote that stole the thunder from another actress, Kiki's chief rival, Zainab, who had just announced her plans to become the film industry's first unwed mother—father unknown. Or at least, officially so. The gossip press had narrowed the field down to five potential fathers, each of whom had coyly admitted to a 'relationship' with Zainab. But she'd surprised everybody by declaring that though she had been 'friendly... very friendly' with all five at about the same time, she was certain that the father of her child was not amongst them. He was a mysterious stranger. A foreigner who, she hinted, was a 'very important person' not connected with showbiz at all. And did the privileged man know about this momentous event? 'I'll let him know when the time comes,' was Zainab's enigmatic reply.

But now, with Kiki going public with her 'confessions', film monthlies had their schedules thrown completely out of gear. Cover stories had to be switched, headlines altered and hoardings repainted. Overnight Feroze had become a household name all over India. Her photographs with Kiki were splashed everywhere—laughing, kissing, holding hands, relaxing. One magazine had gone to the extent of screaming—'Wedding bells for the industry's first lesbian couple. Secret marriage confirms the rumours.'

Feroze's family had all but gone into hiding. Several members were reportedly under sedation. Nosey reporters had been badgering them for days, asking all sorts of peculiar questions. The old uncle continued muttering, 'It's that woman, the mother. It is her influence. It is God's curse on us for allowing Naval to marry her.' Feroze tried to get back home once (she had 'officially' moved in with Kiki) but she found the doors of her family home closed to her.

'You are dead to us,' her aunt announced. 'We never want to see you again.'

She spotted her mother in the background who was desperately signalling to her—'Take me with you.' Feroze pushed the aunt aside roughly and grabbed her mother's hand. 'Let's go,' she said and both of them jumped into Kiki's waiting car.

It worked out OK. Mama Mehta took charge of Kiki's crazy household and sacked all the staff. Feroze became the Man of the House and Kiki's manager. She handled her finances, appointments and contracts with ruthless efficiency and announced a couple of block-busters with the top hero of the industry, with herself as the director.

Kiki looked radiant. The arrangements suited her perfectly. She had finally managed to escape her dominating mother and overbearing half-brother, and found a real family instead—a person who loved her and guarded her interests plus a director she could relate to. It couldn't have ended better in any pot-boiler the industrywallahs could have come up with.

The alliance worked well for us too. Pebbles had known Feroze since their schooldays, and he contacted her. Roping Kiki in for Mrs Sippy's textiles was a major coup. And with Bollywood's top actress and the most sought-after playback singer, Tanya, we watched our ideas take shape—into one of the most successful ad campaigns the agency had produced.

All of us worked very hard on this one, Kawla and gang in particular. This was our 'biggie'—the campaign that would showcase our collective talent and garner a few awards at the next ad club shindig.

Kiki was co-operation itself. And with Feroze's persuasion we managed to bag practically the entire new breed of bold bimbettes who'd taken over Bollywood. As Feroze put it, 'They're OK, these kids. Show them the right amount and they'll flash anything—boobs, ass, cunt.' So there was Kiki as the main attraction (shot at her seductive, luscious best by Pebbles) surrounded by all the semi-clad lovelies who, as Feroze had correctly predicted, dropped their clothes obediently the moment Roy sanctioned the lolly.

The final product was a cross between an MTV hit and a BBC Clothes Show clip—slick, sexy and exceedingly effective, much more so than Mrs Sippy's straightforward masala would've been. It became the most talked of campaign of the year.

God was heartbroken. But not for long.

'One bitch is as good as another,' he said morosely, trying hard not to let his remorse show. But in typical God fashion he didn't remain down for too long. Other distractions claimed his attention. And I didn't waste too much time worrying about him either.

# Twelve

My relationship with God was following its familiar hot and cold pattern. We still saw each other sporadically but the intervals between our meetings were getting longer. There were times I cancelled after fixing up a date. There were times he did. Neither of us moped. It was understood we'd catch up when it was mutually convenient. On the infrequent occasions when we did get together, it was pleasant enough but hardly exciting. God had begun to treat me like a sexless person. I wondered if he even regarded me as a woman any longer. Sometimes I felt hurt by his attitude—the grand poses he struck. At other times I felt indulgent and amused. Physically, we had stopped having a relationship though occasionally he still made a tired pass, needlessly explaining, 'Just for old times' sake, *yaar*.' I preferred it this way. The old uncertainties and tensions had melted away. I felt at ease with God, perhaps for the first time in our relationship.

My weekends were pretty free too. I wasn't really seeing anybody. Just the chaps at office. I had become one of them—one of the guys. Most times I didn't really mind. But there were days when I missed male attention. Specific male attention.

I rang Anil on the spur of the moment. I got his answering machine. Here we go—another yuppie acquisition, I thought to myself. Oh well—it at least proved that he hadn't as yet installed a wife in the flat to take his phone calls. His voice on the recording sounded metallic and phoney. I could picture him running through a variety of cheery-sounding greetings and finally settling for the very American, 'Hi! You've just reached Anil Bhandari's flat. I'm out at the moment. . .' and so on. I didn't feel like talking to a machine so I hung up.

I tried God at the *Plume* office. He wasn't in either. I got Chandni instead.

'Hi-yeee,' she shrieked. She sounded genuinely pleased to hear my voice. 'Where have you been hiding? What's happening? We hardly see you these days. New boyfriend or what? Come come come—let's have a chai. *Aa jao, yaar.* Haven't been to the Surai in ages. Let's *gupshup* about the world.' It sounded like a good idea. The alternatives were hardly more attractive. I would've had to go home and meet a grumpy father and a sulky Didi. My mother was hardly home these days. So, the Surai it was....

Chandni's skin had improved and she was dressed in a wildly colourful ghagra and tunic which made her look like a horny *banjaran* or a sexy sweeperess. 'Don't you just love it—my new outfit. I got it directly from Kumudini. She's exporting heaps of them. Guess what—I'm off....'

'Where to?'

'Well, Paris initially—*aré yaar,* I got onto this Festival *chakkar.* There's a meet of some sort, don't know, poets, writers, all the big-big intellectual types. But I am going in my own right. You know my small anthology about alienation and sublimation was very well received, some feminist types in France want to translate it into French and all that. It's one of those women's lib publishing houses that encourages this type of writing. It's OK, *yaar.* I get a free trip in the bargain.'

'That's terrific, Chandni. When do you leave?'

'In a fortnight. That's why I'm buying all these ethnic outfits, *yaar.* They are a big hit with the *phirangs.*'

I spotted Iqbal just then. He was sitting at his usual table having his fifth cup of pudina chai. The other four cups were lying on the table attracting flies. He was alone for a change and obviously looking for company. I thought he wouldn't recognize me. 'Hello! Hello!' he called out. 'What's up?'

'Everything's OK,' I replied, a little embarrassed at having the entire café whirl around to see who Iqbal was greeting. He picked up his half-empty cup and walked over. Without so much as a by-your-leave, he sat himself down and stared with great interest at Chandni's nosering. 'Unusual,' he said while reaching across to touch it.

She giggled and mumbled, 'Jaisalmer.'

'I thought so,' Iqbal continued.

It was as if he had begun his countdown. He generally gave himself seven minutes to make a play for someone. If it worked great. If not, he moved on. He had already exhausted three. Suddenly, I felt his naked big toe climbing up under my sari. I nearly jumped up and screamed. What was most disturbing was the absence of a tablecloth. Everybody could see his toe travelling up my leg. He hadn't bothered to interrupt his conversation with Chandni. He was busy telling her about his last trip to Jaisalmer. I felt paralysed and enraged. The only thing I could think of was to excuse myself and say I had to go to the loo.

Before I could utter a word, Iqbal put a restraining hand over my arm and pulled me down. 'Sit down... where are you running off to?'

Chandni was quite oblivious to what was going on and hadn't stopped discussing her nosering. Iqbal had fixed me with his penetrating stare and stopped listening to her. In a couple of minutes, he got up and dragged me up with him. 'We are leaving,' he said to the stunned Chandni, whose finger was still on the nosering. He signalled to the waiter that he'd settle both the bills later. *'Chalo,'* he said and took me home. His home.

What had I expected out of this encounter? New insights? Or an out-of-the-body experience? Who knows. But there I was in Iqbal's anarchic studio waiting for him to finish peeing noisily into a dirty pot. He hadn't bothered to shut the rickety door.

Iqbal came back smiling. Why did all men adopt a goofy, self-satisfied expression after a long pee as if they'd achieved something significant?

'Aaah… can't screw on a full bladder,' Iqbal explained, drawing me close to him and sticking his extra-long tongue down my throat. I tried to push him away, but his knee was in my groin, hurting me. He'd shut his eyes. And obviously, his ears as well, since he behaved as if he couldn't hear my muffled cries of protest. Once his tongue was out of my mouth, he stuck it into my ear, covering the lobe with spittle. His rough hands were tearing at my blouse while his knee was still locked between my legs.

'Let's do it standing up,' he said unzipping his stained jeans.

'Let's not,' I insisted, 'I really don't want to … if you don't mind.' Stupid me. Imagine being polite— POLITE—under the circumstances. Iqbal was now down on his knees in front of me, pulling up my sari, raising

the petticoat, dragging my panties down roughly. I knew
it was time to scream, shout, yell, run. But I couldn't
do it. I was far too scared of this madman whose eyes
had dilated, whose nostrils were flared. He reminded
me of a doped horse running madly on much after the
race is over. I shut my eyes and clenched my fists. Iqbal's
tongue was rooting between my thighs. That ugly,
nicotine-stained, hot tongue of his, probing wetly while
the rough hairs of his beard bruised my skin. His hands
were at my breasts—pinching, squeezing, hurting. A
voice within me kept repeating irritatingly, 'You asked
for it. Don't say you didn't. You knew when you climbed
those stairs with him and entered this place exactly
what was in store for you. Don't blame him. Blame
yourself, you little fool.'

Now he'd pushed me down after kicking his cans
of paint to one side. He climbed onto my rigid body,
animal grunts escaping from his wide open mouth. I
could see the cavities in his teeth... and infected hair
follicles with pus-heads in his beard. He looked revolting.
I felt his fingers trying to enter me. Just his paint-covered
fingers. Nothing else. I wanted to laugh. I visualized
what the insides of my legs would look like later with
streaks of green, blue, vermilion. I waited... expecting
something else to happen. It didn't. Iqbal, the great
womanizer, was limp. He looked pathetic at that moment
with his jaw open and eyes shut in pseudo-orgasmic
bliss. Gently, I pushed him away and fixed my clothes.

I looked around at Iqbal's famous nudes. There was nothing even remotely erotic about them anymore.

❉

I phoned God when I got home. There were no wisecracks this time. Just a cold, stony silence. A year ago he would have been incensed and cursed Iqbal's progeny for seven generations to come. He would have railed against me too and hurled the vilest abuse. But this was a changed God I was dealing with. Not that he was unmoved by what I'd just told him. Or indifferent. But his emotions were more under control and the old temper had obviously been reined in. I was disappointed by his tepid reaction. I had expected fireworks. Nastiness. Contempt. Not this. It just proved to me exactly how far we'd drifted apart. We were no longer immersed in the minutae of one another's lives.

He dropped by at the office the next morning. 'So? How was it? *Kaisa laga?*' he asked sarcastically, lighting up a beedi. I was glad it wasn't a Dunhill. I tried to get rid of him. *'Bolo na,* tell me, Nasha, was it good?'

I tried to change the subject by talking about his latest celebrity-interview and asking after Comradesaab's health. 'He's alive. That's all I know.'

'Why? Don't you live there any more?'

'Forget it, *yaar*. I have my own digs now.'

'You didn't tell me you'd moved....'

'Looks like we've stopped telling each other anything, haven't we?'

'Well... we hardly meet these days. How's Bijli?'

'Sold.'

'WHAT?'

'You heard me—I sold her.'

'How could you?'

'It was easy, *yaar*. I didn't need her anymore.'

And a cliché immediately came to my mind—'like you don't need me anymore'—but I didn't say it.

'So... how do you get around?'

'Car.'

'Wow! When did you buy it?'

'Haven't bought it... I... well, I sort of use it.'

'But whose is it?'

'A friend's.'

'Which friend? I didn't know you had such richie-rich friends who had spare cars lying around.'

'You don't know very much, Nasha. Forget it. Tell me... feel like moving in? I need someone... you know... to cook and everything.'

'Why don't you hire a maid in that case? With the kind of money you seem to be making, you can afford not one but half-a-dozen of them surely.'

'It's not that, *yaar*. These maid-shaids are a hassle, *yaar*. I need my own woman. If you want, I don't mind a shaadi-waadi—I know that will make you feel better. *Theek hai*—we can be bourgeois and go through with that marriage rubbish. You *can* cook, can't you? After all, you are a corporatewallah's daughter. Have you ever set foot in a kitchen? Can you fry puris without burning your fingers? Can you make rice that isn't sticky? What about mutton-chicken that doesn't stink? Better to get all this straight from the start, *hai na?* No *lafda* later on. Don't expect me to treat you like a rich bitch. I'm a *seedha-saadha* fellow—you know that. Give me my daal-roti, a warm bed, twice-a-week *maalish* and a daily screw. That's all I expect. So tell me—are you interested?'

I was too stunned to respond. One part of me was laughing. The other, feeling sorry for this man. He was obviously deranged—or the world's biggest egotist. He actually expected me to jump at his offer. He looked so comic. So vulnerable, standing in the lobby, trying to look nonchalant and heroic. I picked up my bag and said, 'Let's go and listen to Hariprasad playing his bansuri. I presume you have stopped playing yours.'

'You presume too much,' said God, and pulled out his flute from his leather satchel.

After the brush-off, God didn't waste much time finding a replacement. She was a much older woman. A *'ghatan'* as he dubbed her. But an unusual one.

Pramila was a non-conformist. She had a divorce to prove it. A divorce that had been icky, messy and perfectly traumatic. A divorced *ghatan* was still a rarity. But then, Pramila was rare in more ways than that. A Nagpur girl, she was one of those small-town products with a big-city hang-up. Married to a boring mechanical engineer from Pilani at an early age, Pramila strained against the kind of life he had to offer. In quick succession, she produced a boy and two girls, after which she considered her duty towards her husband over and done with.

Unfortunately, Vilas had different ideas about holy matrimony. He saw them putting down roots in Nagpur, drawing from his provident fund to buy a bungalow there. He wanted to see his son follow in his footsteps and become a PWD engineer when the time came for him to retire. For his daughters he could only foresee a stable middle-class marriage to doctors (preferably g.p.'s with a 'decent' practice) or lawyers. As for Pramila—why, she had everything a woman could ask for—a husband with 'solid' job, security, lovely children, a moped of her own and all the time in the world to pursue her interests, join the local Mahila Mandal, attend *haldi-kumkums,* organize Sarvajanik Ganapati festivals and show off her latest sari brought by him from Bombay while on 'tour'. Yet, Pramila was wilting. He thought she was ill. She was, but not in the way he assumed.

Pramila was suffocating with boredom and frustration. She'd taken to writing. Vilas didn't know that. But each day after he left for work and the two older children were at school, Pramila would grab some paper and start scribbling furiously, feverishly. It started with poetry. Intense, erotic and enraged. She used a pseudonym and began sending it off to various publishers of pulp. There were several of them, particularly during Diwali when the Marathi *ank* market boomed with literally hundreds of annual publications crammed with articles. Pramila found it remarkably easy to get her stuff published. And she hoarded the paltry sums she received, dreaming of the day she'd make enough to catch a train to Bombay and never return.

She did just that—within a year of starting her literary adventure. One fine day, Pramila upped and disappeared. Vilas was totally bewildered. He just couldn't believe what had happened. He was convinced his wife had been lured away by a hypnotist or a tantrik who had cast a spell over her. The children were still too young to understand that their mother had deserted them. The youngest one whimpered for a week and refused to eat. Vilas' widowed mother left her other son's home and moved in to look after the family. She told Vilas that Pramila was a witch—a woman possessed. And that he should forget her. Vilas didn't want to. Foolishly, he set off for Bombay without knowing where to begin looking for his absconding spouse.

The people in his office had laughed at him. They had called him an ass and told him he was wasting his time. 'She's gone. You'll never find her,' they had jeered. But Vilas had refused to believe them.

He came back a week later. His colleagues had been right. His mother had been right. He hadn't found her. Pramila had gone. Disappeared from their lives. Bombay had claimed another victim. Or trophy.

A few months later, they received a letter from Pramila. She had found a job in a Marathi fortnightly and was staying as a paying guest in Dadar. She was sorry, she said. But she couldn't bear to live in Nagpur. How are the children, she asked. And you? Yes, of course she missed all of them sorely. But she had no choice. She was happy. And was planning a trip to Nagpur shortly, as soon as she could get leave. There was no forwarding address.

Nearly a year after her departure, Pramila went back to Nagpur. Vilas was stony-faced and hostile. The youngest child ran and hid behind the grandmother, while the older two rushed eagerly towards her and asked for presents from Bombay.

Pramila was in Nagpur on a specific mission. She wanted a divorce. And the children. Vilas was stunned. His mother wasn't. 'Give her the divorce and keep the children,' she advised.

Vilas consulted his lawyer friend. 'Your mother is right,' he said. But Vilas was adamant. 'I want her,' he moaned. They arrived at a compromise. 'Take the girls,' the mother screamed. 'The son is ours. He bears our name.' And so it was that after battling for ten days, Pramila took the train back to Bombay with two very frightened little girls with her.

Of course it didn't work. She couldn't cope. The job kept her away for long hours. The older child went to a grimy nursery in the morning while an untidy, illiterate bai managed the younger one at home. Then both of them collected the school-going kid and came back to the room where they remained locked up till their mother came back late in the evening, exhausted, irritable and in no condition to deal with emotional problems. They had worked out a dabba arrangement with a neighbourhood eatery. This was heated and reheated twice a day and fed to everyone. The bai went home at night, leaving Pramila to cope with bed-wetting, crying spells, hunger and tantrums. Then there were frequent small illnesses to deal with. Flu, upset tummies, colic, small cuts and all the other 'inconveniences' that go with raising children. Pramila decided it wasn't going to be possible for her carry on with this crazy situation. She packed the younger kid back to her father which left the older resentful and sulky. 'Why can't I go back to Aji also?' she whined constantly, making Pramila feel even more exasperated. Soon, the bai walked out on her as well. Which meant applying for leave without pay and staying home to look after the little girl while searching frantically for a substitute maid.

Her bosses were understanding but even they couldn't stretch privileges endlessly to accommodate Pramila's problems. It was time for her to look around and move on—which she promptly did. But not before she'd sought audiences with various ministers at the Mantralaya and secured a cosy little place for herself in Kala Nagar, an unpretentious colony near the airport reserved for writers and artists. It was said that her desperation had pushed her to appeal to the C.M. himself who had been so moved by her plight that he had asked for her file and personally sanctioned the place to her. Pramila was certainly getting around in the right circles and making the right moves.

It was at this point that God ran into her through Yashwantbhai, who was trying to induct her into politics.

'We need women like you,' Yashwantbhai leered at their first meeting, scratching his groin thoughtfully. 'Politics... women's issues... you are the right person. You could head our Special Cell. It is a good job. Good pay. We will look after your daughter's education... everything. Also... you will be protected. This city... it is not Nagpur. Full of bad people... *badmashes*. They can harass a single woman... a helpless woman... anything can happen. You have to think of your safety... get my point?'

Pramila got the point. Very quickly. She quit her job and started working full-time for 'the party'. But she continued writing. First for Marathi publications and then venturing timidly into English ones.

God was assigned to translate her early poems for *Plume* and interview her for a newly-launched city magazine that wanted to be 'different' and feature people outside the incestuous celebrity circuit. Pramila's quotes were refreshingly original. She didn't dramatize her life in a vulgar fashion like some, especially the other women spearheading the feminist movement in Bombay. She spoke with a restraint and dignity which appealed to the middle classes who found it impossible to relate to the gut-wrenching catharsis of socialites who had almost succeeded in making battering a status-symbol. Pramila was emerging as a 'Woman of Substance' (that's what God titled his piece, rather unimaginatively). Their attraction was inevitable and also understandable. Soon God took to spending weekends at her Kala Nagar home, actually playing daddy to her little girl and often taking her for outings without her mother. The little girl was relieved to have a man around the place after so many months. The poor child usually couldn't wait for Pramila to get home.

The arrangement at Kala Nagar was no better than the previous one. If anything, it was worse. Shruti, at age seven, was given the key to the lock on the front door. Her meal was left in a tiffin box on the kitchen table. After school, she walked home, let herself in, ate from the tiffin box and waited for the mother to return. Sometimes, she was even locked in 'for safety' before Pramila left again for an urgent meeting at night. It was then that Shruti began to develop phobias and immense fears. She'd wait in the dark, by the barred window of the small room, searching the dimly-lit street in front of their house for some signs of her mother.

God was moved by her plight. 'How can you do this to her?' he asked Pramila angrily. 'It just isn't fair. If you don't have the time to raise a child—send her home to her father.'

Pramila stared at him impassively and said, 'I would gladly do that—but he doesn't want her.' Shruti, in the bathroom, heard this conversation clearly. It was one conversation she never forgot.

God took to visiting Shruti on the days he knew Pramila would be away attending to distress calls from various women while ignoring the distressed victim she'd left behind at home. God would play the flute for Shruti and engage her attention with tales made up on the spur of the moment. On an impulse, he decided to buy her a television. Shruti was ecstatic. Her mother wasn't.

'I don't approve of such things,' she sternly admonished God.

'And I don't approve of you,' he responded.

'You have no right to decide what is good for my child,' she screamed.

'And you, my dear, have no right to be a mother,' he countered. Whether it was predominantly a sense of compassion for Shruti or a genuine feeling for her mother, God, in one of his usual impulsive moments, proposed marriage to Pramila. She wasn't interested. At least, not immediately. Besides, she was worried about Yashwantbhai's reaction. He had been so generous, so kind, often making sure his car dropped her home after a late-night conference. If God knew about his involvement, he didn't discuss it.

Meanwhile, God himself was completely immersed in Yashwantbhai's various operations, frequently planting positive stories about his good works of charity. He had rapidly moved up in Yashwantbhai's hierarchy... even a trouble-shooter for the champion fixer himself. Yashwantbhai did not belong to any political party—he preferred to finance candidates instead. Candidates of any and every hue, provided they had a large enough base. 'I am not interested in seeking any office for myself,' he'd boast, 'I'm bigger than any chief minister.' Which in a way was true. No matter how 'big' he was Yashwantbhai needed God to deal effectively with the press. God was perfectly aware of this and used it to his own advantage, becoming for all practical purposes, Yashwantbhai's chief minder and henchman. In return Yashwantbhai made sure God was comfortable—out-of-turn allotments of precious commodities such as cooking gas, telephone and now... a brand new Maruti.

Initially, God used to feel a little sheepish when any of his new acquisitions were mentioned. But the embarrassment soon wore off and was replaced by a devil-may-care cockiness. 'I deserve all this, damn it,' he'd snapped, when I'd teased him lightly about his smartly-tailored suit made from a premium suit material manufactured by a mill Yashwantbhai's name was associated with. 'Licenses,' people would whisper referring to his clandestine involvement. But God chose to concentrate on the arch rival of this mill and carried on an organized campaign against him. It was all so blatant and depressing. Only God didn't see it that way. *'Chhodo, yaar,* that's the way the game is played. If it's too hot for you... shut up.' While I didn't exactly spend sleepless nights worrying over God's future, there were times I felt severely disturbed by his drift. It seemed a dangerous game. And I wasn't sure he knew all the rules. He only thought he did. Like the time he got mixed up in the messy lives of the Khannas. And dragged me into the muck with him. The Khannas were trying hard to woo Yashwantbhai, whose goons were making trouble for them at their suburban factory. God was playing mediator. I went along for the kicks.

The Khannas lived in a swanky highrise. Their apartment resembled a hot-house with glass and plants everywhere. Dharam and his wife Ruki were in trouble. Marital and financial. God got to know about both. 'Such info is useful, *yaar*,' he told me, 'it can be used as leverage.' As it eventually was.

'Once a bitch, always a bitch,' Dharam snarled, his lips curving maliciously over his nicotine-stained teeth.

'Yes... darling...' Ruki purred back, exposing her fleshy thighs though a transparent nightie, 'just like... once a bastard always a bastard.'

'Don't call me that... I warn you,' he tried to make a move in her direction, but with all the whisky in him, he couldn't get beyond two sloppy steps.

'Did I call you something?' she asked arching her eyebrows, one hand busy filing her long nails.

'Why did you accept the watch—BITCH!' he bellowed.

'Which watch?' she asked sweetly, curiously.

'You bloody well know which one.'

'Oh that? Piagets make such darling post-coital gifts, don't they?' she said absently and went back to her nails.

'You have to stop your affair... or else... or else....'

271

'Or else what, sweetheart? Don't be so dull. Let's have some intelligent conversation for a change. Tell me... how did you perform at the AGM?'

'I'm talking about that bloody watch and the fucking man... you have to stop seeing him.'

'Tch! Tch! Back to the same old thing. Like a broken record. Let's flip the side at least. Or are we listening to a CD?'

'Why do you do this to me? What sadistic pleasure do you get out of it? Wasn't it enough that I rescued you from the gutters. Where would you have been if I hadn't married you? Whoring away somewhere.'

'Stop sounding so holier than thou, darling, it doesn't suit you at all. I am what I am—you married a bitch, now learn to live with one.'

It was Sunday morning as usual for the Khannas. A Sunday morning like dozens they'd seen before. And were likely to in future. They'd been married five years now. Five stormy, tempestuous years. It was the second time round for both of them. His first wife had left him for his best friend, while Ruki had driven her husband to suicide. Murder, insisted her friends. When the two of them met, it seemed inevitable that they'd latch on to each other. She was looking for a home. Not just any home. Preferably, a penthouse. He wanted a glamorous woman to prove to the world he wasn't impotent. He actually was. Luckily for both of them, there were no children from their respective earlier marriages. And, of course, there was no question now of having any in this one. Ruki was a vibrant, bright person who attracted all sorts. At that moment, her most besotted admirer was a small-time businessman with big-time plans. Her husband's associate actually. He plied her with presents painstakingly planned and organized from all corners of the world. If it was a Piaget today, it could be a Cartier tomorrow. Ruki had expensive tastes and habits. She often washed her hair with Dom Perignon, just to get the right bounce into it.

Her husband, Dharam, was a pathetic man with a nervous giggle. The giggle disconcerted everybody since it emerged at the most unexpected moments and without any apparent reason. She was considered outrageous, witty, sharp and sexy. She flirted, oh yes, she did, but in a way that was seductive rather than cheap. He just drank. That was it. He drank. And smoked compulsively, of course. 'The two things go together,' he'd giggle, while she tickled his leg with her bare toe. Yet, the Khannas were considered a great couple. 'Such fun to have at parties,' everybody said.

The Khanna dogs were as famous as they were. 'Love me, love my dogs,' said Ruki as she walked into parties with the two Great Danes dogging her footsteps docilely. Many nasty stories did the rounds as to how 'close' the relationship of the mistress was with her pets, but she laughed it all off: 'Why, sweethearts? Are there no men left in Bombay?'

Their 'best friends', the Baroohas, were another dissipated couple who had been married for twenty years and survived. They all had one thing in common—booze. As Ruki in her brighter moments would point out, 'More marriages in Bombay are destroyed by booze than by infidelity.' She was probably right.

The Baroohas had one anthem—'Our children terrify us.' Which they did. Their son was nineteen, their daughter seventeen and between them they had succeeded in terrorizing their parents to a point where they were actually frightened of being in the same room with their offspring. Servants reported with glee that often Vikki-baba threw assorted *objets* at his mother and called her names ranging from 'nympho' to 'bitch'. The daughter, Sweetie, adopted different tactics—she killed her parents with cruelty. Cold-blooded mental cruelty. It was a constant refrain, an unending taunt, 'Where were you when I got my first period? Where were you when they threw me out of school? Where were you when I met with an accident? Where were you when my boyfriend knocked me up and I nearly bled to death on some quack's operating table?' She stared at them unblinkingly, each glance rapier-sharp.

'I can't bear to look into her eyes,' her mother confessed. 'She has a hypnotic effect. I feel she is constantly accusing me of something... and waiting... waiting for what?... perhaps to kill me.'

They'd tried everything including bribery. It didn't work. 'Our kids are far too smart,' they'd laugh uncomfortably in public. 'You can't buy them.'

'Try love,' someone finally suggested.

'It won't work, it's too late,' Mrs B admitted swiftly, candidly.


Into their world came a black man. Literally, black. He was with the American Consulate. His designation was unclear. People suspected he was a C.I.A. agent which he probably was. But Stash sure got around in the city's high-flying social circle. Stash was laid-back, charming and a stud to boot. And, it was whispered, he had this scar.

'What scar?' innocents would ask.

'Oooh... this *magnificent* scar,' the socialites would groan.

'Where did he get it?'

'He doesn't say. Maybe he was a gangster in Chicago before he joined the foreign service,' said one woman moonily.

'Maybe he's a Vietnam vet who was slashed by a guerilla,' fantasized another.

'Maybe he was with the D.E.A.... you know those drug chaps who do all sorts of heroic things in Colombia,' volunteered a third.

'Maybe he just fell off a ladder in his backyard,' laughed a fourth and that just about clinched the debate. It didn't matter where Stash had acquired his dramatic scar which started at his left shoulder and travelled all the way down his hard-as-steel belly. But each time he went for a swim at the Breach Candy pool, a hush would follow his graceful dive, as others would freeze all activity to stare at his scar. Stash seemed to genuinely like India and Indians. He cultivated all kinds—from drop-outs to socialites looking for a good time. His 'open house' Sunday brunches used to attract everybody from art film types to painters like Iqbal. And of course, the Rukis and Sweeties of Bombay.

It was at the home of the Sachs that the Baroohas ran into Stash (and discovered that he had been dating their daughter). The Sachs were an interesting couple—he a German, she a Goan he'd met on the sands of Baga beach when both were stoned. Their parties were considered fun, because they combined Bavarian beer and sausages with spicy Goan prawn curries... with a crowd that was as interesting as the cuisine.

Cheetah, the Goan girl, had begun to look and sound German with her bleached blonde hair and black leather outfits worn through Bombay's sweltering summers. Some said unkindly that she looked like a hooker from Hamburg and behaved like one, while her husband resembled a Neo-Nazi with his close-cropped hair and manic blue eyes. Herr Herman was a strange man (kinky, according to insiders). He'd been in India for ten years and obviously had no intentions of going back. How he managed to stay on, nobody knew. But the Sachs lived well, in a house full of brooding etchings (most Teutonic) and cheerful Madhubanis. They entertained often, preferring Friday nights, so that hungover friends could stick around and surface at noon the next afternoon. Or sometimes even later... in time for a tall drink to take in the sunset on the balcony and listen to the sound of the waves crashing on the rocks downstairs.

Stash was cool... real cool, when Mrs B confronted him.

He tried being polite, 'Lady, your daughter isn't a little girl any longer. She knows what she's doing.'

But Mrs B wouldn't let up. Mr B looked foolish as he bit into a frankfurter and asked for a can of beer. He could sense his wife's mood. She was egging Stash on... and he wasn't sure why. But he could guess. Perhaps she was jealous. She did have this competitive thing with Sweetie. And of late, she'd been making her rivalry pretty obvious. It happened with him too. If he ever paid Sweetie one compliment too many his wife would come down on him heavily, 'That girl's head is big enough. Why do you keep showering her with stupid compliments?' If Sweetie sensed her mother's attitude (and Sweetie was a sharp girl), she chose to ignore it. Though there were times when it appeared as if she was flaunting herself, flirting with her father or any male present, just to torment Mrs B.

Mrs Khanna would tell her friend not to panic. 'Look, love, it happens to all of us. We all have to face age… wrinkles, fat thighs droopy boobs… so what? Sweetie is a beauty. Be proud of her. Enjoy her. Don't try and keep up with her, or you'll end up with slashed wrists in a bathtub.'

Mrs B agreed with her and yet she couldn't resist the temptation to camouflage her years. She'd giggle at parties, 'My, my, it's so silly… but whenever Sweetie and I go out, people stare at us and say, wow… who is the mother and who the daughter?'

Sweetie would glare at her and snap, 'I've never heard that.'

Or Mrs B would walk into Sweetie's room and ask casually, 'Mind if I borrow your white sweater? In any case, white doesn't do much for you… it looks better on me.'

Her favourite stories about shopping abroad revolved around all the times Sweetie and she went looking for clothes together only to be told by astonished shop girls, 'Hey! You two mother and daughter? Man… that's real neat.' And Mrs B would go on to describe how she could fit perfectly into her jeans while Sweetie had to have hers altered. 'Imagine... I haven't worn skirts since I left school... my legs are nice and all that... but in those days girls switched to saris by the time they were sixteen. And last year when we were looking for things for Sweetie, the shop assistant said, "Why don't you try on one of these?" And guess what it was? A tight skirt... really clingy! I thought, "My God—how can I wear this? What will hubby say? And Vikki-baba?"

'But the woman insisted, so I said, "Fine, no harm in trying it on." Do you know when I walked out of the changing room, people stopped and stared! Too much, *yaar!* The woman said, "It looks great on you. Take it in all colours." They had six.

'So, again I thought, *"Koi boat nahi...* if I feel bad to wear these things in India, I'll pass them on to Sweetie." So I bought all six. Wore them all through the holiday. People didn't believe I was married. I went to a bar wearing the red one. At least two fellows tried to pick me up. Gave me cigarettes and what not. It was fun, *yaar.* After so many years I could feel the sun on my legs.' Someone asked her what her husband thought of her new wardrobe. 'I don't say anything about his ridiculous Polo shirts which are three sizes too small for him. At least I don't have a paunch. My figure is still good... so why hide it?'

To go with the new look, she'd also invested in snazzy accessories, and a complete make-over starting with her hair. She now wore it close-cropped and permed. It looked OK with her skirts, but when she wore saris and huge bindis, she looked like a transvestite. But nobody dared tell her that.

Now, here she was giving Stash the eye, staring intently at his crotch whenever she thought he wasn't looking.

'I don't like my daughter dating foreigners,' she said imperiously.

To which Stash retorted, 'Foreigners, ma'am? Or just blacks? Would you have objected as much if I'd been a white American?'

'What cheek!' said Mrs B. 'How dare you ask me something like that?'

'Be honest,' Stash carried on. 'It is the colour of my skin that scares you, doesn't it?'

'Rubbish!'

'It's happened to me before... don't worry. Especially in India.' And then he told her about the time he was asked by his white boss to stand in for him at some official function. When Stash got there, the Indian hosts waiting in the reception line refused to let him in! Finally, he produced his business card. At which point, one of the people from the welcoming committee had the grace to apologize but not before blurting out, 'Oh no... so sorry... but we were not expecting a negro. Never mind... come in, come in.'

'So you see,' Stash continued, 'it is the "never mind" attitude that betrays people. I didn't feel bad. Amused, maybe. But you Indians are the most colour-conscious people in the world.' And then, looking Mrs B straight in the eye, Stash turned on the juices: 'How about a swim this Sunday? Your daughter does great in the pool. I have a feeling you'll do even better.'

Mrs B found herself blushing. 'Oh… I don't know… I can't really swim… I don't have a swimsuit….'

Stash smiled and waited for her to finish. 'All that can be fixed… let's say eleven-thirty at the Breach Candy? I'll sign you in….'

Mrs B had finally scored one over her daughter… and this time she hadn't even tried. But it was Ruki who got Stash first. It was a cakewalk for her. And as she put it later, 'Every woman *must* have a black experience at least once in her life. And Stash is mine.'

Getting pictures of them cavorting in the swimming pool had been easy for God. All it took was a small bribe. An obliging servant from a neighbouring apartment that overlooked the pool took them with a simple telephoto lens. God was gloating as he showed them to me. 'That will take care of the Khannas. And that black bugger,' he said. 'The *langoor* will lose his job. And the Khannas their reputation.'

'How? Why?' I asked, genuinely puzzled.

'Everybody knows Ruki screws around…. So what's the difference this time?' God wiggled his eyebrows enigmatically, lowered his voice and said, 'C.I.A. Ever heard of it? C.I.A.'

I was still trying to figure that one out, when I overheard his call to Yashwantbhai's office. 'No problem… no problem. Yes we have the pictures. Yes they are clear. Yes, I can deliver enlargements by tomorrow. Yes, they will be in Dharam's office immediately. OK OK.' The strategy was simple—and as old as the hills—blackmail. I couldn't quite visualize Ruki as a modern-day Mata Hari, somehow. But those dreaded initials—C.I.A.—were enough to bring her husband crawling to Yashwantbhai with an offer to make permanent peace in exchange for the negatives. God had notched up another triumph. And impressed his boss. I wondered what his reward was this time? A mini-factory of his own?

# Thirteen

God had managed to infiltrate the super-exclusive 'Highness' Club. To those outside its hallowed precincts, it didn't exist. To belong to it, one had to have blood bluer than the Danube coursing through the veins. It was regarded as something of a joke to those who were aware of its existence but weren't a part of it. How God managed to wangle an invitation to a swanky party thrown by a derelict princeling eager to impress other equally derelict royals, I'll never know, but it had something to do with his being commissioned to write a lengthy piece by some Brit paper. The Raj had never gone out of style for a section of nostalgic readers residing in England. So much so, that editors short on ideas for weekend supplements invariably fell back on Raj-related stories with 'fresh' angles. This one wasn't very different. But it was a first for God.

'This is big time... phoren paper, *yaar,* everybody dies to write for them. One article and five thousand rupees.'

I tried to look impressed. 'So how are you planning to tackle the story? New angle?'

'Depends on the brief... will you help me?'

'I'll have to chuck up my job first.'

'Why don't you? Such a bore... writing shit for shitty people.'

'It pays.'

'*Theek hai...* so will some other job.'

'OK.'

'OK what?'

'OK, I'll quit.'

'You mean it?'

'Test me.'

I did just that. Quit. It was quite painless. Roy asked whether I'd like freelance for them and I agreed. Kawla and the studio boys decided to give me a farewell. They asked the typist to make out a list with a separate column to fill in contributions.

'Must keep proper accounts,' Kawla said.

'Yes, that's important,' I agreed.

I felt embarrassed when the peon came around to each table and everybody reached for their wallets. They didn't feel at all shy as they debated on whether to shell out ten bucks, fifteen or twenty. At the end of the exercise they had managed to collect one hundred and eighty-five rupees. Kawla pondered over the menu for the treat. He was keen on chivda, samosas, barfi and bananas. The others preferred bhajiyas and pastries. They compromised by knocking off barfi and including pastries. But that left a shortfall of thirty-five rupees. Everyone grumbled and the calculations started all over again. I intervened and offered to make up the deficit.

'No, no, no,' they protested in a chorus, 'that is not allowed.' Someone pulled out a calculator and decided it would mean two rupees more per person.

'What about cold drinks?' someone else piped up. 'Gold Spot? Limca? Thums Up?'

'Yes, we must have cold drinks... so hot otherwise.'

'That means another two rupees,' the amateur accountant said. Eventually, the cold drinks were dropped and the canteen boy was instructed to produce an extra round of tea.

The whole thing was rather sweet and touching. Especially the part when the typist hesitantly produced a gift.

'It is from all of us,' she said. 'I hope you like it... open it, open it.'

I didn't really want to, but they would have been disappointed. It turned out to be a crocheted bag with bamboo handles. The kind Goan maids brought to Dhobi Talao market for vegetables. I tried to look enthusiastic and gushed over it. 'Just what I needed,' I said.

'Liar,' a voice hissed in my ears. It was Willie. I winked at him. I was going to miss him.

The executives asked me for a free date so that we could all meet up at Aarti's place for drinks and Bhendi Bazaar biryani. I got the feeling they were just being formal and hoping I'd decline. For a perverse moment I felt like accepting—just to see their crestfallen expressions. But decided it wasn't worth it. So I made up a story about a long holiday abroad, picked up the hideous crochet bag and left, Aarti staring quizzically after me, her hands busy as usual tugging at her underarm hair.

❉

God had been granted a pretty generous travel allowance. Or so he claimed. Besides the article on royalty for the Brit paper, he had been commissioned a couple of times by an NRI lifestyle glossy, and he'd successfully managed to squeeze additional funds out of the commissioning editors. As he put it, 'These fuckers try to short-change local writers while paying the top buck to their own *chootiyas*. I know how this game works now. It's all a question of getting that first byline. In any case, it's cheaper for them to pay someone like me than send out a reporter.'

I was pretty impressed. Most Indian journalists felt so privileged just to be asked to write by some cruddy foreign publication, they ended up doing it for peanuts. But not God. 'Time is money, *yaar*,' he'd say lazily, adding,

'Besides, I like screwing those fuckers.' God was getting to like his newly-acquired status.

*Plume* had acquired the reputation of being India's first major literary journal. One that looked as good as it read. And God was justifiably proud of his role in its unexpected success. Its monthly schedule left him plenty of time to take on other assignments—like the current one. Professionally at least, things were beginning to look up for God.

On the personal front we had graduated to being buddies. Maybe both of us preferred it that way. I missed the old passion and romantic tug sometimes, but this version of God was easier on my heart and mind. We met frequently enough—but without the old accusations, demands and fights. God was more relaxed (and more secure) about himself. So was I. It made it easier for both of us to occasionally work on a piece together.

He was trying to swing some more lolly out of his publishers so that I'd be covered. I was looking forward to going exotic with him, visiting palaces and interviewing royalty. The only rajkumari I knew was broke and batty. She'd come to our home a couple of times along with some ladies' group raising funds for saving Tehri Garhwal. It could have been Red Cross charities. Or starving Ethiopians. Despite her tacky appearance, I'd been fascinated by her. Hooded eyes, hooked nose, overpainted mouth, dyed hair, faded chiffon sari and strands and strands of pearls ('Fake,' said the corporate wives knowingly). Yet, she'd taken over the proceedings and filled the room with her presence. She'd behaved like she was holding a durbar and the rest were handmaidens. Imperious, arrogant and penniless. When she had asked for a tenner for a taxi back home, it was a royal command that nobody dared to refuse. Lots of handbags had flown open and she had picked up all the takings. The act was so stylishly performed that the women looked almost flattered and grateful.

I was keen on God featuring her. 'That zombie? No, don't be crazy. She doesn't have a dime to her name and faces eviction. Her children have disowned her... so have the other Highnesses. She isn't allowed into the club as she hasn't paid her dues. Wonder who pays for her hair dye... or maybe she uses shoe polish.'

'If you don't want to do her... I will,' I said spontaneously.

'Who for?'

'Oh... I don't know. I'll just do it and then worry about flogging the piece.'

'*Theek hai*, but don't try and palm it off on me. I don't want to blow my first big assignment for these phirang guys.'


Her Highness Kanwal Kumari of Dhogragarh, was considered a joke—an unfunny one.

'She is a royal pain in the ass,' said a Maharaja to God while he was being interviewed and photographed.

'A scrounger,' his wife chipped in.

'That hag-bag—I wouldn't have her in my house. She probably has fleas,' bitched another princeling— a minor one.

'Her "state" even in the old days, was the size of my handkerchief,' sniffed a Maharani with pink hair.

'She isn't even legitimate... one of several bastard children,' claimed an erstwhile sardar.

'Nothing but tall claims. Anything to sponge a meal off someone,' insisted an ex-bridge companion.

And yet, I found her compelling. She had more class than the lot of them. And she was still striking in her sixties, or seventies or eighties. It was hard to tell.

'What do you find in that old bag?' God asked with great irritation, after I'd spent three hours with her. It had cost me a lunch at a nearby Irani's, but I didn't mind. I'd enjoyed watching her stately progress through the over-crowded restaurant full of office-goers and share bazaar brokers. She'd sailed through them all, majestically, regally, till she'd commandeered a convenient table for the two of us. I was amazed at her appetite. She'd run through an egg curry, two naans and a plate of chicken biryani, before asking for a tall glass of falooda. Then with great panache, she'd wiped her greasy mouth, reapplied bright orange lipstick and stuck a cigarette holder between her lips. I fumbled around for matches—I always carried them for God. She waited patiently till I found them.

'Ashtray,' she'd whispered throatily to a passing waiter, who was totally foxed. Everybody there just flicked ash into the nearest dish. 'Filthy habit, don't you think?' she'd asked me.

I'd nodded in agreement and echoed, 'Filthy.'

I sent her story to the Sunday supplement of a local paper. It was accepted. I was astonished and delighted. They needed pictures. I thought of Pebbles and decided against it. His rates had zoomed into the stratosphere and he had become a one-man industry cornering just about every assignment in the market. God recommended a comparative newcomer, a brooding, bearded, silent-as-death, bear of a man. He was so hairy and so quiet, it disoriented me. Had he opened his mouth and spoken, I wouldn't have had to concentrate on the forest on his forearms. It was amazing, the fuzz all over D.D. (nobody ever asked him what D.D. stood for and nobody knew). I often wondered how he encashed cheques and what the name on his passport read. I even asked once. But he stared at me intently and looked away with a stricken expression.

Kanwal Kumari of Dogragarh ate out on the story for weeks after that. There was something so poignant about her kind of poverty that she soon had the media creeping up to cash in on it. The little piece on her got picked up by the biggies. She made it to a television clip on a popular news-cassette magazine. And it wasn't long before the Raj-hungry Brits got her. Her Highness found herself the subject of a Channel 4 documentary. What's more, she got paid handsomely for it. And they threw in three French chiffons too. I was glad for her. But even gladder for myself I had finally found something to do. Something more interesting than fooling around with a semi-colon for a fortnight and then finally scrapping the ad.

My first freelance assignment for the agency was a crazy one. De Boss called me in one morning. He was at his favourite pastime, playing with balls—if that sounds like a cheap joke, it is. He was doing it all the time, one way or the other. Under the desk or over the billiard table.

'Aah… Nisha. How are things?' he asked, still playing.

'OK. The usual.'

'Well… I was just wondering… remember Mrs Bhalla, the client-who-wasn't? Well… she's having this party… I understand it's THE thing these days. Theme parties… been to one? She wants us to co-ordinate it, suggest an appropriate theme, work on the cards, help her out with the guest-list… that sort of thing. I thought

I'd put you on the job, you have a good head for stuff like this.'

I stared at his bare toes (he always knocked off his shoes the moment he entered his cavern). The man sure had strange notions about my abilities. Theme parties and I? I told him theme parties were old hat and had gone out with bell-bottom pants and blue movies. The 'in' thing as I understood it, were tequila parties where everybody got boozed up and danced the Mexican shuffle with the cook.

I called and told Mrs Bhalla as much. She was silent for a while and said, 'Yes, yes, yes, but in our circle we only drink is-kotch and sherry.'

Did she have a theme in mind?

'Our friends like to dress up.'

'Fancy dress?'

'Not like clowns, that is for children… we like to wear different-different clothes. Clothes we don't usually wear.'

She didn't mean drag, did she? She hadn t heard of it. So I tiredly suggested fantasy… and she jumped.

'*Kya* idea!'

I felt obliged to tell her that fantasy parties had been done to death. It was Mrs Bhalla's turn to remind me that there was, after all, no limit to fantasy.

'Anything is possible,' she gloated.

'So it is,' I agreed, 'Why not a Rich Bitch Party,' I asked her. She thought it over carefully and said, 'But what about the men?'

'They can come too... haven't you met male bitches?' I volunteered.

'I will have to ask my husband... he is quite conservative you know,' she giggled.

'Tell him it will be the talk of the town and he'll agree,' I suggested.

'Yes... we can also serve tequila along with the is-kotch... that way, we'll have both—theme and tequila.'

We worked on her party with Kawla feeling more than a little inspired. He came up with a cut-out card. A black pom with a diamond collar. The wording in doggy-speak ended with a 'Bow wow back on 671892 if you are attending. Dress: Any bitch way you can.'

God was dying to gatecrash. I hadn't been to a party with him in ages. As a matter of fact, I hadn't really been seeing him all that regularly. I'd realized by then that it was impossible to tie someone like God down to a socially-correct relationship involving daily meetings, phone calls and exchanges. There was no question of a commitment from his side. Perhaps there never had been one. I'd accepted the premise—reluctantly at first and then with tolerant resignation. God was a free spirit. And, in my own way, I suppose, so was I. The 'Pramila' chapter had upset me... even hurt me. But I hadn't kept up with it on an obsessive level. I didn't even ask him whether it was on or off when he strolled in unexpectedly one wretchedly hot day and lit a beedi cheerfully. I watched him sweat all over my table, I even held his clammy hands in mine. It was good to see him again. And this party was exactly what we both needed to unwind and have some fun together.

'*Chalo,* let's check it out,' I said but refused to dress in anything but my usual party sari. God was keen on playing the part and asked my advice. 'Why not something sexy? Like, how about a silver bikini?' I said.

'I don't want to spend any money.'

So Kawla and I came up with a crushed foil tube outfit that we stapled into place on him. It looked rather spectacular if absurd. God was worried about his hairy legs and chest. He should've relaxed. That mad evening saw hairier men in lamé bikinis. If anyone stood out, it was I. Someone came up and asked me why I hadn't dressed up.

Before I could reply, God interjected, 'Because she isn't a rich bitch. Only a poor one.' He was helping himself to one tequila after another even after I'd warned him that tequila was different from *bewda.* 'Get off my case, *yaar,*' he snarled. 'Always spoiling my fun.'

I wandered off to talk to a woman in slinky black. She had stuck on a poodle's tail and made a poodle puff out of her hair. She looked pretty stunning. I don't know how she'd rigged it, but with a flick of her finger, she was able to wag her tail. I instructed the photographer to click her. Mrs Bhalla was determined to have her party splashed in a society glossy that featured 'happenings' like this one.

The poodle turned to me and said, 'Don't I know you from somewhere? Where?' I looked blank but interested. 'Aren't you... wait a minute... aren't you Verma's daughter... the one who used to win all those prizes at school? Of course, you are. And how you have changed. What do you do these days? And why are you so peculiarly dressed? I'm surprised Kamlesh let you in wearing that sari.'

'There's nothing wrong with my sari. And talking of being peculiarly dressed, how about you?'

'Don't get so touchy, my dear. I wasn't being bitchy... sorry... I shouldn't admit that tonight. But you do seem rather out of place. A drink?'

'No thanks. And do I know you?'

'I'm not sure... unless your father confided all his secrets in you. And knowing Champ-oh... that's what I called him those days... as well as I do, he couldn't have told you. I was his dirty little secret before that smelly Sindhi took over. But we were discreet, your father and I. We didn't flaunt our affair the way that bitch did. You talked to me over the phone several times... now do you recognize me... or at least, my voice? I'm Flora... remember me now? I was your father's secretary. I was the one who kept track of your birthday and your parents' anniversary. You'd got lost once—remember? The car didn't reach your school on time and you started to walk home? Your father was panic-stricken. I had to phone your mother to inform her. Anyway—now you know.'

Just then, God lurched up and pulled Flora's tail. She whirled around to see who it was... and then laughed. 'It's you! I should've known. Ever ready to chase a piece of tail, huh? How have you been?'

God put his paws on her bare shoulders and tried to kiss her mouth. 'Down, boy, down,' she said, 'Ron might be looking... and he's a very jealous man.'

'Who's this Ron-Shon, *yaar?*' God demanded.

'He's... he's my husband. There... that's him,' she said pointing to a huge foreigner drinking beer.

'That bastard... how come you married him?'

'I fell in love with the bastard,' Flora laughed.

'You would,' God sneered. 'What does he do with himself these days... he's out of the team, isn't he? Bloody fool. Fighting with umpires. Abusing players. Where did you meet him?'

'At a match... naturally,' Flora said.

'Stop your bullshit. You must've been one of the girls lined up for the cricketers by that goddess. What's her name?' God asked, turning to me.

'I don't know.'

'Of course you know! Stop playing dumb. She's the one who *lagaoes* a lot of *bhav...* married to the TV joker. Forever throwing parties for visiting jocks,' God continued.

'It's not important,' I said, adding, 'I can see the bastard heading towards us... and he doesn't look very happy.'

'Back off, Deb,' Flora warned, looking nervous. 'You know what Ron is like. Hurry. But you might trip... watch your step.'

God had borrowed a ridiculously high-heeled pair of sandals from a model-friend of his. The only girl in town who wore a size nine. Now he was unable to take two steps without stumbling. In any case, he was far too sloshed. He just stood there leering while Ron approached us making his way through the crowd. He was looking pretty ridiculous too, dressed in a sequinned gown with two red balloons stuffed into the neckline. He came directly up to God and without a word, tore off the foil. God's hands flew to his crotch.

Ron bellowed, 'Just one hand will do, mate. You don't need the other. Not much of a man are you?'

I felt very sorry for God at that minute. He looked so puny, miserable and ridiculous, standing there starkers on his high heels, his beard full of bread crumbs, a half-smoked cigarette in one hand, a glass of tequila in the other. The party continued to whirl around us, with just the bartender gazing intently at God's exposed genitals.

Flora, in one graceful gesture, took the cigarette from God's limp fingers and pulled at it briefly. Once the tip was glowing again, she flicked off the ash, raised her arm languidly and burst the red balloons stuffed into Ron's gown. Bang! Bang! The sound attracted some attention but not much. Ron blinked and looked down at his deflated breasts with a puzzled air. The neckline, without anything to fill it, flopped down his chest—exposing a bright red wart. Flora returned the cigarette to God's mouth, tweaked my cheek and started to walk away.

'Where do you think you are going, bitch?' Ron hollered after her and lunged for her tail. He managed to grab it just as she pulled away. It came off in his hand and he stared at it stupidly. God had taken refuge behind the bar by now. Ron chucked the tail at him and said, 'Here... you went sniffing after Flora's tail... you've got it. Go frig with it, cunt.'

The bartender replenished God's glass and gave him his apron to wear around his waist. And that's how we left the party, with God's naked bum wiggling past Mrs Bhalla at the door as we went in search of a cab.

❋

Writing for Sunday supplements was fine. And fun. But it didn't fetch me too much money. And money was what I needed. Badly. Besides, freelancers are the real pariahs of journalism—nobody pays them either on time or sufficiently. Yet, everybody needs them. I had assignments galore. I even got to travel.... Well, mainly to hick places the staffers didn't want to go to. It was enjoyable... but hardly rewarding in monetary terms. But I went along for the ride, covering abandoned monuments, abandoned wives, abandoned pets and abandoned dreams. Something was clearly wrong—I was working harder than ever before in my life, but my bank balance was dismally low. And horror of horrors, the importance of money had begun to dawn on me... finally.

I also discovered to my utter surprise that I had business sense. This was by accident. A schoolfriend showed up unexpectedly from Dubai. 'Can you supply basmati rice and chick peas to a few grocers there?' she asked. Rather a strange enquiry addressed to someone who was neither a farmer nor a shopkeeper. Recklessly, I agreed. And that's how I became a trader. Did it really represent much of a progression from being a lowly ad agency hack? Not really. But selling chickpeas to the Arabs was more fun than selling cigarettes to the locals.

My new-found career also brought with it a whole bunch of fresh friends—the 'Gulfies' as they were called. It was a loosely-knit fraternity of people who had once lived in the Gulf and were dreaming of the day when they could pack up their dishwasher and micro oven and take the first Gulf Air flight to anywhere—Muscat, Bahrain, Kuwait, it didn't really matter.

I met Harsh and his terrifyingly talented wife, Bubli, die-hard Gulfies who now lived in Bombay and were engaged in some highly dubious trading activity, at one of the first 'Gulfie' parties I attended.

'So long as they aren't selling little boys to sheikhs, whether for camel racing or buggering, they are all right,' God warned me. He had just done a major exposé on that vile practice and was full of moral outrage, huffing and puffing about cruelty to kids and exploitation. He was still close to Pramila's daughter and perhaps their closeness had something to do with his tenderness towards children.

Bubli was anything but bubbly. She was an incredibly ugly woman with a cave-like mouth, painted mud brown. She designed ferocious-looking jewellery using bone, horn, metal scrap, ropes and other rough stuff. For some perfectly irrational reason her chunky ornaments had become the rage, both in Bombay and New York, where she was selling to ritzy stores like Sak's. Using all her old Gulf contacts, she'd set up shop at the Hilton in Dubai with one of the wives of one of the sheikhs as a local partner. It was unclear what Harsh was selling besides himself. 'A male whore' was how I'd heard him described at a party. Theirs was certainly a strange marriage. What in their circle was referred to as a 'Typical Bombay marriage, *yaar*. She goes her way and he goes his'. Both of them were sharp dressers and known for their good taste. They'd survived in the Gulf without succumbing to synthetics. At one point, he had sold trendy cottons to Australia and by that transaction alone, he called himself a 'designer' with his own label. She too designed clothes—one-of-a-kind garments, painstakingly put together from bits and pieces bought from a jari-puranawalla. They looked sensational and sold very well with women who wore them once and chucked them into storage.

'In any case, darling,' said a TV star who specialized in quiz shows, 'her finish is so atrocious, the clothes just fall apart after one wear. I was deeply embarrassed one day at the studios. There I was introducing last week's winning team to everybody on camera, when I heard the first rrrrip. I ignored it and carried on with my arm extended. Then I heard the second rrrrip... and with it, the sleeve fell off. Yes! It just fell right off and lay there on the floor. The contestants didn't know what to do. I saw a giggle being suppressed, so I decided to make a big joke of the whole thing. I said, "Oh, oh... aren't you relieved? Bet you thought I still had a few tricks up my sleeve—right?"'

While Bubli looked morose and menopausal, Harsh was the extrovert, reaching out, grabbing hands and kissing everybody, literally everybody, including a few startled male guests. At first it was assumed that he was suffering from a Middle-Eastern hangover. Arafat, Gaddafi and other celebrity Arabs were always seen kissing other men. It was only when a particularly

outraged designer came spluttering out of the loo, that
the story finally got out. Harsh swung both ways. And
so did his wife though she was far more restrained about
her inclinations.

The designer had been attacked by the couple at a
party in their own home, but separately. He'd fobbed
off Bubli's advances by lying, 'Sorry, darling... I prefer
boys. Especially those in dhotis.' It wasn't definite whether
she'd passed this vital piece of info on to Harsh, but
minutes later Dhruv the Devil (his clothes label also
carried this legend) nearly fell out of his crushed cotton
kurta when Harsh grabbed him from the back, twirled
him around and planted a wet slobbering kiss full on
his wide open mouth (open with astonishment, not
desire, he clarified to whoever wanted the real story).
Did Dhruv stomp out of the party in a rage? 'Are you
kidding?' he countered, 'And miss out on the best
cannelloni in town?'

Bubli filled her non-working hours with manic physical
activity. She jogged, swam, rode and did aerobics. In
the little time that was left, she attended religious
discourses on the Gita. She went to bed with her favourite
guru's taped voice droning into her ears through hi-tech
headphones. The background music at the workshop
was restricted to bhajans.

Harsh found all this nauseating. Especially her party pronouncements on the subject. 'I am not a religious person,' she'd sigh, 'but I am deeply spiritual.' Most people ran towards the bar before she got any further. She treated me to a long lecture on divinity and Hindu awakening once. I rather enjoyed listening to her borrowed philosophy. It was a peculiar pastiche of recycled Rajneesh, Krishnamurti, Parthasarthy and B. R. Chopra's *Mahabharat*. But it touched me. She asked whether we could walk together in the morning and I readily agreed. Unlike Bubli, I couldn't work out or exercise on my own, and my waistline was beginning to expand alarmingly.

She had a fixed routine. Three brisk rounds of Oval Maidan at precisely 6.20. 'I have timed it, this way I get home at exactly 7.40... that's when Harsh likes his first cup of coffee in bed.'

'Why don't you get him to walk with you? Doesn't he work out? He looks pretty trim,' I said.

She looked at me with her ringed eyes and replied, 'We tried it. But he wanted to walk counter clockwise. And I prefer clockwise. It was then that I realized how that simple preference symbolized our marriage—we both wanted to go in different directions.'

'Did you tell that to your husband?'

'No way.'

'Why not?'

'It was already too late. At that point he was having an affair with his marketing manager—a lovely girl from Kerala we'd both met in Dubai and brought back to Bombay with us. She's a top model today. I'm sure you know her—Annu Joseph.'

'Of course, I know Annu. She did a couple of assignments for us. Gorgeous hair. Great eyes. Very sultry.'

'Yes... I sort of liked her too... you know....' Bubli left it at that. I imagined Harsh and her fighting over the dark beauty, with Harsh winning in the end. Perhaps reading my thoughts, she added, 'Harsh is very attractive... to women too,' I didn't say anything. 'Do you think so as well... that he's attractive?'

I was in a fix. How do you tell a woman you don't find her husband attractive... or even that you do? I changed the subject. 'Do you still see Annu?'

'No, but Harsh does. On the sly, of course.'

'How do you know?'

'I know. We sacked her, naturally... that's when she started modelling. She's even done a couple of catalogues for Harsh's clothes. I used her once for mine.'

'Didn't you feel anything?'

'Not really. She is the best right now. Besides, I didn't have to meet her or anything. Pebbles handled the assignment on his own. 'You know Pebbles, don't you?' Bubli asked.

'Yes, of course... from my agency days.'

'Does Annu still affect Harsh and you?'

'Let's put it this way... the other day I saw a photograph of her modelling jewellery in some Sunday supplement. I had to dispose of a used S.T. I deliberately wrapped it in her face before throwing it away. Silly? Maybe. But it gave me some sort of a thrill. Later, when I went to the evening Gita discourse, I meditated over my action and felt very small. But for that moment, I'd got my own back. I'm only human. Does this disgust you?'

I'd been dying to use Deborah Kerr's immortal line from *The Night of the Iguana* for years. I looked solemnly at Bubli and declared, with my nostrils appropriately flared, 'Nothing human disgusts me.' She looked very impressed.

I still ran into Chandni at the Surai on afternoons when I'd pop in there between striking deals with grain merchants. She had moved on a bit. Though she continued to be the D.O.M.'s pet, she now took on other assignments and successfully at that. For a while she'd attached herself to a glossy as a production assistant but had left after a particularly dramatic fight with the powerful editor, who was a tarantula with lethal charm.

When I met Chandni after a gap of nearly six months she was full of her new job at a large publishing house.

She'd been taken on to co-ordinate a series of extravaganzas that had been planned to coincide with the proprietor and founder-editor's sixtieth birthday. Chandni's head was brimming over with bright ideas and she'd been given free rein to execute them. She squealed at the sight of me.

'Nishaaaaa... I've been looking for you. Where are you hiding these days, yaar? Deb says you two hardly meet. What happened? Don't tell me you fought about Iqbal! By the way... I'm waiting for him. We have planned a maha-show as part of our celebrations. It is a terrific hit idea, yaar. Sit, sit, let me tell you. But tell me, what are you doing nowadays? Someone said you are selling khana-daana to the sheikhs... is that true? Too much, yaar, from where to where! If you have some free time—join us. Do it on a one year contract basis. It'll be a lot of fun.'

As we were catching up, Iqbal strolled in and as usual, attracted a lot of attention. He was wearing a psychedelic jumpsuit and had a stunning black girl with him. He walked up to us, one hand waving a black flag, the other caressing his companion's left breast. After an elaborate adaab to both of us, he tweaked my nose and said with a naughty smile, 'Remember?' I looked away and started feeding a white cat, blind in one eye, who'd crept up for some titbits. The black girl's eyes were like live coals, her breasts like torpedoes. Iqbal continued to fondle her, staring down Chandni's neckline all the while.

'So… what are the plans?' he asked Chandni. She pulled out a file and started shuffling papers. He slammed his free hand down on her wrist and snapped, 'Don't look at the papers, woman. Tell me only what I want to know—how much?' Chandni looked nervously at me.

I decided to leave her and tried to push back my chair to get up. Iqbal shoved me down roughly. At that point, Boxer came waltzing up humming 'Singing in the Rain'. It was pouring outside. 'What's all this?' he asked ruffling Iqbal's hair. 'Discussing obscene subjects like money, are we?'

Chandni got out a smart, sleek calculator. 'Let's see… the helicopter hire will cost quite a bomb. And the horses… Iqbal only wants white ones. I'll have to hire them from some circus. We also have to get police and municipal clearance. The ad campaign is running into quite at bit.'

The black girl asked for a soda and started sucking at the straw noisily. 'Good girl. Good girl, keep practicing,' Iqbal said to her, 'by tonight you will be an expert.' His hand was near her crotch. Boxer continued to hum. Iqbal turned to me again. *'Chalo, chalengey?'* Let's leave all these stupid people to figure out how much I'm worth to them.' I shook my head. *'Chalo na,'* Iqbal coaxed. Let's go back to my place and play *ek, do, teen,'* Iqbal challenged, yanking the black girl to her feet abruptly. I felt Chandni's eyes on me. She was far too seasoned to give her own reaction away. Her look was studiedly amused... my discomfort far too apparent.

I summoned Raju, my regular waiter, and said, 'Get an iced tea quickly—someone here needs to cool off.' It wasn't a particularly clever exit line, but it was the best I could think of. I recognized the scorn in Iqbal's eyes. But I didn't wince, or look away. The topic was swiftly changed. And the black girl resumed her noisy sucking.

*Sahakari Samachar's* Iqbal extravaganza was being billed as the event of the decade in the cultural calendar. Chandni told me later that she'd been inspired by Salvador Dali's antics and had suggested something similar to the Entertainment Committee at *Samachar*. It involved a retrospective of Iqbal's work hung up all over Apollo Bunder. The opening was to be spectacular with Iqbal arriving for the show at the appointed time dressed in black and riding in a white helicopter from which he'd be air-dropped into the crowd. The triumphant ride past his exhibits mounted at various levels in front of the historic Gateway of India, was to be in a grand chariot drawn by six white horses painted over with Iqbal's trademark whores—'The ultimate erotic image'—as the promotional catalogue described it. Riding with him in his golden chariot would be his five favourite prostitutes dressed in period courtesan garb. The big argument was over this. Iqbal was insistent that he wanted the whores at the functions. In fact, he wanted his long-time steady as the chief guest. The *Samachar* people were worried this would cause a furore and that some stuffed shirt somewhere would object. Iqbal refused to budge. 'My women have to be there, that's it,' he told Chandni. His idea of period garb was equally outrageous. He'd designed their clothes himself and they were designed to shock. Chandni suggested a compromise.

'Why don't we dress them like world famous courtesans instead?' she asked him. 'We could do a Cleopatra, an Umrao Jaan and so on.' Iqbal wasn't entirely convinced, but kept her idea on hold. He wanted the festival to be called "Randiyon Ka Mela", and plaster the city with deliberately gaudy posters celebrating the Immortal Whore. Nobody at *Samachar* dared contradict him. And nobody broke the news of this bizarre strategy to the old man. Instead, Iqbal announced at a packed press conference that he had come up with this idea because Bombay the City, was the Ultimate Whore, drawing hundreds of customers to her hungry bosom daily, exploiting them and getting exploited in turn.

'Think of the visual impact,' he chortled. 'I'm planning a gigantic cut-out of my favourite *randi*, which will hang over Chowpatty and dominate the city. I have plans to float an inflated balloon over Juhu. Breasts the size of twin moons. Buttocks bulging over the skyline like pink hillocks. Wonderful! Wonderful! The foreign press will love the spectacle. And all my friends from Kamathipura will thank me. Thank me for recognizing their contribution to this city. Later, we will hold a prostitute's ball in Azad Maidan. All my girls will be there, dancing and singing, looking bewitching. *Kya khel hoga!* We can have souvenir mugs with the mela's symbol—exposed breasts. We can hold a fashion show with girls in golden brassières and boys with *lal rumals* around their necks....'

Iqbal was hard to stop. The press lapped it all up and slavered for more. Tarantula the Editor featured Iqbal on her next cover with the headline "Salaam Prostitute". The photograph showed him lolling on his favourite palang in Pila House, the madam bending over him with a paan in her hand. At his feet, two young Nepali girls in bridal finery, smiled coyly into the camera. His interview, full of devastatingly decadent quotes, was impossible to run in the original, forcing Tarantula to modify it sufficiently to satisfy her readers' prurient taste and yet, chaste enough not to give offence.


Tarantula's reputation far exceeded her off-print persona. She was really a pussycat playing tigress with enormous success. Especially at work. And she was never at play. Nobody in Bombay knew too much about her except that she'd been married to an eccentric British travel writer at some point. Nobody could guess her age either. Estimates ranged from thirty-five to fifty, going by the number of years she had put into the profession. Starting as a checking clerk in an ad agency in the days when most agencies had British bosses and executives (that's how she'd met her husband) she'd moved on, doing assorted jobs till she found her niche in magazines. It was said that she'd also found a sugar-daddy in the field, a high-profile wheeler-dealer who floated from one publishing house to the other, buying, selling, hiring, firing and getting very pompous and powerful along the way. She'd met him at a press conference she'd gone to cover for one of Bombay's early society magazines. He already had a sleazy reputation around town as a rake who'd make a lizard pregnant if he could. It was inevitable that he noticed the oomphy young reporter desperately taking notes. He sent for her after the event and asked whether she was interested in an exclusive. She wasn't. Not then. Or she was playing hard to get. Her coolness worked instantly. R.B. Bose (know simply as R.B., or Real Bastard, in publishing circles) wooed her with red roses and wine from that moment onwards, till she quit her job and started working for him. He lost interest soon after and moved on to other young things, 'my sweeties', but in the process, Tarantula's future was made.

She moved up swiftly till she impressed her bosses enough to be nominated editor-designate. She was to take over from a senior editor who was something of an institution. But the older woman refused to quit, and no hints were strong enough to make her move on. The management found itself powerless since sacking her would have led to an uproar in media circles (that was in the days when the media actually stuck together and rushed to the defence of scribes they thought were being victimized). Tarantula waited in the wings patiently, plotting her career moves with canny precision. She knew it was only a matter of time before she'd be crowned queen.

Back in her tidy apartment, she worked on dummies with a sidekick and a paste-up artist. They designed new logos, new formats and new typefaces to replace the outdated old ones. She changed everything around starting with the name. She added snappy features, daring columns and sexy fashion, the likes of which hadn't been seen before, at least in India. She wanted to stage a quiet coup by presenting the management with an eye-popping alternative that was bold, gutsy, provocative and above all, commercially gilt-edged. If the senior editor knew about the conspiracy, she pretended otherwise. 'Madam' (as the staff addressed her) was far too busy planning yet another issue on how to recycle kitchen left-overs to pay much attention to the machinations of her rival.

And then, Tarantula decided to strike with all the ferocious ambition at her command. She asked for and promptly got, an appointment with the board. Her presentation was sleek, professional and convincing. 'Madam' got her official marching orders the next morning. And Tarantula the Editor was born.

'Slave driver', 'Monster', 'Queen Bitch' were some of the kinder epithets she was known by. Once she took over, she revamped the entire show starting with the top. 'No deadwood in this joint,' she declared and fired the G.M. via the M.D. of course. She also fired the staff she'd inherited and hired her own team—a bunch of brash, cocky, good-looking, fresh (in every sense of the word) graduates, who, inspired by her style of functioning, sailed forth for interviews like they were doing the interviewees a favour. That they skewered them in print later, added to their arrogance.

Tarantula pampered her favourites. She derived her inspiration from another editor—her male counterpart, who kept his harem happy (he only hired attractive females—Krishna's Gopikas, as they were dubbed) by remembering their birthdays, sending flowers, cakes and occasionally a bottle of (Indian) champagne. This obvious ruse blinded them all to his even more obvious flaws. They forgot that he was a petty bully, a foul-mouthed two-timer and a lousy editor, who made them do all his dirty work and then hogged the credit for himself. Instead, they doted on him slavishly, behaving like groupies hovering around a rock star, overlooking his paunch, premature grey crop, and halitosis, to say nothing of a suspicious, hostile wife with artistic aspirations. Tarantula couldn't have picked a worse role model, yet she made her act work and she shoved, pushed and kicked ass till she got her desired results.

The circulation of *Femme* ('Sounds like a sanitary napkin,' sneered rivals) shot up dramatically, while Tarantula, predictably, acquired the 'fatale' tab to go with her magazine's title. She played the part all right, particularly when she went hustling. She had to do that often in the early stages when *Femme* was negotiating its steep climb to the top of the heap. 'Compromise, darlings, isn't a dirty word in my dictionary,' she'd remind her awestruck staff. 'To get ahead and stay there, you need two things in your armoury—talent, oodles of it, and guts. But, if the adversary isn't impressed by either—seduce. Climb down. Sacrifice pride. In other words, compromise.'

One sell-out issue after another and Tarantula was ready to launch herself. She decided to throw a coming-out party at the 'in' club in Bombay. A dark and dingy dimsum den that had been the brainchild of a canny Chinese with remarkable business acumen. It didn't matter that dimsums weren't considered haute cuisine in a city like Bombay where the 'paisa vasool' mentality prevailed over everything else. Diners usually emerged hungry after a meal at The Dragon's Den, but nobody went there for the food anyway. It was its 'exclusivity' that counted. An exclusivity that had been carefully created over the five years of its existence. That kept the 'riff riff' at bay and that encouraged only bored wives of rich playboys to become patrons. Tarantula deliberately chose the place for her party since it bestowed a 'you're-good-enough-for-the-DD' honour on invitees. Plus, Mr Lee, (the owner), had shrewdly offered her a huge discount for the bash, calculating cleverly that she'd be able to rope in the right people (some more bored, rich wives, in other words). He was dead on in his assumption. Tarantula's guest-list included the most photogenic people of Bombay. Those who'd provide *Femme* with at least four colour pages of party pictures and those who'd persuade their busy husbands to buy an ad campaign in it.

Tarantula's staffers worked round the clock to ensure the party's success, making phone-calls, checking on flower arrangements, sampling a new range of vegetarian dimsums ('there'll be so many Gujjus around the place') getting a booze company to provide crates of complimentary blended whisky and, of course, running around for Tarantula's party outfit. She didn't want anybody to upstage her, not even Bombay's socialite queen.

'Don't worry,' the socialite's arch rival phoned Tarantula to reassure her, 'She's looking like a sack of potatoes these days and wearing dowdy outfits. Shapeless denim dungarees and that sort of stuff.'

Tarantula was vastly relieved. Nobody stood a chance when that siren came slinking into a party clad in clinging jersey outfits that made it abundantly clear she didn't have a stitch on underneath. Tarantula had once done a devastating profile on her in *Femme* claiming she had plastic boobs and capped teeth. The siren had thrown a purple fit and threatened to sue till well-meaning friends warned her off, insisting that in a defamation case, the onus of disproving the charge would be on her.

'Do you want to bare your tits in Esplanade Court and have a surgeon come in and testify to their silicon content?' they'd asked.

The siren had sulked for months in her sylvan retreat before emerging in a modest sari that covered her boobs.

Tarantula insisted she'd done the piece to put the siren in her place. 'Do you know what she did to a good friend of mine?' And then she recounted the story of what had happened to Kiki when she bared her breasts for a foreign film.

In her pre-Feroze days, Kiki had been picked up by 'The Crook', as the American director was universally known, for an Eastern-Western with a mystic message. He assured her the nudie bits were exclusively for foreign audiences and that not a word or a shot of Kiki's *Kamasutra* shenanigans would appear in India. Kiki happily went along, shooting porn disguised as arty erotica. The Crook lived up to his image and reputation, exploiting those sequences to the hilt. His entire publicity for the film revolved around a shot of a nude Kiki in a very complicated pose, where one didn't know where her arms began or her legs ended. This was plastered over posters all over Europe. The siren managed to get hold of a few on one of her frequent foreign jaunts. She came back triumphant. She had several scores to settle with the tarty little bitch who had seduced her husband in her own home, at her own party and on her own bed. And she knew just how to put Kiki in her place and show her up for the hypocrite she was.

She decided to throw a grand reception to celebrate the success of Kiki's film abroad (it had received respectable reviews, much to everybody's amazement). Naturally, Kiki was to be the chief guest being the star of the film. Right at the entrance of the socialite queen's sprawling duplex at Worli, was hung Kiki's sexy poster with a spotlight shining brightly over it. Early guests stood around tittering waiting for the big moment when Kiki would arrive for the party. 'I'd like to see her face... wouldn't miss this chance for anything in the world. I cancelled my Pune trip for this. Imagine—with the races on.' The few Kiki supporters who wanted the hostess to remove the poster were shouted down by the rest. 'Don't be such spoilsports, *yaar*. Kiki wasn't drugged when she acted in the film. Why all the fuss now?'

Kiki's Contessa drew up to the porch of the swanky apartment complex. She couldn't figure out why the security fellows were sniggering (even they were in the know thanks to the driver grapevine). Not at that point. She was far too excited about the party. In the lift taking them up to the granite and glass hot-house full of steamy sex symbols from Sin City, Kiki stood up on her toes and kissed her newest escort. 'To us, darling,' she whispered and goosed him mischievously. The party sounds floated out to them as the elevator stopped on the seventh floor. Kiki straightened her shoulders, stuck her bust out, adjusted the undercup wiring of her black bra and stepped out.

Mahesh, her escort, was decidedly nervous. He knew he'd be all over the gossip columns the next day after this evening. What would Pappaji say or do? Kiki quickly asked him to check her teeth for runaway lipstick. Through the open door (a heavy wooden affair inlaid with transluscent agate chunks) she saw the hostess making her way towards her. The socialite queen was dressed not just to kill but commit a gruesome murder. It was a slithery gown covered with sequins.

Very Forties and very vampish. Someone had told her recently that she resembled Rita Hayworth. The queen had promptly changed back the colour of her treated red hair to its original black, making sure one eye was permanently covered with a tantalizing lock placed over it.

Kiki said to Mahesh, 'God! Just look at her. Gorgeous, isn't she?' He gulped and straightened his bow-tie.

'Daaaarrrrling,' gushed the queen, her arms outstretched dramatically, 'so good of you to come... and this must be Mahesh, your latest.' With that she leaned over to kiss the startled man passionately, just missing his mouth by a whisker. 'Mmmmm—he smells good. He looks good. He *must* be good,' she concluded approvingly. 'Come along the two of you, this is your night.'

Kiki beamed and took Mahesh by the arm. A band from within started playing. "Congratulations", while some of the guests began joining in the chorus. The three of them linked arms and strode in, dancing a little gig from time-to-time.

The shock of seeing the life-size poster registered after the first few heady-giddy moments. It was as if Kiki had been in a trance till then. She'd passed the poster without really noticing it. But it hadn't escaped Mahesh's attention. His eyes had widened and his entire body tensed up, with the white of his knuckles showing

319

up sharply against the smooth black of the tuxedo. He nudged Kiki sharply. So sharply, in fact, that she let out a small scream of pain.

'Look,' he hissed. She looked again, and that's when it hit her. She started to giggle helplessly and then as all the guests watched, the giggles turned to tears and the tears to angry screams.

'Bitch! Bloody bitch! How could you do this to me! Whore! Slut. I'll kill you for this.' She lunged wildly at the queen who swiftly ducked and hid behind a marble stand. Kiki went after her like a wild cat, her claws tearing the air in front of her. Nobody could restrain Kiki, not even Mahesh. She took off her stilettoes and flung them at the queen's face. One got her, the other didn't. Kiki reached for an onyx vase next and aimed for the veined Venetian mirror behind her.

Through all this mayhem, the queen continued to laugh loudly, vulgarly, repeating all the time, 'Serves you right, serves you right.' Kiki's risqué evening dress had all but come apart by then and her hair was a mess. Mahesh, paralysed by the scene, stood by the door, unable to do anything besides gape in bewilderment. It was only when the queen's consort finally showed up and dragged his wife off that the messy affair came to an end. Others present insisted the two women were quits now.

'An expensive way of settling scores... but so exciting,' said a satisfied voyeur when, after a lavish banquet of

smoked salmon and quail breasts, the exhausted invitees
finally trooped home.

❋

It was strange that Tarantula's loyalty had been roused
sufficiently to actually feel sorry for Kiki. But tonight
was going to be her night—she'd fix the siren and all
those ugly bitches with rich husbands who'd sneered
at her in the past. She'd dieted for weeks in order to
fill her pricey designer ensemble (a black crochet coat
with a body hugging cat-suit underneath) that showed
off her new curves to advantage. Tarantula was feeling
right on top of things. Kiki would be there, of course.
And God. Tarantula had concluded (rightly so) that
God was attractive to other women. It was arrogance,
his scruffy unconventional appearance, plus the promise
of violent sex he held out, that made him irresistible.
Compared to the wimpy moneybags married to those
screechy socialites, God was quite a man. A status symbol.
And Tarantula was going to strut him around shamelessly.

At the party, God behaved true to type. He threw up
on a socialite's tussore ghagra and insulted half-a-dozen
prominent people. He even attempted to boogy on
the tiny dance floor, picking the sexy (but hugely
pregnant) wife of a young industrialist (the sort of man

321

who is invariably described as a 'scion' in newspaper reports). Far from being embarrassed Tarantula was rather pleased. 'One needs a few ghastly scenes to perk up these affairs,' she'd chortled gleefully at the post-mortem. 'Now people will be talking about my party for weeks.'

She was right. With one obnoxious high-society appearance, God had ensured his permanent place on the A-list of socialites hungry for cheap diversions. Nothing could have suited Tarantula better. *Femme* gloated about the party's success in the next issue which featured God in every second photograph.

# Fourteen

I'm not sure when and where God and Tarantula met up. His and her versions varied on that score. He insisted it was in Yashwantbhai's office where Tarantula had turned up to do a pre-election interview. Tarantula's memory went back further to a time when God had landed up in her office in search of a freelance assignment.

'He tried to sell me a love poem along with himself,' she giggled. 'I rejected both.' And now, here they were collaborating on getting a political weekly off the ground.

'It's all a matter of great timing, *yaar*,' God drawled when I asked him about it. 'The time is now.'

'Is Yashwantbhai involved?' I asked.

'You ask such obvious questions, *yaar*—grow up. If I say "yes" he will deny it. If I say "no" you won't believe me.'

'And where does Tarantula come in?'

'She is a wizard, *yaar*. She is one woman who can get anything done. She says "jump" and everybody jumps.'

'Have you jumped for her yet?'

'*Kamaal hai*. Again, the same response as the Yashwantbhai one applies here, OK? Guess what, Nasha… we are trying to use both your ex-boss and ex-boyfriend for this project.'

'That's interesting. Why are you leaving me out in that case?' I asked.

'At this point we don't need a female baniya, since we aren't selling basmati and besan but a *bhaari* magazine.'

'Chick peas, Deb, chick peas.'

'Same thing, *yaar*.'

'Not exactly. But then, you aren't a great one for details. So… when is the launch?'

'Everything depends on the election date. Your ad boss is handling the campaign and advising us on other things.'

'Is he selling Yashwantbhai? God knows that man could do with some positive promotion. Or is he relying entirely on Tarantula for that?'

'This is where that yuppie-creep, Anil, comes in. By the way, how did you two screw? If you did, that is? Via his answering machine?'

'Don't get personal, Deb.'

'How can I get impersonal with you, Nasha, *jaan-e-man*? Who are you seeing these days? I'm sure there's somebody.'

'Nobody.'

'Impossible. Vow of chastity?'

'There aren't any interesting men around. Or haven't you noticed?'

'There's me.'

'I'm looking for someone wonderful and new. Someone who makes me feel good.'

'Actually, so am I—but not now. After the elections.'

'I believe someone was mad enough to make you the Bombay bureau chief for that Delhi fortnightly for some time? What's the name—*Capital Voice?*'

'That was only for a few months. I needed a break from *Plume, yaar.* I was getting stifled by all that artistic shit. But those Delhi guys couldn't handle my copy.'

'How come?'

'My sources are so good that I could blackmail the entire cabinet.'

'Thanks to Yashwantbhai?'

'Why are you after him all the time?'

'He is your main contact. Why don't you admit it? What has he given you now—a bungalow in Lonavla?'

'None of your business, Nasha. He has been good to me. And I have been useful to him. *Bas*—it's a straight deal. No nonsense.'

'Wasn't he behind the story you did that ruined Ingle's career?'

'What if he was? That man deserved to be exposed. He was not only corrupt, he was a rapist as well.'

'What about Yashwantbhai's scandals? I hear he doesn't leave a single female alone.'

'But can you prove anything? Has anybody caught him?'

'Does that make him less of a villain? What about that young typist who'd been victimized by her boss at the Mantralaya who'd gone to him for help? And that battered wife of the IAS officer who wanted to let the world know what a beast her husband was? Everybody knows the price Yashwantbhai extracted from both of them before he lifted a finger.'

'Such things happen all the time in politics. Who cares?'

'And you don't feel anything's wrong with being the stooge of such a bastard?'

'What stooge-fooge? We understand each other.'

'I'm sure you do. I've heard that you supply girls when Yashwantbhai is hard up and there aren't any helpless women at his door.'

'A few times I have rung up some friends and called them for a meeting, that's all.'

'That's all! That's disgraceful. So now you can add pimping to your other professional credits.'

'Look, *yaar*, I don't have to listen to any *lecturebaazi* from anybody. Your father is no better. He is just doing the same thing on a smaller scale. Chasing secretaries, stopping increments, holding back bonuses. We know how he functions. Yashwantbhai has a file on him. You can let him know. My father knows everything too.'

'Just leave my father alone, OK? He is a troubled man as it is.'

'Don't worry. He's small fry. We are after bigger fish. Your ex-boss... he's quite a *chaalu* chap also. I bet you don't know anything about his activities. The travel agency he floated. His other offences and violations.'

'A travel agency? This is new!'

'Yes, he had to find a way to make that ex-chauffeur rich enough to support his darling daughter and his first grandson. Now Janine is living in a posh flat, bought by Roy's ill-gotten gains of course.'

'Then why are you going to him? There are other ad agencies in town.'

'Maybe, but for this sort of dirty work, the fellow is good. Besides, we are talking about a multi-crore budget... any agency would jump.'

'Where does Anil come in?'

'We want him to conduct the pre-poll surveys. To get an idea of voter expectations. He's quite good at his work, we are told. He came over to Yashwantbhai's office for a brief.'

'How is he? How did he look?'

'Still interested?'

'Not really. Just curious.'

'Same old stupid face, *yaar*. All that gell-vell shit in his hair. Bloody pansy if you ask me. Don't tell me you didn't find out even that much? I mean, didn't you two screw?'

327

I let that pass.

'Is he married now?'

'Who knows and who gives a fuck? OK, enough *bak-bak*. Back to work.'

'Is Yashwantbhai giving you a ticket?'

'I don't need a ticket. I don't want to be a neta. I'd rather make netas.'

'Call me if you need a good headline or visual. I'll try and come up with something between selling rice.'

'*Theek hai phir milengey,* OK? By the way, you're looking *kafi* sexy.'

'Thanks. You too.'

'*Jhooti* bitch!'

'Capitalist *kutta!*

Iqbal's retro, 'Dedicated To the Whores of Bombay... Or Bombay the Whore of Whores', as it was called, went off wonderfully well, even if the sixty-year-old birthday boy wasn't exactly amused. His brash son, Parthiv, who could barely conceal his impatience at having to hang around in the wings waiting for Papaji to cop it, chose the occasion to make his debut and shove his father out of the limelight, perhaps forever. While this was hailed as a move long overdue by *Samachar* veterans who had had it up to there with the old autocrat's overbearing ways, there were those amongst them who were even more cynical about the son's modus operandi. *'Yeh to saala sab ko kha jaayega,* he'll certainly eat us all up,' they said as they gathered around greasy thalis in the staff canteen.

The young scion didn't waste too much time trying to woo anyone. He decided to bare his fangs right at the start by firing the powerful editor of his respected daily and hiring an unknown corporate man, Amar, in his place.

'We need new blood to shake us up,' he declared at a hastily summoned meeting of senior staffers. 'Anybody who disagrees with the changes I have in mind, may feel free to walk out right now.' Parthiv didn't believe in winning popularity contests and he made that perfectly clear. 'I am not here to be liked or admired by any of you. I'm here to get results. The only people I am responsible to are my readers. You deliver and you stay. You don't deliver—you go. I hope I've made myself clear.' With his fancy foreign degree in journalism from some obscure American university, Parthiv felt he knew all that there was to know about running a publishing empire. He decided to close down three established magazines for starters and launch two new ones in their place. 'We need futuristic journalism in India,' he announced at the weekly edit meet that he had commandeered after his coup. 'We need to think big, talk big and write big.' Nobody had a clue what he meant by that but nobody dared to contradict him either.

'The man is cuckoo,' said incredulous reporters as he stalked the corridors, ducking unannounced into cabins, walking into the newsroom, peeping over shoulders and even doing spot checks of the loo.

Some of Parthiv's moves were very smart, like the one that successfully blocked Tarantula's plans for a new political weekly and, incidentally, derailed God. When he got wind of their plans, he immediately got working on counter moves of his own starting with the distributors. He called an all-India sales conference in Bombay and treated the lowly vendors of his publications like they were royalty. It was one area his father had never bothered about, considering it below his dignity to involve himself with menials. But Parthiv knew better. At the two-day affair, he worked on the vendors systematically, cajoling and bullying by turns. The message was obvious: Lift the rival magazine and we'll freeze ours. There was far too much at stake with *Samachar* for the vendors so they couldn't object to blackmail of this kind. Besides, he told them he would hike their commissions and even came up with incentive schemes. 'Press Baron Plays Dirty With Rivals,' screamed a tabloid, but Parthiv just laughed it off. 'These guys are such amateurs. Don't they read about Murdoch and his methods? American media is full of dirty tricks. That's how the game works these days.'

His new appointee, Amar, was playing little games of his own. Games that involved terrorizing old-timers and reducing them to being office furniture. His methods were crude and direct. If the staff he inherited didn't go along with his bizarre editorial plans, he just pretended they didn't exist, and hired freshers to do the job. This led to enormous antagonism, especially since the freshers demanded the sort of perks that had been unheard of in the stuffy office previously and got them. Amar wanted to prove himself in a hurry since he was more than aware of what colleagues were saying about him.

'What does he know of journalism? He's an outsider pitchforked into the profession. Give him a year or two and he'll go right back where he came from. Where was it, by the way? Wasn't he selling motor-oil or spare parts or something?'

Amar's greatest asset was his gift of the gab. The man could talk. And sell. Plus, he wasn't a quitter. He was determined to stay on and fight it out to the bitter end, tripping over a battlefield full of corpses along the way. 'The route to victory isn't easy. There will be casualties amongst you,' he cautioned the staff. 'Make sure you've got your ass covered and aren't among them.' His style of functioning was bull-doggish and belligerent. He didn't disguise the fact that he preferred to hire girls—pretty girls. 'It's a matter of aesthetics,' he declared in an interview to Tarantula (before the conspiracy to scuttle her plans got out). 'Women, beautiful ones, are easier on the eye. I'd rather have a gorgeous-looking reporter around than some ugly toad who can file brilliant copy. For that I hire freelancers.'

Later, Tarantula predictably insisted he'd made a pass at her, which she had disdainfully dismissed, but this much was true, she'd got some great quotes out of him. Not that that was difficult. Amar always spoke for posterity, his conversation laced with pompous pronouncements and grandiose statements.

'It's a case of over-compensation, *yaar*,' said others who'd known him as a corporate small-timer. 'He has to prove himself in Parthiv's and the watching world's eyes. Plus, he has a complex about his looks. Do you know he wears a toupee to cover his bald patch and that his front teeth are false?'

Nobody, not even the girls from his harem, got close enough to him to find out one way or the other, but it became a major sport at media parties to try and get him to stand under a fan or to have him hang on to his head at a windy poolside bash.

'One day I'll get my dog to chew on his wig,' wowed Tarantula darkly. 'And it won't be in private. I'll have a battery of photographers ready.'

Tarantula should have known just whom she was taking on when she decided to launch a broadside against the *Samachar*. It was when she bared her fangs and dug them into Amar that the shit hit the ceiling. In Amar, she had an adversary more than willing to play the game as dirtily as she did. And Tarantula had got him where it hurt the most. She'd doubted his manhood and implied that he was in reality, impotent. Someone who strutted around as a stud just to keep his secret from getting out. She quoted ex-secretaries, models and society women who'd been linked with him. All of them testified to his 'no-can-do-ness' with sadistic glee.

Yashwantbhai didn't want to get involved when Amar started exposing Tarantula. At least, not initially.

'Forget all *this jhamela, yaar,'he* said to God when he asked for his intervention. *'Saali ko marne dey... tera kya jaata hai* (Let the bitch die... what do *you* have at stake)?' Which was, in fact, a most pertinent question.

Everybody was amazed at God's sudden concern and said so. Soon blind items began appearing about God's connection with Tarantula. Was there more to their relationship than just a shared byline? God dismissed it as garbage but continued to lobby on her behalf. For the first time Tarantula herself was shaken and running scared. She stopped going to work and staffers were told to say she was on leave and had probably gone abroad for a vacation. The truth was Tarantula had dived underground. She'd actually gone into hiding. From her unknown destination she kept in touch with God and a few trusted friends, checking on the scene and

333

asking about the overall atmosphere. God assured her that he was working hard on her case and that a breakthrough with Yashwantbhai was round the corner.

'But you know the man, *yaar*. He doesn't do anything for nothing. Are you willing to pay him his pound of flesh?'

She was. Even though she didn't know what form it would take. She pleaded, 'Just get those goons off my back. Tell Yashwantbhai to settle my case with them. I can't live like this forever.' It was most uncharacteristic for Tarantula to be reduced to begging for favours. But she was obviously under extreme stress. Amar and Parthiv had kept up the pressure, letting dirty little stories leak out about her hitherto closely-guarded private life. They unearthed the ex-husband tucked away in the foothills of the Himalayas, a current boyfriend young enough to be her son, and a messy story about her sleeping her way to the top of her profession, using every man along the way. The usual garbage that men employ to assassinate a woman's character.

But the story that really destroyed her was the one about her mother. *Samachar* sleuths had managed to track down the old lady to Dehradun where she lived a lonely life in a small house on a farm, eking out a miserable existence by doing odd jobs on neighbouring farms and getting by with what little produce her own patch of land yielded. 'My Daughter Disowned Me,' screamed headlines from hoardings all over the city, while print ads carried a pathetic picture of a little old lady with lost eyes, sitting near a well, holding a billy-goat close to her bosom. They quoted her as saying her daughter was a merciless, selfish woman, who kicked her out of her own home when she needed it after her (Tarantula's) divorce.

'My husband was dead. I was a prisoner and a servant in the home he'd left for me. My daughter tortured me physically and emotionally. She used to hit me if I ever objected to her way of life. I told her to find some other good man and settle down. Was that wrong? She abused me and threatened to turn me out. It was a cold winter that year in Chandigarh. I was too scared to open my mouth after that. All sorts of men used to visit her—army generals, politicians, government officers. The neighbours used to gossip and taunt me while she was away, I felt so ashamed. I tried to stop her. I even tried to hang myself. But my dupatta tore when I tried to tie it to a fan. She was furious when she discovered it and warned me never to do such a thing again. I wept and told her I wanted to end my misery. And she shut me into the small coal-room next to the kitchen without food or water. The men who came used to get drunk and behave badly. Once the neighbours complained. But the next day the police came and told them to withdraw their complaint. After that everybody kept quiet. Then she met that man. I don't remember his name now. The one who took her away to Bombay and gave her some job. She used to send some money home at first. Then she stopped even that. I had to look for work as a cook or an ayah. My late husband would have died another death. Imagine me working as a *naukrani*, when my daughter was such a famous woman. Then she started telling people that I was dead. I wish I was. It must have been some curse on me. I must have sinned in my last *janam* to have given birth to such a *shaitan*. But I am not like her. I hope she will find God (irony!) and make her peace. Tell her I forgive her.'

Tarantula was livid with the revelations. But more than livid, something died inside her. She lost her fighting spirit. She finally stopped running. There was nothing left to hide anymore. She threw in the towel. And went crawling to Yashwantbhai.

It was already too late. Amar realized he had finished Tarantula. He didn't need to waste a minute of his time talking to scum like Yashwantbhai. Victory was his and he wanted to revel in it. He told God as much when the latter called to fix an appointment for Yashwantbhai. 'Bloody pimp... fuck off... why should I spare time for the likes of you two? And that too for that bitch who tried to destroy me! Tell your boss to go suck his cock. I have better things to do.'

God should have known right then that Amar was on to a big thing. A major exposé that would establish Yashwantbhai's nexus with powerful brokers manipulating stocks on the exchange and defrauding the public of millions. God's contacts within Amar's office had leaked a few confidential papers and dropped several hints. It was possible that Amar was open to 'negotiations'. As his flunkey put it, 'All that matters is the price.'

God was aware that Amar and Parthiv were vulnerable too, involved as they were in shady newsprint deals, to say nothing of tax evasion on a massive scale. He should have passed on all this to Yashwantbhai. He missed the signals and failed to report matters to Yashwantbhai—thereby becoming suspect. In any case, God was far too busy politicking. The state elections were round the corner and more than just Tarantula's tail was at stake. Yashwantbhai was fielding his men and there were still a couple of tickets going. God was certain he was in the running. Yashwantbhai's sweeping the elections was taken for granted by everybody including Yashwantbhai.

'My boys don't lose elections,' he boasted in various newspapers. 'And neither do I.'

God's father was in the fray as well, and was sure of his chances in a predominantly labour constituency. Yashwantbhai's candidate from the same area was a notorious goonda, a small-time bootlegger who had graduated to big-time smuggling. Yashwantbhai was going to save money on this one, since there was no real need for official campaigning. The candidate's men had terrorized the electorate sufficiently to get them into the polling booths and stamp his symbol—a boat ('He feels boats are lucky for him since his first consignment of silver went out on one'). God's father who had limited resources was hoping his good work with the mill workers in the area would pay off. He was getting old and frail now. He hardly attended any gate-meetings these days, except those in the immediate neighbourhood. God looked in on him occasionally and left money behind in a battered old tin near the old man's bed. That was about the only contact they maintained after God had moved out.

Yashwantbhai was counting on God's press contacts to get positive pieces written on him. It wasn't easy for God to sell Yashwantbhai these days, particularly since Yashwantbhai had stopped doling out largesse to junior reporters, and cut off the booze supply to the informal press centre that was run by the chief reporter of *Samachar* at his own home. God was always reminded of Yashwantbhai's early words of advice to him, 'Corrupt them at the top first and then work your way right down to the peon and chaprasi level... that way you keep everybody happy.'

Unfortunately, Yashwantbhai discovered a bit too late that not everybody was happy. In fact there were two people who were most unhappy. And they were at the top. Right at the top. The fall-out was bad. Very bad. Especially for God.

When ugly stories about Yashwantbhai's underworld connections began to circulate in the press, it was God who was pulled up.

'Can you explain to me, you nincompoop, what is going on?' Yashwantbhai snarled. 'It's your job to fix these things—people like that swine Rathod, and who's that other fellow? Borkar. Chief reporter *hai*—so what? Kill the stories or kill them. That is if you aren't on their payroll yourself.'

God was stunned by these accusations. And deeply offended. Yashwantbhai had called him a two-timer, a double-crosser.

Had he slipped up somewhere or was there an enemy in the camp poisoning Yashwantbhai's mind? Maybe this person was feeling threatened by God's power, access and success. The message was clear: God's countdown had begun. It was only a matter of time before he too became a discarded victim. God had to move quickly. And he tried. But it was already too late.

❋

I'd known all along that God was messing things up for himself by getting involved with Yashwantbhai. He didn't see it that way, of course. He thought he was being smart and clever. Staying ahead in the race. A race to nowhere and nothing. There were no winners in this kind of competition. And the losers often ended up dead.

Meanwhile, the writing bug had bitten me. Perhaps it was God's indirect influence. Or maybe I was trying to upstage him ('Anything you can do, I can do better.') But I was enjoying fooling around with words, more so when I saw them in print.

Getting a break wasn't tough, I discovered. Most editors were hard up for fillers. Anything reasonably well-written and neatly readymade was fit to print. Besides, even if I do say so myself, my stuff wasn't bad at all. It was different. And easy to read. Gradually my byline became a familiar one and I joined the ranks of the poorly-paid but widely-read freelance hacks. I had no political savvy to speak of—and didn't pretend to have any. My pieces worked chiefly because of this—politicians tended to treat me patronizingly. And I in turn played up my naive image. They dropped their guards—and I got my quotes.

I did one such piece on Yashwantbhai and perhaps because of it I was asked to see Amar and Parthiv when they went on a mad talent-shopping binge for their publications. Initially, I'd played it cool, not wanting to give up my chick peas business for another full-time job, this time in journalism. Like some of my old friends at the agency would often sneer, 'In this business we only lend our ass to the client. In journalism you sell your soul to the proprietor.' Both alternatives were equally revolting, but selling basmati wasn't particularly challenging, even if the sight of my own Kawla-designed logo on a gunny sack still continued to thrill me. As Aarti finally pointed out, 'You can do both even if you join the *Samachar*... or you can hire someone to sell your stuff to the Arabs for you... like me, for instance... I'd love to check for myself what they are like... the sheikhs. In my fantasies they are all Omar Sharifs.' That was an idea. Hiring Aarti solved several problems... and created a few, but those weren't terribly bother-some. She needed extra money. I needed extra help. Besides, I wasn't the sort to get too involved in the nitty-gritties. Aarti must have been ripping me off—at least a little. It was fine by me.

The *Samachar* interview was unreal. I wasn't prepared to answer questions that had nothing to do with my abilities as a writer. Amar leered and stared pointedly at my breasts, while Parthiv mumbled incoherently into his coffee cup and spoke about his grand plan, which included an investigative tabloid—along the lines of the *Sun*. I was tempted to say that it wasn't a very original idea, when I remembered that nothing in Indian journalism was all that original anyway. They had decided to call their tabloid *Bharat,* a name they were immensely pleased with.

'The first state-of-the-art paper,' Amar stated, rubbing his crotch with an agate egg.

I'd heard that description before—every new journal claimed it was just that these days. Eventually, it was the hardware that survived the publications.

'But I'm not familiar with computers,' I said. All the while, I wanted to do nothing more than wipe the smug smile off Amar's face with a mailed fist.

'The paper needs bright young people with ambition and insight,' Parthiv droned on.

My eyes wandered to the walls of his impressive room. They were covered with contemporary art. A lurid Iqbal on acrylic stood out from the rest of the confused display ('eclectic collection' critics had dubbed it in innumerable write-ups). There was also a self-parodying portrait of Parthiv, done in sombre tones by Basu. It depicted him as a bejewelled, chained dog. Parthiv caught me staring at it, 'Yes... rather appropriate, isn't it?' I smiled.

Amar had switched from the agate egg to a lapis one (it matched his jeans). 'I liked what you did on that shit-head,' he drawled.

'Which one?' I asked.

'You mean you have rubbished so many of them?' he asked, his eyebrows raised in fake astonishment.

Parthiv intervened. 'He means your profile of Yashwantbhai. We thought of hiring you after we read it. That's the sort of stuff we want in *Bharat*. Corruption and incompetence are the two biggest bureaucratic crimes. We want to expose both.'

Amar continued smoothly, 'How much are you making selling rice… five grand? Ten grand? We can make you an offer you can't refuse.'

'Fine,' I said. 'But I'd still want to continue to sell my rice.'

'Why?' Parthiv asked.

'Because I enjoy it… and I like being my own boss. If I consider joining you at all, I'd prefer to work out some sort of a loose arrangement. Maybe you could consider a retainer. I don't want to give up my business… and in case you are interested, it makes me a great deal of money.'

Amar and Parthiv exchanged glances. 'We had a package in mind actually. Plus, a fancy designation. You would be features editor with complete control. The only people you'd be reporting to is the two of us.'

'Well, like I said, I'll have to think this thing through. I don't know how much time I'll be able to spare.'

'Why don't you do one thing while you are making up your mind—*Bharat* is going to be doing dummies for advertisers over the next few weeks. We need some fillers… we'll pay for them, of course. Why not eight profiles over three months from you?'

'That sounds reasonable… and I'm interested.'

Amar got up from his chair and came over to shake hands. Parthiv got busy on the intercom bawling out his marketing manager who'd goofed on some important details in the promotional letter sent out by him. The language employed to berate the man was worse than God's.

Amar walked me to the door and tried the old schoolboy trick of reaching over to flick some imaginary dust off my shoulder. He waited till we were in full view of the editorial department before doing it. I saw his secretary smirking. She'd probably witnessed it a thousand times before. I told Amar I'd get back to him and left.

The Yashwantbhai piece had created bad blood between God and me. He'd stormed into the house and yelled, 'Nasha! *Yeh tuney kya kiya? Kyon kiya,* huh, why the hell did you do this?' This had been fairly soon after a run-in his father had had with Yashwantbhai's goon-squad, so I was a little surprised by his reaction. God continued, 'You don't know that man the way I do... he will never forget this. You'd better watch out. Tell that *baap* of yours also.'

'Why the sudden interest in our welfare, Deb?' I said. 'You are doing well, being his lap-dog. You may have bartered away your conscience for the price of a Maruti... some of us have other priorities.'

God had stared at me thoughtfully and said tiredly, sadly, 'It's not a case of priorities, Nasha. Don't be dumb. And don't put on your holier-than-thou act with me. If Yashwantbhai is corrupt, so are we all, in varying degrees. So is your father. And so is mine. And so are you. Our means may be different, but the ends are the same. You will regret this. Rather, you will be made to regret it.'

'Are you passing on some sort of a sinister message? Have you been reduced to this? This is disgusting. I do believe you are threatening me. Why don't you just come out with it, spell it out, huh? What is that man planning—to kill me? Kidnap me? Rape me? Or all of those?'

'Let us just say that whatever happened between us in the past is why I am here today. Had you been some unknown broad acting smart, I wouldn't have bothered. But I know that man and what he's capable of. Once he decides on something—that's it. Today, you happen to be his target. I'm here to warn you as a friend—be careful. Don't fool with him.'

Was that some sort of a goodbye, I wondered. God and I were meeting after weeks—it felt like years since we'd last laughed together at one of his silly jokes. We no longer spoke the same language.... We barely recognized each other... or our shared past. I'd even forgotten when exactly it was that we had officially 'broken up'. I doubted whether God remembered—or cared—either.

God's shoulders had slumped. He looked weary and for the first time, defeated. I asked him to play the flute, just to cheer him up.

'It broke,' he said flatly, and left.

So, the flute had gone too. There were times I thought of God as he was when I had first met him nearly six years ago. I remembered Bijli and our joint adventures. But if God had changed, so had I. I missed *me* too. The old me. My parents rarely spoke, either to each other or to me. Didi was far too frail to do anything more than shuffle weakly around the place, dreaming of returning to her beloved Darjeeling one day. My mother's hair had started to grey and she didn't bother to dye it anymore. She'd stopped bothering about her physical appearance for some time now. And my father had stopped bothering her about it. We lived our lives in near-isolation, the conversation rarely going beyond mundane pleasantries. If they were at all concerned about my single status ('The Vermas' unmarried daughter,' was how I was often introduced by corporate friends of my parents as if there were half-a-dozen other married daughters) they didn't show it, though my mother vaguely talked about some 'nice boy' she'd been told about.

I thought about Anil sometimes. But couldn't get myself to pick up the phone and talk him into an evening. My social life, such as it was, was dominated by girlfriends, divorcees, widows and other singles. We met up once or twice a month, generally at a five star bar. After far too many tequila cocktails, we drifted to dinner at one of the fancier new restaurants. Occasionally, we went to the disco at the Taj and danced with each other, making

Pickering Public Library
Central Library
One The Esplanade

Automated Phone Renewal
905-831-8209

Today's date   5/10/2011 12:37:00 PM

33081007596894
Sultry days /
Due back on 5/31/2011

33081007468870
Ghuban /
Due back on 5/31/2011

33081003999803
Shikhron se aage /
Due back on 5/31/2011

Phone: 905-831-6265
www.picnet.org
Note: For security, client barcode
information has been removed

out as if we were having the time of our lives. At the end of it all, plastered and depressed, we'd land up in one of the homes to sum up the evening and our lives. What wrecks we looked with our smudgy kaajal, twisted mouths and half-eaten lipstick. The group conceded in more candid moments that these outings were pointless, expensive and frustrating. But what alternative was there? Like Mona would say in her hard-edged, almost metallic voice, 'Let's face it girls... we are hard up. No men, no future. We work, we earn... we deserve some fun. And who knows... maybe, one day while we are sitting at Lancer's a group of gorgeous guys will walk in and marry us all.'

She'd put her finger on it neatly... we lived with that one hope—that we'd be 'saved' by some man. Most of us hated to admit this, but it was true. Being single wasn't such a hot alternative, though many of our married friends thought so. But even those women could sense our desperation, our loneliness, and feel smug that they had husbands to call their own. They were Mrs So-and-So.

It was at such a party that I met Lotika, who introduced a new perspective into being single. 'I was an apsara in my last life,' she giggled, fiddling provocatively with a strand of hennaed hair. The kitty party was in full swing and most of us were punch drunk.

'Oh, how sweet, darling. Who told you that?'

'My numerologist,' confessed Lotika popping a prawn pakora into her mouth. 'He told me I was so ravishing that I disturbed a rishi's meditation.'

'Too much, *yaar.* It's sounding more and more like the *Ramayana*... or is it the *Mahabharata*,' someone giggled, reaching for a ciggie.

'You don't believe me? All his predictions have come true so far... including Ravi's death. He had told me about it a few months before my Bobby died.'

There was a hush in a room... the silence broken just by the crackle of potato crispies and the metallic click-clack of diamond bangles as they clanged against each other on fat wrists and into delicate china.

'What else did he tell you, darling?' the hostess urged Lotika to tell her tale.

'Oh... so many things. The rishi's curse will trouble me in this lifetime. That's why I left my first husband—all because of the curse.'

We held our breaths and reached for the sev-puris. 'The numerologist told you that also?'

'*Hahn baba*... that man is too much. Next time, let's have a numerology kitty.' Everybody agreed. 'The rishi was so angry with me for seducing him, he said, "You will marry two men. The first one will leave you. A lover will die. And the second husband you will leave." Now I'm waiting for that... it is my destiny.'

'After that what will happen?'

'I will only have one night stands… and then I will commit suicide. This fellow doesn't go wrong. I know this is how it will be.'

After a pause, the hostess said, 'It doesn't sound too bad—at least you will have a lot of fun before you die. Why not forget about a second marriage and concentrate on your one night stands, *yaar?*'

'Be careful,' someone laughed, 'one of those might turn out to be your husband.'

Lotika was a sought-after woman on the social circuit. Contrary to our own sorry state, her biggest asset at the moment was her single status. Especially as, after a certain age, it was hard to meet attractive women who weren't already married to creeps. Lotika was attractive in her own way. But it was her colourful past that sent out signals. And in the recent magazine interview for a women's monthly that specialized in horror stories about 'victimized' women, Lotika hadn't left a single sexy detail of her life to anybody's imagination. So, now the whole town knew that she was the victim of child abuse at age eight ('I was very desirable even as a kid'), that a raunchy cousin had raped her at age fourteen ('At least he was cute looking'), that she'd been married off to husband number one at age nineteen (*'Chalta hai,* he was into booze and dogs'), that she divorced at twenty-four ('Please note, I didn't ask for alimony or anything. I walked out in my bare feet wearing a nightie') that she'd had an unhappy affair two years later which ended with her lover's death ('Suicide? What nonsense. He had me to live for'). And now here she was, ripe and ready, curse or no curse. It went without saying that there were enough takers to keep her in one night stands forever. The old rishi must have had one hell of a foresight. Lotika had successfully converted his 'curse' into a 'boon'.

❄

Nothing happened after God's visit. I waited for a signal from Yashwantbhai. I expected a midnight phone-call, a letter or even a goon in person threatening me with acid bulbs, rape and murder. Weeks went by and I relaxed, thinking to myself that God had over-reacted. God had felt protective and responsible. I was too much of a small-fry, after all; Yashwantbhai had big-time adversaries to combat with. Why would he bother with a rookie like me?

'Yashwantbhai has a long memory. He remembers everything and everyone. Top to bottom. Do you know he was once insulted by some minister's chaprasi? This was when he was a nobody. Just a *maamuli* clerk in the fisheries department. But he did not forget the insult. After he earned his millions and became powerful, he tracked down the fellow, had him sacked—and that's not all. He sent his men to the guy's village near Sangli. They burnt his small paddy field and the sugar cane he had harvested. They threatened his wife and children. That's the sort of man he is. He may not do anything to you just now. But you wait... just you wait,' a well-meaning lackey had warned me.

I was far too preoccupied for a while after the Amar-Parthiv offer to pay much attention to the threat hanging over my head. *'Dekha jayega,'* I said airily to Chandni when she called. The media grapevine had rapidly spread the word. Aarti phoned as well. A blank item had appeared in a weekend tabloid that specialized in muck.

*'Yaar,* this is too much,' she said, 'who could imagine you'd get into such a mess? Why don't you ask Deb to help you?'

I ignored the calls and threw myself into the profiles on hand. The first one I tackled was, naturally, Iqbal's. We'd worked out an easy equation. I'd forgiven him for the 'incident' and he had stopped making his obligatory passes.

I knew I couldn't compete with Tarantula's tantalizing number on him. I also knew I couldn't do an arty piece full of high-sounding shit that conveyed nothing. Iqbal himself was co-operative but insistent on a shocker. I reasoned with him that it had become rather predictable and passé to do eye-poppers on him. I needed a different angle—an original one.

His dirty mind offered two options: 'Why don't you cover a session where I paint Boxer buggering

351

one of the Cuffe Parade fishermen—Billoo allows him these peccadilloes these days, provided it isn't too often. Or if that is too boring for you we can make it an orgy. Throw in a fisherwoman. Or let me think... I have a still better idea. Let's set up a lesbian orgy with my whores.'

I politely suppressed a great big yawn and nearly said, 'So what else is new?' Iqbal had tripped into his familiar world and as usual, everything else had melted away leaving him to masturbate with his own ego for inspiration.

Without much real interest, I started asking him stray questions about his early years... his childhood, memories of his place of birth. Something suddenly clicked at some point and I got to see the real Iqbal. Or, at any rate yet another persona. This one was almost likeable, almost human. The whole thing worked. It was innocent, revealing and touching. Behind the fancy facade, the great Iqbal was not special at all. He was one of us.

The other profiles took longer and required much more leg-work. But I was enjoying them. And discovering myself in the process. Discovering a cold-blooded, ruthless voyeur who had no qualms about digging out all the small details that most celebrities take such pains to bury. I found I had a knack with people. I could disarm them and get their tongues rolling. It was surprisingly easy to get the most intimate revelations. I also found that my eyes and ears missed nothing—the small gestures, the tiny tics, the nervous laughs, the unguarded comments. People trusted me. They thought I was a friend, a well-wisher, someone they could open up to. For my part, I tried not to betray them. But the temptation to do just that was often far too great.

The reception to my interviews was positive, even flattering. While I enjoyed flirting with this kind of writing, it wasn't important enough for me. People, however, viewed it as a powerful implement....

God came over to tell me, 'Nisha... you have now become the city's *nasha*.' He wasn't bitching.

# Fifteen

Yashwantbhai struck when we were least expecting it. It started with threatening calls at home which my mother answered and hastily passed on to my father if he was around. '*Aapki ladki ki jaan khatre mein hai* (Your daughter's life is in danger),' a muffled voice would whisper and ring off. Next came the standard, typed letters asking in crude English: 'Have you felt acid on skin? Your face your fortune will not be soon.' It was getting to a stage where life was beginning to imitate a Hindi film. I expected to see Shakti Kapoor in white shoes and gloves, lurking near the house with a snub-nosed pistol.

God wasn't amused. 'Don't be a bloody fool, Nasha,' he told me. 'You don't know that *harami* like I do. Anything could happen.'

My father was terrified but could not think of what to do. 'Shall we go to the police?' he asked my mother, who shook her head firmly and said scornfully, 'Police?

Huh! What will the police do? They are all on Yashwantbhai's payroll. No... we will have to think of something else.'

'But... but... do we have the time?' my father blubbered. My mother gave him a withering look. 'Of course we don't... but we'll have to think of something.'

This reversal of roles was most interesting. Suddenly, my mother was in full command after the first few nervous days. She'd answer the caller in a firm voice and look at the letters without betraying any emotions. 'Cowards!' I heard her telling Didi who was stone-deaf now. I continued my routine without letting anyone but God know about the developments. God wanted me to hire bodyguards.

'Don't be absurd,' I said, dismissing the suggestion.

'Let me send you a couple of my chaps,' he offered. At that point, he probably didn't know who the real target was. I flatly refused to have some scruffy fellows hanging around me.

My father was aghast. 'How could you refuse Deb's kind assistance?' he demanded. It was amusing to see how Papa's attitude had altered. Suddenly Deb was no longer the streetside ruffian out to ruin his pristine pure daughter. My mother was more realistic and foresighted.

'I still think this is a trick. Yashwantbhai is bluffing. He is using Nisha. So what if she wrote an unflattering piece. So many others have appeared which have been far more damaging. No, Yashwantbhai isn't after Nisha. There has to be something more to this.' This hadn't occurred to any of us. My mother was the only one who was thinking straight. I was so absorbed in noting the dramatic change in her, that all the phone-calls and letters became incidental. She even looked taller and heavier. There was an assertiveness in her voice that I'd never heard before. It was Papa who shocked me. He seemed like a crumpled-up ball of paper, his shoulders sagging, his eyes haunted, his gait a listless shuffle.

God had other business to attend to. Tarantula, amazing creature that she was, had bounced back with a new project backed by yet another ambitious promoter (a political maverick this time). It was being readied for a super launch with a massive ad campaign that used Hanuman as its symbol.

'Why Hanuman?' I asked God.

'We are capitalizing on the current Hindutva craze,' he replied shamelessly. 'Besides, it's a symbol that's understood all over India. We want reach and penetration.'

'But isn't it all terribly down-market?'

'We don't care about such superficialities. The symbol was something I came up with and shoved down the ad agency's throat. Left to them, they would've come up with Superman or King Kong.'

'Will the paper back your mentor?'

'At the moment the policies are fluid, and alignments are being worked out. It's all very new for our bosses.

They aren't old hands at this game—just monied amateurs, with mighty ambitions to set up a publishing empire.'

'What about Yashwantbhai's own ad campaign? How's Anil handling it? And my ex-boss?'

'Fine. Just fine. I've spent quite a lot of time briefing Aarti.'

'Oh… have you? Briefing her on what?'

'What do you think… the fucking campaign… what else?'

'What are his chances? How do you rate Yashwant-bhai's popularity?'

'I've been busting my ass trying to tell him to cool it… your wimpy boyfriend's survey didn't present a positive picture. The agency people are pretty disappointed. They were hoping to make quite a killing out of us.'

'They still can and will. After all, what is Yashwantbhai to them? Another product to be flogged, along with boot-polish and toilet-cleaners.'

'This is their first political account… they don't want to blow it.'

'What has your strategy been?'

'I don't want to tell you… you might use it in one of your pieces and spoil the impact.'

I'm not that hard-up for copy… don't tell me if you don't want to. Had I still been with the agency, it would have been my account.'

'Point is, you aren't with them… so let's not discuss hypothetical situations.'

❋

The news that God had been shot reached us at breakfast. Papa came back after answering the phone and stood dumbly at the table with a burnt toast dangling from his limp fingers. I looked up, saw his face and went back to my coffee, thinking it was one more mad call, perhaps a dirty one this time.

'It's Deb…' I heard Papa say flatly.

'Dead?' my mother asked.

'Don't know. Shot,' my father replied. It still didn't sink in. I continued sipping my coffee and reading my newspaper. 'Didn't you hear me… Deb has been shot,' Papa repeated.

My mother nudged me gently and said, 'I think we should go to the hospital immediately.'

'Is he… ?' I asked her and she shook her head.

'Intensive care… Nair Hospital. Come on… we'd better rush.'

In the car, I sat by the window staring out at Bombay during rush hour. It was oppressively hot. I had, rivulets of sweat streaming down the length of my body. I cursed the muggy weather as my damp clothes clung to me. I couldn't stop cursing the heat that was burning up my insides and preventing me from breathing normally.

It hadn't registered at all. I didn't even *want* to know the details. Instead, I concentrated on the dabbawallahs charging out of the railway station and hurtling down the street, bearing home-cooked lunches for thousands of down-town office-goers. All sorts of pictures flashed through my mind: I thought of the wives who woke up at five a.m. to start cooking for their husbands so that lunch would be ready at 8.30—the time the dabbawallah arrived at the doorstep to pick up the lunch box. And I wondered what sort of lives these couples led. Did they communicate or merely talk. Did they have intense relationships or just matter-of-fact ones? Did they relate to one another or did they merely tolerate their mates? Did their kids get their share of 'quality time' or did they have to make do with whatever scraps that came their way? Did the husbands appreciate the lunch and share it with colleagues proudly? Or did they go home complaining about the thickness of the chapattis? Did the dabbas occasionally get mixed-up? Did a vegetarian Tamil sometime find a chicken leg in place of an idli in his lunch-box? And if so, did he eat it?

What about the wives and their lives? Where did they work? At the Mantralaya? LIC? The Bank of India? Forward Markets Commission? What did they do with their Diwali bonuses? Buy twelve Vimal saris? A

Raymond's pant piece for the hubby and shiny shirts for the son... no, maybe a cricket bat? And for the little girl? A Barbie doll in a pink disco dress? Plus, a salwar-kameez with mirrors on the yoke for themselves?

I envied these women their uncomplicated lives. All they had to bother about was getting the dabba ready on time for the dabbawallah. Nobody of theirs ever got shot. Nobody threatened them through the mail or over the phone. They didn't have to ferret out interesting little nuggets about people in order to write hot copy. They didn't have deadlines to torment them and moustaches to bleach. I felt enormously tired. And sixty years old.

The streets were full of people... crawling out of their dirty little holes and scurrying around till nightfall, when they crept back into their garrets. They ate pao-wadas from streetside vendors and drank sugar-cane juice infested with flies. The trains were crammed with them, hanging out precariously from the compartments, occasionally getting knocked off their perches and landing in a bloody pulp on the tracks. These people used perfumed hair oil on their heads, but it was their 'wash and wear' shirts that stank ('Wear-and-wear, no time to wash,' as the clerks from the State Bank laughed, biting into over-ripe bananas bought from saucy women who beckoned passers-by with suggestive gestures). Watching shoppers buying nylon underwear from pavement hawkers and plastic buckets from over-stuffed kiosks that sold just about every conceivable 'consumer item', I felt sorry for them. And for myself. God was dying on an iron cot somewhere. And here I was racing to meet him in a Contessa (yes, my father's car had been upgraded) with white towelling seat covers.

The fatal bullet had entered his stomach and lodged itself in his spinal cord. When I saw God lying there with tubes coming out of his mouth and nose, I felt nothing at all. This man wasn't God. He was frail, fragile and helpless, like the rest of us. I watched the monitor as his heart beeped away on the tiny screen, little green signals that looked so deceptively cheerful. 'Look folks, I'm still beating,' it seemed to say. There was nobody around. Or so I thought till I spotted God's father and Toro. They were walking down the long, dark corridor with a policeman and a doctor flanking them. Comradesaab was arguing ferociously with both of them while Toro looked on. I could hear him clearly twenty feet away.

'I want to know what is going on. Where is the FIR? Who is responsible? If anything should happen to my son, I will burn down Yashwantbhai's office and have him killed. He did this. Arrest him. I say, arrest that scoundrel. He ruined my son. Finished him. He nearly finished me. But I will not be defeated by a street dog like him. This matter will reach the press—my

Shobhaa Dé

son—he is an important presswallah. There will be an
uproar, not just in Bombay—all over India. You wait
and see. Where is the senior doctor? I want to see the
medical bulletin. How did you give my son a blood
transfusion—did you know he has a rare blood group?
Show me the bottles. Let me see the syringes. I will
expose all of you. My workers will gherao you....'

By now they'd reached our small group. I couldn't
stop my tears. I could feel my mother's soft, pampered
hands caressing my hair. She was busy looking around
for the registrar on duty. My father just stood there
looking awkward. 'Why did he do it?' God's father kept
repeating. I couldn't answer. I really didn't know. After
a while, we both calmed ourselves down and retreated
to a corner. We had to assess the situation. Chalk out a
plan of action. I thought of ringing up Amar or Tarantula
but God's father told me not to bother. 'Do you think
those people will help you? No, no, no. My dear, you
will have to fight this by yourself. Nobody will want
to get involved. Try and phone anyone now and see.
They will all be busy.'

God's condition was still precarious and he was on
the 'serious' list. I told my parents to go home, but
my mother insisted on staying. I think Papa was relieved
when he saw we didn't really need him. God's father
had walked up and embraced him. I'd seen my father
cringing. I was glad when he left after telling all of us

awkwardly, 'Let me know if you require something. I'll be sending the car back.'

It took about ten days for God to recover. Not completely, but enough to get out of the ICU and into the General Ward. He made it to a one-column, five-centimetre mention on page three in most local papers. There weren't any follow-up stories and Yashwantbhai's name didn't appear in any of the news reports. I wasn't surprised. But God certainly was.

'This cannot be true,' he kept saying. 'His men did it, everybody knows that—even the cops.'

'Why did they want to kill you?' I asked him.

He shook his head forlornly. 'He thought I was going to stab him in the back, *yaar*. I was the man who knew too much. You know... all that Pramila *chakkar* and everything. His land scams and other deals. Forget it, the bloody bastard didn't need me any more, plain and simple. He also thought I had helped you with your story, given you most of the details. He'd been after my butt since that appeared. I tried to tell him... it was no use.'

'You mean he thought you were going to blackmail him?'

'Must be, *yaar*. It's all very complicated. And I know so much about him. You don't know what he did to Pramila.'

'You mean they've broken up?'

'Long ago, *yaar*. He found a new chick. But that's not the real reason. Before he decided to throw her out, a lot had already taken place.'

'Like what?'

'You know, the usual shitty stuff. He fooled her into believing he was going to marry her. That mad woman actually fell for the story. When she told me, I told her to forget it. He would never leave his family. She was so sure of herself. She didn't care what happened to Shruti. Just took it for granted I'd look after her. She was determined to go through with this rascal. He made one big mistake—he knocked her up. She came to me crying, "Help me, help me. What should I do now?" I told her to get an abortion since I knew this man's mind. Instead, she went and told him and then tried to force him into marrying her.

'As you know, Yashwantbhai doesn't have a son. Only three daughters. She lied to him that she'd had that sex-test done—what is it called? Amnio-something. She said she was carrying his son. He got taken in, but not for long. They made a deal. He said he would make the whole thing legitimate after confirming the sex of the child in the fourth or fifth month. She said OK. She was so desperate, she bribed one of those sidey doctors into certifying that the baby was male. Next thing Yashwantbhai knew, she had summoned a priest, got a few garlands, lit a fire and was all set for the wedding. She'd also taken care to have me as a witness along with a video cameraman and still photographer.

'Yashwantbhai felt trapped. He went through the *faltu* ceremony… but told me privately to get the films from the cameramen. This part was OK. But when he also told me about his plan to harm Pramila physically and force a miscarriage on her, something in me protested. It was sheer cruelty. I felt sick listening to the man. But I didn't say too much to him. I decided to keep quiet and warn Pramila about his plan. That bloody woman went and blabbed to him. All you women are the same—bloody bitches. Imagine! I was trying to protect her and she went and fucked things up for me. One of Yashwantbhai's bouncers told me that Pramila became hysterical and started threatening him with exposure. She mentioned my name—and yours. She said she knew enough people in the press who'd help her. She started abusing him and creating a scene. She even made up a story that I had kept copies of the video tape and the photographs that I would use if Yashwantbhai didn't play ball.

'He didn't say anything to her. He played it smart. He only mentioned that he had checked up with the clinic where she'd had her sonography and found out what she had done. He told her that he knew that the baby was a girl—another *kutti* like herself—and that he didn't want either her or the unborn child. He reminded her that she had nothing to go on. Nobody would believe her story, and she was free to make a fool of herself if she wanted. "Think of your future and Shruti's future," he said to Pramila, "And I will deal with Deb directly."

'That was it. Pramila panicked and came to me that night. I told her to get the baby out at the earliest and shut up about the whole incident. I knew my goose was cooked. But I had no escape. Neither did you. I tried to warn you, but you didn't listen. If Yashwantbhai's men had succeeded in bumping me off, it would have been explained away easily as a vendetta killing. I'd been doing so much of his dirty work for him, especially with the builders. Now, with all the election nonsense going on, it would have been another "party worker shot by unknown assailants" report. I don't know what he would have done to you. Probably nothing. Or maybe he would have sent some ruffians to frighten you or your family. Now the game has changed a little. That silly bitch Pramila, she's the one who has really botched everything up. She tried to get the Marathi press to carry her story, but nobody dared to pick it up. Yashwantbhai's men made sure of that. I can assure you that even your Amar and Parthiv won't touch it. They have far too much at stake. Remember all those raids? And how their new machines got stuck in the docks? They know better than to mess with this man... *chalo ek* beedi *to pilao.*'

God suffered a relapse four days later. It was a touch-and-go situation during which the doctors couldn't really say whether or not he'd pull through. He was back again in the ICU. Back again to lifelines emerging from his mouth and nose. The sight was truly horrible. The bullet had penetrated a vital portion of God's spine and was still sitting there refusing to be dislodged. Surgery was scheduled, rescheduled, cancelled and finally performed. God's overall condition wasn't strong enough to withstand it, and he collapsed soon after, lapsing into a semi-conscious state with scattered moments of lucidity.

His father and I took turns staying by his side. Toro drifted in and out as he also had to look after his mother who was bed-ridden with arthritis. Meanwhile, it was my mother who'd got really busy. The first thing she did was track down Pramila. I didn't believe her when she told me.

'I had to, dear,' she explained patiently, like one would to a slow child. 'How else could we mobilize public opinion?'

'Public opinion? What are you talking about?' I questioned her, alarmed by her determined expression.

'Well, dear, it was really Pratimaben's idea. She meditated on the problem for hours and finally found a solution in the Gita. You know something—the Gita has all the answers. You just have to know where to look for them. Anyway, we both agreed that Yashwantbhai had to be exposed thoroughly. She has been very active with a *mahila mukti* group for the last few years. She contacted a lawyer attached to their legal cell and asked for her opinion. The lawyer thought we had a pretty good case. But for all that we needed Pramila's help and co-operation. I had to find her.'

She made it sound so straightforward and simple. Yet, I knew the trouble she must have put herself through to locate Pramila who had gone underground after the fiasco. She'd been threatened by Yashwantbhai's men to lie low and preferably disappear altogether. They'd hinted that Shruti's life would be in danger if she squawked.

My mother, displaying enormous resourcefulness and enterprise had tracked down Pramila to some obscure *gali* in Girgaum, where she was holed up with Shruti. She was back with her old Maharashtrian publishing cronies. Back to the people she had arrogantly rejected before moving on to the glamorous world of English language journalism. Shruti was going to a neighbourhood Marathi medium school and Pramila was busy putting together a collection of Marathi poems in tortured metre. Initially, she reacted to my mother with hostility and suspicion. It was after she met the lawyer that she was persuaded to come out of hiding. The plan was neat. Pratimaben's activist acquaintances had decided to take a morcha to Yashwantbhai's house with prominent placards calling him a murderer, sadist, scoundrel and other names. There was another programme chalked out for later. A series of street plays showcasing Pramila's story in symbolic terms. There were a few press conferences lined up as well. Pramila had a fairly busy schedule of her own, talking to various women's magazines and writing her version for weekend papers. One of the more militant activists had recommended a hunger-strike ('fast unto death') at Hutatma Chowk to focus attention on the 'atrocities' she had suffered.

The press lapped it up. Pramila made it to a video magazine brought out by a sensationalistic tabloid. There was talk of a TV film based on her experience. But this was still in the planning stages. At one point, I received a frantic call from Amar who wanted an exclusive. 'Do an inside job on this,' he instructed. 'Nobody will be able to beat your angle. Imagine you could be sitting on the hottest media story without knowing it. Believe me, I'll really play it up. Cover page and all that. Star treatment. Nothing less. What was your precise role in this mess—you were the "other woman" at some point, weren't you? Take it from there.'

I half-listened. I was feeling too exhausted with all the sleepless nights to get my mind working. Besides, the whole thing stank. Was I going soft? Or just getting cynical? Of course Amar was right. There was a major story in there somewhere. Only, I didn't want to write it.

A few months earlier, I might have jumped at a story like this one. Particularly since I did have privileged access. But this time I wasn't even tempted. I was only concerned about God's recovery. My God! That was it. I WAS ONLY CONCERNED ABOUT GOD. I thought he was dying. He looked so weak and helpless. As I sat on an uncomfortable, bug-ridden wooden stool at his bedside, my mind couldn't stop itself from going into flashbacks. It was just like in the movies. An anxious woman, once thwarted, sitting at the bedside of a man she loves, hoping against hope that he wouldn't die on her. Praying that he'd pull through, wishing desperately to crawl into the soiled bed with him to cuddle his fragile body under the grimy sheet... I was longing to hold this impossible man in my arms and whisper to him, 'Dear God... be mine.'

Yashwantbhai was staying cool. The press had been badgering him to issue a statement, say something... anything... a denial, clarifications... but the wily fox kept silent. His men scoffed at the charges when contacted by reporters.

Among the things they said were, 'A frustrated woman will go to any lengths to embarrass a man, particularly a powerful man. Yashwantbhai is not bothered by such petty things. He has more important issues to deal with. Remember, he is launching a major "Safe Drinking Water" scheme in his village next week. Yes, yes... all of you are invited. Air-conditioned video coaches, overnight

stay in a new hotel—three star. Plus, Yashwantbhai has
some other surprises for you. We are planning a lucky
draw for journalists. The prize is *zabardast*—a Maruti
1000. Why do you people want to waste your time on
useless women with *bekaar* stories? She is doing all
this to get cheap publicity for herself. After all, what
does she have to lose? Nothing. A divorced woman of
bad character. No morals, nothing. Left her husband,
left her children. And now she wants to destroy a
respectable man's career and private life. Why don't
you ask her about her relationship with that no-good
fellow, your colleague Deb? Did you know he was living
with her? And her young daughter? *Aré,* who knows?
She may be the person who tried to kill him. That
woman is dangerous. She is friendly with all sorts of
people—dadas, goondas, smugglers. She was once the
mistress of the Silver King who now lives in the Gulf.
*Baba, yeh sab mamla ajeeb hai* (All this is really strange).
*Jao, Jao...* you don't involve Yashwantbhai in this nonsense.
He has nothing to do with it.'

Some sections of the press bought this story and
painted Pramila as a borderline whore who exploited
men to get ahead, suggesting that she had tried to get
rid of Deb because he was playing the jealous lover
and spoiling all her fun with the others. Yashwantbhai
was portrayed as a well-intentioned middleman who,
in trying to protect his protegé, Deb, got inadvertently
caught in the crossfire. There were several separate

pieces about God, too. Most of them harsh and unflattering. He was described as Yashwantbhai's *chamcha* and pimp. A scribe who had sold his soul to stay on a politician's payroll. One of the papers went so far as to suggest that he deserved to die. A couple traced his rise to the top of the heap starting with his lowly chawl beginnings. A few pot-shots were taken at his father and a couple of well-aimed ones at me. The most amazing version of the episode was done by Tarantula, who wrote an 'I was there' piece, falsely suggesting that she had been in the know all along, thanks to her 'closeness' to God (She'd slyly hinted at an affair). Her 'treatment' was different too. Steamy, personalized and provocative. She was also the only journalist Yashwantbhai had 'agreed' to see and though there was no meat in his limp quotes she'd played up the stray sentence or two, making out as if he had opened his heart to her and revealed all.

I wanted to protect God from all the dirt flying around. Particularly from the hurtful bits about his father and him. There was one nasty story calling God a spineless lackey, Yashwantbhai's hit-man, a self-seeking opportunist, who had orchestrated a savage attack on his own father. In any case, God was in no condition to read anything. Our anxiety over his deteriorating health kept mounting. There were days when he hovered precariously between life and death, getting delirious from time to time, his limbs twitching

violently, his eyes rolling back, his face turning ashen.
There was no question of moving him. And, in any
case, there wasn't much money left. Between his father
and me, we'd managed to get enough together to keep
him where he was and buy most of the expensive
medication required. I was beginning to resemble a
ghost myself.

It was my mother who held things together. Hers
was a constant and reassuring presence, fetching and
carrying mosambi juice and other nourishment. The
activists were getting restless and fading away. They'd
flogged the story for all it was worth and had found a
new cause to support. Pramila had run out of quotes.
And Yashwantbhai's camp was all set to make sure that
he romped home victorious at the hustings. Even the
media was beginning to lose interest in God, and they
were through with flashing his bloodied photograph
all over.

Amar called to remind me. 'The story is dead now,
baby. Why don't you get back to work? Parthiv isn't
going to sit around waiting forever for Your Highness
to make up your mind, you know.'

Of course I knew. But I didn't really care. I had
put everything on hold since the shooting. And the last
thing on my mind was the golden carrot so tantalizingly
dangled under my nose by Amar. In any case, I wouldn't
have been able to deliver. It was only the chick peas
and rice business that couldn't be ignored. I was thankful

to my mother and Aarti for taking that off my hands too. Chandni called a couple of times to enquire after God. So did Aarti and Anil. The D.O.M. surfaced out of the blue at the hospital and read out his new poems to God's non-hearing ears. Shruti arrived unexpectedly with some new 'uncle' in tow during one of God's lucid moments. And that was the last time I saw God smiling.

When the final moment came, I wasn't there. Neither was his father. We had both stepped out to attend to urgent matters. Comradesaab to touch one of his Lal Nishan cronies for money for his son, and I to see my father who had chosen that very day to suffer a minor heart attack. I never forgave him for his badly-timed cardiac infarction. Though sometimes, when I look back on that dreadful day, I feel it was better that way. God had probably picked the time to die with care—defiant and alone. I found a packet of beedies smuggled in by an indifferent night-nurse under his pillow. And a half-smoked one on the floor. God had gone off in a puff of foul-smelling smoke without saying goodbye to anyone. Died like a dog. Or like a god... if you prefer to reverse the letters like I do. It was yet another mercilessly hot day in Bombay when we removed him from the hospital.